William Makepeace Thayer

Charles Jewett

Life and Recollections

William Makepeace Thayer

Charles Jewett
Life and Recollections

ISBN/EAN: 9783337148065

Printed in Europe, USA, Canada, Australia, Japan

Cover: Foto ©Raphael Reischuk / pixelio.de

More available books at **www.hansebooks.com**

INTRODUCTION.

THE Life of Dr. Jewett is not a mere record of his labors in the Temperance Reform. His precocious boyhood; his struggles for a livelihood and education; his early hardships; his brilliant scholarship; his skill in the Fine Arts, as music, poetry, drawing, and oratory; his inventive genius; his success as a physician; his experience in agriculture and horticulture; his pioneer life in the far West; his tact as a lecturer, teacher, and preacher; his efficient service in the church, together with his wit, humor, talents, and aptitude in every relation, — all constitute a remarkable career, outside of his temperance work.

It has not been an easy task to produce on paper the *real* life of such a man as Dr. Jewett, so versatile, humorous, and genial; all of whose acts were made specially emphatic by his presence and manners. The volume needs that wonderful eye of his, which possessed more

3

language than the eye of any man whom we ever knew. He spoke with his eye. He laughed with his eye. He joked with his eye. He pleaded with his eye. He hurled sarcasm and invective with his eye.

We have known men of marked versatility of talents and genius, but never one among them possessing a larger variety of natural gifts, qualified even by nature to succeed and shine in so many positions, with such seeming contradiction of qualities; so intensely witty and profoundly wise, so merry and serious at so nearly the same time; appropriating humor and solemnity with equal fervor, his soul as elastic as rubber, yet solid as granite — all apart from literary culture. Add to this native versatility the refinement and charm of intellectual growth, and we have a bird's-eye view of Dr. Jewett as he was. Think of one man as a physician, artist, agriculturist, horticulturist, inventor, temperance lecturer, mechanic, music-teacher, pioneer, legislator, professor of chemistry, Sabbath-school teacher and superintendent and preacher; and in all these relations successful! Tuckerman's description of Sydney Smith is such an exact portrait of Dr. Jewett that no language of ours is so much to the point. He says:

"A pioneer of national reforms, without acrimony or fanaticism ; prompt to 'set the table in a roar,' yet never losing self-respect, or neglecting the essential duties of life ; capable of the keenest satire, yet instinctively considerate of the feelings of others ; the admired guest, yet contented in domestic retirement ; born to grace society, and at the same time the idol of home.

"In him, first of all and beyond all, is manhood, which no skill in pen-craft, no blandishment of fame or love of pleasure, was suffered to overlay for a moment. To be a man in courage, generosity, stern faith to every domestic tie and professional claim, in the fear of God and love of his kind, in loyalty to personal convictions, bold speech, candid life, and good-fellowship — this was the necessity, the normal condition, of his nature. . . . It made him an architect, a physician, a judge, a schoolmaster, a critic, a reformer, the choicest man of society, the most efficient of domestic economists, the best of correspondents, the most practical of writers, the most genial of companions, a good farmer, a patient nurse, and an admirable husband, father, and friend. The integrity, good sense, and moral energy which gave birth to this versatile exercise of his faculties, constitute the broad and solid foundation of his character ; they were the essential traits of the man, the base to that noble column of which wit formed the capital and wisdom the shaft."

Dr. Jewett came upon the stage of active service when he was needed for a special work. Born with singular tact, wit, and ingenuity, as well as marked talents, invincible will, and

humane feelings, culture easily fitted him for
"the niche he was ordained to fill." Starting
out, not for wealth or fame, but at the call of
DUTY, he accomplished most for himself by
doing what he could for God and humanity. Believing that "our reward is in the race we run,"
he bent all his energies to the race, and thereby
became an accumulating force in the social and
moral progress of his time. Discarding the popular ideas about "luck," "accident," and "fortune," he never became the "sport of circumstances," but their master. Like all great, good
men, he did not stand so much for the dignity
of his work as he did for its fitness and quality.
Unlike many public men, who are found both
for and against the same principles at different
periods, he, from first to last, with single purpose and persistent labor, defended the same
principles, for the reason that his Christian heart
controlled his intellect, and, with it, stood firmly
for the right.

The period covered by Dr. Jewett's public
career was the most exciting and marvellous of
our nation's history; and he participated per-
sonally in the grand contest. The Anti-Slavery
and Temperance reforms began in his early
manhood. The Kansas and Nebraska con-

flicts enlisted his whole heart. The war against slavery in the District of Columbia, the opposition to the Fugitive Slave Law and the rendition of runaway slaves, drew largely upon his humanity. The era of the Prohibitory Liquor Law occupied the best half of his public service. The late "Civil War" absorbed his whole soul, and he was an important actor in its scenes. The amazing progress of the Arts and Sciences in the last half century deeply interested him, and he kept posted therein. A man of such intense personality, humane sentiments, and practical knowledge, could not mingle in such unusual scenes without investing his life with a kind of fascination.

Most men of mark infuse their own leading qualities into whatever they do. Dr. Jewett was pre-eminent in this regard. His speeches, writings, acts, conversations, letters, and verbal counsels, all were permeated by his wit, humor, logic, and genial nature. A vein of pleasantry, like a ray of sunshine, enlivens his life from childhood to age.

Incidents in the life of such a man, next to his actual presence, show what the man is; therefore we let them tell much of the story. A human life was never more crowded with incidents than Dr. Jewett's. From boyhood to the end of life, varying and fascinating as pictures of the kaleidoscope, the scenes of his life multiply.

The task of preparing this work has been more difficult because Dr. Jewett was not in the habit of preserving documents. It was more convenient, in his itinerant life, to commit letters, articles for the press, newspaper notices, and reports of lectures, to the flames, or send them to the paper-mill, than to be burdened with their preservation. Friendly hands, however, preserved valuable correspondence, newspaper articles, &c., which we have found of great value in our work. Neither did he keep a diary. He believed in *deeds* rather than the record of them. The latter was too small a matter for him to think of in his earnest, matter-of-fact methods. A small percentage of personal ambition to be chronicled after death, would have insured the careful preservation of important material.

The public appreciation of an intensely interesting and useful life, and Dr. Jewett's unselfish use of his powers to make the most of life by making the most of himself, have made his biography a necessity in the literature of the land.

CONTENTS.

LIFE OF CHARLES JEWETT.

I.

JEWETT AND TRACY.

EDWARD JEWETT emigrated to this country
from Lincolnshire, England, in 1638, and settled in Rowley, Massachusetts. His youngest son,
Eleazer, removed to Griswold, Connecticut, and
was the founder of the thriving village of Jewett
City — a man of sterling worth, marked business
tact, and as enterprising as he was honest.

From the *History of Norwich*, by Miss Calkins,
we extract the following:

" Eleazer Jewett, to whom this beautiful village is indebted for its origin and its name, was not a man of finished education, but active, persevering, and of a genial,
kindly temperament, happy in doing good, and opening
paths of enterprise for the benefit of others, without laboring to enrich himself. Beginning with only a small farm
and a mill-seat on the Pachaug River, he lived to see a
flourishing village spread around him, enriched with mills,
stores, mechanical operations, and farms in an improved
state of tillage, to which the public gave the familiar name

of 'Jewett City,' a popular substitute for Jewettville, or Jewett Farms.

" He had at first a grist-mill, and to this he added a saw-mill, and sold out portions of land to induce others to settle near him. About the year 1790 he was joined by John Wilson, a clothier, from Massachusetts, who married his daughter, whom he encouraged to set up a woolen-mill. We learn from Wilson's advertisement that he was ready at his mill to accommodate the public in December, 1793.

" In the village graveyard a plain slab marks the burial-place of this founder, bearing the following inscription :

"IN MEMORY OF MR
ELIEZER JEWETT, WHO
DIED DEC 7th 1817,
IN THE 87th YEAR OF HIS AGE.
IN APRIL 1771 HE BEGAN
THE SETTLEMENT OF THIS VILLAGE,
AND FROM HIS PERSEVERANCE AND INDUSTRY
AND ACTIVE BENEVOLENCE, IT HAS
DERIVED ITS PRESENT IMPORTANCE.
ITS NAME WILL PERPETUATE HIS MEMORY."

Eleazer Jewett, whose career we have just noted, was twice married, and had six children. His fifth child, Joseph, father of Dr. Charles Jewett, was born December 12, 1762. He settled in Lisbon, Connecticut, and was married to Sally Johnson, October 13, 1785. Their first child, Sally, was born September 3, 1786. The mother died November 18, 1786, and the child died March 18, 1787. On March 4, 1790, he was married to Betsey King; and their children

were as follows : Betsey, born November 20, 1790 ;
Sally, December 25, 1792 ; Lydia, December 26,
1794 ; Ann, October 19, 1796 ; Eleazer, January 11,
1799 ; Henry, April 2, 1801 ; Joseph R., December
18, 1802 ; Thomas M., September 30, 1804 ; Charles,
September 5, 1807.

Lieutenant Thomas Tracy emigrated to this country from England before 1636, in which year he was
admitted an inhabitant, and had lands assigned to
him, in Salem, Massachusetts. He was the grand-
son of Samuel, the youngest brother of Sir Paul
Tracy, the first baronet of Stanway. In the latter
part of 1639 he removed from Salem to Saybrook,
Connecticut, where, in 1643, he was one of the
committee to divide the township into quarters. He
removed to Norwich, with his family, in 1659. He
was one of the witnesses to the deed by which
Uncas, sachem of Mohegan, conveyed the township of Norwich to the proprietors, thirty-five in
number.

He had seven children, one of whom, Solomon,
married Sarah Huntington, of Norwich, November
23, 1676. They had two children, son and daughter. The son, Simon Solomon, married, and removed to Canterbury, Connecticut. He had eight
children. His sixth child, Phineas, born in November, 1721, married Mehitabel Adams, a descend-
ant of Miles Standish. The descent is traced thus :

Captain Miles Standish came to this country, in
the Mayflower, in 1620. He was twice married,
and had six children, Josiah being the third. Josiah

was twice married, and had nine children, the oldest
of whom he named for his grandfather — Miles.
Miles married, and had a daughter, Mehitabel, who
married Eliashib Adams; and it was her daughter,
Mehitabel Adams, who married Phineas Tracy, of
Canterbury, son of Simon Solomon; so that here
the Miles Standish family unites with the Tracy
family.

Phineas had five children. His son, Eliashib,
married Zeruah Adams, and had two children,
Phineas and Fanning. The latter married Lucy
Adams, daughter of William and Phyllis Adams,
September 26, 1802. Their children were:

William, born in Lisbon, November 18, 1803;
Solomon Fanning, in Canterbury, August 25, 1805;
Charles, in Canterbury, June 5, 1807; Thomas,
in Canterbury, May 12, 1809; Lucy Adams, in
Lisbon, September 21, 1811; Eliashib, in Lisbon,
December 6, 1813; Jabez Ensworth, in Canterbury,
February 21, 1817; John Cushman, in Windham,
1830.

It was Lucy Adams Tracy of this family who
married Charles Jewett. Her grandfather Tracy,
who was a strong-minded but uneducated man, died
suddenly in a fit. His wife, in her great sorrow,
decided to educate their only living son, to accomplish which she mortgaged her farm. The son was
graduated at Yale College, in the class with the
late Professor Silliman. He was one of the finest
scholars in college, a superior mathematician; but

poor health embarrassed him through his whole course.

He went immediately from college to Virginia, as a teacher, where he distinguished himself in that profession. He returned to Connecticut after a time, and established a school for young ladies in New London. Subsequently he established a similar school in Killingly. Both of these schools were popular and successful. At the time his daughter Lucy married Dr. Jewett, he was assistant editor of the New York Observer. Lucy's mother died when she was five years old, in consequence of which she became a permanent member of her grandfather Adams' family.

Thus, by the marriage of Dr. Charles Jewett and Lucy Adams Tracy, two eminent families united their genealogical lines without detracting one iota from ancestral worth, ability, and renown.

Their children were as follows: Charles, born in East Greenwich, R. I., April 2, 1831; William Adams, in Norwich, Conn., October 25, 1832; Richard Henry Lee, in West Greenwich, R. I., July 10, 1834; Levi Nelson, in Warwick, R. I., May 24, 1836; Levi Nelson, 2d, in Natick, R. I., June 4, 1838; Lucy Tracy, in Providence, R. I., January 13, 1840; John Hampden, in Newton, Mass., August 10, 1842; Frank Fanning, in Newton, January 8, 1844; Sarah Elizabeth, in Newton, January 20, 1846; William Parker, in Plainfield, Conn., August 25, 1848. A twin brother of William died at birth.

Anna Maria and Mary Louise, twins, born in Mill-bury, Mass., April 23, 1851.

Just a baker's dozen — THIRTEEN! At the tenth birth, as will be noticed, twins were born. Dr. Jewett remarked to his wife that she had introduced a new rule into arithmetic, namely, " to carry *two* for ten." Notice that the first twins were boys; the second were girls.

II.

A GOOD START.

CHARLES JEWETT'S father was a man of the Puritan stamp, tall, broad-shouldered, grave, and dignified. Physically he was strong and powerful, able to perform hard work, which he did without complaint. Emphatically he supported his growing family by the sweat of his brow; and it required a great deal of brow-sweat to support so many dependants. He was a nailer by trade, though he owned a small farm, the latter being noted for nothing in particular, except that it could boast a huckleberry-bush that yielded *white* berries.

The accompanying illustration is an exact representation of the Jewett homestead as it was at the birth and during the early life of Charles. The original sketch was furnished by Mrs. Mary A. Jewett, widow of Eliezur, an older brother of Charles, and was drawn from memory. The house was one story high, gambrel-roof, and had eight rooms — a small house and large family when the youngest child, Charles, was born. It required some study of adaptation to circumstances to make so large a family fit so small a house. But the thing

2

was accomplished, and that, too, without compressing a single cranium, as future mental developments abundantly proved.

On the right stands the small nail-shop, an ash-tree in front and an apple-tree in the rear. Here the support of the family was mainly achieved. Then nails and tacks were made by hand; and, what was specially remarkable, Mr. Jewett invented and manufactured some of the most effective tools that he used. Here the sons rendered good service at a very early age. There was one thing in the shop which they could do at seven or eight years of age, and even earlier. As the nails were cut, a small boy could pass them to the workman who headed them, laying them with the end to be headed towards the workman. Here the Jewett boys took their first lessons in manual labor really, though they early assisted about the farm in the farming season. Charles took his turn with his brothers, and was never known to call it "small business." Evidently he did not regard it "small" to pass the unfinished nails to his father for heading, laying them just right. We have heard him remark respecting reforms, since he was fifty years old, that "the beginning of a good cause is never small."

Doubtless, in his estimation, nail-making was a "good cause," whose beginnings were not to be despised. The celebrated English merchant, Samuel Budgett, used to set boys, whom he received into his warehouse, to work straightening old nails picked up about the establishment. If a boy

THE BIRTHPLACE OF CHARLES JEWETT, LISBON, CONN. — Page 19.

straightened nails well, it was proof that he could do something else well. Whether this principle was a known law of the Jewett nail-shop or not, Charles adopted it, unconsciously or otherwise. He passed up those nails *well*. In due time he was promoted. Before he was twelve years old he could head nails with considerable efficiency. Though rather small of his age, his blows were steady, heavy, and direct. From that time he has been rather noted for "hitting the nail on the head." In this regard, perhaps, no man ever beat him.

We turned aside to call attention to the homestead. There is no doubt that the house in which a person was born, the grounds on which he played and romped, and the shop in which he worked, all exert a degree of influence upon life and character. A single hour's interview with Dr. Jewett, turning his attention to the home and scenes of his boyhood, was sufficient to satisfy the most sceptical on that point. That sharp eye of his glistened with new lustre, and his enthusiasm kindled afresh at the recollection of the old hearthstone where he knew that he was made a man. If Wellington won the battle of Waterloo at Eton, then the hero of this volume won his fame for ability and usefulness on the homestead, where parents commanded and children obeyed.

But to return to father Jewett. He was a man of strict integrity and honor, possessing those sterling virtues of endurance, perseverance, and industry that distinguished his Puritan ancestors. What he

lacked in pecuniary ability he made up in character — the latter being better than a fortune for his
children. There was no humor in his composition,
but he was thoughtful, reserved, and practical.
Consequently he was not so familiar with his children as some fathers. His air rather than his spirit
hindered that freedom which some children indulge
in the presence of their fathers. Still he was a kind
and considerate parent, strongly attached to his
sons and daughters, for whose mental and moral culture he would tax both his muscle and his brain.
He hated idleness and meanness so vehemently, that
his children, at a very early age, had no doubt at
all upon the subject. He accepted hard toil as
necessary and honorable, and often said, "God
helps those who help themselves." He despised
laziness and viciousness in man or boy, and never
lacked adjectives to express his detestation of them.
His counsels to his children were more or less colored by these well-defined views.

He was an indulgent husband, less demonstrative
in that relation than his son Charles proved to be,
but no less appreciative of wife-worth. He understood full well that the mother of his children was a
remarkable woman, his "better half" in the highest
sense of the term, whose influence was light and life
in the home. Not for the world would he interpose
a barrier to that maternal influence at his fireside;
for he knew that it was both culture and character
to his offspring. Often his confidence incidentally
appeared in his answers to the children seeking in-

dulgences of some sort; "What does your mother say about it?"

He was a man of real mental force, qualifying him for positions of trust in the town, which he filled honorably for many years. His intellectual sharpness, united with his sound COMMON SENSE, which Dr. Emmons used to say, "is the most uncommon kind of sense," made him a prominent man in Lisbon.

He was a man of such justice, ability, and integrity, that his aid was often sought in the settlement of estates, even before he was a justice of the peace. His good sense in this position is illustrated by a single fact. Charles asked him one day what rules he had to guide him in writing the various documents. He replied, "Find out exactly what the parties want, and then express it in the briefest and clearest manner possible."

He did not become a Christian, and unite with the church, until three years after Charles did. All this time, however, he was an important member of the parish, intellectually convinced of the truth of the Orthodox faith, and a strict observer of the external things of religion. At his house the Sabbath was observed with scrupulous exactness, and all unnecessary labor dispensed with. His Sabbath commenced at sundown on Saturday evening. Beds were not made nor rooms swept until after sundown on Sunday evening. On the Tracy side of the family even more strictness was observed; for "Grandfather Adams" would not go ten rods on Sunday to inquire after his grandchild that was very sick. He would frequently address his grand-daughter in the most serious manner, " Lucy, are you not encroaching upon the Sabbath? " So careful were all to obey the very letter of the commandment.

Father Jewett was converted in the year 1831, by listening to a sermon from the text, " I beseech you, therefore, brethren, by the mercies of God, that ye present your bodies a living sacrifice, holy, acceptable unto God, which is your reasonable service." (Rom. xii. 1.) After his conversion, he wrote as follows to Charles, who had become a practising physician in Rhode Island. The letter details the circumstances, and photographs the man.

"LISBON, April 16, 1831.

"DEAR CHILD: I scarcely know how to address you at this time. God is passing before us in such a wonderful manner as to astonish the world. The great revivals of religion that we hear of at a distance, and those in places around us, are calculated to arouse every Christian to look around him, and learn how he can become a worker with God in this work. We have had what is called a ' three days' meeting ' in the neighboring towns, at which there has been uncommon exertion, and uncommon success attending them. This week we have had one in this place, and, wonderful to tell, God has, by his Spirit, turned a number from darkness to light, and from the power of sin and Satan unto God. And shall I say, I hope among the number is your aged father! Oh, Charles! when I look on my past life and my advanced age, that God should constrain me to come in at the eleventh hour, what astonishing grace and mercy! when his goodness has been following me all my days; that he

has thus provided for me in a temporal manner; his goodness and mercy in calling eight of my children, as I hope,
and made them trust in a Saviour, and all without any
assistance of a father; oh, what goodness! I am ashamed
of myself; but would say with the psalmist:

> " ' Wonders of grace to God belong;
> Repeat his mercy in your song.'

Then, my dear child, you will come to the footstool of
your God, and pray that his grace may be sufficient for
me.

" Your mother says she wishes also to be remembered,
that she may renew her covenant with God that bought
her."

Mrs. Jewett was unlike her husband in some important traits. She possessed a native humor that
imparted a sort of sparkle to much of domestic life,
and drew her children to herself like a magnet.
In this regard Charles was very much like his
mother, as the sequel will show. She was strictly
a religious woman, but her religion was cheerful as
sunlight. If her husband sometimes forgot that he
was ever a boy, *she* remembered vividly that she
was once a girl. This one thought tempered her
views of childhood, and helped to make her a dis-
creet and wise disciplinarian. She sincerely lived
for God and her family. She was a sensible woman, bright and keen mentally, contented and
happy with her lot, tender and loving in her nature
— a genial orb around which the children revolved
in joyful obedience. That her hands were full of

work, and her thoughts busy with plans, we need scarcely say. The mother of nine children, sixteen eventful years intervening between the oldest and the youngest, must be pressed with cares and labors. Yet her tractable disposition and buoyant spirits carried her through royally. Her children never forgot her tender advice about good behavior, correct principles, and the " narrow-path life."

We see that Charles Jewett was born of good stock. He once remarked, in a public lecture, of an American statesman, who had stood up squarely and firmly for liberty and temperance, " I knew his father ; he descended from good stock ; and stock is everything in human life ! " So we say of him, that he came from good stock, and that is the first factor in the problem of true manhood.

Turn now to his surroundings. First, the town in which he was born. Reformers are not often born in large places. Charles Jewett was not. Lisbon was formerly a part of Norwich, and was set off and incorporated in 1786, nearly one hundred years ago. The only church in town (Congregational) was organized in 1723, being now one hundred and fifty-six years old. Before a preaching service was established there, the inhabitants attended meeting at Norwich, eight miles distant. Men and women travelled thither on horseback, and many of the young people on foot. They were constant and punctual, too, according to the habit of that day. The Newent Church, as it was named by the Perkinses, whose ancestors came from a town by that name in England, was organized with seven members only, all males, the first pastor being one of the seven. In that day many churches were formed with that number, seven. Importance seems to have been attached to that number because it is prominent in the Scriptures. Perhaps this explains the fact that not a man brought his wife with him; not even the minister. The charm of that particular number, seven, would have been dispelled by such addition.

Charles Jewett was born during the ministry of Rev. Levi Nelson, who was the fourth pastor of the church, the pastorates of the four covering almost one hundred and forty years. Mr. Nelson was pastor more than fifty years. He was the only preacher with whose ministrations the early life of our subject was identified. Mr. Nelson was a clergyman of the olden type, a man "of great simplicity and purity of life," who "never had an enemy," it was said. He preached Divine Sovereignty, foreordination, election, and the decrees with as much solemnity as any other divine of his day, though he was more tender and practical than many of them. He was a clear, plain preacher, in whom the young people were interested with their fathers and mothers. Indeed, more than many ministers of that time, he drew the children to him, both in and out of the pulpit. They revered and loved him. He believed in the Catechism thoroughly, as a text-book in the family, school, and church. He taught it, at stated times, in the public schools, as well as in the house of God on "catechising Sunday;" and he counselled his people to use it, with the Bible, in the family. So, between the three institutions, — the family, school, and church, — Charles Jewett was pretty well *catechised*. And he never forgot his catechetical lore. We have heard him draw extensively from it many times, and think that he could have repeated the catechism the last year of his life as accurately as he did at twelve years of age.

The meeting-house where Charles worshipped so long as he lived in Lisbon, was one of the ancient style, made for temporal and spiritual good, like the catechism. The Norwich historian describes it thus :

" The pulpit was high and contracted, with a sounding-board frowning over it, and a seat for the deacons in front of it below. The pews were square, with high partitions ; the galleries spacious, with certain seats more elevated for the tithing-men or supervisors of behavior. The venerable structure is believed to be the last specimen of the old New England sanctuary that lingered in the ' nine-miles' square. It was demolished, and a new house of worship dedicated, September 15, 1858."

To this house Charles was taken when he was " too young to understand a syllable of the preaching, but old enough to cry." Everybody went to meeting then. Whole families went, including the babies, and often the chorus of baby voices spoiled the music of Dundee and Balerma.

When Mr. Nelson preached his " half-century sermon," in 1854, he alluded to the change that had been wrought among the people in respect to this habit. "Many a time," he said, "while passing over the town, has my attention been arrested to notice the paths, now given up, where they used to make their rugged way to the house of God almost as surely as the holy Sabbath returned. . . . To this day I love to think of their appearance in the house of God, of the seats they occupied, and of their significant motions to express their approbation of the truth." Every Sabbath for many years, that town, which never numbered over six hundred inhabitants, crowded that place of worship with men, women, and children. Our hero was a constant attendant in his boyhood, youth, and early manhood.

Mr. Nelson regarded the Sabbath with all the veneration that the clergy of those times cherished for the holy day; and he honestly sought to instruct and lead his people to cultivate similar reverence for it. With him and his people Sunday began at sunset on Saturday, when all secular cares and labors ended, and the solemn, serious observance of "holy time" began. It was Sunday on the farm, in the store and shop, in the house and by the way, in the front yard and back yard — Sunday everywhere. At one time, for some reason, the Jewett children took a short walk on Sabbath afternoon, just before night, and they walked up the hill past the parsonage. Mr. Nelson beheld them with mingled surprise and astonishment. Such desecration of the Sabbath must not be repeated, lest the wickedness spread, and the Newent church become a "hissing and by word." Early on Monday morning he proceeded to the Jewett homestead to discharge the painful duty of reproof and warning. He declared that such an act was "not only a flagrant violation of the Sabbath, but an insult to himself." The Jewett children never did such a thing again. How such a nervous, wide-awake, fun-loving urchin as Charles Jewett survived such a strait-jacket discipline, we can scarcely understand; but he did, and evidently profited by the rigid treatment. For we recall remarks and acts of his, within twenty years, that indicate the moulding influence of Mr. Nelson's ministry upon his life. On one occasion he remarked to a gentleman, who said that his church were looking for a pastor:

"Get one whom the children can love and listen to. It is a great mistake in societies to consult the tastes of parents only, and forget the children. To compel the little ones to sit in meeting, Sabbath after Sabbath, under the preaching of one who has no real sympathy with children, and no tact to interest them, is just the way to make them dislike the house of God, and shun it in after-life."

Dr. Jewett was a severe critic upon anything like affectation or pedantry in the pulpit. The two qualities in a minister that seemed to impress him most were sincerity and earnestness, just the qualities prominent in the character of the pastor of his boyhood. We can but think that there was an intimate connection between that and his admiration of Cowper's description of a minister, which we have heard him repeat with signal pertinence and force:

" Would I describe a preacher, such as Paul,
    Were he on earth, would hear, approve, and own,
    Paul should himself direct me : I would trace
    His master-strokes, and draw from his design.
    I would express him, simple, grave, sincere ;
    In doctrine uncorrupt ; in language plain,
    And plain in manner ; decent, solemn, chaste,
    And natural in gesture ; much impress'd
    Himself, as conscious of his awful charge,
    And anxious mainly that the flock he feeds
    May feel it too ; affectionate in look
    And tender in address, as well becomes
    A messenger of grace to guilty men."

As we shall learn hereafter, Dr. Jewett was very
familiar with the standard poets of Great Britain and
America, and frequently enforced a sentiment, in
conversation and lectures, by a singularly apt quotation from them. In this respect he excelled all
men we ever knew.

The natural scenery of Lisbon was in keeping
with the social and moral aspects described. The
inhabitants made no attempt to improve upon it even
in their door-yards. It was rugged, yet beautiful :
a hilly country, where valleys nestled between the
frequent elevations, and forests relieved the grand
perspective with their leafy glories. Rocks abounded on hill-side and in valley, sometimes existing in
such profusion as to elicit remarks from strangers.
Here *men* were reared. The genealogy of a class
of families, such as Perkins, Tracy, Jewett, Bishop,
Morgan, Adams, Brown, and others, will show
that this little town has furnished more than its
quota of men who " were not born to die." Their

influence has extended throughout this and other lands, and been felt in the marts of trade as well as in all the learned professions. Who will deny that the influences enumerated did not give them a START ? They seemed to grow up naturally, like the trees around them. They were neither budded nor grafted — the natural product of an intelligent and substantial ancestry.

Dr. Jewett was an expert in horticulture, as we shall see. We have seen him take from his carpet-bag a package of scions, gathered in his travels, and say, "That is the way to raise apples. Only *set* them well, and let them have a good *start*, and they are sure." We think that Charles Jewett was well *set*, and, for such a boy, had a GOOD START.

III.

BOYHOOD.

THE boy Charles Jewett was "father of the man."
Bright, intelligent, witty, genial, magnetic, he
was the centre of juvenile circles in his boyhood,
just as he was of adult, graver circles, thirty years
thereafter. The component parts of his make-up
were such as attract and even fascinate associates,
whether in early or later life. That he was roguish,
in the proper sense of that term, is but another way
of saying that he was natural — himself. He could
not help being roguish. A lamb will jump and frisk;
a kitten will play, must play, or die; and so young
life everywhere is jubilant and overflowing. If
Charles Jewett, the boy, could not have bubbled over
occasionally, and that exuberant nature of his rev-
elled in a good time now and then, he never would
have lived out half of his days. Crowd young,
buoyant nature back into itself, and the insult will
be felt through life; not even time can repair the
damage. A boy is a boy, and he ought to be, as
truly as a man is a man. That " Charlie," as he was
called, was a boy, neither parent nor neighbor ever
doubted; for he gave "full proof" of his boyhood,
impetuous, gushing, and tireless as he went along.

We have no doubt that his father sometimes looked on with much anxiety, and said seriously, " What will become of him?" That dear, good, Christian mother, who saw her own self remarkably reproduced in the boy, must have carried his case often to the Lord. Doubtless she made her Father in heaven very familiar with the child's necessities. That the right sort of a man could be made out of such a boy, she did not doubt; but the Lord must do it.

There is little doubt that an impulsive, brilliant boy like him, fond of sports and novelties, charmed by humorous and comic entertainments, would be very likely to go astray in the city. Such a little steam-engine, with the steam always on, would be quite likely to run off the track where so many theatres, dram-shops, and kindred lures embarrass the way. But in Lisbon, where temptations were comparatively few at a period when they put a quart of Catechism into a pint of humanity, there was little danger to be encountered. At any rate, he survived all the moral perils to which his impulsive nature subjected him, and was as conscientious as he was full of fun. We have heard the doctor himself say that if he had been born in a city, where access to the theatre is easy, he would have been a play-actor. The reason for this remark will appear more clearly when we speak of his admiration of Shakspeare, and his own remarkable dramatic powers. The staid old Puritan lessons and manners of his native town cheated the play-house out of a star. 3

We have said that he was conscientious. He *was* truly; and very tame for so wild a boy. Conscientiousness was his regulator. He devised fun, but not mischief. Supposing that a man so jocose, humorous, and witty as Dr. Jewett, must have been a mischievous boy, we inquired of one of his townspeople, when surveying the grounds over which his young feet danced:

"Can you tell me about his pranks? Such a boy as he must have been inclined to 'cut up.'"

"Not at all," was the reply. "He was a good boy, full of life and fun; but you will find nothing bad said of him."

After a few moments' deliberation, my informant continued:

"He was roguish in school, sometimes, but such a bright, happy lad as both teacher and scholar liked. The worst thing that I ever knew him to do — and that was nothing but Charlie's genuine love of frolic — was this: When about eight years old, his teacher caught him at play in school-time, and she shut him into the wood-house leading out of the schoolroom. The key-hole became a source of still greater amusement, for he could observe the location of the teacher through it, at the same time that he kept the scholars in a titter by the manipulations of a small stick that he would withdraw from the hole whenever her attention was directed thither by the laughing of the pupils. He kept up the entertainment some time before the teacher discovered what was the cause of the merriment."

The teacher concluded that Charles Jewett was born to fun "as the sparks to fly upward," and she released her prisoner with the conviction that what was in him would come out; and she loved the little fellow more than ever.

As already hinted in the first chapter, mother Jewett was responsible for this element of fun-making in her family. It was not limited to Charles. Henry was as complete a mimic as Charles, and, in some things in that line, was his superior. Any man in the town who possessed an eccentricity of manner or action, he could "take off completely." Joe could not do that, but he could get off a pun, crack a joke, or bandy wit equal to Charles. Here is a single example. His father was appointed justice of the peace in the place of a neighbor who retired from the office. On being qualified officially for the office, he brought books and documents from the ex-justice in a bushel-basket and set it under the bed. Desiring some service done soon after, he ordered Joe to do it. The latter delayed, for reasons not explained, whereupon his father spoke as "one having authority," as he was wont to do at times. Joe felt the censure keenly, and turned to Charles, saying in an undertone that his father might not hear, "*Esquire* Jewett needn't feel so crank if he is appointed justice of the peace, with his office in a corn-basket under the bed."

Although Charlie loved a book better than he did work, he was very accommodating and helpful generally. Among Tom's daily duties assigned was that of bringing in wood for the night. One night he said to Charlie, who was then about eight years of age :

"Come, Charlie, help me bring in the wood to-night, that's a good boy ! "

Putting on an air of dignity, and looking very much as if he had repressed the imp of fun that was in him long enough, he replied :

" Let every man skin his own eels."

Each boy had his own work about the house and farm to do, and he thought it was best to stick to the original plan.

His school opportunities were limited. Public schools in the rural towns of Connecticut were poor at that day. They were short, and rudimentary as they were short. "Reading, writing, and arithmetic" constituted the curriculum of a common-school education. Charlie added a branch to his course before he was ten years old, though he pursued it only when the teacher's back was turned. It was DRAWING. He practised the art on his slate, and sometimes on the fly-leaves of his books. Portraits, of the scholars, and pictures of animals, were among his favorites. His mates were surprised to see how accurately he drew their profiles, and how easily it was done, as if he were an adept in the art. Occasionally these artistic dashes were varied with something comical, as a dog arrayed in man's apparel, with hat and boots ; and many a titter was started over one of these productions, as a stolen glance at it was enjoyed when the teacher was un-observant.

Charlie was apt to learn, quick to understand, prompt to recite, and fresh and animated in all that he did. History says that Newton was a dunce in school until a classmate kicked him in the stomach, when he sought revenge by outstripping his assailant at every step in the schoolroom. Charlie needed no kick to arouse his energies, for they never slumbered. He began life *aroused*, and no school committee ever saw him in seat or class without thinking, "that is a *live* boy." He was one of the few pupils whose brightness and readiness attracted attention. It was easy for him to acquire, so that he was not obliged to study hard in order to have good lessons. His conduct in school was usually good. Roguishness does not necessarily spoil good conduct. He had great respect for his teachers. That male or female should know enough to teach so many pupils, some of whom were almost men and women grown, rather caused him to wonder. Years afterwards he thought that Goldsmith's description was an exact representation of his case, and he would repeat the lines with much effect:

> "Beside yon straggling fence that skirts the way,
> With blossomed furze unprofitably gay,
> There, in his noisy mansion, skilled to rule,
> The village master taught his little school.
>
> .   .   .   .
>
> "While words of learned length and thundering sound
> Amazed the gazing rustics ranged around;
> And still they gazed, and still the wonder grew,
> That one small head could carry all he knew."

In school and elsewhere he was a peacemaker.
Strongly attached to his schoolfellows and playmates, he never had any difficulty with them. He
could not endure to witness quarrels among them,
and usually managed, on such occasions, to step in
with his wit or tact, and parry all warlike demonstrations. It was quite impossible for the most
evil-disposed urchins to pick a quarrel with such a
"budget of fun." As well attempt to convert a ray
of light into a thunderbolt, or to extract sour from
sweet. Nor was this quality confined to the schoolroom and playground; it pervaded the home. He
was the life of the family circle. He never had
trouble with brothers and sisters. "Let us have
peace" was the motto on his banner. Always happy, always ready with a word of cheer, there was
little opportunity for disputes or encounters when he
was about. Indeed, there was little disposition to
disagree in that family, for the cheerful element
was in the ascendency.

This quality manifested itself also in another direction. His sympathy for the poor, sick, and suffering was always manifest. An unfortunate or sick
companion drew tenderness from the depths of his
soul. Sickness in the family awakened both anxiety
and affection. He was ever ready with words of
comfort and hands to assist. The sight of a beggar,
homeless and friendless, tattered and hungry, coming to his father's door, drew a whole bucketful of
sympathy from the deep well of his humanity. Unlike many children, he never ran from beggars:

he ran to them; and the first thought seemed to be, What can be done for them? Even poor, dumb animals shared this gracious element of his being with the nobler race. The abuse of a dog, cat, or fly distressed him. Stoning frogs in the mill-stream that ran close to his father's house, elicited his reproof. It was well understood by the juvenile fraternity that " cruelty to animals " must not be practised when Charlie was around. He had a "Society for the Prevention of Cruelty to Animals" in his own heart, with a constitution that God wrote on its immortal tablet; and the older he grew the more distinctly could its Divine principles be read. It was a genuine pathos and tenderness at the sight of suffering or wrong in man or beast that beautified his boyhood. Within a few years this prominent element of his being asserted itself at a railroad depot in Boston, where a crowd of thoughtless men were teasing and making fun of Daniel Pratt. Dr. Jewett withstood the spectacle as long as possible, when he rebuked them in a manner that shamed every soul of them. His point was, that it was shameful for men with reason to subject to disrespect and ridicule a man bereft of reason. Blair said, " Graceful in youth is the tear of sympathy, and the heart that melts at the sight of woe."

He was a great reader, with only a few books to read. There was no Sabbath-school at that time, and consequently no Sunday-school library for the young. Indeed, very few books for children were then published in the country. There were none in the possession of the Jewett family. The Bible, Psalm Book, Westminster Catechism, American Preceptor, Columbian Orator, and the Norwich Courier, constituted his library, small but substantial. We believe, however, that Robinson Crusoe was in possession of the family, and that Charlie read it over and over until he could well-nigh repeat it. Without question, this dearth of books was better for a boy like him than such a deluge of them as now floods the world. With his taste for reading, and his love of stories, particularly the dramatic and marvellous, a great supply would have surfeited his appetite for reading at the expense of thinking. If society was at one extreme of this subject sixty and seventy years ago, it is at the other extreme now. Real profit was the object sought then ; amusement is the object now. It is no longer a quart of profit to a pint of pleasure, but a small gill of the former to a hogshead of the latter. Charlie would have shrunk mentally under such a regimen instead of growing into vigorous action. His intellectual faculties would have been dwarfed on such a bottle of watery pap ; and he would have made a fluid sort of a man, instead of the man of iron that he was.

The Columbian Orator was a source of exquisite pleasure to him. Both as a reading-book and a book of declamations it proved a treasure to him. Hours of unalloyed satisfaction he spent with that volume. He was born an orator, and very early showed a strong passion in that direction. He committed declamations from it before he was eight years old, and spoke them at home and by the roadside. His reputation was so well established in the community for oratorical ability that neighbors would invite him to speak when they met him by the way. Sometimes a man meeting him would stand him on the wall for an exhibition of his forensic powers. It was not simply a recitation that he furnished; any boy could do that; it was real, fervid eloquence that poured from his impassioned soul. It was this quality that led people to prophesy that Charlie would be a minister. No one thought he would ever become a doctor. Even when, ten years later, he decided to qualify himself for the medical profession, one citizen said:

"It's no use, Charlie. You can't make a doctor if you try. You are cut out for a minister. Public speaking is your forte. If you study medicine, you will come around into the pulpit after all."

The man was not so far out of the way, for he came around so far as to preach the Gospel of Temperance in hundreds of pulpits. Indeed, as we shall learn hereafter, he ministered to people, on many occasions, in the place of an ordained preacher.

The first proof that there was a poet in the Jewett family occurred on this wise. It was when Charlie was nine or ten years old. The boys would come home from school ravenously hungry, a state of affairs very common in large families, and the good mother usually provided for the rush. Often, on returning from school, they found mother employed in frying doughnuts, and a generous distribution followed. It was not always so, however, when Fanny, a redoubtable old maid who lived many years in the family, officiated at the fry-pan. Instead of distributing the doughnuts, and saying, as their mother did, " There now, you have enough ; run away and be good boys," she would meet their modest demands with a flat denial, — " Not one doughnut. Clear out, and don't bother me ! "

On one occasion their best bow and plea failed to extort the doughnuts from Fanny, whereupon Charlie played the poet extemporaneously, more to annoy her than to carry his point. He extemporized a verse containing the names of all the children and others, with volunteer advice to Fanny to escape from single blessedness as soon as she could. The verse ran thus :

> " Betsey, Sally, Lydia, Ann,
> Eleazer, Henry, Joe, and Tom,
> Charles, Maria,* and Mary Ann ; †
> And Fanny, marry if you can ! "

This unexpected dash of poetry caused an ex plosive laughter all round the juvenile camp, and Fanny, surprised and pleased that such a " tot " could get off such a poetical hit, joined in it heartily, and proceeded to distribute doughnuts with a liberal hand. The boys could not forget that achievement. The doughnut problem was solved now. Charlie's

---

* A girl brought up in the family.
† A tailoress who worked much in the family.

rhymes would insure a full supply. He must ply his art with a will every time. And he did; but the doughnut-maker was inexorable again. Her heart became steeled against poetical effusions; and, instead of doughnuts, they got the broom. Fanny declared that she " hated boys," and Charlie thought *that was the reason she never got married.* But the war on the doughnuts was not yet ended. Charlie's tactics were equal to the emergency. The boys held a council of war, at which he proposed a covert attack on the doughnuts. Each one should sharpen a stick and run it up his sleeve out of sight, and when assembled about the fire in happy converse, at a given signal each should spear a doughnut and bear it away in triumph. The plot was gloriously successful, but proved to be one of those victories that destroy the victors. For Mother Jewett thought that hostilities had proceeded far enough, and her proclamation ended the siege. From that time, however, it was settled that Charlie was poetical, if not a poet.

With all the rest, he was very ingenious. With his jack-knife and some tools that his father's nail-shop furnished, he could construct windmills, water-wheels, kites, sleds, and miniature tables, bureaus, carts, and articles even more elaborate. The stream of water near his father's house was utilized to run water-wheels that he made, and the corners of barn and shed were adorned with specimens of his wind-mills. No one could beat him in the manufacture of whistles, and bows and arrows. His ingenuity,

too, was used in a benevolent way, often, to interest
and please children younger than himself. Here and
there are persons, if now living, who could testify
to the genuine kindness of the boy Charles Jewett,
in making water-wheels, windmills, and whistles for
them. He seemed to possess an inborn inclination
to do for others. It was a sort of passion with him
to please and help others. Within two or three
years we heard of his gymnastics in a railroad depot
to relieve a worn and weary mother. She had a
sick child with her, so restless and worrysome as to
trouble her exceedingly. The doctor came to her
relief, and by motions and noises, imitating birds,
beasts, and perhaps fishes, he succeeded in gaining
the attention of the child, and holding it until car-
time arrived. Any person acquainted with the
doctor will say, "That was characteristic."

We are told that the ingenuity of Newton's boyhood foreshadowed his manhood ; that he constructed
water-wheels, windmills, kites, and other articles,
and was mender-general of toys in the neighborhood ; that he drew profiles of friends, including that
of his favorite teacher, and wrote verses ; and that
he loved a book so much more than he did work,
that he would pilfer time allotted to labor for the
purpose of reading. All this was no more remarkable than what we have seen was true of Charles
Jewett's early years, except the latter needed no
"kick in the stomach" to start him in the race of
life. We are not making Dr. Jewett an equal with
the great philosopher ; but the boyhood of the latter

no more foreshadowed later life than the boyhood of the former did. We believe that —

> " God gives to every man
> The virtue, temper, understanding, taste,
> That lifts him into life, and lets him fall ;
> Just in the niche he was ordained to fill."

The evidence of this truth begins with childhood and youth, though much more distinct in some lives than in others.

One who knew Charles well, says, " He kept his eyes open ; " that is, he was a keen observer. For this reason he was learning when other boys were wasting time. Observation, discriminating and sharp, is one of the most practical and valuable elements of success. Dr. Johnson said, " Some men will learn more in the Hempstead stage than others in the tour of Europe." It is so with boys. On a journey, one will notice every tree, house, field, bird, stream, herd, hill, and valley, while another will scarcely observe anything but the animal which draws him. One will observe a steam-engine only to take in its size and general appearance, while another will study every valve, wheel, rod, and pipe, comprehending the actual construction of the machine. One will commit a lesson in school and recite it glibly, parrot-like, without raising a single inquiry as to its meaning, or understanding it at all ; while another is surcharged with inquiries, and his enthusiasm and interest appear in every question and answer. The difference is found in observation. Ferguson was gifted with observation in his

boyhood. A toy, tool, or other article was thoroughly understood by him. By taking them to pieces and
putting them together again, he understood their
mechanism. His father's watch especially interested
him. He longed to know how it was made. He
would have taken it to pieces, but his father's eye
was too watchful. One day a gentleman was riding
by on horseback, and he stopped to inquire of the
lad about the way. While directing him, young
Ferguson observed that the traveller had a watch.

" Will you be good enough to tell me what time it
is?" he asked.

The gentleman very kindly responded

" Would you be willing that I should look at your
watch?" continued the boy, after learning the time,
which was only a ruse to examine the timekeeper.

"Certainly," replied the kind-hearted man, passing him the watch. His first question was :

" What makes that box go round?"

" A steel spring," the owner replied.

" How can a steel spring in a box turn it round so
as to wind up all the chain?"

The gentleman explained.

"I don't see through it yet," young Ferguson
answered.

"Well now, my young friend," said the man,
becoming deeply interested in the boy, "take a long,
thin piece of whalebone, hold one end of it fast
between your finger and thumb, and wind it round
your finger; it will then endeavor to unwind itself;
and if you fix the other end of it to the inside of a

small hoop, and leave it to itself, it will turn the hoop round and round, and wind up a thread tied to the inside."

"I see it! I see it!" exclaimed Ferguson, expressing thanks and his enthusiasm at the same time. And he subsequently constructed a wooden watch, which he put into a case about the size of a teacup.

Blaise Pascal was a similar boy. When about ten years old, at the dinner-table one day, he was amusing himself by striking his plate with his knife, and then listening to the sound.

"What are you doing with that plate, Blaise?" inquired his sister, without dreaming that the boy was unwittingly studying the science of acoustics.

"See!" he replied, "when I strike the plate with my knife, it rings; hark!"

And he repeated the experiment.

"When I grasp it with my hand *so*," — suiting the action to the word, — "the sound ceases," he continued. "I wonder why it is!"

His sister could not enlighten him, and she only smiled at his childish interest. The boy, however, did not stop his researches. He went on dinging various articles, in order to study the laws of sound, until in manhood he produced a remarkable treatise on the subject.

We have cited these two examples of observation to illustrate our point better than we could by simple description. Charles Jewett was precisely such a boy. He had an irrepressible desire to know the

reason of things. Before he was old enough to comprehend the philosophy of his action, he was investi-
gating the nature, tendency, and relation of things.
Whether he was a born inventor, mechanic, chemist, artist, or not, his discriminating powers led him
in that direction. Says one who saw him much
before he was twelve years old, "He was a natural
mechanic, very ingenious, and when he had perfected one thing he would turn and invent another."
Very few boys can do that. There must be native-
born tact, genius, and perseverance, to secure such
results.

His critical observation went hand in hand with
his conscientiousness. He early saw the *tendency*
of acts; — that the youth who drank intoxicating
liquors might become a drunkard; that the profane,
reckless youth was despised by good people; that
doing low, mean things was unmanly and detesta-
ble; — and so, with a heart full of life and joy, and
a soul on fire with enthusiasm, and his impulsive
nature in love with the humorous side of humanity,
he steered clear of rocks and shoals, and fairly
earned the reputation of being a "good boy." Pro
fanity, vulgarity, and kindred vices, did not lure
him, nor flaunt their colors in his presence. Though
just the boy, with a class of his qualities, to fall into
such ways, he was just the boy, with another class
of qualities, to shun them. Any amount of roguishness may be carried safely by a youthful soul that
is controlled by conscience. A small amount may
wreck a soul that ignores conscience.

No doubt that poverty was one of his greatest blessings. He spent no money because he had none to spend. With his generous impulses, and craving for a merry time, a rich father might have made him a degenerate son. Money would have gained for him the facilities that imperil and ruin. Many a lad is spoiled by his spending money. To all this class, having none to spend is a real godsend. True, boys had not the temptation to spend money at that time that they have now. In Lisbon especially this was true. Confection and baker carts did not run in there. Travelling shows and exhibitions of every kind shunned the town. So that, while Charlie had no money, he had no particular need of any.

Hugh Miller said, "It was necessity that made me a quarrier." Whether it was " necessity " that made Charles Jewett economical or not, he was all this from birth till death. Greater men than he spent money very foolishly in early life. Even Franklin paid all his for a whistle, and Samuel Drew for a purse. The latter wrote, in mature years : "When I was a boy, I remember I got a few pence, and coming into St. Anstell on a fairday, laid out all on a purse. My empty purse often reminded me of my folly; and the recollection has since been as useful to me as Franklin's whistle was to him." But our hero could not have been so foolish if he would; for he had not money to buy the whistle or purse. Poor, indeed, was he. Blessed poverty !

One very painful experience came to Charlie's boyhood. His eldest sister married, and removed to the state of New York. She was sixteen years older than he, and was a sort of sister-mother to him in his babyhood. She was specially charged with his care, so that there existed an extra reason for his strong attachment to her. He was seven or eight years old when she married and went away. Charlie was hardly reconciled to the event; but his opinion of the man who would perpetrate such an outrage as to capture and bear away his sister, was never committed to writing. His feelings, however, were sadly wrought upon. A part of himself was carried off; and how lonely one must feel with a part of himself gone! For a time the event took the fun out of him, as rain takes starch out of linen. He brooded over it, and grieved. But the cloud broke after a time. Such a boy could not live long under a cloud. He would oust it if relief could come in no other way. But relief came; the old sun shone out brightly, and his bounding spirit made as much of life as ever.

IV.

LEAVES HOME.

CHARLES was familiar with work at twelve years of age. He could turn his hand to the demands of the farm or nail-shop with much efficiency. Out of school his time was quite fully occupied with labor. His father believed that it was better "to wear out than to rust out;" and his opinions were reduced to practice. Rust was scarce about his premises. His boys and girls did not corrode; they had no chance for that. "Work before play," was a family motto.

Charles took to the farm more than to the nail-shop. He was in love with Nature, and farming gratified that love more than nail-making. We do not mean to say that his heart was set upon raising corn and potatoes, grain and fruits, though he did all this with commendable tact. Horticulture especially interested him. Cultivating trees and flowers yielded him a large percentage of genuine satisfaction. He early learned the art of grafting and budding, and practised it thereafter as long as he lived. His acquisitions in this regard served him a good purpose in manhood.

At this time, however, an event of great moment to him occurred. His parents went on a visit to their daughter, in the state of New York; and they took Charlie with them. It was her request that Charlie should come. We have seen that a strong attachment existed between brother and sister, and the reason for it. This visit brought them together again. "Was there ever such a sister?" he thought. "Was there ever such a brother?" she thought.

It was a new world to Charles. Herkimer County, New York, then, was as new a country as Wyoming or New Mexico are now. The soil was rich; and such vegetation, forests, and timber, as met his wondering eye, were marvels. Farming on such an extensive scale, too, was entirely new to him. To a boy of his sharp observation the scene was fascinating. His whole attention was absorbed in the panorama about him.

He had not been there long before his sister expressed a desire that he should remain and live with them. "Live here always?" inquired Charles.

"Yes, always," was the reply.

Had the proposition come from any one but his sister, he would have declined it at once. Home had too many attractions for a boy like him to be sacrificed hastily.

The facts of the case were set before him, — the opportunity to acquire a thorough knowledge of farming; the pleasure of driving horses and having charge of so many cattle; the help it would be to his father, who was poor; and the satisfaction it would afford his sister.

The parents were consulted of course, and the

subject was thoroughly discussed in the family. Charlie's father expressed himself candidly and fully. He thought it was a good opportunity for a boy twelve years old. Nor was it going out of the family to avail himself of the privilege. Next to his mother, his eldest sister would care for him with tender interest. It was clearly a providential opening that ought to be occupied. The question was settled. Charles would stay with his sister; nor had he any tears to shed over the decision. He accepted the situation with his wonted cheerfulness. The fact that his parents favored the object, and the thought that it would aid his father to bear the family burden, reconciled him completely to the result.

No boy ever took up his abode among strangers sharing better counsels than Charles did. The tender and timely words of advice which his parents gave him were "apples of gold in pictures of silver." "It will depend on yourself," said his father, "whether you make a good man. If you succeed, it will be because you do the best you can. Nobody can make a man of you without your noblest efforts. A boy can make almost anything he wants to be, if he will work hard enough for it. Industry, perseverance, and sound moral principle will do for you what all the money in the world can never do."

This counsel was not put with the grace and beauty of Bacon, though it is not less practical and pertinent. Bacon said, "Men seem neither to understand their riches nor their strength; of the former they believe greater things than they should: of the latter, much less. Self-reliance and self-denial will teach a man to drink out of his own cistern, and eat his own sweet bread, and to learn and labor truly to get his living, and carefully expend the good things committed to his trust."

In his counsels, Father Jewett met Bacon's idea of the best advice: "He that gives good advice builds with one hand; he that gives good counsel and example builds with both."

So Charles was left behind when his parents returned; and he found himself settled in Fairfield, Herkimer County, New York, — a boy-farmer. As it proved, he was introduced to an experience of which he scarcely dreamed. He found a splendid farm, but not a bed of roses. His sister was the same dear, loving, and lovable woman that she always was, but her husband would scarcely answer to the description of being a kind and genial man. He was a hard worker, a worshipper of the almighty dollar, and he wanted everybody around him to be the same. Franklin's couplet was his Bible, Catechism, and Prayer-Book:

> " Early to bed, and early to rise,
>   Will make a man healthy, wealthy, and wise."

Boy or man, with religion enough to rise at break of day and toil until dark, with an occasional night spent at the coal-pit, answered his *beau idcal* of a man for this world and the next. Had his views and practice been in full accord with physical laws, he himself would have been the healthiest, wealthi-

est, and wisest man in Herkimer County. But, unfortunately, he was at loggerheads with Nature,
and did not know it. Physiology could not find a
place on his farm to rest the sole of its foot. The
only ology that was tolerated there was workology.
From dawn to setting day, it was work, work, work !
scrub, scrub, scrub ! Yet Henry Dexter did not
mean to be unreasonable or cruel. He was born
to run a farm with all his might, so he appeared to
think. John Adams' motto was, " Sink or swim,
live or die, survive or perish, I am for the Declaration." Henry Dexter's was the same, except that
he was for *farming* instead of the " Declaration."
He cared not a fig for the latter ; but the former
was his country and his little world.

Judge, then, of Charles's introduction to a farmer's life. He struck right into the business at
once ; he was obliged to do it. He did not stop to
learn — he began without learning. It was a service without the voluntary, a sermon without introduction, a book without a preface. He began without a beginning. He struck in where boy-farmers
usually find themselves after three or five years'
service. It was a good-bad thing for him, no doubt,
— good for his tact, self-reliance, and energy, but
bad for his physical powers. Over-work is to be
deprecated as much as under-work, though hard
work is a much better discipline than no work.

Charles was better qualified for such service than
most boys. His remarkable tact and dispatch fitted
him for the emergency. He " obeyed orders " like a

soldier.   He was wont to do this.   Much work did
not scare him.   To milk cows before sunrise and
after sunset did not sour him.   He would sooner
crack a joke over it than scold and complain.   That
was less onerous and wearying than logging in the
woods, in winter, or tending cóal-pits at other seasons of the year.   Before he was fifteen years old
he at one time tended coal-pits fourteen nights in
succession and worked at haying each day.   He
cherished his own thoughts about the cruelty of
the exaction, but not a word of complaint or remon-
strance escaped his lips.   His sister, who was a
woman of real mental ability, deeply sympathized
with him, and tender words were dropped into his
ears occasionally, though she well understood that
a woman's interference would not be tolerated on
that farm.

Late in the autumn and early in the winter he
carried wood to market.   Sometimes he went to
market under unusual orders, namely, the wood must
be sold at such a price [a stiff price], and the boy
return at a given time or be flogged.   He had no
taste for the latter antidote, and so he generally sold
the wood and returned whistling.   We once asked
a successful book-agent, "What is the secret of
your success?"   He replied, "Going home whistling
when I have not sold enough to pay for a dinner."
Whistling came to Charlie's rescue a great many
times.   His buoyant spirits often lifted him out of
the "slough of despond;" nay, rather, his merry-
making nature kept him from falling into it.

One of his tasks was frequently to go to the woods early in the morning, cut half a cord of wood, carry it to market, and sell it before coming home at night. The penalty of failing to do this was a flogging. At that time there were no bridges in that region, and rivers had to be forded; and a river lay between the woods and the market. Frequently it was very dark before he reached the river, so that he could not see his way, and he was obliged to give loose reins to the horses, and " trust to luck" in fording the stream. Fortunately, he never met with any misfortune in these hazardous adventures, though this fact did not mitigate the cruelty of his employer.

Once, in the spring of the year, he was ordered to drive a four-horse load of coal to market, when the river to be forded was unusually swollen. Everybody about the farm protested against such a hazardous undertaking. The neighbors did not dare to ford the stream even in a pleasure-wagon. But expostulation availed nothing. Mr. Dexter said that he must go, and that settled it. The boy went at the risk of his life. He was threatened a "licking" if any accident befell the team. Realizing fully the perils of the trip, he obeyed orders; and when the horses plunged and trembled in the swift, swollen river, with voice and whip he urged them forward with the load. It was pitch-dark when he returned, so that human vision and skill were powerless at the stream. The only alternative was to commit himself to the instinct of the horses, and urge them for-

ward.   The stream was so full and the current
so rushing that he expected to perish in the attempt
to cross.   But a kind Providence watched over the
heroic lad, then only fifteen years of age, and he
reached home, escaping both a "licking" and a
watery grave.   There is no doubt that such heavy
responsibility laid upon the boy served to develop
his courage and efficiency, and thus bore some part
in qualifying him for the grand things of his manhood.   But for all that the hardship was cruel.

The "bargain" was, that Charlie should attend
the winter school a term of ten or twelve weeks.
Nominally he did, although his schooling was often
interrupted by a pressure of work.   Mr. Dexter did
not appreciate the value of education as he would
have done if he had not been avaricious.   The loss of
one or two days of schooling in a week was of little
account with him.   Indeed, a whole week at a time
Charlie was kept out of school to drive the work on
the farm.   But such time as he had for school was
faithfully improved.   A schoolmate writes that he
"was a bright, smart scholar, always happy, popular with teacher and scholars, and the best declaimer
on the stage."   It seems that declamations and dia-
logues were spoken in school and at evening exhibitions; and Charles stood foremost in the exercise.
The resources of his Lisbon home served him a
good purpose here, and were just as good as new to
the people of that region.   He distinguished himself
to such a degree in the elocutionary art that he became the subject of remark and conversation in the

community. Everybody was interested in him. His popularity extended to the old as well as to the young. He was so genial and witty, that all hearts were drawn to him. Says Colton : " There is no quality of the mind, or of the body, that so instantaneously and irresistibly captivates, as wit." The remark is true, whether it be the wit of a boy or man.

In this case, also, it drew sympathy from the hearts of those townspeople who thought he was having a hard time on the Dexter farm. They expressed their sympathy in various ways. Sometimes they hailed him with a kind salutation on the street ; sometimes they sent goodies to him by their children to school. Again one would go to him in the field with an appetizing lunch. These facts show that Charles Jewett was a marked boy in that neighborhood.

One thing that particularly gratified his associates was, his gift in song and speech-making. He was a good singer for one of his age, and he easily caught lively airs, and delighted in humorous songs. Of these he had many at command, with which he would entertain his companions, as circumstances favored. He often gratified them, too, by speech-making, usually upon topics that were uppermost in the locality. In this respect he was regarded as somewhat of a prodigy, so that he was often invited to mount a stump or rock and deliver himself of a speech. The young people almost idolized him on account of these and other characteristics.

An incident occurred when he was fourteen years of age that deserves special notice at this point. Mr. Dexter employed quite a gang of men at the coal-pits, and often youth and young men of the town were among them. Night and day were spent there during the period of coaling, the laborers occupying cabins erected for their convenience. Their evenings were often made attractive by games and sports. On a certain evening one of the men was casting about for something new to interest them, when his eye rested upon the "big beech stump" near by, that had previously elicited some remarks.

"Capital pulpit!" exclaimed the man. "It only needs a preacher, and we could run a service."

"And here are Bible and hymn-book," responded another, who chanced to have a diminutive copy of each in his pocket.

"Who will preach?" called out the first speaker, designing to get sport out of the affair.

"Charlie!" answered several voices.

"Yes, Charlie!" was unanimously repeated.

There was no excuse to be accepted with that company. Charlie hesitated, but was forced to respond. So he mounted the stump, with a resolve in his heart that scoffing men should not get much sport out of that affair. He gave out a hymn, reading it with marked pathos and power, and a few of the number united in singing it. Then he proceeded to preach, with an appearance of earnestness, and even solemnity, that caused jokes and facetious remarks

THE BOY CHARLES JEWETT PREACHING ON A STUMP AT
THE COAL-PIT.

to seem out of place. He announced for his text,
John iii. 14, 15 : "And as Moses lifted up the serpent in the wilderness, even so must the Son of man
be lifted up ; that whosoever believeth in him should
not perish, but have eternal life." With singular
tact he proceeded to explain the meaning of the passage, availing himself of his home drill in the Catechism and Scriptures to add point and force to his
discourse. He told his audience that they were in
the condition of the Israelites who were bitten by
the fiery serpents, and their only relief and hope was
to look to Christ. Failing to do this, they would
sink to hell. The plan of human redemption was

unfolded just about as clearly as he had heard it from the lips of his honored pastor, Mr. Nelson.

For fifteen or twenty minutes he continued to pour out his fervid eloquence, to the utter astonishment of his hearers. They knew that he was an orator, and a boy of rare abilities; but such a powerful appeal from his lips was wholly unexpected. They hung breathless upon his lips, losing all desire for sport, captivated by the boy's earnestness and remarkable gifts. When he closed, there was not a thoughtless face among the listeners. All jollity and trifling had disappeared. What began jocosely, ended seriously. Young Whitman, a youth about Charlie's age, the son of a Baptist deacon, of the town, was in tears, totally unable to control his feelings, though all eyes were upon him. A more thoughtful group of laborers never retired to rest than were Charlie's hearers on that night.

The fame of the young preacher spread. Every one who heard him carried the story of it abroad. Young Whitman reported to his father, and the good deacon said:

"He must be a minister. We must educate him for the ministry."

The affair became so notorious that there was much talk among Christian people about educating him for the pulpit. The matter assumed such a serious aspect, that Deacon Whitman conceived this plan to enjoy the opportunity of hearing Charlie preach. Then he could judge better about his fitness for the clerical profession. He proposed

that his son should invite a company of young people
to his house on a given evening, when Charlie should
be requested to preach. The deacon and other brethren would be in an adjoining room, unperceived by
the speaker, where they could hear the sermon.
The invitations were sent out, and on the eventful
evening a large number for that place assembled.
But Charlie, having heard what the ruse was, did
not put in his appearance.

When he was fifteen years old another incident
occurred, illustrative of the boy in another direction.
Wrestling was a very popular sport with young and
old in that region. Charlie was initiated into the
practice soon after he took up his abode there. At
school, at noontime, in the woods and field, on holi-
days, and on various other occasions, men and boys
tried their skill and strength in this way. Charlie
was not opposed to the sport; he was rather taken
with it. He proved an apt learner here, too, as
elsewhere. He did it *well*. That was a rule with
him. "Whatever is worth doing at all, is worth
doing well," — he believed it fully. So he wrestled
well. On a certain holiday, in Charlie's sixteenth
year, quite a large company assembled to see the
wrestlers try their strength. Among the wrestlers
was a bully — a young man of twenty-one or two
years of age, who was generally successful in laying
his comrades on their backs. The bully had succeeded in throwing quite a number who were so
presumptuous as to risk an encounter, when one of
the number proposed that Charlie should enter the

ring. He hesitated, and excused himself at first, but finally yielded to solicitation. On entering the ring, the scene presented was a second edition of David and Goliath. The bully was more than a head taller than Charlie, and nearly twice his weight. Yet the bully claimed the "under-hold," but relinquished his claim when the crowd cried "Shame!" in derision. The contest began; and Charlie, who believed that successful wrestling depended on skill more than strength, allowed his antagonist to exert and worry himself until quite fatigued, when, watching the favorable moment, he tripped the bully's feet, and laid him on his back. Such a yell of surprise and applause went up from the assembly as made the welkin ring. Cheer upon cheer, laugh upon laugh, shout after shout, followed, until the crestfallen bully slunk away out of sight, and was never known thereafter to court notoriety in that vicinity.

It was Charlie's tact and skill that gave him success. He was neither large nor strong of his age. Rather he was small of his age, though wiry and athletic. He had scarcely grown at all in New York state. The neighbors said that his excessive labor prevented his growth. Be that as it may, he brought down the Philistine without any parade or boasting.

When Charles had been there about four years, the sympathy for him in town attained its climax. People said it was "outrageous for a boy to be worked as Dexter worked him." Many insisted that the authorities ought to interpose in behalf of the boy. Finally, the excitement reached such a pitch that the authorities did interfere. They waited upon Dexter, and expressed the sentiments of the people plainly and candidly. The result was, that Charles returned to Lisbon, Connecticut. Dexter gave a final illustration of his generosity by presenting the boy with *one dollar* to pay his passage home. Here, again, Charles was equal to the occasion; for he walked nearly the whole distance, occasionally catching a ride with some passing traveller, using his money to buy food and lodgings as far as it went, and then begging these the remainder of the way.

5

V.

HOME AGAIN.

IT was a glad welcome home that Charles received. It was a joyous greeting that he extended to the old hearthstone. He was fully satisfied with pioneer life; and a boy was never happier than he to escape from a hard lot. Still, he had learned to endure hardness as a good soldier; and the experience had proved a benefit to him. His self-reliance and efficiency were developed by his relentless service in New York. There was a manliness about his methods that was unusual. He undertook labor as if he thoroughly understood it. There was a promptness and dispatch in his movements that indicated both acquaintance and ability.

The nail-shop had attractions for him now which it never possessed before. It was paradise to him in comparison with the drudgery and hardship of his farm-life. He turned off nails with a relish and facility that caused his father to smile. The prospect was that he would be a nailer by trade. We think that the farm and nail-shop did more to make him the practical man that he became than college could have done.

During the winter following his return, he again attended the district school. An incident occurred at that term of school illustrative of his politeness. In his presence, a boy indulged himself in vulgar remarks before the girls. Partly in a vein of pleasantry, and partly as a rebuke, Charles seized the lad by his coat-collar, and whirled him round and round. In his circuit through the air, his head hit the stove-pipe, cutting quite a gash over his temple. The blood flowed freely for a few moments, and Charles poured out his regrets in profusion at what he had done, proceeding at once to bind up the wound and put matters on a peaceable footing. His genuine politeness, however, was manifest, notwithstanding the accident. He had no sympathy with pranks or language that smacked of rudeness or vulgarity. In the presence of ladies, he thought every youth was put upon his good behavior. This was a noble trait.

In the spring following, Charles and his brother Thomas had an opportunity to work in a nail-shop at Norwich, where they could board with a sister. The opportunity was improved, and they remained there some ten months. Both pleased their employer by their unremitting industry and tact; and both studiously labored to improve themselves mentally in their evening hours. There was a small circulating library in the village, where books could be had at a few cents per day each. As a matter of economy in their straitened circumstances, they took out but one book at a time, reading it together

by the light of one tallow candle.   Sitting side by
side, they would read a volume, turning the leaves
to suit each other, soon learning to read a page in
about the same time.   In this way, volume after
volume of biography, history, and travels were
carefully read, and their contents treasured in retentive memories.   They purchased Weams's " Life
of Washington," in which both were specially interested, reading it again and again, until both could
repeat a good part of it.

During their ten months' residence in Norwich
they scarcely spent an evening away from home,
but improved every moment in reading.   Neither
of them had much taste for light reading at that
time.   Charles had developed rapidly, and now he
thirsted for knowledge as never before.   He began
to think about becoming a doctor.   He had no idea
of making nails for a living all his days.   He could
not understand exactly how the object could be accomplished, but he knew that poorer boys than he
had become doctors, lawyers, and ministers.   He
was earning money slowly, and he could earn more
as he grew older, and possibly his father might render him some aid ; at any rate, he could lay out the
road to the medical profession on paper, though he
might never travel it in reality.   Difficulties, however, did not discourage him — he was not that sort
of a youth.   Like Sir Charles Napier, " difficulties
made his feet go deeper into the ground."   Though he
did not have the sentiment clear cut and well-defined
in his soul, — namely, that " necessity and not facility

is the secret of success," — the gist of it was there, nevertheless. If Wilkie could learn to sketch on a barn-door with a burnt stick; if Stothard could acquire the art of combining colors by studying the wings of a butterfly; if Ferguson could make a clock with a common pocket-knife; if Gifford could work out his first problems in mathematics on scraps of leather pounded smooth; if Rittenhouse could calculate eclipses on his plough-handle; if Hugh Miller could carve the fortunes of a geologist out of the "Old Red Sandstone;" and if hundreds of others could win the object of their highest ambition in spite of poverty, obscurity, and difficulty, — then there was a chance for him to exchange the nail-shop for a doctor's office.

His ten months' residence in Norwich proved of great service to him. We think that really it determined his course into the medical profession. From that time his mind was eager for knowledge, and all his thoughts and aims seemed to turn in that direction. With all his mirth he possessed an indomitable spirit, that, once directed in a given course, knew no faltering. Buxton, the English philanthropist, said, "The longer I live, the more I am certain that the great difference between men, between the feeble and the powerful, is *energy*, invincible determination — a purpose once fixed, and then death or victory. That quality will do anything that can be done in this world; and no talents, no circumstances, no opportunities, will make a two-legged creature a man without it." That

Charles Jewett possessed this quality in an eminent degree, the story of his life fully proves. From the time that he served in the Norwich nail-shop it took direction, growing more and more intense from year to year, until finally it was "death or victory."

He must have saved nine or ten hundred hours for reading during that period, the value of which cannot be estimated. From fifteen to twenty thousand pages must have been read in that time, which is equal to forty fair-sized volumes. This amount of reading, divided between history, biography, and travels, provides a fund of information that the retentive memory will carry into future years.

It was a rich vein that he struck here; it was a mine. When a youth understands that leisure hours need not, and must not be, idle hours, he has taken a long step upwards. Just here thousands of youth make a fatal mistake. Just here Charles Jewett made a significant strike. He found an inspiration in leisure hours that not only fired his brain, but nerved his arms for manual labor. The more he thirsted for knowledge, the more he was willing to work for it with his hands. Brain-work reconciled him to hand-work, and hand-work stimulated brain-work. Both together laid the foundation of his success. Neither of them alone, in the circumstances, would or could have made him what he became.

Carlyle once wrote to a young man who sought his advice: "It is not by books alone, nor by books chiefly, that a man becomes in all parts a man.

Study to do faithfully whatever thing in your actual situation, there and now, you find, either expressly or tacitly, laid to your charge; that is your post; stand to it like a true soldier. A man perfects himself by work much more than by reading. They are a growing kind of men that can wisely combine the two things, — wisely, valiantly can do what is laid to their hand in their present sphere, and prepare themselves withal for doing other wider things, if such lie before them."

If this counsel had been written especially for Charles Jewett, he could not have reduced it to practice more thoroughly than he did in youth and later life.

It was this principle and spirit, as we shall see, that enabled Charles Jewett to improve his mind when engaged in manual labor, to explore science and study English and American literature, after entering the medical profession, and to acquaint himself with various branches of knowledge and arts of industry when his time was occupied by philanthropic labors.

Soon after he closed his labors at Norwich, he entered the Academy at Plainfield, Conn., a few miles from his native place. It was an era in his life when he became a member of the Plainfield Academy. It was his first actual step towards the medical profession. The school was good and popular for that day, though its curriculum was limited to the English branches. Latin even was not taught, and, of course, youth were not prepared for college there. Nor was Charles looking collegeward. That was out of the question, owing to his poverty. He could continue but two terms in the Academy, and he must make the most of that; and he did. They were two terms of close application and rapid progress. He enjoyed it. His teacher enjoyed it, too. A more popular and brilliant student had not attended the Academy. His rare social qualities drew many firm friends around him, while his sparkling wit made the scene lively and happy. In composition and declamation he excelled. Unlike many students, he never shirked these important exercises, nor any others. His compositions were always characteristic, possessing a vein of humor that charmed, while they abounded with thought. He wrote one upon "The Cradle," that has been remembered for its originality and ingenuity. The hearers supposed that it was the familiar and useful thing for rocking babies, as they listened to its serio-comic description to the very last paragraph, when their sobriety was turned to laughter by learning that it was the common implement for cradling grain. The whole school soon learned to expect real entertainment when Jewett read a composition. And it was equally so with declamations. He carried his audience every time. His power of imitation enabled him to make his speech seem reality. His face spoke as well as his voice. Indeed, he spoke all over; for he threw his whole soul into it, just as he did into everything. His reputation at the Plainfield Academy, when his

academic career closed, was that of a talented,
witty, genial, promising young man.

On returning to his home, the all-important question was, What next? For a season he applied himself to labor on the farm and in the nail-shop, improving his spare hours in study and reading. It
was settled, finally, that he should study medicine
with Dr. Elijah Baldwin, a physician of considerable note in South Canterbury, three or four miles
distant. The doctor had several medical students
pursuing their studies with him, attending medical
lectures at Pittsfield, Mass., or elsewhere, in the
winter. But he must acquire some knowledge of
Latin first. An interview with the pastor, Rev.
Levi Nelson, resulted in the arrangement to study
Latin with him. Mr. Nelson had already engaged
to teach Miss Frances Calkins, a teacher in Norwich, a young lady of acknowledged talents and
literary taste. It was settled that the two should
study Latin together, and commence at once.

" It is claimed," said Miss Calkins to young Jewett, " that females do not possess the ability of males ;
and that so high scholarship ought not to be expected of them."

" I don't know about that," answered Jewett;
" but I feel quite sure that some females have more
talents than some men, and make better scholars."

" Nor is that much of a compliment," replied Miss
Calkins, " since some men have not much ability to
boast of."

Jewett laughed, and suggested that the present

might be a good opportunity to settle the question between the sexes — that he would represent the male portion of humanity, and she the female part, the result of the contest determining which sex possessed superiority of intellect — a sort of Adam and Eve arrangement, with the forbidden fruit left out, and much pleasantry put in.

Miss Calkins accepted the proposition in high glee, and the contest began about May, 1825. It was a short, animated, sharp contest, brimful of fun. In three weeks, Jewett was so far in advance of his fair contestant that he was reciting alone to his pastor. The young lady did nobly, and proved herself to be an excellent scholar; but both she and her teacher were surprised to witness the strides of her opponent over the Latin race-course. He carried off the prize, though it rather annoyed his gallantry " to beat a woman." This young lady became one of Connecticut's most accomplished women, and several years ago she wrote the "History of Norwich."

In six weeks Mr. Nelson reported that young Jewett had mastered the amount of Latin required at the commencement of a medical course; adding his opinion that it was a very remarkable feat! The amount required was the Latin Grammar and the whole of Virgil.

All this time Charles was at home, and found more or less work to do on the farm and in the shop. Every day a portion of his time was given to physical labor, both as a necessity and for needful exercise. The celebrated Dr. Arnold held that pupils would accomplish a great deal more by devoting a liberal portion of their time to physical labor. He once remarked: "I would far rather send a boy to Van Diemen's Land, where he must work for his bread, than send him to Oxford to live in luxury, without any desire in his mind to avail himself of the advantages. . . . If there be one thing on earth which is truly admirable, it is to see God's wisdom blessing an inferiority of natural powers, when they have been honestly, truly, and zealously cultivated." There is no doubt that Charles Jewett made a stronger man intellectually because he was under the necessity of laboring with his hands in early life.

VI.

THE MEDICAL STUDENT.

ABOUT the time that Charles began the study
of medicine, rumors reached the family of
opposition to the sale and use of intoxicating liquors
in some localities.   This rumor caused discussion
upon the subject at the fireside, all regarding hostility to the traffic as just and wise.   Father and sons
knew that intemperance had made sad work in Lisbon families, and that many of them procured the
agent of their ruin at the liquor-shop near by.
Everybody drank intoxicating liquors at that time,
and most people regarded such beverages as indispensable to health and longevity.   They were considered indispensable, also, as a pledge of friendship !   They were found on every sideboard, and
were used by all classes.   Ministers used them as
freely as their people.   Christian men, and even
deacons of churches, sold them without the least
compunction of conscience.   They were used on all
occasions ; at parties, weddings, funerals, ordination
of ministers, military trainings, when visitors came
and went, when neighbors met, in field, and house,
and shop, everywhere, these fiery beverages were
used, and scarcely any one had raised the question

of impropriety or wrong about the custom. Here and there might be found a person who refrained from drinking them because of some natural aversion. There was one such person in Mr. Jewett's family. His son Joseph could never be prevailed upon to take a swallow of the stuff. He abominated the taste of it, and declared that he was better off without than with it. When a party said to him, " But, Joseph, you cannot stand it on water alone, through these long hot days, and in the midst of such severe labor, without a little stimulus. You will be faint and give out before night," he replied, " Well, when I do you will know it."

No one ever saw Joseph "give out;" so that in the Jewett family the common theory that intoxicating liquors would promote endurance by imparting strength, was not exactly current. Then a man was found occasionally, like Charles's father, and Mrs. Jewett's " grandfather Adams," who took but one glass per day, and that at eleven o'clock A. M. But such cases were exceptional. Moderate drinking was universal, and immoderate drinking was fearfully prevalent. Drunkards were more numerous than saints. Charles could count " one-tenth of the male population of his native town who were occasional or habitual drunkards."

One evening Mr. Jewett was discussing the subject with his sons, and deprecating the ravages of intemperance, when he said to Charles :

" Charles, you are always scribbling about something, and for the most part, I think, on matters of very little importance; and now, if you have any gifts in connection with the use of the quill, try your hand for once on a subject of some consequence."

"What would you have me do?" inquired Charles.

"Go into your chamber to-morrow morning, and write an address to the authorities of this town, and endeavor to show them the folly and wickedness of granting men license to destroy the peace and happiness of the neighborhood by selling liquors; for that is the result of the sale any way; and men with but half an eye ought to see it."

It is quite evident that Charles's father had his eyes open to see the curse of rum at that time, although he was not an abstainer. It is clear, also, that Providence was disciplining the son, through the father, for a temperance career second to that of no man who ever lived; and it was a good beginning.

Charles adopted his father's advice, and on the next morning went to his room, where he produced, at one sitting, an "Appeal to the Town Authorities in Rhyme." The following is an extract that shows its pith and point.

We are not to read this and other subsequent poetical effusions to learn their intrinsic value, but for the *look* it affords us into the soul of the youth. His aspirations, aims, and principles appear as unmistakably in these rhythmic efforts, as they would were he the sweetest poet of the land.

"Most of the evils to this fount we trace,
  Which blast our pleasures and destroy our race.

For *this* the widow mourns her husband dead;
For *this* the starving children cry for bread;
For *this* the wife sits waiting for her spouse,
At midnight hour, and ponders o'er her woes;
While he, poor wretch, all power of moving fled,
Sleeps by the fence, or in yon crazy shed.
In vain she goes and listens at the door:
The sighing breeze, the torrent's distant roar,
Are all she hears; now, where her children sleep
She casts one look, and then lies down to weep.
Now, tell me, what on earth can comfort bring?
Or from what source shall smiling pleasure spring?"

It closed with this appeal to the fathers of the town :

"Oh banish grog-shops, and suppress the ill;
Delay no longer, but your part fulfil :
Rescue the fallen, sinking age regard,
And Heaven's rich blessing be your great reward."

His father was highly pleased with the production, and posted off to Norwich, where he had a hundred copies of it printed. The next Saturday night, after counseling secrecy in the matter, he and his sons tacked up copies of it in different parts of the town. Some were tacked to front gates; others were carefully folded and slipped under door-knockers or thrust under front doors. One was tacked to the box on the whipping-post, that still stood in front of the meeting-house, — a relic of olden times, when crimes were punished by flogging.

The excitement occasioned by this first assault upon the liquor traffic was novel for those times.

Many were pleased with the demonstration; others condemned it. Church-goers crowded about the whipping-post, Sunday noon, to read the remarkable production, that was so hard upon a business which most of the readers considered respectable. Charles elbowed his way through the crowd, as eager as any of them to read the document. His manner and remarks were well suited to cause men to look away from the Jewett family to discover the author. The poetical effusion was discussed more on that day than the pastor's sermons. At nearly every hearthstone it was the subject of remark and criticism; and, on the whole, it proved a very efficient method to arouse the community to the evils of intemperance, and set people to thinking upon the subject and discussing it. It startled like a bombshell unexpectedly thrown into the enemies' camp.

We judge that the pastor was not an indifferent spectator, because one year thereafter he caused the organization of a temperance society, though the pledge prohibited only the sale and use of spirituous liquors. Charles was one of the first to sign the pledge, the members of his father's family doing the same. Mr. Nelson also preached upon the subject, taking advanced ground for that day. A year later we find that Mr. Jewett wrote to Charles, who was attending medical lectures at Pittsfield, Massachusetts, as follows:

"Mr. Nelson gave the young men a lecture on ardent spirits this afternoon (November 9, 1828), from the text, 'Young men, I exhort to be sober-minded,' which I hope will make all the inhabitants temperate, if they do not wholly refrain from drinking spirits."

Charles was nearly or quite nineteen years of age when he began the study of medicine. He boarded with Dr. B. when he studied with him, going home on Saturday nights to spend his Sabbaths. At the same time that he pursued his medical studies, he turned his hand to farming, especially in hay-time, whenever Dr. B. needed additional help upon his large farm.

Several other students were in Dr. B.'s family, among them Reuben Crandall, who, subsequently, espoused the anti-slavery cause, and was imprisoned in Baltimore for aiding slaves to their freedom. He was brother of Miss Prudence Crandall, whose school for colored girls in Canterbury was broken up by the pro-slavery mobocratic spirit that possessed the defenders of slavery at that day. These things may have exerted a strong influence upon the heart of Charles Jewett, subsequently, to make him the fearless advocate of emancipation that he became.

Charles "took to medicine surprisingly," as a person remarked. The only profession that most people seemed to think God made him for was the clerical, provided he became a Christian; so that it was a surprise to many that he applied himself to medicine as if he meant business. Sharp discrimination and nice analysis, for which he was qualified by nature, prepared him to appreciate this new branch of science. Even this, however, could not

6

absorb his interest in agriculture, horticulture, music, and other departments of knowledge. He criticised the methods of raising fruit that were generally adopted, especially the method of raising peaches. He begged Dr. B. to allow him the opportunity to graft and bud in order to illustrate the truth of his statements. So Dr. Baldwin gave him full scope on his farm, and the young thinker worked with a will to establish his views upon the peach crop. The result was that ten or fifteen years thereafter Dr. B. had the finest peach orchard anywhere in that vicinity, and just as enduring as it was prolific. Dr. B. considered that the result was a proof of the correctness of Charles's ideas of budding and grafting, as well as of the selection and quality of original fruits. Samples of his grafting are to be seen in extra apple-trees on the Baldwin homestead to-day.

His interest in botany, too, rather increased. Very often he would come down from his room in the morning, and go at his medical lesson, as one who had other irons in the fire awaiting his attention ; and in an incredible short time his lesson was learned, and away he would go to experiment in his profession, or to botanize in the fields, gathering specimens, and pushing investigations. He became in later years a skilled botanist, and yet made no pretensions in that direction. Few men or women ever excelled him in knowledge of plants of every description, flowers of every hue and color, and herbs of every sort, whether possessing medicinal qualities or not. The methods of preserving plants and flowers, the soil best adapted to their culture, together with their habits and nature, whether sturdy or otherwise, were all familiar to him.

He became a fast friend of " Old Buck," a favorite dog in the family. It was in his line to befriend the canine race; and such a venerable and clever canine as " Old Buck" wrought largely upon his sympathies. They would do anything for each other that was reasonable. But Charlie's fondness for experimenting in the uses of medicine got the better of his tender sympathies one day; and he administered a dose of asafœtida to the confiding animal. His object was to study the effects of the nasty drug upon the brute, which he did to his satisfaction. The poor dog expressed his disgust for the nauseating medicine by all sorts of canine contortions of the face, and by lively exercise over the yard. He cut Charlie's acquaintance, and never more allowed himself to play the role of patient for a young doctor to experiment upon.

During the first season of his study with Dr. Baldwin, he rendered some service at manual labor in hay-time. Then, it was not thought to be possible to make hay successfully, or do any other farm-work well, without rum. Medical practitioners generally recommended its use to impart strength; also, to keep out the heat in summer and the cold in winter. But Charles discarded the whole rum theory; he did not believe in it. So that, on the very threshold of the study of medical science, he began to doubt and even to reject medical theories.

"You can't labor at haying on cold water alone, without giving out before night," said Dr. B. "It might be possible in cold weather, but in hot weather hard labor is impossible without spirits."

"The proof of the pudding is in the eating; wait and see," replied Charles. "I can work as long and as hard as any man on the farm without rum. There is my brother Joe, who never drank a glass of rum in his life, — he will endure as long, and perform as much hard work, as the stoutest rum-drinker; and I can do the same."

"And do as much work, like mowing, raking, and pitching, as the men I hire?" inquired Dr. B.

"Yes, do as much work — mow as much, rake as much, and pitch as much," answered Charles.

"Well, I shall believe it when I see it," retorted Dr. B. "You will have ample opportunity to test your theory in the hay-field."

"Of course," said Charles; "and if I do not do as much work as your man Brown, and keep at it as long, then I will yield my hostility to rum, and own that it is good."

The discussion was long and animated, and much more was said, of course, than we have space to record. But it was settled that Brown should have the rum, and Charles should have the water, except that the latter stipulated for a given quantity of milk porridge.

He plunged into haying with all his heart. The scythe flew, and the rake flew, and the pitchfork flew, and Brown flew also, to keep out of his way.

He neither lagged nor faltered under the blaze of the hottest sun ; and his excellent humor withstood the racket of the race well. He was as bright, chipper, and jolly at sundown as he was at sunrise, while Brown looked tired and lank, as if he wanted to take another glass and go immediately to bed. Charles was ready at the close of each day for a jump in the door-yard, or to go and see the girls. We have no doubt that " he put the best foot forward ; " he would have been extremely foolish to have done otherwise. It was a match between cold water and rum : and the latter came off second best. Water and porridge found a noble champion in the unfledged doctor. So did rum find an heroic worker in Brown ; but rum cannot give what it does not possess. It had no more strength to bestow fifty years ago than it has now.

From that time until his death the subject of this memoir was at war with the doctors as to the vitalizing effects of alcohol, though he never denied that there is a place for it in the materia medica. We shall learn hereafter how far these views of his youth were carried out in his medical practice and public teaching.

Charles was the same fun-loving and fun-making fellow as a student of medicine that he was everywhere else. He made merry times for the group of students and for the family. He sang and played the flute well. He could also play the violin and bass-viol, although these latter instruments were not in use at Dr. B.'s. His musical talents came in to augment the general fund of pleasure, as well as to dignify some humorous scenes that might not have been so well enjoyed without them. All his other resources of fun-making were drawn upon to contribute to a good time generally. His remarkable powers of mimicry became increasingly popular. It spread into the neighborhood. The young people could not enjoy a party without Charles. His presence was "as good as a play" anywhere. A lady about his age, one of the girls who knew him well fifty years ago and upwards, writes:

"I well remember that first essay on temperance that he wrote, addressed to the selectmen of the town, and what a commotion it made. He was much given to writing poetry about that time on various subjects. He was a youth of rare talents and ability, brimful of fun, and the most perfect mimic I ever saw. I have in my mind two or three instances where the acting was perfect. It was not done with the intent to ridicule or disparage the characters of the persons represented, but for a little pleasantry and fun."

Allusion is made here to his ability to imitate the eccentricities of persons. At that time he would exactly represent persons in town, men and women, noted for a peculiar gait, a peculiar voice, a peculiar motion of the body or use of language. This power became of great service to him in his future philanthropic labors.

There was a girl in Dr. Baldwin's family, not older than Charles, who did much of the spinning for the household. The spinning-wheel was an indispensable article of furniture at that day. She was not fond of the business, and often gave expression to her dislike when the work troubled her. Fretting was common with her, accompanied with a singular tone of voice and jerk of the body that indicated the soured spirit within. One day, in the presence of the students and the family, Charles took his seat at the spinning-wheel to imitate the girl. He could spin almost as well as she, and he made the wheel buzz for a time, but soon got into trouble with it as the girl did; and he proceeded to mimic her snarling and fretting, imitating the very tones of her voice, using the expressions and reproducing her movements of body so perfectly that the whole roomful of persons burst into a loud laugh, enjoying the scene hugely. The poor girl, who had often been counselled upon the matter, was too mortified to laugh and too vexed to cry; but she was never known to fret and scold over the spinning-wheel again. It cured her.

Charles could then imitate with surprising exactness the voice of any person, the tones and general appearance of any public speaker to whom he had listened, the notes of birds, the bark of dogs, the squeal of pigs, the bleating of sheep, the lowing of cattle, and much more that we need not mention. One day Dr. Baldwin returned from visiting patients, and, on alighting from his carriage, he heard a sound behind his barn like the cry of a bird in distress. He went thither to learn the cause. Looking over a high wall, he discovered Charles imitat-

ing the carol of a bobolink so perfectly that the bird
was fluttering and screaming above his head as if
he had one of her own family in his grasp. When
the doctor had watched him a few moments, Charles
looked up and saw him, remarking :

" That fellow has two notes that I can't get."

The doctor thought he got them all, however.

At the time in question, Lisbon had made some
advance, and a Sabbath school existed; there was,
also, a small town library ; both of these were pat-
ronized by Charles with real enthusiasm. He loved
to study the Bible, although he was not yet a Christian. He attended the Sabbath school, not because
he felt compelled to attend, but from choice. And
he was a close, thoughtful, discriminating student
of the Bible.

The little circulating library was a treat to him.
He interspersed his medical studies with reading from
it. Among the volumes that he especially enjoyed
was Young's *Night Thoughts*. He read it over and
over, and committed much of it to memory. His
interest in the volume never abated. We have heard
him recite passages from it within ten years, accompanied by remarks upon its beauties and real worth.
Baxter's *Call to the Unconverted* was another volume that he read with much interest : a very singular selection for a youth of his make-up, but just
the sort of a work to mix up with his mirthfulness,
that the latter might not always be in the ascendant.
This volume set him to thinking more seriously
about religious things. It appealed to his better

judgment, and sounded an alarm to his heart, that he could not altogether dismiss. Still nobody knew by his appearance that he was at all inclined to listen to the " Call."

At this time the young people had frequent parties in town, at which it was evident that girls and boys belonged to the fallen race of Adam in spite of Puritanic customs and close 'udy of the " Assembly's Catechism." Games and plays were current at those times, and usually a fascinating dance terminated the " good time," often quite late into the evening. For music, there was usually some young man of their number who could play the violin sufficiently to lead a country-dance. That was hedged in so effectually by Orthodox discipline as never to run into what was called a " ball." The old people, who sometimes trembled at the worldliness of youth, and wondered what would become of them, made a plain distinction between "*tripping the light fantastic toe* " in a neighbor's dining-room or kitchen, and doing the same thing until two or three o'clock in the morning in a public hall. The class of youth of whom we are speaking never ventured to cross that Puritanic line, and appear at a " ball."

At these sociables *manners* were taught. This was an important feature, and the thing was done somewhat on this wise. Two parties would go into another room, from which they would return in due time, when one of them would introduce the other to the whole company, one after the other. This was varied with other forms of etiquette, in order

to cultivate ease and grace in manners, and make
all familiar with the demands of the best society.

Charles enjoyed such occasions hugely ; and they
enjoyed him. It seemed as if he were made for
such occasions, and that such occasions were made
for him. At any rate they were just adapted to
each other. So long as he mixed up medical
science, Young's "Night Thoughts," and Baxter's
"Call to the Unconverted" with them, together with
frequent excellent paternal and maternal counsels
at home, there was not much danger that these
scenes of gayety would lead him astray. It is certain
that they did not. Perhaps his interest in these occasions was deepened by the fact that a certain young
lady, of whom we shall hear more, was the best
dancer of the company and the most accomplished
in manners; so graceful and fairy-like as to well-
nigh bewitch his tender heart. It was she who took
the "Scottish Chiefs" from the Library to read,
causing much gossip and criticism thereby, because
her "grandfather Adams" was a deacon of the Orthodox church. Sinners' children might read novels, but the children of saints could not do it with
impunity.

Agriculture, horticulture, medical science, music,
botany, and some minor branches of knowledge
commanded his attention about this time, but astron-
omy did not appear to fascinate him. We do not
hear that he studied the heavenly bodies at all.
But there was one little terrestrial body that performed its daily orbit at "grandfather Adams's," on

the opposite hill, a third of a mile distant, that he studied with somewhat more interest than he did medicine or horticulture. He was wont to go out a few rods distant, near sunset, and seat himself under a splendid oak on the highest point of land, where he would play on his flute the most loving airs that Cupid could suggest. He claimed that he went thither to enjoy the magnificent panorama that nature spread out before him (and at this time, after the lapse of more than fifty years, any person who has visited the spot, as the author has, can readily believe the young student) ; but his fellow-students declared that his observations related to the aforesaid brilliant little orb, in full view from his position, rather than the celestial horoscope, and that his dulcet notes were "the music of the spheres." However, no amount of teasing ever destroyed our young friend's equilibrium. He was independent by nature, and he meant to be by practice. He had great respect for girls in general, and it was nobody's business if he singled out one to respect in particular. So the matter ran along, while dame rumor circulated reports, both true and false, though subsequent events proved that the true were far more abundant than the false. At length an event transpired that confirmed the suspicions of the aged, and afforded both proof and merriment for the young folks. Quite a number of the girls devoted an afternoon to a huckleberry trip. In their enjoyable wanderings they encountered a hornets' nest unexpectedly, the denizens of which attacked the fair intru-

ders with mad haste. The girls fled precipitately
from the foe, pulling down their calashes over their
faces for protection. Unfortunately Lucy (the sat-
ellite mentioned) pulled her calash over her face
just in season to shut in a hornet that stung her
without mercy, as hornets will. Some of the girls
got into a worse hornets' nest years thereafter; but
Lucy never did. A few days after the rather serious event, she received the following poetic effusion
from Charles, designed to be, without question, a
" very precious ointment " for healing purposes.

TO L—— *.

The little bee, whom you thus sorely blame,
  While gazing on thy beauty, lovely girl,
Was so intoxicated with love's flame,
  That giddiness made his little cranium whirl.

And, quite unable to remove the charm,
  Around thy head he flew, yet knew not why;
He thought no ill, nor wished to do thee harm,
  But with a random stroke he hit thine eye.

Ah, then, what sorrows filled his little breast!
  My muse was listening, and she heard him say
He'd power to cure thee, and, at thy request,
  Would come and kiss the anguish all away.

C—— * *.

This Bee-in-the-bonnet-affair, together with a ride
or two with the young lady, convinced people generally that the embryo doctor was in earnest, and

that Miss Lucy A. Tracy would one day be Mrs. Dr. Charles Jewett, — all of which occurred in fulfilment of numerous neighborhood prophecies.

We shall see that this was one of the most important transactions of young Jewett's life. We smile or laugh over so-called "love affairs," as if they were trifling matters incident to early life only, when in reality they bless or curse the whole future existence on earth, and perhaps beyond. No graver matter ever engages the attention of a young man than the choice of a life-companion, save his personal relations to Christ. His choice of a profession may dwindle into insignificance in the comparison. In the instance before us, the mutual choice proved the greatest blessing. Dr. Charles Jewett, the philanthropist and reformer, never could have accomplished his great work without the co-operation and supporting sympathy of his wife. How many times his intimate friends have heard the veteran affirm as much, when worn and weary with the heat and strife of battle! How many times have still more intimate associates observed as much in his actions, that "speak louder than words"! If "matches are made in heaven," then heaven had something to do with the hornets' nest and what followed. If the husband was made for a doctor, agriculturist, horticulturist, teacher, temperance lecturer, and defender of the right, in spite of contumely and reproach, then the wife must have been made to stand side by side with him in all of these relations; for she did it with the wisdom, fidelity, and heroism of the noblest women who adorn the page of history.

In his admiration for Shakspeare, in later years, he maintained that " Romeo and Juliet " is the most perfect description of love-making that was ever penned. No doubt that Shakspeare hit his case exactly.

At Dr. Baldwin's, Charles furnished additional evidence that he was a born artist. He amused himself and the family by drawing profiles of the members and of the neighbors. These profiles were not caricatures, but rare specimens of artistic skill. No professional could produce better likenesses. Some said, "they look as if they could speak." Many persons insisted upon keeping the profiles of themselves and friends, because they were so natural. At the Baldwin homestead we saw a number of them, drawn fifty-four years ago, somewhat faded it is true, but the outlines still traceable. Aunt Polly's profile — an old woman in the neighborhood at that time — all said was perfect. And so they have been handed down, and are sure proof of the taste for the fine arts that Charles possessed. He did not hesitate to undertake the profile of any living mortal, except the particular young lady on the opposite hill. She was too fair a subject in his eye, no doubt, for his inexperienced pencil to try.

In the winter following, Charles attended medical lectures at Pittsfield, Mass. Here his medical proclivities found ample scope. No part of his literary course was more enjoyable to him than this. He scarcely left his boarding-place for an hour, day or evening, for pleasure. Time for needful exercise he took, of course, but nothing beyond. An occasional public lecture drew him out for an evening, but nothing in the way of pleasure commanded an hour of his time. His undivided attention was given to his medical studies.

In the lecture-room he was sharp and inquisitive. He did not hesitate to disagree with the doctors if the weight of evidence seemed to be against them. Each day an invitation was given to the class, that as many as pleased would take the front seat to be questioned. This was after the regular lecture. Charles never failed to be on that seat; and he enjoyed that part of the exercises best of all. He could ask as many questions as any professor, and he could answer questions as easily as he could ask them. He was the life of the class; and to-day there are physicians living who recall and rehearse the occasions when his wisdom and wit were a rare entertainment for the class. Nor was he at all opposed to an occasional freak of sport among the young men who were qualifying themselves for the soberest practice.

In the class was a " swell," as the boys called him, — a young fop, who seemed to think that what he did not know was not worth knowing. He was very unpopular, and the students loved to annoy him. One day he came to the lecture pompous as ever, and took his seat in front with his hat on his head. It was not quite lecture-time, and the professor had not arrived. A student behind him knocked his hat off, causing some satisfaction and not a little merriment. Charles improved the moment to provide another covering for the young man's head. He seized a feed-basket that happened to be under one of the seats (such as oxen and horses eat from), and quicker than we can tell it, thrust it on the fellow's head, crowding it down over his face until his quite prominent nasal organ prevented its removal by himself alone. The professor appeared upon the scene when the poor fellow was doing his best to remove the unusual head-gear, and seemed to enjoy the comical side-show as much as his pupils, although he did not say so. This single exhibition of frolic satisfied Charles for the whole time he spent in Pittsfield. He had many and grave duties to perform, and to their discharge he bent all his powers. We have sought in vain for other spurts of his roguish nature while he attended upon the medical lectures at Pittsfield. He spent two seasons there; and, as the second season was so much like the first, we shall not have occasion to recur to it, and so shall dismiss his residence at Pittsfield with one more fact.

During the first winter of Charles's student-life there, the Rev. Dr. Hewett visited the place to lecture on temperance. His fame preceded him, and Charles heard the two lectures that he delivered. With his previous hostility to the sale and use of intoxicating liquors, he was roused to fiery enthusiasm by Dr. Hewett's eloquent appeals. From that moment Charles Jewett was a determined and uncompromising temperance reformer. He resolved to denounce and fight the evil henceforth and forever. And he kept his word. Forty years afterwards, Dr. Jewett delivered a temperance lecture in Bridgeport, Conn., the home of Dr. Hewett, who was old, infirm, and feeble; and he had the pleasure of welcoming him to the platform, where he opened the meeting with prayer.

We are reminded that the causes of Dr. Jewett's espousal and advocacy of the temperance cause are akin to those which led William Lloyd Garrison to the espousal and advocacy of the anti-slavery enterprise. The two young men came upon the stage about the same time, though Garrison was three or four years the senior; and the earthly career of both closed within a few weeks of each other. The one sympathized deeply in the reform work of the other; each esteemed the other for his hearty and heroic defence of right. On his dying-bed, Dr. Jewett inquired tenderly of the writer after Mr. Garrison's health, and expressed his admiration of the unselfish and unfaltering spirit with which he had contended for universal freedom. Immediately afterwards, in response to a call for a Jewett testimonial fund, Garrison wrote as follows:

" I would be willing to have my name appended to a circular to the public upon the subject; and I pledge ten dollars toward the fund aforesaid, hoping that the appeal

7

will be widely responded to, and to the full extent at least of the necessities of the case.

"The temperance movement, in a radical sense, has never had raised up in its support a more devoted, untiring, disinterested advocate than Dr. Jewett; and now that his noble life-work is near its close, and his translation to another sphere of existence a matter of hourly expectancy, it is most fitting that his family should be kindly and promptly assisted by the friends of temperance in the manner proposed."

With previous well-defined opinions, Garrison beheld the slave-pens of Baltimore, and his heart was fired with an unconquerable desire to rid the land of the crime. Jewett beheld the liquor-shop near his father's house where the slaves of appetite suffered worse than Egyptian bondage; and this, with the ringing philippic of Hewett, aroused his indomitable spirit to do and dare against the traffic the remainder of his life.

Charles studied another season with Dr. Baldwin. Some time in that period an accident occurred near his father's house, illustrative of the youth's zeal in the study of medicine. He happened to be at home when the accident occurred. A boy was kicked by a horse so seriously that his skull was broken, and some of his brains were scattered upon the ground. Charles was on hand to assist almost as soon as any one, and when the doctors had cared for the sufferer as well as they could, he gathered up the scattered brains and carried them home for critical examination and experiment. The doctors saved the boy, and Charles told him when he recovered, "If any-body says that you have no brains, tell them that I know better, for I have had some of them."

The writer was introduced to the party a few months ago, and concluded that he did not miss the few brains that Charles took for experiment.

During the second season at Dr. Baldwin's, also, Charles's inventive and mechanical skill found inter-esting play. He constructed a miniature bureau, the apartments of which were ample to hold jewelry and knickknacks; and he presented it to the young lady who had the contest with a hornet. It is still extant — a piece of cabinet-work that honors his skill. He made, also, a gem of a pocket-knife. The handle was wrought out of an old silver spoon, the blade being the best of steel, nicely finished and polished. This is still as good as new, although its possessor, who would not exchange it for any knife in the United States, dates her ownership of it back to the next year after the hornet difficulty.

We omitted to say, that, during the second winter of Charles's stay at Pittsfield, he made a set of dental instruments for his own use. At that time, regular physicians did all the teeth-pulling and teeth-repairing that was required by the public. Therefore, dental instruments were indispensable. Subsequently, he provided himself with surgical instruments by the use of cash instead of brains. The dental instruments were manufactured in the shop of a villager, who kindly granted him the use of his tools. When Charles had completed his work, the proprietor of the shop, who had watched him with the deepest interest, remarked, "*It is a pity to spoil a good mechanic to make a poor doctor.*"

In the last year of his medical studies, Charles became a Christian, an earnest, faithful follower of Christ. Various causes operated to bring about this event, not the least of which was his pastor's fidelity. From the time that he read Baxter's "Call to the Unconverted," his thoughts were more particularly turned to his personal obligations to love and serve God, while Mr. Nelson's faithfulness unwittingly supplemented the deep impressions made by that book. He stepped forth boldly upon the Lord's side, and from that time never faltered in Christian work. He united with the Congregational Church in Lisbon, on the first Sabbath of May, 1828.

Nothing remains to be added to this chapter, except that Charles studied medicine a short time with Dr. Eaton, of Norwich, before he took his medical degree. Dr. Eaton was an eminent physician, which fact, together with another, that he could board with his sister in the city, caused him to take this step.

VII.

THE SUCCESSFUL PHYSICIAN.

DR. CHARLES JEWETT commenced the practice of medicine in East Greenwich, R. I., in 1829. He was only twenty-two years of age, — pretty young for a physician, but old in tact and ability for one of his years. His personal appearance, too, was very much in his favor. With a splendid physique, tall, well-proportioned, muscular, graceful, with a dignified and manly bearing, the intellectual and refined element radiating from his lustrous eye and beaming face — few young men ever possessed more personal attractions at the threshold of public life. He found this advantage in going to his new field of labor, that the people had an exalted opinion of Connecticut teachers, doctors, and ministers. To receive a doctor from that state, who was so genial, sensible, and able, was a source of great pleasure to them. There was but one physician within five miles, and he was an old gentleman who was approaching the end of his career. His reception was all that he could desire; and he stepped directly into a good practice.

His sharp eye read the people very soon, and he found many of them uneducated and superstitious, and well settled in the notion that "ignorance is

bliss." A large number were mill operatives. Most
of the good people preferred ministers who worked
all the week at manual labor, and preached on Sunday as they were moved by what they called the
"sperit." Whether they wanted the doctor to practise by the "sperit," is not recorded. The leading
denomination of that region was the "Six-Principle
Baptists," whose creed was derived from the sixth
chapter of Hebrews, — a well-meaning class of people, but ignorant and superstitious. They had a poor
opinion of other denominations, with little disposition
to fraternize with them. Dr. Jewett found no difficulty, however, in mixing with them. He attended their
meetings. He participated in religious services with
them, doing his share of the labor efficiently, thereby
proving to them that he was a true Christian man.
Occasionally he rode five miles on the Sabbath to
the nearest Congregational church.

He was fortunate in his boarding-place, the family
of Mr. John Pitcher. They were kind, sensible people, though not cultivated. Mr. Pitcher was ready
to co-operate in every good work to the extent of his
ability. "Mother Pitcher," as the doctor always
called her, was the very soul of motherly care, interested deeply in every good thing proposed. Dr.
Jewett must have indulged his artistic propensity
soon after becoming a member of the family; for a
profile of the good lady lies before us, which he
executed very early in his Rhode Island life. Good
judges called it perfect. Mrs. Pitcher was delighted
with the work of art.

There were several boys in the family, whom the doctor soon drew to himself by his methods of entertainment. He interested himself in their pastime as well as in their work. Seeing them turning a grindstone for their father, he suggested to the boys that the small stream of water near by might be utilized to do that work. The boys could not understand how such a wonderful feat could be accomplished, but they were anxious to see it done. So, with such assistance as they could render, he employed some of his spare time in constructing a water-wheel, and setting it up in the stream. It was not long before the boys had the pleasure of seeing the grindstone turned by water, more rapidly, too, than their best exertions could secure by hand. Subsequently this water-power was utilized for other purposes.

Dr. Jewett found opportunity also to gratify his grafting ability. He demonstrated to Mr. Pitcher's satisfaction that his fruit-trees might be improved immensely by grafting choice fruit into them. He did the work, too, with as much enjoyment as he would have done if the trees had been his own.

Crops on the farm, too, commanded his attention. The rotation of crops, and the adaptation of certain soils to certain crops, were familiar subjects to him; and Mr. Pitcher was benefited by his intelligent suggestions. Choice seed-corn and potatoes, also, were introduced by his advice. And the benefits of these improvements spread, in time, through the town. Other fruit-growers and farmers adopted them, so that the improvement became somewhat general. That a physician should know more about agriculture and horticulture, as well as machinery, than the wisest among themselves, appeared to set them to thinking and acting.

There was little regard for the Sabbath. At that time Rhode Island was rather famous for desecrating the Lord's day. Many people labored on Sundays as on other days of the week. Many others used it for a holiday. It was a time for visiting, hunting, fishing, and ball-playing. Only a small part of the population attended meeting. The moral status of such a community is well understood. A profane, vulgar, rowdyish, intemperate population, as a whole, was the inevitable result. Drunkenness abounded. What Dr. Jewett had witnessed hitherto scarcely prepared him at all to behold such scenes as were enacted in his adopted state. Everybody used intoxicating liquors. It seemed to him that a majority of men used them excessively. There was not a temperance man in the whole town. The doctor found himself alone in this regard, and he felt lonely. He was not a teetotaler at that time. The pledge he had taken did not prohibit fermented and malt liquors, though he did not allow himself to drink any intoxicants but wine and cider, and these not habitually. He set himself to work to convert the family with which he boarded, and he was successful. Then he extended his temperance labors carefully, coveting the accession of only one person at a time, in the circumstances. Forty years thereafter, he wrote as follows of his policy in that day of small things:

" Often, while waiting to watch the operation of medicines on the sick, there would be opportunities to talk about something, and somehow it would frequently happen that the conversation would turn on the fearful prevalence of intemperance and on the serious injury therefrom to all the best interests of the community. Careful not to give needless offence, I sought thus to influence those with whom I daily came in contact. With a little medicine I mixed a little temperance; and despite all my skill and caution in compounding the latter, I found it more difficult to render it agreeable to certain parties than even my pills and powders."

He witnessed scenes of suffering and woe in his practice that touched his heart. Here is one that intensified his hostility to strong drink. He was called to see a girl fourteen years of age, who was wasting with consumption. Her parents were intemperate and very poor. Dr. Jewett found the sick daughter a Christian girl, and her " sweet angelic temper of mind " soon endeared her to him. One morning he called to see her earlier than usual, and found her sitting up in a chair with a blanket wrapped about her, and trembling from head to feet.

" Martha, what makes you tremble so? " the doctor asked.

" I am very cold," she answered.

" But why are you not in bed?"

"I have had one of my distressed turns, and could not lie in bed." ·

"How long have you been sitting here, Martha?"

"Almost through the night."

Seeing there was no fire in the apartment, the doctor continued, "Have you been sitting here alone, and without fire?"

"Yes, sir; there is no wood in the house."

"Where is your father?"

"He is in bed."

"And where is your mother?"

"She is in bed, too."

"Both drunk," thought the doctor; and his soul was moved to the lowest depths. "While I live," he exclaimed, "may a merciful God spare me from another such trial of my feelings."

Fifteen years afterwards, Dr. Jewett referred to the sad incident in a public lecture, and said: "I have lived more than forty years, and I have never witnessed the operation of any other power than that of alcoholic drinks, capable of conquering a *mother's love.* It may not be said of *drunken* mothers, in the sense intended in an old couplet, that,

'A mother's *a mother* all the days of her life.'"

At another time he was called to visit an intemperate man who was injured in a drunken fight. His antagonist bit out a piece of his lip, and the poor fellow was in a sad plight. Dr. Jewett saw that, owing to the mangled condition of the lip, he

must cut out a piece in the shape of a **V**, bring
together and sew the parts, and leave it for nature
to do the rest in spite of rum. Fortunately the
fellow had more lip than he actually needed, so
that the operation was easily performed. The doctor charged him to keep perfectly quiet, not to leave
his house on any account, nor to drink a drop of
liquor. Early in the morning he called to see him,
but he was gone; he was at the grog-shop. The
doctor sought him out, when the wretch said, by
way of apology, that he "thought his lip would be
benefited by wetting it with rum." Dr. Jewett did
not hate the liquor traffic any less after this exhibition of lost manhood.

With all his prudence the doctor occasionally
awakened opposition that was difficult to allay.
But opposition did not scare him. Good Mrs.
Pitcher would say : " Now, doctor, look out ; don't
be hasty ; you will lose your practice if you do ;
better not say quite so much."

But the doctor condemned himself sometimes for
not saying more. He believed it to be the duty of
every Christian man to wage an uncompromising
warfare with every curse of society, and he had not
inaugurated much of a war after all. But the opposition was increasing. There was more and louder
hostile talk at the end of six months than there was
in the beginning. He continued to criticise the
drunkenness of the times and to denounce the liquor
traffic. He grew bold and uncompromising as the
opposition increased. The fear of losing practice

by his fidelity to principle never influenced him at
all.   He would have despised himself if such a servile fear had controlled his actions.   There was a
great .evil in the community, and he struck at it.
Had he not been a very popular physician, whose
genial face was a better passport in that region than
his medical degree, the opposition would have been
hotter and more vituperous.   But he had won a
good reputation in his profession, and was generally
regarded as an unusually promising young doctor.
Still, by the end of his first year's practice, the opposition aroused was considerable.   He was prepared
to meet it, however, in his Christian manhood.
He buckled on his armor and enlisted for the war.

The reader may judge somewhat of the severe
trials to which temperance advocates were subjected
at that time, from the following letter of Dr. Justin
Edwards to Rev. John Marsh, who was appointed
district secretary of the American Temperance Society at Boston, in 1833:

"If you think it to be the will of God that you
should accept the appointment, I should rejoice to
have you do so, but not without; because, without
such a conviction, it would not be comfortable to
endure the privations and labor and trials to which
it will call you.   These, as you know, must be
great; and nothing else will sustain you and carry
you forward perseveringly, but the conviction that
you are probably accomplishing more for the final
good of men than you possibly can in any other
way."

About this time, May 5, 1830, he consummated
the hornet affair, and Miss Lucy Adams Tracy became his wife. It was altogether a new scene to
which Dr. Jewett introduced his bride. Such
Sabbath desecration, such ignorance and supersti-
tion, such immorality and intemperance, she never
witnessed before. On the first Sabbath after their
marriage they rode four or five miles to a Congregational church. On the way men were working
in their gardens and fields, shearing sheep, playing
ball, pitching quoits, hunting, fishing, and fooling,
as if Sunday had no claim upon their regard. Mrs.
Jewett was shocked at such an exhibition of heathenism in Puritan New England. The doctor assured
her that she was not yet a witness to the worst side
of the reality — that she would find Plymouth Rock
morality only here and there on the " Providence
plantation."

The doctor's temperance talks had done good
execution. He set the temperance ball rolling, not
only in Greenwich, but also in the neighboring
towns. The best people were aroused, and so were
the worst. The former reasoned, expostulated, and
prayed. The latter swore, raved, and threatened.

Just before the doctor's marriage, Elder Meech,
who preached in the town of Exeter, five miles distant, delivered a temperance sermon of the most ·
radical character. The elder was a man of decided
native ability, and fearless as a lion. He never did
things by halves. With him it was the whole or
nothing. He looked over this evil in his discrimi-

nating way, and concluded that drunkards were
made out of moderate drinkers, and therefore that
moderate drinking was a sin.   He went into his
pulpit and denounced the sale and use of rum with
out stint, and raked down moderate drinkers until
they felt that something more than a flesh-brush was
applied to their backs.   They were mad.   They
insulted and threatened the elder.   His popularity
did not save him from their wrath, and the excitement ran into bitterness and acrimonious strife.

Dr. Jewett heard of the temperance hostilities in
Exeter, and he sent word to Elder Meech that he
would deliver a temperance lecture in Exeter on any
day he might select.   The elder was delighted with
the kind and friendly offer.   Such reinforcement
was unexpected to him, and all the more welcome
on that account.   He appointed the lecture on
the second day of June.   The doctor's friends
were not pleased with his volunteer service.   Many
of them regarded it as a Quixotic and unnecessary
attack upon an old custom, and that the address
would cost him his practice ; and they told him so.
Some said that the effort would expose him to the
violence of intemperate men, who would be incensed
enough to shoot him.   But the doctor's head was
level and his heart brave.   He had not yet given a
public temperance discourse, and here was a capital opportunity that he would not lose for the value
of his medical practice.   He carefully prepared a
lecture for the occasion, writing it out in full, from
beginning to end, and was on hand in Exeter, June

2d, enforced by the presence of his young wife. He did not know exactly what sort of a "mare's nest" he might find; but his wife was his partner now in joy and sorrow both, and she was resolved to share that trip with him.

A crowd of people assembled, filling the lecture-room to its utmost capacity, while more congregated outside than inside, backing up wagons against the windows, that they might both see and hear. The chief liquor-dealer of the town was there, — a tall, dare-devil sort of a fellow, — and he took his stand in the doorway directly in front of the platform, as if he expected to terrify the young doctor.

Dr. Jewett delivered his lecture without the least interruption, expressing his own views frankly about the curse of intemperance, dilating upon the abuse of liquors by physicians in medical practice, and setting forth the duties of citizens in the plainest language. The audacious rumseller who planted himself in the doorway to scare the speaker, was himself scared. The following paragraph rasped his hardened soul, and turned all eyes toward him curiously, much to his discomfiture :

" To those who are engaged in the business of manufacturing or distributing among your fellow-citizens intoxicating liquors, I would address a few words. Among a Christian people it is, I believe, a settled principle, that men ought never to engage in any business upon which they cannot consistently ask the blessing of God. I now ask you if, when you take the jug or the bottle from the hand of the poor little ragged son or daughter of the drunkard, and go behind your counter and turn your faucet to draw for a drunken father his daily quart of liquor, you can, while the measure is filling up, improve the passing moment to lift your heart to God, and crave his blessing on such a calling? You dare not do it. You would fear the vengeance of insulted Heaven against such high-handed wickedness added to such daring impiety. But you may say, perhaps, that you do not sell to the drunkard. What then? You sold to him while he was a sober man. He was, perhaps, educated in the school of drunkenness at *your counter*, but when he had lost his property, and could no longer meet his payments, all at once your conscience became exceedingly tender, and when the poor, besotted victim of depraved appetite begs you to furnish him but one glass to satisfy his insatiate longings, you can then vociferate, in loud and determined tone, ' *You shall not have it !* ' and the poor wretch, as he turns disappointed and unsatisfied away, mutters his curses against you, as one of the prime authors of his destruction."

Elder Meech fairly effervesced with gratitude to the doctor for this brave co-operation. Seizing his hand, he exclaimed:

" This is friendship indeed, to throw yourself into the breach with me at such a time as this ! "

Well, the doctor survived that Thermopylæ. He was neither shot nor stabbed. He came off with flying colors. Instead of tar and feathers, he received a very urgent request for a copy of his address for publication, proving unmistakably that it was a convincing document. So the doctor's first temperance address went into print forty-nine years ago, and was widely circulated and read.   Friends read it, to see what a powerful reformer he was; enemies read it, for proof of his folly and fanaticism.

From this time Dr. Jewett's labors were sought in the temperance lecture-field.   Friends in the neighboring towns waited upon him often, and set before him their most urgent necessities.   To many of these invitations he responded — to so many, as to interfere with his professional duties.   Often he resolved to deny all applicants, and attend more closely to his practice; but it did not require a very earnest or eloquent appeal to cause him to forget his resolve, so great was his interest in the temperance reform.   Night after night he would ride five, and even ten miles, to lecture in hall or schoolhouse, returning late at night, weary and worn, yet feeling well paid if he got ten, twenty, or thirty names upon the pledge.   At one time the temperance battle waxed so warm that his friends advised him to cease lecturing, saying, "You run great risk in being out nights.   Some of the desperate fellows will waylay you, and they just as lief shoot you as not."   But the doctor concluded that he ran no more risk in going to lecture in the evening than he did in going to see a patient at a distance.   So he persevered in his work, guarding against surprises by putting a loaded pistol in his pocket.   In the course of three or four years he had the satisfaction of seeing temperance societies organized in many towns in that part of Rhode Island.   This was his pay; for his labors were without money or price.

8

That the doctor had some anxiety lest his family should be visited by ruffians in his absence, is evident from the fact that he provided his wife with a gun, and taught her how to use it.   Under his instructions she soon learned to handle a gun without fear, and became a good markswoman.   From that day to this woe to the ruffian or wharf-rat committing depredations on her premises.

Schoolhouses were often shut against him, and sometimes he addressed the people who gathered, upon the steps outside.   On one occasion he was announced to speak at a schoolhouse, but on going thither he found that the committee-man " who held the keys, and acted in the capacity of St. Peter," as the doctor said, refused to open the door for a temperance lecture.   " What shall be done? " inquired the doctor of the people assembled.   " Go to my house," replied the nearest neighbor ; and they went.   The lecture was delivered in spite of the opposition.

As yet Dr. Jewett had not signed the total-abstinence pledge.   The pledge circulated did not prohibit the use of wine or cider, and occasionally the doctor drank both.   But a brief interview with Ben Johnson, an intemperate man, one day, resulted in his discarding wine altogether.

"Halloo, Ben! I want to see you," cried the doctor, one day, on meeting him.   Ben stopped in the road, and turned about.   " I want you should abandon your gin, and join our temperance society. What say you? "

Ben grunted out something that the doctor did not understand.

"You know that the fiery stuff does you no good, but a great deal of hurt. Come now, give it up and join us."

"Don't *you* drink wine, doctor?" Ben finally inquired.

"Why, yes," answered the doctor; "but what has that to do with gin?"

"Why do you drink wine instead of water?" persisted Ben.

"Well," replied the doctor, "when I have been out riding for hours, and have been broken of my rest, and feel exhausted from excessive labor, a glass of wine refreshes me."

"That is it, doctor. You are right!" shouted Ben. "When I have been chopping or sledding wood all day in the cold, and come home tired and chilled through, a glass of gin refreshes *me* wonderfully."

Dr. Jewett drank no wine after listening to Ben Johnson's temperance lecture.

Assisted by his wife, Dr. Jewett turned his attention to the improvement of the people morally. He established a Sabbath school in East Greenwich, obtaining question and reading books of friends in Providence and elsewhere. At first considerable opposition was aroused against the movement.

One said, "Dr. Jewett is a Congregationalist, and he does this to introduce his creed."

"It is an ingenious way of his to teach Infant

Baptism," said a suspicious old woman ; "and I ain't goin' ter lift the end of my finger for it."

"It's just the way to spread heresies and isms," remarked an ignorant preacher ; " and that minister the doctor had with him 'tother Sunday will help him, no doubt," — referring to a clergyman who stopped with Doctor Jewett over Sabbath, and preached a sermon in the hall.

But the doctor took little notice of their opposition except to laugh at them in his inimitable way ; and finally it wore away, and the Sabbath school flourished as well as could be expected in such a community. The doctor superintended the school, and his wife taught a class. Here he enjoyed a favorable opportunity to preach "lay sermons" for the benefit of the young, not omitting temperance by any means. This school exerted a wide and decided influence upon the community. There is no doubt that, for real Christian results, awakening intelligence, and impelling to nobler living, it was the best institution the town had ever enjoyed to that time.

All the people sung by the "sperit," as they claimed, in religious meetings. But the singing grated harshly upon the feelings of Dr. and Mrs. Jewett. What could be done to improve them? The question was no sooner asked than answered. The doctor resolved to run a singing-school. He could play the flute, bass-viol, and violin, and was also a capital singer. He belonged to a musical family ; his brothers and sisters were good singers; the latter rather superior.

Notice was given out that the doctor would teach the young people singing, and older people if they desired, without charge. To practise for the Sabbath services they would meet on Saturday evening, and all who were disposed would stop after meeting on Sunday for general instruction. So, in due time, Dr. Jewett was converted into a singing-master. He run the school some time, playing the bass-viol, and he also led the singing on Sundays. One Sabbath, a member of the congregation, who thought there was too much note and rule in his teaching, called out, "Doctor, let 'em sing with the ' sperit.' "

"That is what we are doing," replied the doctor, with a roguish smile; "with the spirit and the *undcr-standing*, according to Paul."

Dr. Jewett had no idle moments. He improved every minute that he could snatch from public service in reading the latest and best medical works, and the study of general literature, though English literature especially interested him. The standard poets occupied much of his time, particularly Shakspeare and Burns. He made himself quite familiar with these, committing to memory those parts which seemed to him especially chaste and beautiful. In this way he was a growing man intellectually as well as professionally. The first five years of his professional life developed him remarkably. He became a marked man for intellect and medical skill in that time. When he was thirty years old he was a man of note. Few young physicians enjoyed a wider fame than he, and few public men of his age were considered so talented. He kept two horses, and often rode a long distance in critical cases. Sometimes people would come for him in a hurry when he was absent, and they would intercept him and secure his services before he returned home. Once, in this way, he was absent two days and nights from home.

In 1835, the leading citizens of Centreville, in the town of Warwick, R. I., formally invited Dr. Jewett to settle in that village, and take the place of Dr. Knight, an old and popular physician, who was about to retire from practice. Centreville was five miles from East Greenwich. The result was that Dr. Jewett bought out Dr. Knight, and removed thither with his family. The foregoing fact proves that he was held in high estimation as a medical practitioner. His prospects for fame and wealth in his profession were flattering indeed.*

Dr. Jewett reduced his views, respecting the medical uses of alcohol, to practice. He spoke and wrote his sentiments fearlessly, though they were in direct conflict with the views of the medical profession.

---

* Within a few years, a Rhode Island journal said : " At Centreville is a doctor's office that has been the property, successively, of three physicians since the year 1836. The first of the three was Dr. Charles Jewett. He was then a thorough rigid abstainer from all intoxicating liquors. He still lives in good health, and enjoys life as well as when he occupied the premises referred to. His two successors were both able, well-educated men, enjoyed the public confidence, and were eminently useful to the public for a while. But they both drank intoxicating liquors, were enslaved by them, and died, years ago, intemperate."

His own practice accorded with his opinions expressed below :

" The old notion of dealing out for every feeble patient, convalescent from fever or other disease, a little colombo or gentian root, a handful of camomile, and a little orange peel as a tonic, and ordering ' a pint of West India rum,' or ' pure Holland gin,' wherewith to extract their virtues, and perhaps make a drunkard of the patient, is a mere relic of barbarism, as much so as the ancient pillory or whipping-post. I deny that there is any *such* necessity for the use of alcoholic stimulants, as should lead to the licensing of any particular establishment for their sale, any more than for the sale of gamboge or blue vitriol ; and I deny the right of any physician, in country practice at least, to order the article, and post his patrons off to a grog-shop to obtain it. All that is really necessary he should provide ; and that he may do, in ninety-nine cases out of a hundred, from a fountain not more extensive *than a four-ounce vial.*"

That " four-ounce vial " was always found in Dr. Jewett's saddle-bags ; and he claimed that patients could be more safely trusted to go after rhubarb or castor-oil, than they could after liquors, since they would be more careful to abide by the prescription for the former than the latter. He was as far in advance of his medical brethren on this question, as he was in advance of his temperance brethren on the subject of prohibition. And he never modified his views. He was more confirmed, if possible, in the last years of his life, that his views of the medical uses of alcohol were correct. We have heard

him quote Cowper upon the subject with decided
effect :

> "O madness, to think the use of strongest wines
> And strongest drinks are chief support of health,
> When God has these forbidden ; made choice to rear
> His mighty champion,* strong above compare,
> Whose drink was only from the limpid brook."

He won the reputation of being a skilful surgeon. Such cases as the following are cited to this
day. A boy seven years old fell from a tree and
broke his leg diagonally at the thigh (a bad break).
Dr. Jewett set and cared for the limb, and the boy
recovered speedily, with a leg so sound that he did
not even limp. The lad is now one of the wealthy
citizens of Providence, a deacon in the First Baptist
Church, and thinks that "Dr. Jewett made a mistake
in giving up the practice of medicine to become a
temperance lecturer."

In 1834, an Irishman attempted the murder of a
whole family on the "New England Pike." All
were stabbed by him except the daughter, who fled
and alarmed the neighbors. The wounds of all
were dangerous, one or two of them alarmingly so.
Dr. Jewett was called to them, and by his skill and
unremitting attention saved every one of them. The
happy result added very much to his fame.

It was at Centreville that he came near losing
his life. The hand and arm of a patient were singularly diseased, and physicians were in doubt as to
the nature of the disease. Complete ulceration of

---

* Samson.

the parts, with profuse discharge, was its general appearance. Dr. Jewett was called to the patient, and he examined and dressed the parts. Soon after reaching home, his hand, arm, and shoulder began to pain him severely, attended with great chilliness and high fever. He understood the symptoms at once, and supposed that he must have had a scratch on his hand when he dressed the patient's arm, and was badly poisoned by the virus. Calling in a gentleman to assist his wife, he went to bed and ordered the most active remedies to be used. All through the night the two worked over him with great anxiety, executing his orders promptly. Towards morning he was relieved, and in three or four days recovered. A physician less cool and self-reliant would have lost his life.

In the course of his systematic reading, Dr. Jewett became deeply interested in the development of the agricultural resources of the West. He studied the subject of prairie farming with more than ordinary interest, particularly the methods of irrigation and supply of water for stock and family use. There being no springs or streams on the prairies for miles often, even large farms depended upon wells. When parties could afford it, windmills were used to pump the water therefrom. The doctor learned, however, that the usefulness of windmills was much impaired for the want of some method to regulate their speed. He became so enthusiastic over the subject that he invented a " regulator," and actually put up a windmill, rather larger than a door, to test the practicability of his invention. It operated perfectly, and friends advised that he take measures to introduce the invention to the West. But his battle with disease and intemperance occupied his attention so thoroughly that he had no time to instruct western farmers how to run the prairies by water.

Dr. Jewett was scarcely settled in Centreville before he was invited to address the temperance society on a stated evening. He accepted the invitation ; and, as several rumsellers were prosecuting their destructive business in that and neighboring villages, he paid his addresses to them in no ambiguous way. Van Amburg never stirred up his cage of lions more effectually than the doctor did those rumsellers.

When he removed to Centreville, two barrels of cider were carried with his effects and put into his cellar. Although the doctor had not yet signed a total-abstinence pledge, he did not drink cider except occasionally when he called to see a patient. The two barrels were intended for vinegar. Not long afterwards, however, a man called at his door to inquire if he had a barrel of cider to sell. The doctor thought a moment, and concluded that one barrel would make all the vinegar his family could use. "Yes, I can sell you a barrel," answered the doctor. The bargain was concluded,and the stranger took the cider away.

A few days only elapsed when the superintendent of a factory in the neighborhood called and said,

"Doctoi, there is a man in the upper part of the village in a deplorable state, and I want you should go at once to see him. His name is Wilcox."

"What is the matter with him?" the doctor asked.

"I should call it a sort of drunken craziness," the superintendent answered.

The doctor thought at once of the rumsellers he had stirred up, and inquired further, "Where did he get his liquor?" — evidently resolved in his mind that the offending dealer would "catch it."

"I aon't think he has had any liquor," replied the man.

"No liquor!" exclaimed the doctor, surprised. "On what, then, did he get drunk?"

"Why, somebody sold him a barrel of cider a few days ago, and he has been pouring it down ever since. He is not so drunk as to prevent his moving about, but he is fierce as a tiger, and the moment he goes into the street the neighbors shut their doors and bolt them."

This was enough. The doctor was on the track of the rumseller. It was very evident where the man got his liquor. Years afterwards, writing of that occasion, he said:

"What a revelation was here! The superintendent did not know that I sold that barrel of cider, but I knew it, and if I ever felt like getting into a very small place, and shutting the door after me, it was then. Could I have been bought that morning at the then present valuation, and afterwards sold at former estimates, somebody would have made a speculation."

Dr. Jewett lost no time in seeing the unfortunate man.

"Sell me what cider remains, and I will give you what you paid me for the whole," was the first thing the doctor said to him. But the poor fellow did not wish to traffic, so that the doctor could not get possession of the cider. His object was to empty the barrel at once, but he did not succeed. He prescribed remedies for the man, and assured him that he should see him again early the next morning. The doctor was hardly out of sight before the drunkard's wife glided down cellar, and set the cider to running. The barrel was soon empty.

"That incident taught me," wrote the doctor, ' that there is but one consistent course for any real friend of temperance to pursue, namely, to wage uncompromising and indiscriminate war on all intoxicating liquors, no matter by what *name* they may be called."

At one time the temperance battle waxed so warm in consequence of the doctor's fearless attacks upon the liquor traffic, that he was often insulted and threatened. Along from 1834 to 1840, a mobocratic spirit seemed to pervade the land. In many of the large cities and centres of influence, as Boston, New York, Syracuse, Baltimore, &c., temperance, anti-slavery, and other meetings for reform, were broken up by mobs. Even Dr. Graham was mobbed in Boston for undertaking to lecture upon diet. It seemed as if a Satanic spirit were aroused against all opposers of wickedness and wrong every-

where. Men's lives were threatened, and some were
actually murdered. Their houses were mobbed
by drunken rabbles, and their places of business
burned. The fiendish spirit pervaded Rhode Island,
and temperance reformers were tabooed. Dr. Jewett received his share of abuse and insult from a
drunken class who knew not what they did. Friends
told him that no appeals or persuasion could influence the class who assailed him; that nothing less
than a knowledge of his superior strength would
deter them from violence. He reflected seriously
upon the matter, and decided what to do. He
believed in "muscular Christianity," and he possessed as much of it as any man in the county. He
resolved to make an exhibit of it to his assailants.
Nor was he obliged to wait long. Going into a
place of business where several of his enemies had
congregated, one of them grossly insulted him.
The doctor seized him by the nap of his neck and
sent him head over heels out the door. Before the
fellow picked himself up, the doctor had him by the
coat-collar, and he proceeded to whirl him round
and round so furiously that his legs were out straight
as he revolved, that his associates might understand
he did not fear their threats. Then, setting the man
upon his feet, he said, "You and I are friends; but
this business must be stopped."

Dr. Jewett was never insulted in that community
again. A wrecked sea-captain could not purchase a
canoe of the natives of the island on which he was
wrecked for money; but they sold him one for a
jack-knife. The poor, untaught heathen could not

appreciate currency, but a jack-knife was the height of their capacity. So the doctor's assailants could neither understand nor respect the "Golden Rule," or the simplest precepts of the Gospel, but a "*licking*" was just suited to their ability.

As we are speaking of the doctor's great strength, an incident deserves mention here. Wrestling was common in that part of Rhode Island. Many youths and men prided themselves upon their wrestling ability. Often one was pitted against another. There was one of the number, a worthless bragga-docio, who was boasting of his powers, one day when Dr. Jewett happened along. With some jocose remark he alluded to their sport, and reflected on their want of skill and strength, whereupon the aforesaid boaster challenged him to a trial. Laugh-ingly the doctor accepted, causing considerable mer-riment to the company. In three minutes the doctor flung him, and did it with such force *as to break the poor fellow's leg*. When Dr. Jewett saw what he had done, all the sport in him vanished at once, and he poured out his regrets sorrowfully, took the suf-ferer to his home, and carefully attended him until the broken limb "was as good as new." He never wrestled again; for manufacturing a patient to doctor gratuitously would never make a paying business.

Notwithstanding the opposition and abuse the doctor experienced, he neither faltered nor lost courage. The greater the hostility, the greater was his zeal and pluck apparently. Like tea, his real strength was proved by being in " hot water."

VIII.

ABANDONS MEDICINE.

DR. JEWETT'S efficient labors in the Temperance Reform won a high reputation for him
all through Rhode Island by the time he was thirty
years of age. His talents, eloquence, wit, energy,
and indomitable perseverance made him the prominent champion of the cause.

A short time before he relinquished his medical
practice for the temperance-lecture field, he wrote
"An Address to Retailers of Intoxicating Liquors," in
rhyme, which was published in *Zion's Herald*, Boston.
The friends of temperance in Rhode Island printed it
subsequently in the form of a handbill, and scattered
it by thousands over the state. We have space for
only brief extracts. Evidently he had in view the
death of a drunkard named Briggs, and closed the
article by reference to the following fact. One Mr.
Kelton purchased something for his sisters at the
store, and the trader wrapped it in a leaf torn from
an account-book. On reaching home, a week's
purchase of gin was found on the leaf, charged to
said Briggs, thus :

```
"Monday, Sept. 24, to one quart of gin. [Price.]
 Tuesday,    "   25,  "   "    "    "    "      "
 Wednesday," 26,  "   "    "    "    "      "
 Thursday,   "   27,  "   "    "    "    "      "
 Friday,     "   28,  "   "    "    "    "      "
```

Briggs died on Friday night, and the next charge was :

" Saturday, Sept. 29, to 5 yds. cloth for winding-sheet "

. . . .

" But here the old excuse yet meets us still,
  ' If I don't sell the poison, others will.
  Then let them sell, and thou wilt be no worse ;
  They'll have the *profits*, and they'll have the *curse*.
  If some *will* still do wrong, thou shouldst refuse :
  The sins of others cannot yours excuse.
  Is it, in fact, a privilege to sell
  What kills the body, dooms the soul to hell?

. . . .

" Come now, draw near, my money-making friend ;
  You saw the starting ; *come and see the end.*
  When you first filled his glass *one* would suffice ;
  Next *two* were wanting ; and now *here he lies.*
  Look there into that open grave, and say,
  Dost feel no sorrow, no remorse to-day?
  Does not your answering conscience loud declare
  That *your cursed avarice* has laid him there?
  Recall the virtues which he once possessed :
  How justly honored, and how richly blessed,
  With health uninjured, character unstained,
  While at his hearth domestic comfort reigned.

" Go meet him there.   A smiling wife you'd see,
  And prattling children climbing up his knee.
  His heart was cheerful, and his conscience clear,
  And thus he journeyed on from year to year,
  Till, oh, sad day ! when first he chanced to drop
  Within the confines of your slaughter-shop.
  You filled for him the intoxicating glass,
  Loud cracked your jokes, and bade the bumper pass ;

And while he, thoughtless, poured the ruin down,
You counted future cups from seed then sown ;
And you have reaped even all his earthly store ;
For Death hath snatched him, and your harvest's o'er.

"Now, since the earth has closed o'er his remains,
Turn o'er your book, and count your honest gains.
How doth the account for his last week begin? —
'*Monday, the twenty-fourth, one quart of gin !*'
A like amount for each succeeding day,
Tells on the book, but wears his life away.
Saturday's charge makes out the account complete ;
'*To cloth, five yards, to make a winding-sheet!*'
There all stands fair, without mistake or flaw ;
How honest trade will thrive, UPHELD BY LAW ! "

Another incident turned the attention of leading temperance men in Rhode Island to Dr. Jewett when an agent was required to canvass the state. The liquor-license law had received the attention of speakers from the start, and its inhuman and godless character had been thoroughly discussed. Dr. Jewett was its most powerful opponent. He struck at it on every public occasion, and denounced it in private. Nor were they light blows that he inflicted upon the license system. He never exhibited more power and boldness than in his attacks upon that curse of a law. The result was, that the legislature passed an act allowing the towns of the state to adopt or reject license by vote on a certain day. The friends of temperance went into the canvass with a will. Dr. Jewett was in his element. It was a good opportunity to smite the law — the be-

9

ginning of what he could see was a favorable end.
It was a short, hot, and somewhat acrimonious
contest. In some of the towns "no license" was
victorious; in others, license. On the whole, the
result was full as good as Dr. Jewett anticipated. In
his own town — Warwick — the liquor party triumphed. On the day after the election the leading
rumseller of the place announced that the victory
would be celebrated in the evening at his liquor
shop, and that he should keep open doors and furnish free drinks, and they would have an hilarious
time until the small hours of the morning.

Dr. Jewett understood what such a general invitation meant — the most drunken scene that had
disgraced the town for a long time. The elements of
a bacchanalian powwow existed in the village, and
he knew full well that they would seethe and boil
in that caldron of vice as never before. So he sat
down and scribbled off a few verses, which he sent
into the rumseller's riotous levee in the evening for
the edification of all concerned. The first two
stanzas ran thus:

" Ye friends of grog, rejoice, rejoice !
    The work, the glorious work is done !
  Raise high each trembling, stammering voice ;
    The battle 's fought, and we have won !

" Ye old established bruisers, come, .
    With purple blossoms on each nose,
  My house this day shall be your home ;
    Rejoice with us o'er fallen foes ! "

The communication closed thus :

" What though our wives should scold and fret?
    Blows well applied, will cool their spunk ;
While rum our parching throats can wet,
    Rejoice, and be exceeding drunk ! "

That the poetical effusion exasperated the miserable company we need not inform the reader. But Dr. Jewett had become too well known to be assaulted with impunity. The booziest fellow in the crowd did not dare to vent his spite upon this fearless foe of the grog-shop.

Still another incident, more than those mentioned perhaps, increased the doctor's notoriety. The Providence Temperance Society adopted a resolution recommending the friends of temperance to withdraw patronage from grocers who sold intoxicating liquors. Samuel Young, a prominent grocer and rumseller, attacked the society in the Courier; and his article was sent to Dr. Jewett, at Centreville, with a request that he should reply to it.

The doctor was only too glad of an opportunity to expose the wicked business, and he replied in the same journal. It was the beginning of a controversy that continued several weeks, creating interest on both sides, and causing a great demand for the papers.

In one of his articles Dr. Jewett exposed the *meanness* of the liquor traffic in very strong language, creating great commotion among the liquor fraternity by the following verse :

" I'd sooner black my visage o'er,
   And put the shine on boots and shoes,
Than stand within a liquor store
   And rinse the glasses drunkards use."

Perhaps no one verse was ever more widely quoted in our country than this. Temperance and anti-temperance papers quoted it, the former to indorse and laugh, the latter to condemn and scold. In temperance meetings and families, as well as in grog-shops, it was repeated, in the one case to approve, in the other to denounce. In one liquor store in Providence it proved to be as effective as a sermon. The young man who was running it, read the verse over and over. There was something about it exactly suited to his case. When he rinsed the glass of the next customer, the line, "And rinse the glasses drunkards use," he repeated almost audibly. It was so with the next customer, and the next, and the next, until the conscience-smitten fellow closed his saloon and sought other business.

It was natural, in these circumstances, for all eyes to be turned to Dr. Jewett, when an efficient lecturing agent was required by the Rhode Island Temperance Society. With unanimous and urgent voice the doctor was invited to this new field. It was virtually a request that he would abandon his chosen

profession to become a temperance reformer. The
invitation was unexpected, but no less complimentary on that account. It was a grave question for
him to settle. Wealth and high position were promised in the medical profession. On the other hand,
here was a new and wide field of usefulness, for
which all friends said that he was particularly qualified. The doctor considered the matter seriously,
consulted his wife, went to God for direction, and
finally accepted the new position. Within a few
weeks he entered upon the work of lecturing agent,
with headquarters in Providence. His removal to
Providence was a thorn in the flesh to the rumsellers. They feared him as they did no other man.
They thought his coming to Providence foreboded
ill to their business. It was not strange that there
was a great sensation in their camp. Nor did the
doctor's method of work yield them any comfort.
They took counsel of one another, and some of them
assumed a defiant attitude. They "talked big," as
the Temperance Herald said, and *quasi* threats were
not infrequent. After a time, the doctor received
threatening letters. Some of them promised a coat
of tar and feathers; others pledged a bath or watery
grave in Providence River; and others still hinted
that a bullet would serve him right. But the doctor
pursued the even tenor of his ways.

By a rousing canvass the friends of temperance
secured a vote against granting licenses in the city
of Providence. This result exasperated the rumsellers beyond measure. They swore vengeance

upon leading temperance men, and actually attacked Judge Aplin at ten o'clock at night in the street. The judge was a fearless and uncompromising friend of temperance, who dealt out justice to convicted rumsellers with a liberal hand; and scoundrels wanted to put him away. Two ruffians were employed to seize him on his way home from his office, while a third party, with horse and carriage, stood ready to convey him — somewhere. Their plan was to put him into a sack for convenient transportation, and convey him, no one knew where, probably to the river. But the judge was too much for his assailants, and they failed to accomplish their purpose. In their flight, one of them lost his hat, which the judge retained as a memento. One Smith, the proprietor of a rumselling hotel, was strongly suspected of being one of the assailants, as he appeared with a new hat on the next day.

It was expected that Dr. Jewett would be the next victim of the liquor interest. Friends cautioned him to be on his guard constantly, and advised him to keep indoors after dark. But the doctor never changed his program in consequence of threats, and he was never molested. He said, "My enemies relieved themselves by growling and scowling, and by the utterance of big oaths on the sidewalk in front of my office."

Dr. Jewett had never delivered an *extemporaneous* address when he commenced his labors as agent of the Rhode Island Temperance Society. His first address of that sort was in the town of Warren.

He went thither with a carefully written address, and was entertained at the house of the clergyman. Several rumsellers and one distiller were members of his parish. The minister, of course, was anxious, knowing as he did that Dr. Jewett's method of dealing with the liquor traffic was after the John Knox style. Walking from the house to the church at the hour of meeting, the clergyman's anxiety took form in the following advice, delicately and kindly proffered:

"Be as conciliatory as you can. Denunciation does little good to the bad men who deserve it. It is not well to stir up their ire."

The doctor was troubled. He did not wish to get the minister into difficulty with any of his people, and yet a duty was laid upon his conscience. He must not shirk that duty. What could he do? In this frame of mind he went into the pulpit. Father Bonney, a superannuated clergyman of the Methodist denomination, led in prayer, and such a prayer! It was the cry of a dependent soul for help. He pleaded for the drunkard, and his wife and children, with a tenderness that brought tears to the eyes. He pleaded for the rumsellers in Warren, and for that one distiller, with a desperate earnestness as if it were "now or never" with them. In short, he prayed for just those things the temperance people needed then and there. "No mention was made of the Sandwich or Fejee islands," remarked the doctor, speaking of that prayer, "of the mission to heathen lands, or of any matter entirely foreign to the occasion, as there generally is in the prayers of men who have no hearty interest in the cause of temperance, and yet are asked to pray for it."

When the prayer ceased, the doctor's embarrassment had disappeared; and, casting aside his notes, he spoke for one hour and a half with remarkable power, assailing the traffic, moderate drinking, and milk-and-water methods of dealing with an evil so gigantic.

From that time Dr. Jewett adopted extemporaneous speaking. He said of that experience:

"It taught me that what is really wanting to success in extemporaneous speaking, is that a man discuss a subject in which he feels a deep interest, and one concerning which he has acquired some positive knowledge *which he feels anxious to impart to others*; that he have a tolerable acquaintance with the language he is about to use, and that he shall be so intent on accomplishing some desirable practical result by his efforts, that he will forget himself, and have not a thought of what his audience may possibly think of his performance."

Dr. Jewett reduced to practice the lesson of that hour so thoroughly that his course of scientific temperance lectures, conceded to be the most valuable of any temperance lectures ever delivered, were never committed to writing. Many, many times he was besought to write them out carefully for the press, but he passed away without thus preserving them. The little volume that he published in 1849 contained extemporaneous discourses that were phonographically reported for that particular work.

Speaking of Father Bonney's prayer, recalls an incident in Dr. Jewett's experience. We have several times heard him repeat prayers of ministers who have dodged the main question. We recollect his return from lecturing one Monday morning, when, about the first thing, he said:

"You ought to have heard Mr. B.'s prayer last night. It was 'good lord, good devil,' from beginning to end. He told the Lord about the Fall of Adam, the great wickedness of the human race, the reign of appetites and passions, and other bits of *news*, and he prayed that men might rise to the dignity of true Christian manhood and be temperate in all things; and that was the nearest he came to the subject before us, and the needs of his own people, with the rum-traffic and drink-curse among them."

Then, pausing a moment, he added, sarcasm flashing in his eye as plainly as it spoke in his words, "MOCKERY! MOCKERY!"

In canvassing the state of Rhode Island, Dr. Jewett lectured in Cumberland. On the morning after his lecture, before the stage left for Providence, a lad of ten or twelve years broke his leg. There was no surgeon within several miles, and Dr. Jewett volunteered his services. The boy's mother was very much frightened, and the boy himself was suffering severely. The doctor hastened to set the limb and dress it, calling wit to his aid in order to comfort the mother and interest the lad. All the while that he was repairing the limb, he was cracking jokes and telling stories; and by the time the leg was dressed, the mother was calm and cheerful, and the boy quiet. The lad is a man now, between fifty and sixty years of age, and he remembers, as if it occurred but yesterday, how magically the doctor's wit allayed the fears of his mother and soothed his own pains.

While Dr. Jewett resided in Providence, there was a town meeting, at which both he and his rum-selling antagonist, Samuel Young, were present. Young rose to speak upon the question before the house, when he discovered Dr. Jewett sitting near by. The sight of the man who had pummelled him so with his pen seemed to exasperate him, and he began to berate the doctor, calling him anything but an honest man, and declaring that he would " lick " him if he could catch him on the street. All this time the doctor sat with his eye turned up towards the speaker, and humor that could almost speak twinkling out of its corner, which spectacle appeared to increase the rage of Young. When the speaker ceased, Dr. Jewett arose, with fun beaming out of every lineament of his face, and said :

" My friend Young has told you some things that he will do. He has expressed himself very frankly and fully; but he will not be half so bad as he claims. He says that he will 'lick' me when he catches me on the street; but friend Young won't do any such thing. He wouldn't do it if he could, and he knows that he couldn't do it if he would." And he continued after this manner, interspersing

the most amusing stories and illustrations, until the
whole assembly, both friends and foes, laughed,
cheered, and clapped their hands, to the mortifica-
tion of the rumseller, who took his hat and left the
hall in a rage. Both sides conceded a signal victory
to the doctor.

After the city of Providence voted "no license,"
and the wrath of rumsellers was at its height, a
laughable incident occurred on Christian Hill. A
drunken fellow was seen near the " Hoyle Tavern,"
in the western part of the city, digging away at the
foot of a certain pole.

"Hallo! What are you doing there?" inquired
a passer-by.

The boozy digger looked up and replied:

"Our liberties are all—hic—taken away, and it's
only a mo—mockery to have liberty-poles sticking
up about the—hic—city, when we have got no liberty; and I'm going to dig 'em down."

"Liberty-poles indeed, you blockhead!" replied
the gentleman. "Why, look up and see what is
over your head."

The fellow looked and saw the tavern-sign swing-
ing from the pole. He had taken the tavern sign-
post for the liberty-pole. The doctor celebrated the
event in the Rhode Island Temperance Herald,
which he edited, in verse:

> " Yes, dig it down; ply well the spade,
> And make it bow its haughty head;
> For at its side there hangs a sign,
> That tells of brandy, rum, and wine.

A sign suspended to that pole,
   Tempts oft the throng,
   That pass along,
To come and quaff the poisonous bowl.

   •   •   •   •   •

" When Britain bade your fathers pay
   A paltry tax on tea,
They threw that luxury away,
   And gave it to the sea.
But had that lusty cargo been
Rum punch, *ye* ne'er had thrown it in.

   •   •   •   •   •

" They suffered hunger, cold, and pain,
   To save us from disgrace ;
But ye, their sons, for three-cent gains,
   Would blast the rising race.
Yes, ye would make the widows wail,
Rather than let your *profits* fail."

There were ten or twelve stanzas of the poem,
and the friends of temperance published it upon a
sheet, illustrated with a cut of the " Hoyle Tavern,"
and the drunken man digging down the sign-post.
Thousands of copies were scattered over the state,
pleasing temperance men and shaming the support-
ers of the liquor traffic.

It was believed that this and kindred efforts accomplished much good for the cause. Thirty years
ago, Dr. Jewett wrote in explanation of his use of
verse, while he did not claim to be a poet:

" However severely my attempts at verse might suffer
from a severe criticism, I find pleasure in the belief that

they have sometimes contributed to the gratification of
those who love the cause of temperance, and who dil-
igently labor for its advancement. That consideration
shall still afford me comfort, even though some keen dis-
secter of words and sentences should undertake to punish
me for my presumption, and break a butterfly upon the
critic's wheel. I am not vain enough to suppose that I
have any claim to the appellation of poet, and shall never
go out of my way as a reformer, or spend an hour of the
time allotted me on earth, in efforts to secure even a
sprig of that laurel which belongs to the followers of the
Nine."

That Dr. Jewett was a poet "sown by nature,"
his vivid imagination, delicate sense of the refined
and beautiful, and inclination to express his thoughts
in verse, furnish ample proof. Had he devoted
himself to this rare accomplishment as he did to the
study of medicine, or to the work of reform, he
would have adorned the society of song. What he
did in this line was only "to point a moral or adorn
a tale." Whenever he believed that rollicking verse
would serve his purpose better than staid prose, his
muse spread her "wings" without thought or study.
But his heart was so absorbed in the practical things
of life that he had no time for the cultivation of the
poetic art. No ripe scholar, however, ever possessed nicer taste for genuine poetry than did he;
and he made himself familiar, by the improvement
of odd moments, with many of the best poets of
ancient and modern days.

During Dr. Jewett's agency in Rhode Island, two

incidents occurred in Pawtucket, in which he performed an important part. He went thither one day to the house of Abraham Wilkinson, who was an uncompromising foe to the liquor traffic. While conversing with his host, a gentleman entered in haste, and, taking Mr. W. to the farther part of the room, conversed with him in a low tone. The doctor mistrusted that some rumseller was on the tapis, when he heard the sentence, "We want one man more."

"I am at your service," said Dr. Jewett, stepping up to the speaker. Mr. Wilkinson introduced him, adding, "He will do." The two crossed the street immediately into a store where a convicted rumseller was under keepers. A mob of rumsellers and drinkers had gathered in front of the building, swearing vengeance upon the "cold water fanatics" who should undertake to carry him to Providence. Threats of shooting and killing were uttered in no polished phrases.

The sheriff had three men besides the doctor— five in all. A few temperance men also, with three wagons, drove up to the door at once, when the rumseller was collared, dragged to the middle wagon, and lifted to a seat therein, beside the sheriff and his assistants. It was all done in a moment; and before the crowd was aroused from its wonder, crack went the whip, and the three teams started upon the run. The mob sprang for the middle wagon, in which was the prisoner, intending to upset it, but they were too late, and the teams dashed forward at a rapid rate to the Providence jail, where the rumseller was safely lodged. A part of the mob followed them for a distance in teams, pouring out indignation and wrath. The doctor shall tell the rest of the story :

"I expected a battle on our way back, and for lack of a breech-loader or a Remington six-shooter, I helped myself to a three-foot oak club of reasonable size from the jailer's wood-pile, and so we started. Instead of going back by the way we came, however, our drivers took the old road to Pawtucket, and in about forty minutes we were eating buckwheat cakes and honey at Uncle Abraham's (as Mr. Wilkinson was called), while the poor satellites of the liquor-sellers, who had followed us half-way to Providence, were still lying in wait by the turnpike roadside, to pelt us with stones on our return.

"Uncle Abraham remarked, with a beaming countenance, as he passed the buckwheats, ' There is one less rumseller in Pawtucket.' "

This incident illustrates Dr. Jewett's great courage as well as the facility with which he could adapt himself to circumstances. The other incident illustrates his accuracy in personating character. In this branch of imitation he excelled all the persons we ever knew. Even reformed men, who know by experience what drunkenness is, testify that Dr. Jewett personated the drunkard perfectly.

He went to Pawtucket to lecture. An hour or more before the lecture he stepped into a barber's shop, where he had often been, and while there, two drunken young men rushed in with, " How are you,

Joe? Give us the time of day. Ha, what's up? Put 'em through, my boy!"

Thinking to obtain some information about the traffic, the doctor gave a knowing wink to the barber, and immediately assumed the role of a drunkard, and complained that Pawtucket "had got to be so mighty temperate that a stranger can't find a drop to wet his whistle."

The young rowdies, supposing that he was a man after their sort, replied:

"There's liquor enough in Pawtucket if you know where to find it."

"Just so; but there's the trouble, you see," answered the doctor. "I'm a stranger in the place, and how should I know?"

"Come along," said they, "and we will show you."

Away they went, the doctor in the middle, apparently as drunk as either of them, over Pawtucket bridge, to the Massachusetts side, into the liquor store of one Crane. The young men pushed forward into a room in the rear, and proceeded to draw liquor for themselves, the doctor keeping close to them.

"Now, stranger, what'll you have?"

Thinking to call for something the rumseller did not have, the doctor replied:

"If I take anything, I'll take a glass of ale."

"Sartin," said one rowdy. "All right; the ale is in the front store;" and they led on to the beer-pump.

While the dealer was drawing the liquor, the doctor resolved what to do, and he took occasion to remark :

"I want you to understand now, that I don't go none of your swill stuff. If your beer's all right I shall go it; and if it isn't, I shan't."

"It's all right," said Crane, passing a glass of it all foaming.

Taking, and lifting it to his mouth, he blew off the foam with such a puff as to send it into the seller's face, who took no offence, since it was just the way drunkards did.

"Sour!" the doctor cried out.

"No, it ain't!" said Crane; "it is first-rate."

"You lie!" roared the doctor, like a toper mad clear through. "I guess I know beer." Then dropping his voice, he continued : "But, never mind; we won't quarrel over it. But what do you say *now*, on the whole; had I best drink it or not? You see how it is with me; what do you say? Speak it now like a man; what do you say?"

"On the whole, I guess I would not drink any more. I think you have got enough."

The doctor acknowledged that the rumseller was right.

"But I'll pay for it," he said.

"No," replied Crane; "if you don't drink it, you needn't pay."

"But look here," continued the doctor, "didn't I call for it, eh?"

"Yes, of course you did."

10

" Well, now I want you to *understand* that I'm no sneak, anyhow ; and when *I* calls for things I *pays* for 'em.   What's to pay? "

" If you pay anything, it'll be three cents."

"All right ; " and fumbling in his pocket, he drew forth some coppers with his right hand, and counted out three with great precision, one by one, into the open palm of the left hand, exclaiming, " There you have it !   That's right, ain't it ?   That makes it all square 'twixt you and I, don't it? "

" Yes, all right," answered Crane.

In half an hour from that time the doctor stood before a large audience in one of the churches of Pawtucket, where he rehearsed his adventures in the liquor saloon, thus furnishing evidence against another rumseller.

The excitement of that evening can be better imagined than described.   Before the lecture was through, Crane was informed of the joke played on him ; but he declared " there was no counterfeit about *that* drunk ; that was the genuine article. Do you think I don't know when a man is drunk? You can't cheat me.   A man may pitch and reel about like a drunkard, but he can't make his *eye* drunk.   That man's *eye* was drunk.   Why, I stood close to him when he was fretting about the beer, and my eye wasn't more than two feet from his, and that eye of his was drunk.   You can't cheat me."

However, when Crane found that it was really Dr. Jewett, and that he could not make his own customers believe the doctor was drunk, he contented himself by expressing his contempt for that "humbug of a lecturer," promising to "lick" him before he left Pawtucket if he could find him. The doctor heard of it the next forenoon, and he walked up by Crane's store several times; but the *sold* vender of strong drink made no demonstration.

While Dr. Jewett was in the service of the Rhode Island Temperance Society he spent a night at an hotel in Woonsocket. As usual, he "kept his eye open," studying the characters of parties in the barroom, some of whom were citizens of the place. Between nine and ten o'clock it was proposed to "crack up;" which the doctor found to be a method of deciding who should pay for drinks for the company. A piece of coin was tossed up, and the case was decided by its falling near to or remote from a certain crack. The doctor was a silent but close observer of the game, and he was a stranger to all present. The impression which the scene made upon his mind may be gathered from the following lines that he composed before retiring, and published in the local paper the next day:

"'Crack up!' 'crack up!' The clock strikes nine;
    We have not drank for half an hour;
  Say, will you choose, or rum or wine,
    Or brandy's stimulating power?
        Come, fill the glass,
        And let it pass,
    Till sorrow, care, and thought are gone,
  And exiled reason quits her throne.

" Come, jovial boys, ' crack up!' ' crack up!'
And fill again the maddening cup!
What though our wives sit quite alone,
And muse on hopes and pleasures gone?
Though bitter thoughts their bosoms burn,
And while they wait for our return,
    Let all that pass, —
    Come, fill the glass;
We'll drink to love that never dies,
Till from *our* hearts affection flies.

" ' Crack up!' ' crack up!' Come, fill again
    The accursed cup with liquid fire;
And now its contents let us drain
    To sleeping babes and hoary sire;
To mother dear, though drenched in tears,
And bending with the weight of years.

    " Bid sorrow flee,
    And drink with glee,
Though babes may need a father's care
    From wretchedness and want to save,
And though we bring the time-bleached hair
    Of parents sorrowing to the grave.
Come, fill again the accursed cup,
And let us drain. ' Crack up!' ' crack up!' ' "

No temperance lecture or sermon had ever made
so deep an impression in Woonsocket, at that time,
as this poem. It set many respectable people to
thinking, and actually brought the " crack-up "
game into bad repute.

About this time the doctor was in another part of
the state, when he observed, over the bar, at the

hotel where he stopped an hour, the following information :

NO CREDIT GIVEN HERE.

It was just the thing to start the doctor off upon a
train of original thought. After reflecting a few
moments, he said to the landlord, pointing to the
placard :

"I see that you bring your customers right up to
the chalk, and don't plague yourself with book-
keeping."

"Oh, yes," the landlord replied; "in the sale of
liquors these days, it won't do to give credit. If you
don't get your pay down from the class that buy
liquors now, you will never get it."

"I think you are right *there*," remarked the doctor; "but you might add a few words that would
improve your inscription, and render it more striking and impressive."

"What would you add?" inquired the landlord
with apparent interest.

"Give me pen and paper, and I will show you,"
replied the doctor.

"Just step to the desk within the bar, and you
will find paper, ink, and pen," he answered.

The doctor stepped to the desk and wrote out the
landlord's notice for the first line of the following
verse, and added three other lines :

> "'No credit given here;'
> But I have cause to fear
> That there's a day-book kept in Heaven,
> Where charge is made and credit given."

The doctor returned to his seat, and the landlord went to the desk, and read. His countenance changed, though he was not enraged. He was silent and thoughtful. Evidently the shot struck his conscience. The doctor bade him "good-day," and departed, without another word on either side.*

Dr. Jewett's connection with the Rhode Island Temperance Society was brief. It was a period of great depression in business, when money was scarce, and many laborers unemployed. In these circumstances it became quite impossible to raise money to prosecute the work. Some temperance men, who had pledged generous amounts in the outset, had become embarrassed, and could not redeem their pledges. In these circumstances, Dr. Jewett resigned at the end of a year, to the regret of the friends of temperance throughout New England. His purpose was to return to the practice of medicine.

His reputation as a physician stood high in Prov-

---

* One day Dr. Jewett wanted to send a letter to a Dr. Carpenter, of Pawtucket, living on the Massachusetts side of the river. There were two physicians there bearing this name, one of whom sold rum with his drugs, and he could not recall the Christian name of either ; so he superscribed the letter thus :

"Go, little packet ; seek the home
  Of Dr. Carpenter, Pawtucket ;
Not he who sells New England rum
  To the poor sots who love and suck it,
But he who lends a helping hand
  To drive intemperance from the land
    Of Massachusetts."

idence, and his friends besought him to open an office in that city. The result was that he established himself on Christian Hill, hanging out his sign, "CHARLES JEWETT, M. D."

The doctor was poor now. When he left Centreville he had hundreds of dollars owing to him; but the hard times had shut down the mills and thrown the operatives out of employment. Not a dollar of his debts could he collect. Then, he had received but a part of his stipulated salary in Rhode Island; and he had labored on, economizing even to scrimping his family, without making known his actual necessities to friends. To add to his distress, he had scarcely renewed his practice when his wife was stricken down with hemorrhage of the lungs, and for months lingered on the brink of the grave. At length, however, she rallied, and his practice opened encouragingly. His drug-shop was in the house he occupied; and he had run in debt for the small quantity of drugs it contained, — seventy dollars.

We should have called attention before to a most interesting episode in the doctor's life, while he was temperance agent. He represented the Rhode Island Temperance Society in a very large temperance convention, held in Boston in January, 1839, where more than three hundred clergymen were present. Thinking that he might be called upon to address the assembly, he prepared a poem, called "A Dream: the Rumsellers' and Rumdrinkers' Lamentation." The convention continued two days, and on the evening of the first day Dr. Jewett was invited, with other distinguished advocates of the cause, to speak. At the close of his speech he recited his poem, in which he personated the irate rumseller and boisterous drunkard. He did it so exactly "to nature" that the large audience were almost wild over it. They shouted, stamped their feet, and clapped their hands; men threw up their hats and women waved their handkerchiefs; reporters dropped their pens to laugh and shout, and such a scene was never witnessed in Boston before. The Rev. A. W. McClure, a prominent Orthodox clergyman, thus describes the scene in the "Sons of Temperance Offering":

"We have seen some laughing in our time, but decidedly the most extravagant, uproarious, ecstatical burst we ever witnessed was at Dr. Jewett's recital of his poem, 'The Rumsellers' and Rumdrinkers' Lamentation,' as given at the great convention held January, 1839, at the Marlboro' chapel in Boston. In reading this effusion in cool blood, at this distance of time, and under great change of circumstances, it is difficult to see anything about it sufficient to cause that deafening cachinatory explosion and its long-sounding reverberations. But at that time, when the 'fifteen gallon law' was in all its glory, the satire was most ticklishly *apropos*, and never did ridicule seem keener or more free from venom. Above all, the doctor's delivery justified what the ancient rhetoricians have said of the importance and effectiveness of manner. The whole densely crowded audience was thrown into a paroxysm of laughter such as can never be exceeded in the same length of time. The fat man rolled in his seat like a pudding in a boiling pot. The lean man doubled up into a hard knot, then threw himself back in a rigid spasm, and at last twisted himself into a corkscrew, undergirding his poor ribs with both hands to keep himself from being shaken to pieces. The tremendous roar burst up into yells of delight and shrieks of orgastic merriment. When the most furious stamping and clapping seemed too tame an expression of applause, men seized hold of each other and exchanged mutual thumps of congratulation. Even grave doctors of divinity took to thwacking the pew-rails with their stout walking-staves, leaving lasting mementos of their uncontrollable mirth. For many a day after that did the intercostal muscles of the company retain the sorest reminiscences of that season of unparalleled drollery. We never expect to see the equal of it, nor do we wish to ; one such laughing-spell is enough for a lifetime, and affords ' a joy for memory.' "

In the poem the rumseller began his " Lamentation " thus :

" Alas ! for the days of our glory are past,
   And the long-dreaded evil has reached us at last ;
   We must now our respectable traffic give o'er,
   For our license is out, nor can we get more."

The boisterous drunkard began his wail as follows :

" Nabers and frinds ! and can this be !
   And shall we be no longer free?
   Say, has the time, long dreaded, come,
   When we can't have one drop of rum?"

We have not space for liberal extracts from the

poem. We should say, however, that representatives of the press, who were present, obtained a copy of it, and it was published in several Boston papers; and it was issued, also, in a sheet, which the newsboys sold on the street, crying, "Buy a 'Lamentation'! Buy a 'Lamentation'!" In this way the production had a wide circulation.

In the winter of 1840, at the time to which we have referred, when Mrs. Jewett was convalescent, the doctor received an invitation to prepare a poem for another temperance convention in Boston. The invitation was urgent from a committee of leading temperance men, Deacon Moses Grant chairman. The doctor decided at once not to accept the invitation. His wife urged him to go.

"Impossible!" replied the doctor. "I cannot spare the time. I have that bill of seventy dollars for drugs to pay in four weeks, and I must bestir myself and raise the money, which I cannot do if I sit down to write poems."

Mrs. Jewett suggested that he might be paid something for the labor. At any rate she was impressed that God would provide some way to pay the SEVENTY dollars; it was best for him to trust in Providence, and do the work. Her plea was successful, and he hastened to write the poem, which he did not complete till the evening before the convention. The last eighteen lines he wrote on that evening, in Deacon Grant's parlor, Boston. The convention was to continue two days, with a rousing meeting on the evening of each day. The doctor's poem was advertised for the first evening. The audience on that evening numbered three thousand, in which were several hundred clergymen, presided over by Hon. John Tappan. The reader will understand how the vast assembly received the poetical plea for temperance, when he learns that, as soon as the doctor concluded, a gentleman in the audience arose and inquired if the poem could be printed so that delegates could secure copies some time during the following day. Deacon Grant immediately pledged the audience that the poem should be printed during the night, and be ready for sale at ten o'clock the next day, — the time the convention would assemble.

Rev. T. P. Hunt ("Father Hunt," as he was called), the celebrated advocate of temperance, was present, and he said :

" Mr. President, I am glad the poem is to be printed. I think it is worthy of publication, and hope, when printed, that the delegates present will buy, not a single copy each, but half a dozen each, to distribute among their friends, and that they will be willing to pay a good price for them ; and, in that case, perhaps our friend, the doctor, will obtain some reward for his labor more substantial than the thanks of this honorable body."

The doctor concluded reading the proof-sheet of the poem about two o'clock in the morning, and at the assembling of the convention, at ten o'clock the following morning, Rev. L. D. Johnson, of Rhode Island, offered it for sale. Over twelve hundred copies were sold; and when the net profits were counted out and handed to Dr. Jewett, there were just SEVENTY DOLLARS. We suspect that his thoughts were of his wife and Divine Providence when he pocketed the money.

The poem contained about five hundred lines, and made a pamphlet of nearly sixteen pages. It was a clear-cut use of the salient points of the cause, of which the following paragraph is a sample:

> " Say ye that vice and wrong must be o'erthrown
>   By the persuasive power of truth alone?
>   Then act consistent, and throw down the rod
>   Of penal law; let murder stalk abroad
>   Free o'er the land, with none to make afraid;
>   Be the assassin's upraised hand unstayed;
>   Strike from your statutes every virtuous law
>   That can protect the innocent, and awe
>   The stern transgressor with its penalty,
>   That vice may riot unrestrained and free.
>   Draw out the felon from his dungeon cell,
>   With his red torch, that midnight fires may tell
>   Where falls his smothered vengeance on your land;
>   And when you see him lift the flaming brand,
>   To deal destruction on your own fair halls,
>   Fold up your arms, and as the ruin falls,
>   Beseech him calmly to desist, because
>   He errs against the spirit of your laws,
>   And with their ' general end;' but yet are these
> ' Enforced by no specific penalties.'
>   Ye hypocrites! Ye slaves of *place* and *time!*
>   Ye dare not thus unfetter every crime;

Ye hold a halter for the wretch who slays
His fellow-man in aught but legal ways;
The thief who robs you of your worldly store,
For him ye bolt the prison's iron door;
Say, why inflict your stripes on these, and save,
' Unwhipt of justice,' the still blacker knave?"

The "Journal of the American Temperance Union,"
published in New York city, said of Dr. Jewett and
this poem :

"Dr. Jewett is making himself in various ways one
of the most useful advocates of the temperance
cause. When wit is needed he has it at command;
and when sober argument is the proper weapon he
is not deficient. His former poetic effusions have
been highly comic and sarcastic. This is neat,
chaste, and sober. Some parts of the poem are very
beautiful and touching."

A few weeks after the delivery of this poem, Dr.
Jewett was invited to act as agent of the Massachusetts Temperance Union, — a wider field and graver
responsibilities than ever.

The reader may well imagine that this new call
must have perplexed the doctor considerably. He
had regretfully but honestly abandoned the lecture-
field and returned to his chosen profession. A wide
door seemed to be opened to him for medical practice. Many friends rejoiced to see him reinstated in
his old pursuit. Then, too, he had been disappointed
in pecuniary support. By sad experience he had
learned that philanthropic labors, if appreciated,
were not remunerative. Would he have a similar

experience in the new field to which he was called?
He could scarcely help asking this question. However much he loved the cause, and whatever sacrifice he was willing to make, such thoughts and
inquiries as these were inevitable. That he was
perplexed cannot be denied. The sequel will show,
however, that all doubts soon vanished before the
brightening prospect of blessing the fallen and
saving the tempted.

CALL TO MASSACHUSETTS.

THE large humanity of Dr. Jewett caused him to abandon the practice of medicine, with the prospect of wealth and position, the second time, for the temperance-lecture field. More men were adapted to the former than to the latter, and more were inclined to adopt it. At this point, the appeal of suffering humanity touched his heart, and he was not long in deciding to accept the proposition from Massachusetts. The cry of the fatherless and the widow stirred his soul, and he could not decline.

The doctor was poor — too poor to move his family to Massachusetts ; yes, too poor to pay his honest debts. He resolved to sell every article of furniture and other property, that would command a fractional part of its value, that he might pay his debts, send his family to board with relatives in Connecticut, and when, with his salary of twelve hundred dollars and expenses promised, he was able, to set up house-keeping again in the Bay State. The doctor shall tell the story in his own words.

" My personal property, even furniture, the gift of relatives to my wife before her marriage, was, at her request, sent to the auction-room and sold, that the avails might aid in paying debts which I had contracted while serving the cause of temperance. The time for the commencement of my labor in Massachusetts had arrived, and yet, after employing all available means, I was unable to pay all my debts before leaving.

" That was a gloomy hour. I went down to old India Point to take the cars for Boston, and reached the depot twenty minutes in advance of the time of starting. I had this time to ruminate. In connection with the practice of my profession, and as a laborer in a great work of reform, I had served the state faithfully for ten years, and now must leave it, with a wife and four children to care for, with but little more money than would pay my fare to a new field of labor. I paced the platform, and presently extended my walk along the piles of wood near by, and for a moment I was quite unmanned. I may as well confess it: the boy Charles Jewett got the better of the man. I sat down behind the pile of wood, and wept."

If wit or pleasantry did not come to his aid before the cars started, then it is the only strait we have found him in powerless and disconsolate. It should be said, however, that the bare intimation of his situation to friends in Providence would have brought immediate assistance ; but he kept that to himself.

On that very night Dr. Jewett began his labors in Massachusetts by lecturing in Dedham before a large audience. As he expressed it, " I got another fair opportunity to assail the wicked system I had long been fighting, and in the labor forgot personal griefs and embarrassments."

Three things rendered Dr. Jewett's removal to Massachusetts, in April, 1840, peculiarly interesting.

First, the violent mobocratic opposition to the anti-slavery and temperance movements had spent itself. The spirit that dragged Garrison through the streets of Boston, with a rope about his neck, in 1835, incarcerated Rev. George B. Cheever in Salem jail, and drove Rev. John Pierpont from his pulpit, had been exorcised, though it still hovered about instead of going into the swine. Second, the leaders of the temperance cause were the noblest men of the times, many of them giants in intellect and personal influence. The mention of the names of many of them will even now awaken precious memories of the early struggles of the temperance cause : Sargent, Pierpont, Dr. Beecher, Rantoul, Crosby, Hoar, Gray, Dr. Channing, Hilliard, Sears, Dr. Ide, Mann, Jackson, Bond, Alden, Huntington, Fletcher, Loring, Mellen, Bowles, Walker, Tappan, Drs. Edwards, Gannett, Pierce, Jenks, Perry, Ware, Kirk, and Ballou ; Grant, Hallett, Bartlett, Lawrence, May, Spooner, Thompson, Safford, Palmer, Damrell, and many others, were numbered among the prominent workers then. Judge Nathan Crosby, of Lowell, was secretary of the Massachusetts Temperance Union, that invited Dr. Jewett to the state, and John Tappan was president. No temperance agent ever had an opportunity to associate with such a band of intelligent and able leaders, before or since.

Third, the clamor against the License System, begun five years before, culminated in the passage of the so-called " Fifteen Gallon Law," in April,

11

1838, under which no party licensed could sell less than fifteen gallons at once. This, of course, was indirect prohibition, and it created the greatest excitement. The liquor-sellers were violent against the measure, and their servile patrons joined them in the most resolute opposition. They set themselves to work, sparing neither money nor labor, to repeal the law. In 1839 they found a tool in Marcus Morton, who professed to be a temperance man, and had been president of the Massachusetts Temperance Society. He consented to be the candidate for governor of the liquor party, thus selling his birthright for this "mess of pottage." He was elected to the office, and the aforesaid law was repealed in the early part of the session of the legislature, in 1840.

The repeal of the law left the state of affairs as it was before its passage in 1838, namely, the power to grant liquor licenses was vested in the county commissioners; and in some counties the commissioners refused to grant licenses. Hence, in some localities practical prohibition was tried before the "Fifteen Gallon Law" was enacted.

Immediately after the repeal of the law, the friends of temperance commenced a campaign to secure the election of temperance county commissioners who would not grant licenses. Dr. Jewett removed to Massachusetts just in time to engage in that campaign. Nor could he have found a work more congenial to his taste. He was in advance of many temperance leaders in his views of prohibition. He had publicly declared, again and again, that the only consistent and righteous course was to *prohibit* the traffic. The election of county commissioners who would grant no licenses was next to absolute prohibition, in the circumstances ; so that he engaged in the exciting canvass with all his heart. It was about the first dash of wit and humor the cause had received, and a livelier time than Dr. Jewett's audiences had, the temperance people never enjoyed.

One incident occurred at Dedham under the "Fifteen Gallon Law," which Dr. Jewett turned to good account. At a military muster in that town, a rum-seller pitched his tent, on which, in large letters, was advertised "THE STRIPED PIG, — Admittance Six Cents." He had striped a pig with paint from snout to tail, giving it the appearance of a zebra, as a device to evade the law. Men paid six cents to see the animal, and a glass of rum was given to each patron. While the liquor fraternity were chuckling over this shrewd evasion of the law, as they thought, the sheriff of the county arrested the proprietor, and seized his pig, tent, rum, and all, and carried them off the ground. The anti-temper·ance press spread the news of the "Striped Pig" affair over the country, commenting upon it as a ⌐apital thing, and creating all the merriment possible over it. Dr. Jewett learned of it, and just before his removal from Rhode Island he drew a picture of the scene, which was given to the public in a lithographic print, entitled, "DEATH OF THE STRIPED PIG." His design was to convey by the print an idea of the state of the temperance cause at that time, and Nast himself could not have done the work better. Thousands of them were sold and circulated in Massachusetts and other states. They were posted in shops and stores, on board fences and big trees; and for many years copies were found in different parts of New England. The effect of it was amusement and instruction, exerting an influence for the cause wider and greater than that of any one temperance advocate. People were on tiptoe to see the author of "The Death of the Striped Pig;" nor did they listen to him long before they said within themselves, "Just the man to get up such a capital thing."

About the same time, also, the doctor sketched and published another lithograph, representing rumsellers catching men. A pond was the chief object of interest, around which the rumsellers gathered with fish-poles and lines, their hooks baited with bottles of rum, to catch men. He employed these illustrations, as he wrote temperance poems, to do good. Under the circumstances, he believed that it was one important method of awakening public attention, and causing people to stop and reflect.

One of the first things that Dr. Jewett sought to accomplish was to place the Massachusetts Temperance Union, whose agent he was, upon a sound "financial basis." In addition to salaries, the society needed money for a liberal distribution of temperance literature, in which method of usefulness Dr. Jewett thoroughly believed. The society was publishing the "Temperance Journal," and "Temperance Almanac," (monthly sheets;) the latter designed for the young. In addition to these, the "Tract" was issued occasionally, containing valuable temperance speeches. To give these publications, together with the usual temperance tract, a general circulation, much money was needed. The doctor proposed that the State be canvassed for members to the "Union," who should pay into its treasury one dollar or more annually, and that each lecturer should test the practicability of the measure by pressing it upon the attention of the people, though other agents might be employed specially for collecting money on that plan. Each contributor of one dollar should receive a copy of the "Temperance Journal" gratuitously.

Dr. Jewett's "Plan" was unanimously adopted; and the success of it may be learned from the result of his labors. The first month he obtained seven hundred and sixty dollars from seven hundred and fifteen members, and thirty-three donors — the latter being persons who would not sign the pledge of the "Union," but would pay one dollar each, and receive its publication. The second month he added over *four hundred members.*

A little more than a year from the time this "Plan" was adopted, the "Washingtonian Movement," inaugurated by John Hawkins and his coadjutors of Baltimore, so absorbed public attention and diverted funds to its own support, as to nearly exhaust the treasury of the "Union." Mr. Crosby, the popular and efficient editor of its publications, said, in July, 1842 :

"Our plan was favorably received, and our agents were carrying it forward with all practicable dispatch through the State. Under it, the circulation of the 'Journal' had risen to nearly twenty-five thousand copies monthly ; the 'Almanac' and 'Tract' to twenty thousand more. More than six thousand members and donors had been obtained, the 'Cold Water Army' paper established, and the whole operation of banners, badges, songs, &c., gotten up. The committee and friends, who had watched with much interest and care the successful influence of the plan, were buoyant with hope that we were now to have a somewhat more *systematic* and *permanent* effort in our great enterprise than had ever before been made in the State. . . . . We cannot with integrity conceal the cause of our embarrassment. We should be false to the cause and to ourselves were we longer to remain silent upon a matter of such vital importance to both. . . . The answer to our calls for accustomed aid comes up from most of our towns, — 'We are doing so much for the Washingtonians, you must excuse us this year.' "

The doctor's labors were highly appreciated, and within six months his salary was raised to fifteen hundred dollars and expenses. He removed his family to Massachusetts, residing at Ashland for a time, but removing in the spring of 1842 to the village then called "Newton Corner," but now "Newton," as distinguished from the other divisions of the city of Newton, where he was more convenient to the Boston headquarters.

The pecuniary resources of the "Union" became

so diminished by the "Washingtonian Movement," and still later by the advent of the " Sons of Temperance," that Mr. Crosby withdrew from the society, to the deep regret of the temperance public. From that time the editorial management of the "Union's" publications was committed to Dr. Jewett, though he still continued his labors in the lecture field.

At one time the treasury of the society which Dr. Jewett served was exhausted, and the Executive Committee were devising ways to replenish it.

"Gentlemen," said the doctor, " give me your subscription-book and proper authority, and I will go abroad to-morrow among your fellow-citizens, and get you some money."

" That would be too bad," replied one of the committee, "to subject you to the necessity of public speaking evenings, and begging in the day-time."

" Nevertheless it is honest," responded the doctor ; " and I am willing to perform any kind of service for the temperance cause which a man may, and not do violence to his conscience."

So the subscription-book was given to the doctor, one gentleman remarking :

"You will need a list of the names of such persons as will be likely to aid our cause."

" Never mind that," replied Dr. Jewett; "I shall find out who are friendly. I intend to take the places of business on the streets I shall visit, in course, and if I happen to drop in upon those not friendly to the enterprise, I will endeavor to make them so."

The next morning the doctor began his collecting

tour at the head of Washington Street, and found only friends to the cause in the first few places of business. At length he reached a hat-store, where he met with a different reception; and his tact, humor, and logic, in dealing with the man, are very interesting and instructive.

"I am raising money for the temperance cause," said the doctor, addressing the hatter politely, and passing the subscription-book to him.

"I have no interest in the cause, and I have nothing to give," answered the hatter, rather coldly.

"What, sir!" exclaimed the doctor, assuming an air of surprise, "did I understand you to say that you were not aware of having any interest in the subject I have presented to you?"

"Yes, that was what I said," replied the hatter.

"Well, sir," continued the doctor, with one of his blandest smiles, "I am sorry to hear that; for it affords me evidence that you are not acquainted with your own business."

This was "pushing plainness of speech to the verge of impudence," as the doctor said afterwards.

"If you are better acquainted with my business than I am," answered the man with considerable spirit, "I will take lessons of you."

"I have no doubt that I am, in this matter," added the doctor, with more of his seeming impudence; "and if you please, I will proceed to instruct you forthwith."

Probably, after all, the doctor did not appear so

impudent as his language implied, for here the hatter laughed him in his face.

"Well," continued the doctor, "you deal in hats, and intend to make a little money on every hat you sell?"

"Yes."

"Whatever sends additional customers to your counter, and increases their ability to purchase, promotes your interest, does it not?"

"Certainly."

"Whatever destroys men's ability to purchase, and makes them content to wear old, worn-out hats, does your craft an injury, does it not?"

"Very true."

"Well, sir, if you and I were to walk out an hour or two through the streets and lanes, and along the wharves of the city, we should see scores of men with old, miserable, slouched hats on their heads, — hats which ought, years ago, to have been thrown into the dock or the fire. Now, sir, what hinders those men that they do not condemn the old head-dress, and walk up to your counter and purchase a hat from your extensive assortment?"

"That is not a difficult question to answer," replied the hatter. "The men are too poor to buy a hat."

"Very true, sir. But what, in your opinion, made the mass of them so poor that they cannot buy a decent hat; and has so far crushed their self-respect that they are content to sport old concerns, whose rims have been torn half off, and whose crowns flap up and down as they walk, like the air-valve of the blacksmith's bellows? "

" Well, I do not — "

" Hold ! " exclaimed the doctor, interrupting ; " do not say, I beg you, that you do not know ; but think a minute."

Bursting into a loud laugh, the hatter replied :

" Well, sir, if you must have it, I suppose it was the work of rum."

" Exactly so, sir. I thought you would see the subject in the right light with a very little assistance and reflection. And now, do you not begin to discover that you made a mistake when you asserted that you had no interest in the subject of temperance? There are thousands of poor topers and tipplers in this city who expend every cent they get, beyond what purchases the bread that feeds them, at the dramshops ; and you will never get any patronage from them unless they become sober men. But, sir, let one of them go up to Washingtonian Hall, sign the temperance pledge, take the good counsel which will there be given him, and live up to the principle and practice of total abstinence, and he will not wear the old slouched hat eight weeks. If *he* cannot command means to improve his dress, means will be furnished by interested friends.   He will go to a clothing-store and purchase new garments, and then walk up to your store and buy a new hat. You will put the profits of the trade in your pocket — gains which you never would have received but for the temperance efforts of some of your fellow-citizens. And when I call on you and ask for a trifle to aid the temperance cause, you will, perhaps, give me the cold shoulder, and tell me you are not aware of having any interest in the subject."

The hatter was conquered. He gave the doctor one dollar for the cause, remarking :

" I never saw the subject in the light you have presented it before."

Dr. Jewett always profited by observation and experience, and he made great use of this incident. A Unitarian clergyman says that he heard the doctor use it with great power in Minnesota, fifteen years or more after it transpired, fixing the lesson of his address indelibly in the minds of his hearers.

Another incident, illustrative of the doctor's tact and efficiency, occurred on this wise. One day he dropped into the store of Joseph Breck, a stanch friend of temperance, where he met a citizen of Dorchester. As the latter gentleman was not a friend of temperance, Mr. Breck managed to get him into conversation with the doctor upon the subject without an introduction. The way was soon fairly open, for the man confessed in the outset, " I drink gin daily, think of it as you will."

He urged the common arguments in favor of moderate drinking, and the doctor replied to them so triumphantly, that the drinker felt he was driven to the wall, and he lost his temper, and declared that " the whole host of professed temperance men are hypocrites, who drink behind the door."

" Hold on, sir," responded Dr. Jewett. " You are
an old man, and I comparatively a young one, and
in this discussion I have endeavored to treat you
with that respect which is due to age ; and however
sharp you may be on me, I shall not reply in kind.
But I shall defend my temperance friends from your
charge of hypocrisy, for we have many men in our
ranks as aged and respectable as yourself."

" Well, do as you like," he retorted ; "you have
my opinion. You are all a set of hypocrites ; you
drink behind the door."

Dr. Jewett met him squarely here, and challenged
him to compare the temperance party and the drink
party. He arrayed before him the churches, Sabbath schools, Christian men and women, the clergy,
and benevolent people engaged in the best enterprises, as on the temperance side ; and, on the other,
(after conceding that there was a class of respectable
men,) the occupants of " gambling dens and houses
of infamy," where are the representatives of every
rascally business in the city, and they are all with
your party, sir. Blear-eyed and bloated, ragged and
reeling, hundreds of them hurrying along to their
graves. They are all with you. Why, sir, Falstaff's ragged regiment, which he swore he would
not march through Coventry with, were a set of well-
dressed gentlemen compared with a portion of your
rank and file."

The man looked at him for a moment in silence,
then burst into a loud laugh, and said :

" Well, I don't know who you are ; but you are an

odd one. You talk too fast for me. Yes, yes — too fast for me!"

"You say you don't know this man," said Mr. Breck, stepping forward. "Why, you ought to know him. He is pretty generally known throughout the state, and I will warrant that you have heard of him often enough. This, sir, is Dr. Charles Jewett, the temperance agent."

With a single exclamation of surprise, the man made for the door as if he were escaping from a monster. From prejudiced men he had heard strange things about the doctor, no doubt, and this sudden introduction well-nigh unmanned him.* The interview was ended for that day. Subsequently, when he visited Mr. Breck, the latter rallied him about his contest with that "terrible temperance fanatic."

---

* As an illustration of the grossly erroneous views that many people imbibe of reformers, is the following about the late William Lloyd Garrison. With Rev. Samuel J. May, and many other abolitionists, he was on his way to Philadelphia, to organize a National Anti-Slavery Society. On the steamer from New York Mr. May was drawn into an argument with a pro-slavery passenger, and he managed to shift his part of the controversy upon Mr. Garrison, and stood delighted to hear his manly, clear, and kind defence of the abolition doctrines. At the conclusion of the discussion, the pro-slavery gentleman said:

"I have been deeply interested in your frank and temperate treatment of the subject. If all abolitionists were 'like you, there would be much less opposition to your enterprise. But, sir, depend upon it, that hair-brained, reckless, violent fanatic, Garrison, will damage, if he does not shipwreck, any cause."

Mr. May said, "You are talking with Mr. Garrison, sir."

The reader may imagine what followed.

Months afterwards, Dr. Jewett visited Dorchester to collect money for the Society. He inquired after a certain man, and was told that there were two gentlemen by that name, father and son. He found that the "father" was his opponent at Mr. Breck's. The son was a regular contributor to the "Union," and he proceeded directly to his house. Ringing the bell, he was informed that the gentleman had not yet returned from the city. Reflecting a moment, he decided to call upon the father; it could do no hurt. So he went to his fine residence, rang the door-bell, and the master of the house himself responded. Each recognized the other, and saluted.

"Walk in, walk in, sir; I am happy to see you," said the man.

Dr. Jewett walked in, meanwhile stating the object of his call.

"Well," continued the host, "I was just going to sit down to tea. Come, throw off your coat, and take a cup of tea with me."

The doctor accepted the invitation, and the two men were soon in close conversation about "fruit-culture," the citizen of Dorchester being engaged quite largely in that business, and the doctor understanding the *modus operandi* equally well with himself. Gradually, however, by skilful management, the conversation passed to the inestimable blessings the temperance cause had bestowed on Dorchester, to all of which the reluctant citizen was compelled to yield assent. The result was that he made a fast friend of his host, and, what was more remarkable, *carried away a liberal donation from him to the Union.*

Such incidents prove that the doctor was not above his business. He could stand in the most honored pulpit, and upon the most famous rostrum, to advocate the temperance cause, or he could canvass for money to pay the bills.

It is evident that Dr. Jewett was a plain-dealing and heroic laborer. But for his wit, his fearless speech might have involved him in grave difficulties.

At one time he visited Paxton, where he was to lecture in the evening. Learning that the proprietor of the village tavern was a member of a church in another town, and that when he applied for a license he claimed that he would sell only to travellers, never to residents, the doctor concluded to spend two or three hours in said tavern. He was a stranger to the proprietor, so that he could do it without awakening suspicion. He saw travellers and residents both patronize the bar freely; and finally a venerable, gray-haired man, having the appearance of an intelligent, educated, but ruined man, came in for his drink. As soon as he left, the doctor inquired :

"Landlord, what old daddy was that?"

"That is Dr. Harrison," he replied.

"What! *he* a doctor? He don't look much like one," responded Dr. Jewett.

"Well," continued the proprietor, "notwithstanding his bad looks now, he has been one of the most celebrated physicians in this part of the country, and has in his time done a world of business."

" He will neither bless nor curse the world much longer," the doctor remarked.

"No," he answered; "*his copper is pretty much burned out.*"

This last heartless remark roused the doctor thoroughly. He made it the text of his discourse in the church that evening, describing the scenes of the afternoon in the bar-room, charging the proprietor with selling to residents as well as travellers, criticising his connection with a Christian church, and branding him as dangerous to the community and a disgrace to his kind. He awakened such enthusiasm and hostility against the liquor trade that the tavern-keeper was compelled to quit the business and leave town.

He could not endure a rum-selling professor of religion. In the beginning of his work in Massachusetts, when there were many of this class engaged in the traffic, he exposed one publicly in this way :

" To aid the gentleman and his acquaintances in estimating his claims to Christian character, I will contrast the life and labors of the great Teacher with the life and labors of this professed disciple.

The Master,	The Disciple,
Went about doing good.	Stays at home doing evil.
Fed the hungry.	Takes bread away from the poor.
Healed the sick.	Scatters elements of disease broadcast.
Raised the dead.	Hurries men to the grave.
Cast out devils.	Puts the devil into men."

In the autumn of 1842, the doctor lectured in Worcester. Much interest had been awakened there by the work among the intemperate. Several reformed drunkards had spoken in public, adding enthusiasm to the meetings. Dr. Jewett referred to the reclaimed class, and expressed the wish that some of them would address the audience at the close of his lecture. In the course of his remarks he stated that he had not drank a glass of distilled spirits for more than ten years. As soon as he took his seat, the audience called out:

"Gough! Gough! Gough!"

The president rose and said: "If Mr. Gough is in the hall, will he come to the platform?"

Mr. Gough responded, and his first words made reference to Dr. Jewett's remark.

"Mr. President: I should really like to know exactly how a man feels who has not had a glass of liquor in his stomach for ten years."

And then he proceeded to his experience in living a new life, and, in a speech of real eloquence and power, enchained the audience for ten minutes or more. The doctor saw in the stranger the elements of a distinguished worker, and remarked to the president, at the close of the meeting: "Look well to that young man, for, if I mistake not, you will be able to use him to some purpose hereafter." He was not mistaken.

Notwithstanding the "Washingtonian Movement" crippled the resources of the "Union" so essentially, Dr. Jewett co-operated in that work with all his heart. Few speakers were as efficient as he in pleading for reformed men, and few were so self-sacrificing in personal efforts to save them.

There came to his office one day an intemperate man by the name of Carey, asking for money to purchase food and lodging. The doctor recognized him as a young printer whom he knew in Providence when he labored there. With another young man by the name of Warner, in the same printing-office, Carey indulged freely in strong drink. Dr. Jewett had his printing done in that office, and he pleaded often with them to renounce their cups, but without avail. Both became quite intemperate, and Warner committed suicide by cutting his throat with a razor at the conclusion of a spree. Carey was forced to leave the office because his habits became so dissolute. From that time, Dr. Jewett had not seen him until he came to him in Boston.

The doctor pitied him in his degradation, gave him money to buy food and lodgings for the night, and extorted his promise to come to the office on the following morning.

The doctor went to his house in Newton at night, rehearsed to his wife the interview with Carey, saying that he appeared to desire a better life, and he proposed that they should take him into their house, and save him if possible. Mrs. Jewett, whose heart was ever ready to help the needy, seconded the proposal at once, and the next day Carey became a member of Dr. Jewett's family. The reader will appreciate the kind and benevolent spirit of Dr.

Jewett and his excellent wife, when he learns the actual condition of the man. The doctor shall describe him :

" As the result of long intemperance, offensive ulcers had formed on his limbs, and he was a ragged, bloated, diseased, degraded, repulsive creature. . . . . We had then six children of our own, and this was not a promising child to adopt into one's family; could not bring a certificate of good character; did not look very well, and withal, other senses revolted at his presence. I furnished him a room, made such improvements in his *personale* as soap, water, and clean clothing could do, and he was ' one of us.' It was a bitter pill to swallow. But what else could we do? The widow's son, his former companion, had come to me in Providence, and I had given him — advice. That was all; and rumsellers and the razor had given him — death.

" James Carey was saved; but it cost us five months board at — how much per week? His clothes did not cost much; for he wore those I had cast off; but they were clean, although here and there ornamented with a patch. You would have laughed to have seen the *set* of them, for my weight was one hundred and eighty, and he was as thin as Oliver Twist. But what a struggle the poor fellow had for a week. The presiding genius of that home had to make him a good many cups of strong coffee, and to bake for him a good many custards, and speak to him a good many encouraging words.

" ' Do not leave me, James, however badly you may feel,' she would say. ' Stay with us, come what may, and we will do all we can for you.'

" ' I will, ma'am ; I will stick by, live or die. If I die of tremens, I will die here.'

" ' That is right, James. But you will not die. You

may feel sometimes as if you would die, but you will not. You will live to retrieve the past. You have had a terrible education; but never mind, you'll be a man yet.'"

James Carey became a working temperance man and a Christian, settled in Boston as a printer, married an estimable lady, and went to housekeeping; and his first guests in his happy home were Doctor and Mrs. Jewett. Again and again Dr. Jewett was entertained in his house; and at the time his visits were interrupted by removal, the couple were blessed with a little daughter. Leaving the state, the doctor never saw Carey again; and he lost sight of him. The sequel is soon told.

Twenty years elapsed; and we recollect the doctor's coming into the Alliance rooms one Monday morning, after lecturing in Marblehead on the Sabbath, and narrating the following incident:

"Last night at five o'clock I addressed the crowd at Marblehead, down by the water, on the rocks. At the conclusion of my remarks, a young lady came to me with considerable emotion, and said, 'Dr. Jewett, you do not know me, but I know you. I have heard my father tell so much about you that I thought I must speak to you, and thank you for your great kindness to him.' 'And who is your father?' I asked. 'James Carey,' she answered. You may be sure that I was greatly surprised and pleased; and I inquired, as soon as I recovered from my surprise, 'And where is your father?' 'He is in heaven,' she replied; 'died several years ago, a good man, as he had lived. His death was triumphant. He talked much of you; and I have longed to see you, and tell you how grateful I feel for your goodness to him.'"

"That pays," added the doctor, with tears running down his cheeks.

Months after the reformation of Carey, Dr. Jewett related the circumstances of his recovery to an audience in South Hadley, Mass., as an encouragement to labor for the intemperate. Rev. L. Thompson, the missionary, was present, and he was so impressed with the qualities of a woman who was willing to receive into her large family such a miserable creature, and toil for his salvation, that subsequently he sent her a unique and valuable present, accompanied by the following graceful letter :

"SOUTH HADLEY, March 1, 1845.

" DEAR DOCTOR : Allow me to say that I was greatly interested in the story you gave us, which so admirably illustrated the kindness of your wife. I am anxious, in some way, to signify my hearty esteem for her character, and my gratitude, in the name of human nature, for her ' sweet charities ' to the miserable and unfortunate. Will you accept, for her, as a slight token of my esteem, the small box in the package with the books. It is covered with the *Cedar of Lebanon*, the emblem of strength and beauty combined. I visited the 'Cedars' somewhat over two years since, and with great difficulty and danger brought away with me, over rocks, precipices, and ravines, through throngs of spies, soldiers, and all sorts of foes to the foreigners, a distance of three days' journey, enough of the wood for many such souvenirs. If Mrs. Jewett will accept of one, it will add a little to my happiness.

" In great haste,

Yours truly,

L. THOMPSON."

X.

WORK IN MASSACHUSETTS CONTINUED.

WHEN Dr. Jewett removed his family to " Newton," there was no place of religious worship
in that part of the town. A few Congregational
families had settled there, and the prospect of a
growing, thriving village was encouraging. It was
not long, however, before a movement was made to
establish public worship. At first, service was
maintained in the schoolhouse, on Sabbath evenings.
Sometimes it was a preaching service, and sometimes a conference meeting. But in 1845 a successful movement was made to organize a church,
and establish the Christian ordinances permanently.
A church of thirty-seven members was organized,
Dr. Jewett and wife being two of the number. The
doctor engaged in the enterprise with all the enthusiasm that he usually put into the temperance reform.
He gave his best thoughts, spare time, and money,
to make the project successful. He subscribed one-
twelfth of all his property towards the erection of a
house of worship. He watched the process of building it with an interest that no words can adequately
express. He entered into the plan to secure a pastor, with a zeal and spirit that were born of con-

science and heroic faith. When the enterprise was complete, and a pastor ordained, he was a happy man. A grand thing was done for the public in general, and for his family in particular.

One who participated in those early scenes, writes:

"Citizens were invited to meet at the schoolhouse to adopt measures for the building of a church. Dr. Jewett was present, and expressed much interest in the enterprise. He was among the first to record his name with a subscription for at least one-twelfth of all his worldly wealth, in furtherance of the object. The doctor was almost invariably present at the many meetings called, ere the plans were perfected, and a contract made for the church-edifice, and by his familiarity with churches, seen in his travels, gave valuable aid in securing a neat, substantial structure, at a reasonable cost. Great was the joy of doctor and Mrs. Jewett, that henceforth they were to have the comfort and aid of the sanctuary in educating and training their growing family in the way of holiness; and the place of prayer was hereafter to be the welcome spot, where, in union with their brethren, they were to enjoy communion one with another in prayer for 'that wisdom which maketh rich, and addeth no sorrow therewith.' Dr. Jewett was rarely absent from the weekly prayer-meeting when at home. He loved the place of prayer, and rarely omitted to express his interest by some hearty, tender petition, or brief, pointed, yet kind address."

The doctor built a house soon after he became a resident of Newton, and the street upon which it was erected was named after him — Jewett Street. While building the house, he lectured in Manchester; and the ladies were so deeply interested in his address, that they desired to furnish some special, tangible proof of their appreciation of it; so they presented him with a pump for his new house. The doctor, in turn, desired to show that he valued the pump as highly as they did the lecture; so he magnified the affair in verse, and published the same in the " Salem Register."

Three of Dr. Jewett's children were born at Newton. When Frank was eight or ten months old, the doctor saw a baby-jumper for the first time, somewhere in his travels, and he went home and made one, as attractive and useful as any that he could purchase. In a letter to his son in Japan, January 6, 1878, we find a pleasant allusion to it in his characteristic signature, thus: " Yours decidedly, ever since I saw you in the Baby-Jumper."

Of Dr. Jewett's influence in Newton, the writer just quoted continues:

" I think he had no superior as a temperance lecturer in this country. As a city we are largely indebted to him for the position of *no license* which it to-day holds. His lectures, given to the children and youth of thirty years ago and more, who are the men of to-day, so thoroughly indoctrinated them in the principles of temperance, that no city government would dare to license the sale of intoxicating liquors as a beverage."

Rev. William S. Leavitt was the first pastor of the church, and he says:

" Dr. Jewett was one of the founders of the Eliot Church in Newton, Mass., of which I was the first pastor. He remained there not long, and was absent most of the time upon his temperance work. But I knew him only to admire his untiring energy, his earnest eloquence, his fertile and exhaustless wit, and his perfectly unselfish devotion to the good of his fellow-men. I have listened with the greatest interest and pleasure to some of the lectures and addresses which he gave on the subject of temperance, and especially admired the skill and solemnity with which he brought the teachings of Scripture to bear upon the great theme."

Before leaving his Newton home, we desire to call the reader's attention to what will appear in the course of this narrative. Twelve years after Dr. Jewett assisted to form the Eliot Church, he established a Sabbath school and worship in his own house in the territory of Minnesota, and the society at Newton presented him with a library. A year later, when a chapel for divine worship was erected there by his persevering labors, the society at Newton sent him over one hundred dollars. And since his death, the same society forwarded one hundred and fifteen dollars for the Testimonial Fund, raised as a tribute to his memory. "Cast thy bread upon the waters, and thou shalt find it after many days."

When the editorial management of the publications of the society devolved upon Dr. Jewett, the committee voted that each monthly sheet should contain a poem, illustrated, the doctor's brain to furnish as many of them as was consistent with other duties. At the close of the year, these twelve poems were published in a pamphlet of forty-eight pages, under the title of "Temperance Lyrics," a copy of which is before us; and we find that Dr. Jewett wrote four of them, while all the illustrations are the products of his fertile brain. The names of the four he wrote are: "The Cambridge Tragedy," "Fourteen o'Clock," "The Cotton Speculation," and "Quitting Too Late." The first was the story of a drunkard's wife, who requested the rumseller to desist selling strong drink to her husband. As he did not heed her advice, she entered his liquor-shop, and destroyed decanters, demijohns, and what not, leaving the concern a wreck. It began:

> " Women and facts are very stubborn things,
>   And rule this world in spite of lords and kings;
>   My muse of facts and women therefore sings."

The second was the experience of two drunken dandies on a dark, rainy night, on their way home from the revel. A clock struck the time, which they stopped to learn, and just as it ceased, another clock began. Counting to "*fourteen*," they stopped in amazement; and here the piece closes:

> " They reached at length *fourteen*, and quite amazed,
>   One thus exclaimed, while wildly round he gazed,
> '*Through all my* — (hic) — *life, some twenty years or
>   more,*
>   *I never knew it* — (hic) — *quite so late before.*' "

The third was the story of a rumseller's wife in Fall River, who gave a shirt of her husband to a beggar. Two hours afterwards she found that the recipient tore it into rags, and with other garments served in the same way, sold them to her husband for old rags, taking his pay in rum. To satisfy her liege lord that he had bought his own shirt, she examined the bundle of rags and found a strip with his own name on it. She tantalized him afterwards about his "cotton speculation."

> " Then staring in the face of her liege lord,
>   And suiting well her action to the word,
>   With bitter irony she thus exclaimed:
> ' Dear sir, don't look confounded or ashamed ;
>   For one of moderate means and humble station
>   You've made a splendid cotton speculation.' "

A gentleman recited this poem at a temperance convention in Seekonk, Mass., some months after its publication, and when he concluded, a clergyman arose and said that he knew the parties, and that he furnished Dr. Jewett with the facts.

The fourth poem was the tale of the turkeys which became intoxicated on the liquor-seller's rum-soaked cherries that he threw into the street. Their maiden owners, supposing they were dead, picked off their feathers and threw them under the shed, whence they soon emerged, crying, " Quit, quit !"

> " Poor birds ! " said Hannah, " better seek your pen ;
>   You act as foolish quite as drunken men.
>   And a like fate is yours, for they get tricked
>   By vile rumsellers, are made drunk, and picked ;

And some, like you, cry ' Quit!' but quite too late
To save them from a sad and wretched fate.

" Oh, my poor birds! it makes me melancholy
To think how you must suffer for your folly ;
Your unprotected sides exposed all weathers !
    It would have pleased me more
    If you had ' *quit* ' before,
In time to save your credit and your feathers."

These illustrated poems were altogether a new feature of a temperance journal, and were received with great favor. They arrested attention where graver things would have passed unnoticed.

For the third time he was invited to deliver a poem in Boston, at a temperance convention. It was a tribute to the mission of Law to destroy the liquor traffic, in which he personated the rumseller lamenting over his occupation gone, and experiencing the penalty of broken laws behind bolts and bars. The joy of the reclaimed drunkard also, and that of his wife, is produced, closing with an appeal to Massachusetts to defend virtue and liberty against vice and oppression. Afterwards, by invitation, he delivered it before the members of the Massachusetts legislature, and, subsequently, on going to Portland, Maine, to lecture, the passengers on the steamer pressed him to read it to them, and he acceded to their request. We have space for only the beginning of the vender's lamentation :

" Alack ! alas ! and well-a-day !   In vain did lawyers
    plead ;

Our last appeal has surely failed! There is a God,
  indeed.
I've doubted it this many a day, but now, perforce, I
  see !
There is a Judge who can't be reached with any kind
  of fee."

He delivered a public address in Lowell, at a
time when there was an effort made to arouse
temperance people from their apathy, to attack
the liquor traffic. Having two or three hours of
leisure before the lecture, he wrote a short poem,
"Apostrophe to the Merrimack," with which to
close his address. It represented the priceless
value of its *water* to the city; that it would be
"desolate," "deserted," "dead," without it; and
closed thus :

" Those mighty cotton kings, whose slightest word
  Is now obeyed almost as soon as heard ;
  Who speak the word, and lofty walls ascend ;
  Who stretch the hand, and lengthening streets extend ;
  Who stamp the foot, and like an ebbing tide,
  The very pavement settles at your side ;
  Lords of both men and money, where were they,
  Shouldst thou but turn thy *water* power away?

" Such were the fate of Lowell, shouldst thou lack
  Thy wealth of waters, bounteous *Merrimack !*
  The pulse of life, that beats so full and free,
  Through all her mighty frame, is given by *thee !*
  Then let her own thy power, yield to thy sway,
  And in cold water wash her stains away."

The delivery of it was received with tumultuous applause, and the following day gentlemen of the press solicited a copy for publication.

A social gathering of the friends of temperance in Boston one evening, at the house of Deacon Moses Grant, enjoyed a rare exhibition of Dr. Jewett's ability to read character, and his power of imitation in representing it. He was called out by some one who understood that he was an adept in the art. In the company was Rev. T. P. Hunt, the renowned temperance lecturer from Pennsylvania, and James Haydock, a reformed inebriate from New York, who had lost a leg in blasting rocks when he was drunk. Haydock possessed some eccentricities that attracted attention.

The doctor proposed to imitate those of the company with whom he was familiar; and he began with good Deacon Grant, and passed on to others, to the no small delight of all present. But when he came to Mr. Hunt, short and humpbacked, with a squeaking voice, the imitation was so exact that the company grew wild with excitement. Their laughter was of the explosive kind, and somewhat intemperate. Some were observed to clap their hands on their hips as if to hold the imperilled body together; and "Father Hunt" himself, no longer able to maintain a sitting posture in his chair, took at once to the floor, where the laughter poured out of him in a torrent. The company had scarcely recovered from the effects of the scene just described, when it came Haydock's turn, and the result was a repetition of

the foregoing, with this exception, that the exhausted forces of human nature in the parlor could not do
justice to the occasion.

Dr. Jewett was able to imitate prominent clergymen, lawyers, statesmen, and other public men,
showing peculiarities of manners, enunciation, tones
of voice, gesture, and emphasis. In reading the
standard poets, particularly Shakespeare, he studied
characters, and in reading, he reproduced the characters. For example, many of his friends recall, as
the author does, how well he personated the "fat-
witted" Falstaff in "King Henry Fourth," stretching
himself up to his full height, and appearing, for all
the world, as obese, rotund, and funny as Falstaff
himself; in deep, grum voice, and free-and-easy
action, like another bar-room visitor, discoursing:

"Thou hast the most unsavory similes; and art, indeed, the most comparative, rascaliest, sweet young
prince. But, Hal, I pr'ythee, trouble me no more with
vanity. I would thou and I knew where a commodity of
good names were to be bought. An old lord of the council rated me the other day in the street about you, sir; but I
marked him not; and yet he talked very wisely; but I
regarded him not; and yet he talked loosely, and in the
street too."

He lectured sometimes upon Shakespeare; also
upon Burns. He had a lecture, too, entitled "Evenings with the Poets," in which he introduced the
productions of various poets, as Goldsmith, Byron,
Thomson, Hood, Wordsworth, and others. All of
these were extemporaneous efforts. He quoted from

the poets wholly from memory, thereby gaining
power that is usually lost when the text-book is used.
His memory was not only very retentive, but wonderfully exact. It not only retained the substance
of the author's poem or essay, but his precise words.
Nor did the lapse of time appear to loosen the hold
of his memory upon its possessions. We have heard
him repeat a poem that he committed more than
thirty years before, never having rehearsed it from
that time. This remarkable ability was of inestimable value to him in public lectures, as well as in
social chat, and, added to his great power in personating character of any and every nationality,
imitating dialect, brogue, and other peculiarities
perfectly, made him really an exception among the
best public readers, since nearly all of them render
the text finely, but fail to produce the characters.

On the fourth of July, 1876, the citizens of Wood-
stock, Connecticut, celebrated the national centen-
nial on a grand scale, — oration, speeches, music,
poem, — honored by the presence of several of the
distinguished public men of our country. Among
the exercises that elicited particular applause was the
personating of Daniel Webster, Thomas Corwin,
George N. Briggs, J. G. Whittier, Horace Greeley,
and John Bright, by Dr. Jewett. In selections from
the writings of these famous men, he reproduced
the men themselves so skilfully as to surprise his
delighted listeners.

He regarded Shakespeare as far superior to any
other writer, not alone in the delineation of charac-

ter, but also as preserving *individuality*, so that the ruling trait was always manifest. Dr. Jewett aimed at this in his delineation of character, and he was successful.

A letter just received from a leading citizen of Faribault, Minnesota, R. A. Mott, Esq., who was intimate with Dr. Jewett in Minnesota from 1855 to 1858, says:

" The doctor's dramatic powers were wonderful, and, fed by his exuberant fancies and rich imagination, gave him rare power over a *movable* audience. He gave public readings on both Burns and Shakespeare in our village. His success with Burns, especially Tam O'Shanter and Holy Willie's Prayer, was great. I will give you an incident of rare success with but one auditor. In the winter of 1858 I was invited to attend a temperance meeting at Northfield, in this county, and, if possible, to bring Dr. Jewett with me. We went, and held an evening meeting. We were the guests of Hon. John W. North, proprietor of the town, and roomed and slept together. After a pleasant talk with the family we retired. Our chamber was lighted by an uncurtained west window, through which a Minnesota moon poured her richest flood of light. I got into bed first, and the doctor's undressed profile standing between me and the illuminated window suggested to me a couplet in *Macbeth*, which I repeated. The doctor ignited at once, and stalking through and und the room, and with excited, maniacal, though ropriate gesticulations, he repeated, correctly and aptly, the entire act in which my quotation occurred. It was the wildest, weirdest exhibition of genius I ever witnessed, and the scene will remain with me forever.

13

"In the morning, at the breakfast-table, Mr. North inquired who had been sick overnight, said he heard a great commotion up-stairs, and if he had not known the character of his guests, should have suspected a case of delirium tremens. I told the whole story, as best I could, to the great amusement of the ladies, and utter discomfiture of the doctor, who always afterwards declared that he owed me one."

When he read Burns, he was a complete Scotchman in voice, brogue, and manners. In one town, a scholarly gentleman listened to his lecture on Burns with profound interest. The next morning he sent to the city for a copy of Burns, remarking that "he never appreciated the beauties of Burns before," thus paying a decided compliment to the doctor's ability as a reader. Few public readers cause hearers to fall in love with the authors they personate to a degree that sends them away to study the productions read. Recently we met a clergyman in the cars who remarked:

"I heard Dr. Jewett deliver a course of six scientific temperance lectures in New Hampshire, over thirty years ago, and those lectures have been the basis of my views and labors on the subject from that day to this. At the close of the course of temperance lectures, he gave us a lecture on the poet Burns, the best lecture of the kind I ever heard. The fine points of that poet were impressed upon me as never before, and I went away and purchased a copy of his poems."

The venerable Daniel Kimball, Esq., who was

associated with Dr. Jewett in the beginning of his work in Massachusetts, says : "I have heard him talk for hours of 'Bobby Burns,' filling up all void spaces with snatches of the poet's songs, repeated in Scotch accent, and ever and anon illuminated by the bright scintillations of that laughing eye of his, which gave such point to all he said."

We find what appears to be notes of a lecture on Burns, delivered in Amesbury, Massachusetts, several years ago. Speaking of Burns' youth and inexperience, he said, by way of introduction :

" No just estimate can be formed of the native talent or genius of an individual from the most careful examination of what he has wrought, unless we take into consideration his previous *preparation* for the work, and the *circumstances* which surrounded him during its execution. When we look at a splendid painting, and find there all the excellences which can attach to such a production, we are not surprised at its faultless character if we are told that it was executed by one who had enjoyed every facility for perfecting himself in that art, and was quite at leisure to devote to the specimen before us all the time he desired. But if we are told that the splendid work on which we are gazing with delight was the work of a young man, who had enjoyed no advantages for cultivation, and that the work was executed during brief intervals snatched from a laborious occupation, we are amazed at the native genius of the young artist."

From the notes it appears that he called attention to the different classes of poetry thus :

" *Epistolary.* — A species of verse combining all the

other forms, giving, in combination, History, Philosophy, Fiction.

"*Didactic.* — Written with a special view to instruction.

"*Elegiac.* — The poetry of mourning or grief.

"*Dramatic.* — Poetry adapted to representation on the stage.

"*Pastoral.* — Descriptive of rural life and country scenes; a sort of landscape painting with words.

"*Descriptive.* — Goldsmith's Deserted Village."

His illustrations from Burns were confined to the epistolary class, — "Epistle to Friend Davy," — descriptive and elegiac classes. On the particular subject of the "Tempest," he introduced not only Burns, but, by way of comparison, Shakespeare, Byron, William Gaylord Clark, and Goldsmith. "To Mary in Heaven," "Lament for James Earl of Glencairn," and "John Anderson My Joe," were among his principal selections.

The feeling is irrepressible, that he would have stood before the country as the prince of public readers, had he but chosen to devote himself to that particular department. But with him it was simply a pastime. He had other and greater work on his hands, which his conscience required him to perform.

Now that we are speaking of Dr. Jewett's ability to represent character, we may record several facts illustrating his ability to *read* character.

He went to Faneuil Hall, Boston, to hear John Quincy Adams. Soon after he was seated, he observed a gentleman in front of him who attracted his notice. After a moment's close observation, he called Mrs. Jewett's attention to that marked face, saying, "That man does his own thinking." At the close of the meeting, he learned that the gentleman was Rufus Choate.

Once he stopped at the Delevan House, Albany, with his wife. It was in June, just as strawberries came into market, and the hotel table was supplied with them. There came to the table a well-dressed, portly man, with his wife and daughters; and no sooner did he discover the strawberries than he appropriated every dish of them within his reach for himself and family. Dr. Jewett surveyed the scene with as much composure as possible for a moment, then whispered to his wife:

"That fellow is a Western pork-dealer, I believe, and he has followed the business so long that it has struck in."

On going to the office of the hotel after dinner, he found that the man was an extensive pork-dealer from Cincinnati.

At another time he was travelling in the cars from New York to Philadelphia. Directly in front of him sat two young men whose manners and conversation he observed closely. At a station where the train stopped, a female acquaintance of the doctor entered the car — one whom he had not seen for several years. Each was surprised and delighted to see the other, and they chatted together until the lady left at another station. The lady was rather masculine in appearance, though very intelligent, and her voice was somewhat boisterous. On her departure, the doctor overheard one of the young men drop a remark to his associate that was not intended to compliment the woman, and the appearance of both indicated a disposition to ridicule.

"Young men," said the doctor, leaning forward, and addressing them in a subdued voice, "I think you do not read the character of that lady. She is a clergyman's wife, one of the most talented Christian women of Massachusetts, a person for whom I cherish profound respect. You did not form that opinion of her — did you? Come, now, tell me frankly."

One of them admitted that he did not form an exalted opinion of her.

"Now, young men," continued the doctor, "let us have a familiar talk about this matter; it is one of great importance. I have made character a study all my life. In the cars and stage-coach, on the steamer, in the parlor and public assembly, I have made it a business to read the characters of men; and it has been of great advantage to me. I am often reading a stranger with whom I converse, when he don't know it. Students like you, especially, should study character."

"And how do you know that we are students?" interrupted one of them.

"Ah! that is it," answered the doctor; "I told you that I had made character a study. Both of you are students, I am sure."

"It is so," remarked one, laughing.

"And you are collegians, too," added Dr. Jewett.

At this both of the young men laughed outright, one of them saying, "Members of Princeton College; but how can you tell that?"

"Simply by observation," replied the doctor; "and what may surprise you still more, perhaps, I can tell to what classes in college you belong. You are a Senior," putting his hand upon the shoulder of one, "and you are a Sophomore,"— putting his hand on the shoulder of the other.

The doctor had "hit the nail on the head," as he was wont to do in boyhood; and the young men were as astonished as they were pleased. The conversation continued, eliciting the deepest interest of the students, until the train reached Philadelphia, when the parties separated, warm-hearted friends.

Fifteen years and more elapsed; the doctor was lecturing in the state of New York, where he met a clergyman on the platform one night, who said to him, after the lecture, "Dr. Jewett, I suppose that you do not recollect when we met."

"I did not know that we ever met before," the doctor replied.

"That is not strange," responded the clergyman; "but do you remember the Senior and Sophomore students to whom you gave a gratuitous lecture upon reading character, in the cars, going to Philadelphia?"

"Certainly I do," answered the doctor.

"Well, I am the Senior," continued the minister;

" and I cannot thank you enough, Dr. Jewett, for the good you did me in that interview. It was the first counsel I had ever received to study character, and from that time I profited by it, and the advantage to me has been better than one year in college."

Within a few years Dr. Jewett was waiting at a depot in the city of H——. While there, a young gentleman and lady, richly attired, came in, evidently to take the next train. The doctor read them both within a few minutes, when the young man went out. No other persons were in the room now but the young lady and himself.

" Will you excuse an old man if he shall venture to express his interest in your welfare?" said the doctor to her.

She signified that such an act would not only be excusable, but that she would esteem it a favor from so venerable a gentleman.

" That young man is your particular friend, I suppose? "

She admitted that he was.

" And he is a young man of ability and many noble traits, I have no doubt; but do you know what his habits are? "

The young lady blushed and was silent, and the doctor continued: " Far be it from me to give you pain. God knows that I only want to put you on your guard. But that young man is fast becoming intemperate, whether you know it or not. I think he has gone out now for a dram."

She admitted that she knew he was in the habit of using intoxicating drinks, but added "they all do."

"Well, I have two daughters," the doctor answered, "and I could never give my consent for them to marry young men who thus tamper with strong drink."

The girl replied, "If the young ladies of the city refuse to marry young men who drink more or less, very few of them will ever be married."

These incidents show how great was Dr. Jewett's ability in this respect, and he was constantly improving it. He endeavored, also, to interest others in the reading of character, especially young people. When travelling with his wife and children on car or steamer, and when in the crowded assembly with them, he directed their attention to certain men and women for this purpose. The result of it, too, is seen in the family to-day. It was a trait of Dr. Jewett's character to make those around him familiar with what he was doing. When he budded or grafted trees, he wanted his wife and sons and daughters to understand the process also. When he planted currants, strawberries, and other fruits, he told any persons who were with him just how he did it, and why he did it so, even to the preparation of the soil. So that now even his wife and daughters understand all such things better than three-fourths of the men; and we doubt if they will consider it a compromise of feminine dignity for the author to say that they can exhibit the most cred-

itable proof of their acquaintance with these things
within their well-dressed garden.

The readiness with which the doctor read character was the secret of his singular success in dealing with all sorts of men. He could manage anything human. When he bought his farm in M——.
he was warned against having anything to do with
his nearest neighbor, a selfish, ugly, wicked man,
whose hand was against every one. "The only
way to get along with him is to keep away from
him," said one. "The more you do for him, the
worse he will treat you," added another.

The doctor concluded that he must be a very
peculiar man, if all this were true, — different from
any man he ever saw. However, he resolved to
make a friend of that strange neighbor ; and he did.
He improved every opportunity to do him a favor.
When he saw a chance to render him any service,
he did not let it slip. He carried things to his family. He went over to assist him whenever he saw
that an extra hand would be especially useful. He
let him know how glad he would be to loan him
farming utensils and other articles. At first the
"odd stick" appeared rather crooked, and he was
crusty and gruffy, and the doctor heard of his making
remarks not particularly complimentary. But when
Dr. Jewett saw that his gruffness was passing off, he
knew that kindness was taking effect. The result
was that the doctor completely won him over, so
that he became one of the best of neighbors. When
he became a good neighbor to Dr. Jewett's family,

he was a better neighbor to everybody else, as well as a better citizen, father, and husband. When the doctor removed from the town, this neighbor volunteered to assist him in the extra labors imposed ; and subsequently he drew largely upon his native vocabulary to express to others his admiration of the man.

Here we may add two more illustrations of the doctor's power of imitation, since the knowledge of them may aid the reader to understand some other things that follow.

Dr. Jewett was travelling with a friend in Pennsylvania, when their conversation turned upon his ability to personate the drunkard.

"I have no doubt that I can deceive the conductor of this train," remarked the doctor, "so that he will take me to be a drunken man, and put me off at the next stopping-place, if I carry the matter so far."

"Try it, try it," said his friend, eager to enjoy the sport.

When the conductor appeared for the tickets, the doctor was apparently pretty drunk ; enough so, at least, to be independent and saucy; so that it became an easy matter to get into trouble with him over his ticket, which, if we remember, he refused to show. The conductor denounced him as "a miserable drunken fellow," and declared that he would put him off at the next station. And sure enough, when the train stopped, the conductor dashed into the car, with one of his brakemen, to execute his threat; but he could not find the drunken man. He found his seat, and the passenger whom he thought was insolently drunk; but everybody was sober now. Passengers by this time understood the game played, and they enjoyed the conductor's confusion exceedingly. The latter soon learned, however, from the demonstration around him, that he was the victim of a well-laid plot, and he withdrew from the scene as gracefully as the circumstances would permit.

A few years since, Dr. Jewett attended a national temperance convention at Saratoga Springs. Several clergymen and Christian laymen stopped where the doctor was entertained. At the dining-table some one remarked upon Dr. Jewett's ability to personate the drunkard. This remark led to a trial of his skill on that day. A certain shop near by was selected, where knickknacks were sold, as well as intoxicating liquors. The doctor was to play the role of a drunkard in that shop, to which the clergymen and one or two others would repair in advance. They would be making some small purchases when the doctor should arrive. The programme was carried out to the letter, and the doctor staggered into the shop, waiting at one corner of the room for the proprietor to get through with his clerical customers. Apparently impatient, however, he finally motioned to the trader with his finger, to which no attention was paid. Putting on the air of affront at the intentional neglect, the doctor belched out his opinion of a man who would so treat a customer coming for a glass of brandy ; whereupon the trader ordered him out as one who " was too drunk to drink any more," declaring that he could not " have a drop there."

The clergymen had now reached the uttermost limit of self-control, and such an outburst of laughter as astonished the well-meaning merchant was a revelation to him. At the same time, the " miserable drunken fellow " was suddenly transformed, as if by magic, into one of the pleasantest, most affable, gentlemanly visitors the proprietor ever met.

An explanation of the ruse followed, and the company retired, with the verdict upon all lips, that in personating the drunkard, Dr. Jewett was " perfect."

He was very tenacious in his views respecting the effect of alcohol upon the reasoning faculties of even the moderate drinker. He claimed that any man, however intelligent or able, was blinded by his appetite to the influence of narcotics upon his reasoning powers. In a lecture in Franklin County, Massachusetts, he put the matter in the following characteristic manner, as amusing as it was instructive. He said :

" I doubt whether it be in the power of the strongest intellect to reason as soundly in relation to an unnatural appetite, to which the individual has become subject, as upon other matters. . . . . A good old lady who had been an extravagant user of snuff for many years, when urged to abandon the habit on account of its tendency to injure the voice, exclaimed, with a peculiar nasal twang [here the doctor imitated the old lady perfectly, bringing down the house tumultuously]: 'I do't believe a si'gle word of it, for I hab took s'uff for twe'ty years, and my voice is chest as clear now as it was whe' I comme'ced.' The good lady was mistaken. She could neither hear nor reason correctly in relation to snuff and its influences. Had you consulted her on other subjects, I doubt not that she would have exhibited powers of observation and reason quite respectable.

" Often, while travelling, with my pockets full of choice apples, and in company with some friend, I have offered to share with him their contents, and received for answer, 'No, I thank you, I have tobacco in my mouth.' Poor soul ! and so he must deny himself delicious fruit, that he might masticate a filthy weed, which we put around our squash-vines to keep off the bugs. . . . . Luscious fruits never afford to organs of taste, whose sensibilities have been blunted by narcotics, that exquisite pleasure they afford to a healthy palate.

" A clergyman in Essex County, Mass., who had an abundance of delicious grapes in the autumn, took a friend, from Boston, educated but intemperate, into his garden, to feast him on the ripe fruit. He picked a bunch here and a bunch there, of different kinds, for him, but soon found that he did not eat them. 'My dear sir,' he exclaimed, ' do eat them, and eat them freely ; they are fully ripe, and can't hurt you ; and there is abundance of them.' The unfortunate man looked up in his face, and with the most lugubrious expression imaginable replied :

" ' You are very kind; *but do you not think such things are rather cold to the stomach?* '

" Poor man ! " added the doctor, " he had scorched the coats of his stomach with the fiery products of the still until he had no relish for the most luscious fruits which

God has given for our sustenance and enjoyment. ' Rather cold for the stomach!' Mr. President, you and I, with palates and stomachs uncursed by alcohol, will not complain of the coldness of delicious peaches, or a basket of grapes, whose purple jackets are bursting from the pressure of the rich juices they contain."

Dr. Jewett lectured in a thriving country village one night, when he used "the wagon-maker" for an illustration, not knowing that a prominent citizen on the platform belonged to that craft. The illustration lost none of its force on that account. He said:

"All useful trades and occupations among men, if properly followed, may exist in the same community without clashing or collision, while many of them sustain a truly fraternal relationship to each other. The wagon-maker, for instance — " [Here laughter began, and the citizen on the platform looked as if he was not sitting there to furnish an illustration for the speaker.]

The doctor waited for the sensation to cease, when he continued:

"I am inclined to the opinion, from certain indications, that I have one of that class of tradesmen near me. If so, he will understand my argument. While the wagon-maker is shaping and putting together the various parts which enter into the construction of a wagon, he is thinking only of executing a valuable piece of work, and receiving for it a valuable consideration; and yet he is doing service to his neighbors. When he has finished his work, the wagon must be ironed; and the blacksmith now gets a good job. He also, while performing his part of the labor, is intent mainly on doing a good piece of work, and receiving for it a valuable consideration ; but he in turn is preparing work for another, for now the wagon must be painted. The painter takes his turn ; and before the horse can be attached to it, the harness-maker comes in for his share of the labor and the profits. Thus it is, to a greater or less extent, with all useful trades and occupations ; they are brothers, and work together harmoniously. But let us see. Does the grogseller sustain a legitimate relationship to this family of brothers? By no means. His vocation is that of a perfect Ishmaelite. Its hand is against every man, and every man's hand *should* be against it."

A round of applause greeted the doctor at this point, in which the "wagon-maker" joined with particular gusto.

Dr. Jewett had a way of enforcing an important truth, often, by using the testimony of drinkers themselves. In his lecture, at one time, speaking of the social element in drinking-clubs and parties, he urged the necessity of observing what sort of associates are found in such society. He thought the " game would not pay for the powder," and illustrated his statement by the following incident :

" I stopped at an hotel," said the doctor, " where I saw ' Joe ' and ' Bill ' in the bar-room. The parties were sitting very close together, and at the opening of the colloquy, Bill brought his big, dirty hand down pretty smartly upon Joe's knee, to render him wide awake to the importance of the question he was about to ask.

" ' See here, Joe,' said Bill, ' how much money (hic) do you reckon you and I have spent in this old place, first and last?'

" ' Well, I dunno,' replied Joe.

" ' Nor I, nuther, exactly,' continued Bill ; ' but I reckon we've (hic) spent in this old place, first and last, drinkin' and treatin' and sich like, as much as *six hundred dollars !* '

" ' Well, I guess we have,' responded Joe.

" ' Well, I guess we have, too,' said Bill. ' But what of that? Let her go! Who cares? It's gone, and we can't git it back again ; but we had some pretty good times while it (hic) was goin', — didn't we? and made a good many friends in that way, drinkin' and treatin', and sich like.'

" ' Yes, that's sartin, and no mistake,' replied Joe.

" ' Now, Joe,' continued Bill, ' I'll tell you what I'm thinking of. If, *now*, we could sell all the friends we made in that way, drinkin' and treatin', and sich like, for *one-half* what they cost us, shouldn't we make a speculation? '

" Joe indorsed the opinion, and had a loud laugh over it ; and thus the discussion ended.

" That fellow's head is level, thought I, if he is drunk."

Dr. Jewett sometimes applied the word "suckers," facetiously, to excessive drinkers, though he never forgot to explain by citing the occasion that furnished it, as follows : He lectured in a wide-awake manufacturing village of Massachusetts, where the pond had been drawn off the previous week for the purpose of repairing the dam. The people of the village had enjoyed a good time in scooping up suckers and other fish from the race-way. Bushels of these excellent fish were "scooped" up, and the inhabitants had thought of little but "suckers" for several days, — suckers pickled, fried, stewed, and boiled. When the villagers gathered in the old meeting-house that night (an unusual number of hard drinkers had been button-holed by leading citizens and persuaded to come), a layman, uncultured but good, was called upon to open the meeting with prayer. He besought a blessing on the gathering, a blessing on the town, on "the poor lost ones before him," on everything under the sun, in fact, till it occurred to him that he had forgotten the speaker; so he begged the divine blessing upon him, "to make him instrumental in saving many souls; and may he" — here he was at a loss for the right word, evidently thinking of the habitual drinkers there — "and may he" — hesitating, but soon rallying — "scoop up many suckers to-night! Amen."

The doctor said that no sort of fishing would please him better than "scooping up suckers."

Often the most dramatic and powerful appeals followed Dr. Jewett's wittiest sallies. At the foregoing meeting, in which drunkards and "suckers" seem to have been mixed, his remarks drifted into one of his ablest and most serious exposures of the sin and curse of the license system; and he closed by reciting the following from Cowper's "Task," in a manner so dramatic and eloquent, that his audience seemed to be enthused with his own spirit, and broke forth, at the close, into the most tumultuous applause:

> " Pass where we may, through city or through town,
> Village, or hamlet of this merry land,

Though lean and beggared, every twentieth pace
Conducts the unguarded nose to suck a whiff
Of stale debauch forth-issuing from THE STYES
THAT LAW HAS LICENSED, as makes Temperance reel.
There sit involved and lost in curling clouds
Of Indian fume, and guzzling deep, the boor,
The lackey, and the groom.   The craftsman there
Takes lethean leave of all his toil ;
Smith, cobbler, joiner, he that plies the shears,
And he that kneads the dough, all loud alike,
All learnéd, and all drunk.   The fiddle screams
Plaintive and piteous, as it wept and wailed
Its wasted tunes and harmony unheard.
Dire is the frequent curse, and its twin sound,
The cheek-distending oath.   'Tis here they learn
The road that leads from competence and peace
To indigence and rapine : till at last
Society, grown weary of the load,
Shakes her encumbered lap, and casts them out.
But *Censure* profits little : vain the attempt
To advertise in verse A PUBLIC PEST,
That, like the filth with which the peasant feeds
His hungry acres, *stinks*, and is of use.
Th' excise is fattened with the rich result
Of all this riot.   The ten thousand casks,
Forever dribbling out their base contents,
Touched by the Midas finger of the State,
Bleed gold, for Parliament to vote away.
Drink and be mad, then ; 'tis your country bids ;
Gloriously drunk — obey the important call ;
Her cause demands the assistance of your throats ;
Ye all can swallow, and she asks no more."

Much extra labor was imposed upon Dr. Jewett
in consequence of his ability and prominence. He
was frequently invited to the annual meetings of the
National Temperance Union in New York, and to

kindred conventions in other states. County temperance societies often besought his presence and speeches. Clergymen required his aid on special occasions, to promote temperance among their people. His pen was frequently brought into requisition to answer editorials in anti-temperance papers, as well as to correct grave errors respecting the physical effects of alcohol, and other important phases of the cause. Thus exhausting extra labors taxed his energies severely, though he enjoyed the service as well as they to whom it was rendered.

XI.

INDEPENDENT LABOR.

THE "Union" was so much crippled by the Washingtonian movement and the Sons of Temperance, that Dr. Jewett resigned in 1845, preferring independent labor. More than a year previous his editorial labors ceased; the "Temperance Journal" was discontinued, and Daniel Kimball, Esq., removed his "Temperance Standard" from Lowell to Boston. The doctor's resignation was accepted with sincere regret. The clergy and Christian people, especially, were highly gratified with his efficient work.

A few months after his resignation he was invited to accept an agency from the State Temperance Society of New Hampshire. In addition to lecturing, he was expected to edit the monthly organ of that society, "The Temperance Banner." He accepted the invitation at once, because he saw a wide field of influence there. Most of the Washingtonian societies in the state had become extinct, and there were not a dozen "Divisions of the Sons of Temperance." The doctor removed his family to Concord — his headquarters — and commenced his labors with a hopeful spirit.

At his suggestion the society adopted the plan of labor employed in Massachusetts. Its success enlisted the interest of the temperance public until a crotchety member of the Board interposed substantial obstacles by his opposition. Dr. Jewett withstood the hindrance for several months and then resigned, removing his family to Plainfield, Connecticut. At the next annual meeting of the society the offending member was censured by a resolution unanimously adopted, and he was not re-elected as a member of the Board. A motion was made to add expulsion to censure; but it was withdrawn at the instance of a witty speaker.

Temporarily Dr. Jewett labored in Connecticut, after leaving New Hampshire; but the temperance forces were so disorganized that no systematic way of raising money seemed to be open, and he turned away from the field disheartened. At that juncture he received a very pressing invitation to settle, as physician, in a flourishing town of New Haven County, and decided to accept it, after having made one more lecturing visit to Massachusetts. He wrote his purpose to a temperance paper in Worcester, Massachusetts, adding:

" Before, however, I lay down the *teetotal trumpet*, and take up the *lancet* and the *pill-box*, I propose to visit Massachusetts, and spend a few days on my old battle-ground, that I may meet once more old friends with whom I have so long labored."

Immediately he received several invitations to lecture, one of them from Clintonville, Massachusetts. After the close of his address in that village, a number of gentlemen gathered around him to express their regrets that he was soon to leave the lecture-field.

" Why must you do it?" said one.

" The experience of the last two years proves that my health will not endure the labor of continued public speaking through the summer months; and I cannot support my family without that strain," was the doctor's reply.

" And is there no remedy for that?" inquired another gentleman.

" There might be," answered the doctor, " if I were able to purchase a small farm, from the cultivation of which, in the summer months, I might obtain subsistence for my family, and also recruit my wasted energies for the winter's campaign."

" If that is all that is needed to keep you in the field," responded one of the aforesaid gentlemen, promptly, " *then you shall not leave it.*"

Others present seconded the thought so happily expressed; and on that evening was born a movement which put ONE THOUSAND dollars into the doctor's hands, as a tribute to his philanthropy and ability. With this money, and a few hundred dollars he had saved by close economy, he purchased his little farm in Millbury, Massachusetts, and removed thither in 1849.

One of the first acts of the doctor, on removing to Millbury, was to publish by subscription a little

volume, entitled, "Speeches, Poems, and Miscellaneous Writings on Subjects connected with
Temperance and the Liquor Traffic," *— a long
title for so small a book, if we measure it by dimen-
sions instead of quality.	Estimated by the *quality*,
the title well becomes the book.

During the first year of the doctor's residence in
Millbury, he was employed a month in Hampden
County, to aid in an earnest attempt to elect
county commissioners who would not grant licenses.
Hampden and Suffolk counties were the only ones
that continued to grant licenses; and no attempt
was made to secure a change in Suffolk against the
influence of the anti-temperance class of Boston.

Dr. Jewett always loved "to beard the lion in his
den;" so he enjoyed his labor in Hampden County
greatly.	He stirred up the country towns, and
closed his service on the day (Sunday) before the
election by a lecture in the city hall of Springfield
to a crowded audience.	Workmen were already
engaged in enlarging the county jail, and the doctor
said to his hearers: "If licenses must be granted, I
commend you for the enlargement of your jail, for
the same reason that I would commend the farmer,
who, while planting additional acres, puts an addition
to his corn-crib."	The applause showed that the

---

* The preface to the volume closed with these words : " I commit this little volume to the judgment of the public ; and in doing
so, I will say to the public, concerning the book, as I have often
said of a dose of medicine to a sick friend, ' *If you can only
manage to swallow it, I believe it will do you good.*' "

audience saw the point, and could not or would not withhold their approval, though it was Sunday night.

The doctor returned to his home on Monday morning. On Tuesday morning, however, he was so anxious to hear the result of the election in Hampden County, that he harnessed his horse early, and drove over to Worcester to get the first news from Springfield. As soon as the cars entered the depot he stepped aboard, and inquired if any passenger could let him see the Springfield Republican. No one near by appeared to have a copy, but a gentleman understood at once the cause of Dr. Jewett's anxiety, and he said, "I suppose that you want news from the election yesterday, doctor?"

"You are right, sir," replied the doctor; "that is exactly what I want just now."

"Well," he continued, "I am not one of your cold-water folks, and I did all I could to defeat them, but they elected their ticket by about one thousand majority in the county."

" Thank you, sir, for the information," responded the doctor, "and I thank God for the result." And without cracking a joke, or quoting poetry, he rushed out of the car, sprang into his carriage, and drove home at unusual speed, *to tell his wife*, as Abraham Lincoln did when he received the nomination for President.

Nor was this the end of it. A few months afterwards the friends in Springfield invited him to spend another Sabbath in that city, and lecture at City

Hall in the evening. Mr. Ingersoll, then paymaster of the United States Armory, entertained him, and on Sabbath morning said to the doctor, "I am superintendent of the Sabbath school in our county jail, and if you will go with me this morning and address the prisoners, I will omit the usual exercises."

The doctor promised, and at the appointed hour was sitting before a congregation of prisoners. During the first singing, Mr. Ingersoll whispered to him, "Dr. Jewett, you never addressed such an audience as this."

" Oh yes, I have repeatedly," the doctor answered. " I have addressed the inmates of both state and county prisons, and where my audience was five times as large as this."

" Grant all that," replied Mr. Ingersoll with a gracious smile, "I still insist that you have never addressed *such* an audience."

"Well, what is there so very peculiar about this audience?" asked Dr. Jewett.

Putting his lips close to the doctor's ear, he whispered, "A large portion of the congregation before you are liquor-sellers, sent here for violation of the law."

At that time the penalty for selling without license was imprisonment for the third offence; and the temperance men of the county had been very busy in arresting and convicting offenders.

Dr. Jewett enjoyed the scene after learning the foregoing facts. He had done more than any other

man to stir up the people to punish rumsellers, and
the fruit of his labors was before him. He questioned, however, whether it was not too great an
infliction to add to their incarceration an address
by the man who did so much to put them there, and
who rejoiced to see them in that situation. But it
was a good opportunity to instruct them. He never
enjoyed such an opportunity before, and he improved
it. A large number of the rumsellers of Hampden
County were addressed by Dr. Jewett in 1849!

At the time Dr. Jewett removed to Millbury, he
had visited different portions of our country on lecturing tours. He had spoken in all the New England states, in all the Western states east of the
Mississippi, and in several other states. He had
been several times into the British Provinces. On
one of his visits to the provinces a passenger in the
stage called his attention to a singular tavern-sign,
at one of the stopping places on the route. The
sign was a rude painting of a bee-hive, with this
verse under it :

> " Within this hive we're all alive ;
>   Good liquor makes us funny;
>   As you pass by, step in and try
>   The flavor of our honey."

The doctor proposed, on the spot, an improvement of the sign to his fellow-traveller. He drew a
pigeon *plucked*, and changed the verses, saying,
"You will find that I have preserved a part of the
very pretty rhyme of the original, only exchanging

"honey" for "money," which is not a bad exchange if one is fond of sweets."

> "We've liquors here of every kind,
> And sell them cheap, as you shall find.
> They'll make you feel quite funny;
> Perhaps they'll sprawl you on the floor,
> If so, we'll kick you out the door,
> AFTER we've got your money."

On a visit to Connecticut he was introduced to a scene that served him thereafter as a commentary upon a clause of the passage in Proverbs 23 : 35, — "*They have beaten me, and I felt it not*," spoken of the drunkard who does not realize the work of his ruin.

At the close of his lecture in a thriving town, a gentleman approached him pleasantly and said : "Dr. Jewett, I want to exact a service of you before you leave town."

"If possible, I will gladly perform it," replied the doctor ; "what is it?"

"Well," continued the citizen, with some diffidence and in a low tone, "I have a brother in this village, a man of much intelligence and considerable wealth. He lives yonder" (pointing) "in a large nice house ; he is not a drunkard, but I fear that he may be ; he drinks considerable. I wish you would call upon him in the morning, and talk with him."

The doctor promised, and in the morning called. The gentleman met him at the door with the most cordial greeting, asking him into the sitting-room, and saying, before the doctor had fairly seated himself: "Dr. Jewett, I am glad to see you in our village; and I want to ask you to call on my brother before you leave town; he lives yonder" (going to the window and pointing to the dwelling); "he is not intemperate, though he drinks much; and he is too valuable a man to sacrifice himself in this way."

"Neither of these brothers could see himself, but each could see the other. 'Wine is a mocker,'" said Dr. Jewett.

From the time the doctor became a citizen of Millbury he identified himself with all that was necessary to promote the welfare of town and church. The schools, the lyceum, the library, and whatever else was indispensable to social and intellectual growth, enlisted his deepest interest. Especially the moral and spiritual growth of the community absorbed his attention. He and his family united with the Congregational church and society, under the pastoral care of Rev. Leverett Griggs (now Dr. Griggs, of Bristol, Connecticut). The service which the doctor and family rendered to both pastor and people was highly esteemed.

Dr. Jewett's wit, humor, talents, piety, and tact, became an element in the social, intellectual, and moral condition of the town. How prominent he was in this regard may be learned from a very interesting letter from Dr. Griggs, penned since the preparation of this work was commenced. The letter shows the doctor's remarkable ability to read character, and his tact in dealing with men, while his poetic taste and dramatic powers appear in his extemporaneous lecture upon the great English poet, Shakespeare:

"Bristol, May 28, 1879.

"Rev. W. M. Thayer:

"*Dear Sir:* It is with pleasure I pen a few thoughts respecting Dr. Charles Jewett. He was a parishioner of mine, very much respected and beloved, the few years he resided in Millbury, Mass.

"I had often seen extracts from his speeches and poems illustrating his genius, his wit, and sarcasm; but I had never seen the doctor himself till be became one of our people. When I heard he was in town, negotiating for a home among us, I inquired, with no concealed anxiety, about his religious principles. If he were of that class who have an exalted view of human nature and a low estimate of the character and atonement of the Lord Jesus Christ, I was ready to pray, ' Good Lord, deliver us.' On making his acquaintance, I found the doctor one of the most genial, warm-hearted, child-like, Christian men I have ever known. He was in sympathy with evangelical religion and all benevolent enterprises to spread that religion through the land and the world. He would often speak and pray in our social meetings in his peculiarly simple and familiar manner, so as to awaken a deep interest.

"Important as was the subject of temperance in his view, it was not all that a man needed. Dr. Jewett labored first of all to exorcise the demon of intemperance, and then lead men to Christ. When he came to Millbury, one of his nearest neighbors was almost ruined by rum. He was a man at the head of an interesting family, of fair talents, many noble traits of character, and capable of great usefulness. The doctor made his acquaintance, gained his confidence and esteem, and engaged in earnest for his reformation. He was successful — successful in restoring that man to himself, to his family, and to his God. That neighbor became an honored citizen, the first selectman in the town, a worthy member of the church, and after many years of exemplary and useful life he died in the Lord.

"When abroad on a lecturing tour one time, the doctor met with a brilliant young man who was a skeptic. He spent several hours with him in friendly and earnest conversation on the foundation of our holy religion. Months after, that young man wrote a letter expressing his gratitude to Dr. Jewett for his kindly fidelity, and saying his doubts and difficulties were all removed, and he was rejoicing in that liberty with which Christ makes free. No labor that the doctor ever performed was remembered with more satisfaction than this.

"But few Christian parents are to their households what Dr. Jewett and his most estimable wife were to theirs. They were blessed with a numerous family — *thirteen* children. They endeavored to walk before their house with a perfect heart, and bring up their children in the nurture and admonition of the Lord. The Bible was studied, the God of the Bible was worshipped, and religion was illustrated as something real, good, and unspeakably precious. Their family life was full of enterprise, energy, aspiration, mutual love and helpfulness. What was the result? All the children that grew up to years of discretion, early chose that good part which shall never be taken away from them. One more than half, if I remember aright, preceded the father to that other and better country; the surviving portion are in different and distant parts of the world, serving their generation by the will of God.

" Dr. Jewett was ready for almost any emergency. In Millbury we were generally favored with a course of lectures in the winter. On one occasion a large assembly convened, but the expected lecturer did not come. Inquiry was made of the doctor whether he would consent to address the audience. No one, I presume, expected anything but a temperance talk. He rose and delighted that audience for a full hour, with an exceedingly entertaining lecture on Shakespeare. He quoted lengthy passages, and represented the different characters as but few men are able to do. The lecture was regarded as one of the very best of the season.

" Dr. Jewett's powers of imitation exceeded that of any other man I have ever known. Only suggest what you desired, and you would have it to the life — whether speech of judge, lawyer, doctor, or divine. The last time the doctor was with us he dropped out his teeth and read to us Tennyson's 'Grandmother.' Shut your eyes and you would think it must be the voice of an old woman telling the story of seventy years ago. He also gave us a specimen of Thomas P. Hunt's eloquence. As we had several times heard that wonderful minister and temperance advocate, it afforded us special pleasure. We heard his sententious words, his peculiar enunciation, tones, and inflections. In short, it was Thomas P. Hunt to the life.

" When Dr. Jewett and his excellent family removed from Millbury, one of the strong ties that bound us to that beautiful village was loosened; and now that he is gone to ' that bourn whence no traveller returns,' earth is losing its attractions, and heaven is becoming more attractive.

" Yours truly,

" L. Griggs."

The doctor was lecturing in Vermont in the winter. He had taken his seat in a coach at a certain public-house, when he overheard the driver say to a drunken man, who was trying to get upon the box:

"You will freeze to death up there; you have been drinking."

"How is that, driver?" interrupted the doctor, rather surprised to hear a true temperance sentiment expressed so emphatically by a stage-driver. "Did you say that the man would freeze all the quicker for having rum inside?"

"Yes," answered the driver; "freeze as quick again."

"That's queer," responded Dr. Jewett; "from time immemorial it has been held that rum will keep the cold out."

"Held by people who don't know any better," retorted the driver.

"Do not stage-drivers generally take liquor to keep them warm in winter?" inquired the doctor, eager to draw out more real temperance sentiment from a practical man.

"I suppose they do," replied the driver; "and that is not the only foolish thing that drivers do."

"Well," continued Dr. Jewett, "I will try your theory. The stage is full; I will get out and ride on the box with you; and the man with rum in him shall have my seat."

So the doctor jumped out and assisted the drunken man into his seat, then mounted the box with the

15

driver, rejoicing in his heart to have an opportunity to converse with a teetotal stage-driver, where the thermometer was thirty degrees below zero.

He made himself known to the driver, and assured him that his views accorded perfectly with physiological science. A pleasant and profitable interchange of thought between them on the trip proved better than whiskey to keep out the cold. The doctor was learner as well as teacher on that occasion, for the driver's experience furnished him with many facts for future use.

Afterwards the doctor was in the British Provinces, at a bitter cold time, and he was booked for a ride of thirty miles in the stage. The driver came in, and going up to the bar, dropped a remark about his "warming-up" glass.

"Freezing-up glass, rather," responded the doctor, jocosely, who heard the remark.

"What do you mean by that?" inquired the driver, who was a jolly sort of a fellow.

"I mean that a glass of liquor exposes you more to the cold than anything you can take," replied the doctor. "Better drink a glass of cold water if you don't want to freeze."

"Do you mean to say that liquor won't keep the cold out?" said the driver, evidently surprised at the doctor's statement.

"Yes, that is just what I mean," answered the doctor.

"Well," continued the driver, rather disgusted with what he thought was the remark of an ignoramus; " it is precious little about driving a stage that you know."

" It is precious little about the philosophy of heat and cold that you know if you think that a glass of liquor will keep out the cold," retorted the doctor, pleasantly; and he cited the case of the teetotal driver in Vermont. " Come now, my good fellow," continued the doctor, "just try it for one trip; let your grog go this time, and prove my declaration that you can withstand the cold better without than with intoxicating liquors. It is the last stuff I should think of taking to help me through a cold ride."

" And I shouldn't think of taking it if I rode inside the stage as you do," replied the driver.

"But I will ride on the outside of the stage with you," retorted the doctor, " and we will see if a teetotaler can't withstand as much cold as a rum-drinker."

" You will freeze before you get half-way there," said the driver. " You haven't clothes enough on your back to keep the frost out one hour."

The doctor was clothed with his usual winter dress, though he was not clad for such an exposure. But he was just the man for such an emergency. He went on and explained to the driver the heat-generating powers of the body, and the philosophy of preserving and utilizing the heat, and closed by saying, in his laughing way :

" Come now, driver, just prove by this trip whether I am a fool or not. Good digestion, good circulation, a good conscience, good company, and your buffalo-robe, will keep you as warm as toast."

The result was, that the driver agreed to go without his accustomed dram, and the doctor mounted the box with him, remarking, as the horses started, "If you expect to deliver a chunk of ice at ——, you will be mistaken. I don't propose to end my career by freezing."

Dr. Jewett enjoyed that ride. It was another trial of his teetotal principles : water was pitted against rum. He exerted himself to the utmost to entertain the driver, making heavy drafts upon his wit, humor, and knowledge to accomplish his object, not omitting to preach to him upon "righteousness, temperance, and a judgment to come."

At the end of the route the driver acknowledged that he never rode more comfortably than he did on that day, but naively suggested that, after all, it "might be the laughter instead of temperance." (The doctor kept him laughing a good part of the way.) "At any rate, he was sure that there was no danger of freezing with such a passenger on the box, rum or no rum."

In 1851 Dr. Jewett was employed in Maine for a season, to begin his labors "on the Kennebec, ending them with Calais, on the eastern border of the state." The Maine Law was in complete operation at the time in a large portion of the state, and this champion of prohibition was expected to aid essentially in its execution.

On his way, Dr. Jewett spent a few days with his old friend, Hon. Neal Dow, author of the Maine Law, then mayor of Portland. On the morning after he reached that city, Mr. Dow took him to the basement of the City Hall, where a large quantity of liquors that had been seized under the law were stored.

The spectacle pleased the doctor beyond measure. He had worked and waited long and patiently for just such a result, and he was so full that he could almost say with Simeon of old, "Lord, now lettest thou thy servant depart in peace." But the Lord would not do that, as he had other and great work for him to do in his vineyard. The doctor returned to the residence of Mr. Dow, and relieved his overflowing heart by writing the following article, that was published subsequently in a Portland paper, and was copied into many journals throughout the country :

"A VISIT TO THE SPIRITS IN PRISON.

"While walking down the streets of Portland, this morning, in company with the very efficient mayor of that beautiful city, I was invited to step with him across the street and take a look at the imprisoned 'spirits' shut up in durance vile beneath the City Hall. I accepted the invitation, and in a moment found myself in a large basement room, surrounded on all sides by the imprisoned fiends, which, under the recently enacted and most righteous law of the state, had been arrested in their march from the mouth of the still to the mouths of the wretched men who had become already so far demonized as to desire the further acquaintance and companionship of those liquid devils. Three or four extensive seizures of the spirits had been made, and here they were all gathered together in one group; and a sorry-looking group it was. Their sad plight, piled on each other's backs around the apartment, recalled the language of Hamlet to the skull of poor Yorick:

> 'Where be your gibes now? your
> Gambols? your songs? your flashes of merriment
> That were wont to set the table in a roar? . . .
> . . . Quite chapfallen.'

"I looked upon the strong oak casks, some of them iron-bound, and thought how fortunate it was that the hands of government had arrested them before their fiery and demonizing contents had got spilled into the stomachs of some of its poor deluded subjects. Long and ardently I had desired to see the government, in true paternal regard for its suffering poor, and for the thousands who are being hurried by the liquor traffic to ruin, exert its power promptly and effectually to stay the work of death. And here, at length, I am permitted to see the master-spirit of mischief, the giant curse of the civilized world, chained. A feeling of exultation was kindled within me, which I have no words adequately to express. Aha! thought I, you who, with your kindred spirits, have sent thousands to the watch-house, to the jail, and to the prison; who have bolted the doors upon thousands of my brethren, and shut them out from the society of their families and the world, have gotten into limbo yourself! The angel of justice has at length come down, 'with a great chain in his hand,' and bound you. Here you await your trial, and, if condemned, as you probably will be, you shall be led forth to execution, amid the rejoicing of an injured people, and your blood shall flow, not as ye hoped, down the parched throats of men, but down the gutters, and through the city sewers. Well, you are in a good way.

Mother earth and the waters of the bay can swallow you and not reel, and that is more than men could do.

"How long have you trampled on laws human and divine, taken your own wild, wicked way, and gloried in your might! Ye laughed at 'restriction' and 'regulation;' but stronger words have been whispered in your ears by the legislature of Maine — 'suppression,' 'annihilation;' and lo, ye pause here to consider the import of the new vocabulary. Well, ye will learn it, no doubt, for ye are apt scholars. But how will your friends and adherents, not only in the city, but among the hills, regard your capture and detention? They have hitherto gloried in your strength, and have asked exultingly, 'Who is like unto the beast? Who is able to make war against him?' Maine hath answered in stern and decided tone, and — ye are here! 'The merchants of those things, which were made rich by thee, shall stand afar off, for the fear of thy torment, weeping and wailing, and crying, Alas! . . . for in one hour so great riches have come to naught.'

"What varied forms have ye taken, as I see ye here in your prison; and how varied your destination! Here ye swell out in great bulk, like a corpulent, turtle-fed alderman, and there ye shrink almost to the dimensions of a water-bucket. Let me look at your names, and learn whither ye were bound. 'American Gin, Parsonsfield.' And what business had you at Parsonsfield? Did the parson invite you to visit his field? Nay, verily! He would sooner have sent you to the Potter's Field. But to Parsonsfield you were going; and for what? Ah, I remember! There is a poor widow in that neighborhood, whose husband ye slew, and whose oldest son ye have poisoned until the poor lad totters as he walks. His brain is on fire. He talks incoherently, and strange fan-

cies possess him. Sometimes he curses the mother who
bore him; and those hands which, when a child, she
pressed in hers while she prayed, have been lifted in violence against her. She is almost distracted with her troubles, and knoweth not whither to turn for relief. Despair
has sometimes almost taken possession of her soul. She
hateth thee, and lifteth her eyes, swollen with weeping,
and her feeble hands, to heaven against thee. And thou
wouldst afflict her still more! Heartless, obdurate devil!
Yes, you were journeying to Parsonsfield for that purpose;
but the angel of justice met thee, and — thou art here.
How will that widow rejoice and sing when she shall hear
the glad tidings of thy fall!

"But let me look at thy brother fiend, 'N. E. Rum,
W. A., Bethel.' And what was thy errand to Bethel?
Jacob went up to Bethel, and built there an altar, because
there the Lord met him in the time of his troubles. And
you too have built an altar at Bethel, whereon thou dost
sacrifice to strange gods. But goats and bullocks will not
serve thee for sacrifices. The blood of our sons, 'the expectancy and rose of the fair state,' is smoking upon thine
altar at Bethel. But thou art not there. Iron bands confine, and bolts and bars detain thee. Thine altar at Bethel
will grow cold, and the sweet waters of the rejoicing
heavens shall wash away its stains. 'Old Madeira, 10
gallons, Wm. Baker, Brunswick.' And you, old gentleman, were bound to Brunswick. There is a college at
Brunswick; and did ye covet an education? 'No, ye
were going to teach, and not to be taught.' So I supposed.
A professor of infernal mathematics and languages, *en
route* for Brunswick, to teach the young men big oaths,
subtraction from the pocket, multiplication of miseries,
and reduction descending; ay, and to add thereto important instruction in *your* rule of three direct, to the poor-

house, the prison, and the drunkard's grave. Verily a
rule of *three*, and as *direct* as one could desire. And
' you give instructions in navigation.' Ay, I have seen
your pupils making trial of their skill: and it was indeed
an interesting exhibition!

"But let/us make the acquaintance of your next neighbor, Mr. St. Croix. And you, sir, were bound to *Free-
port*, but — did not get there. It was not a '*port of
entry*' for you, it seems, with all its freedom. And what
do you propose to do now? 'Wait here the arrival of
your friends from Boston.' Very well; we pledge you the
word of the mayor and city marshal, that your friends
shall visit you here immediately on their arrival. Farewell to your devilship; keep cool, and learn 'the uses of
affliction.'"

At Hallowell, there had been little or no effort to
execute the law; but Dr. Jewett's labors there inaugurated an efficient movement. One Gilman, a
prominent rumseller, defied the city government,
and it was proposed to make him an example.

"He is a man of violent temper," said one, "and
has sworn that he will hew down with an axe the
first man who enters his store to execute the law."

"And he would just as lief do it as not," added
another; "he is perfectly reckless."

"I beg to differ from you," said Dr. Jewett; "he
will not strike a blow, if sober, when the officers of
the law, with proper assistance, visit him. I gladly
offer my services to the officer."

Officer and aids were soon in Gilman's store, who
paced about like an enraged tiger in his cage. The
news of a raid on Gilman's shop spread like wild-

fire, and soon a hundred guzzlers or more assembled in front of the building, and backed up a wagon, filled with loafers, against the door, to prevent the exit of the whiskey-seizers.

Fourteen barrels of intoxicating liquor were found in the store, and the conundrum was how to remove them with that crowd of opposers in the way.

"What business have you in my store?" shouted Gilman in a very threatening way to Dr. Jewett.

"I am here at the request of the officer," replied Dr. Jewett.

"You are, ha!"

"Yes, sir."

"Well, get out of this store — quick! or you will find yourself in trouble."

"I shall not leave until ordered by the officer," replied Dr. Jewett, who was now enjoying an opportunity to confiscate liquors that he had coveted for years.

Gilman stepped back and seized an axe. with which he rushed forward, exclaiming, "Do you say that you will not leave my store?"

"Yes; I will not leave your store until ordered by the officer," answered the doctor, coolly and defiantly.

The rumseller cowed and dropped the axe.

"Officer," said Dr. Jewett, "when you say the word, these barrels will be taken away, in spite of cart and loafers at the door."

The officer stepped to the door and said, "Gentlemen, I request you to clear that passage. I have a legal warrant to execute, and you may be sure that I shall execute it."

Several voices defiantly responded by sending him to a very hot place.

Turning to his men, the officer said, "Forward with the liquors."

The doctor and Allen seized a barrel, and away it went.

"Again I command you to clear the doorway!" exclaimed the officer. Again the profane crowd sent him to — a place prepared for themselves.

"Put the barrels into the street!" shouted the officer.

Allen and the doctor sent a barrel into the cart among the loafers, when the imperilled legs scattered, and the way was clear. Gilman saw that his boastful customers failed him, and he sat down in the rear of the cart, thrusting his feet into the doorway. The next barrel was rolled directly upon his legs, holding him fast. The doctor sprang over the barrel, and seizing it by one end, lifted it from the sufferer's legs (which the doctor called "*novel skids*"), greatly to his relief. There was no more resistance. The crowd scattered, the horse and cart were removed, and wagons in waiting received the liquors that were conveyed to the city hall in a sort of triumphal march. For the news of a seizure at Gilman's had spread, and temperance men and women flocked into the streets, men cheering on the officers, and women waving handkerchiefs from doors and windows, glad to witness the reign of justice.

"That is practical," said the doctor when the affair terminated; "*the prohibitory law works like a charm.*"

The doctor was not there when the liquor was spilled; but John Hawkins, the renowned reformer, was; and when the first barrel was emptied, he turned it up on end, mounted it, and made a speech to the crowd. Afterwards the doctor met Hawkins in Boston, who said, rehearsing the incident, " It was one of the happiest hours of my life."

Three days after this seizure officer Smith seized a whole cargo of rum from Boston. Dr. Jewett was assisting in its removal from the vessel, when there was a call for compromise.

" No compromise," said the officer; " the whole cargo goes into the Kennebec unless the ship returns with it at once to Boston."

The vessel returned to Boston with its load of rum.

On the Fourth of July of that year Dr. Jewett delivered the oration in Portland, by invitation of the city government, — one of his noblest efforts.

He completed his campaign in Maine to the entire satisfaction of good people, and the discomfiture of the opposite class. The following letter from the Honorable Neal Dow contains all that it is necessary to add respecting his work in Maine:

" My Dear Mr. Thayer: Our dear and honored friend, Dr. Jewett, did very much in the early days of the

Maine Law to form and strengthen the public opinion of the state in favor of the policy of prohibition to the liquor traffic, by which alone it could be rendered permanent as the fixed and settled policy of Maine.

"I remember very well the eager interest which he took in all our work in this state in preparing the way for prohibition, and the delight with which he hailed its advent. Immediately after the enactment of the Maine Law, he came to the state and labored earnestly and effectively in all our large towns, and in many of our smaller ones, and in our rural districts, in demonstrating to the people the rightfulness, the expediency, and the wisdom of the movement to protect them and their children from the infinite mischief and misery of the liquor traffic. We never had among us any one more acceptable to our people as a teacher in this department of Christian and philanthropic labor.

"It was his fortune to help, in a most important manner, in the execution of the law in its earliest days. He was in an eastern town, holding a series of meetings, when it was determined to suppress the liquor shops with a strong hand. Among the rumsellers there was a Pat Meagher, whose liquors were to be seized. When the constable went to his shop, Pat was standing in the doorway with an axe, swearing that he would kill any one who should attempt to enter, and he kept the constable and his posse at bay. Dr. Jewett heard of what was going on, and went to the shop, asking the constable to call on him for assistance, which he did. The doctor then quietly stepped up to Pat, put him gently aside, and walked into the shop, followed by the constable and some others, and the liquors were put into a cart and taken away. After that the law was steadily and vigorously enforced in that town and neighborhood.

" I never knew a more devoted and unselfish man. His whole heart was in his work for the love of God and of his fellow-men. His purpose was ever to teach the people, not to amuse them. His lectures were full of instruction, even to those who supposed themselves best acquainted with the temperance cause in all its phases. Though possessing the histrionic power in a high degree, he never employed it on the platform : to amuse the people was never his object, but always to appeal to their understanding and conscience. He was always in good spirits ; never discouraged or depressed by disappointments and misfortunes and afflictions, of which he had his full share. No man realized more truly than he that earthly interests and affairs are of small moment when compared with those which relate to the eternal world ; and so he lived mainly for these, which he made the great purpose of life. He was always warmly welcomed to the houses of his innumerable friends all over the country. He brought sunshine and gladness with him whenever he came. He was an admirable conversationalist, and enlivened every circle in which he was. His talk was always full of wit and wisdom, enlivening and instructing all with whom he came in contact.

" He knew the world, and men, and books, and was never at a loss for topics of conversation ; he could contribute his share to the general entertainment and instruction, whatever the subject of conversation might be. He made the temperance cause the purpose and labor of his life, and was as wise in council as he was interesting and instructive upon the platform. His hope was to be able to work to the very last, not to be placed upon the 'retired list,' or to be 'invalided,' but to fall, in full health and strength, upon the battle-field.

" A few years ago he was suddenly taken with some illness, and he wrote me that his working-days were over; that in future he would be compelled to be a mere spectator of the battle, unable to take any part in it; ' but God knows best,' he said, ' and I bow cheerfully and lovingly to his holy will.' But he rallied from this illness, recovered his voice and strength, and was able to go on to the last, thus realizing his wish in that particular.

" No one had warmer, truer friends than he; he won them fairly by his unwavering fidelity, and devotedness and integrity in all the relations of life. There have been few men to whom the temperance cause has been and is so much indebted as to him, and all its friends will cherish his memory as an earnest, devoted, and able worker in it. 		I am truly yours,

" NEAL DOW.

" PORTLAND, Sept. 1, 1879."

Dr. Jewett insisted that no rule for moderate drinking could be established, since a quantity that one man could carry might intoxicate another. On going to a thriving manufacturing town in Ohio, at one time, he found a telling illustration of his position. In the village was a lawyer of considerable note, by the name of Hubbard, who could drink brandy enough to fuddle two or three men, without showing it. There was another man who was in a drunken state most of the time, and yet he did not drink half so much liquor as the lawyer consumed. It appears that the lawyer had abused his intemperate neighbor, once when the latter was drunk, and, in consequence, they were not friendly to each other. Both were present at the doctor's lecture. He proceeded to expose the fallacy of all pleas in

favor of moderate drinking, and ridiculed the popular notion that, "if a man can drink a great deal
without becoming intoxicated, it is because his head
is strong." "That is not so," said the doctor. "The
head has nothing to do with it, but the lungs and
the man's activity will account for his capacity in
this respect. When you inhale the strong odor of
liquor from a man who has been drinking, it is
because his eliminating organs are at work. His
lungs are throwing off its vapor." After thoroughly
and eloquently elaborating his subject, the doctor
closed by making a strong appeal to drinkers, and
particularly to excessive drinkers (if there were any
of this class in the house), to sign the pledge. No
sooner had the doctor taken his seat than the aforesaid intemperate man, who owed the lawyer a
grudge, rose, and drawled out, "that he had listened
to the lecture with much interest, that it was all
true, and he must own to being a drunkard, and
perhaps he was the only one in the house; but," he
added, looking around the hall, "*where is Squire
Hubbard?*"

The audience burst into an uproarious laughter,
and it was several minutes before the doctor could
proceed.

This incident furnished them with a good illustration of his theory, and the doctor used to say, "In
every sense but the physical, the lawyer was the
greater drunkard of the two, but his great lung-
power had enabled him thus far to preserve a re-

spectability which he was doing his utmost to undermine."

Dr. Jewett's health was precarious at this time, and he was obliged to lessen temperance work, and seek relief in physical labor on his farm. The following year he labored in Ohio, and an effort was made in that state, in 1852, to introduce a clause into the constitution, to prevent the legislature enacting a liquor-license law. Three months before the people were to vote upon the question, the friends of temperance entered upon a vigorous campaign. Dr. Jewett was on the ground eight or ten weeks before the election, by invitation of Gen. S. F. Cary, of Cincinnati.

The liquor advocates had imported one of their able debaters from New York city, and had challenged the Executive Committee of the Temperance Society to a discussion of the question before the people. The challenge was accepted, and Dr. Jewett booked for the discussion, before he was consulted at all upon the subject. He accepted the assignment, however, and the discussion opened at Columbus, to be continued at Lancaster, Circleville, and Chillicothe, on four immediately successive days.

At the former place a platform was erected in the open air; and when Dr. Jewett rose to open the debate, and looked into the sea of upturned faces, he concluded that all the grogshops of the city had poured out their "ragged regiments," to hear their imported advocate defend the liquor traffic. Such a

16

bloated, debased crowd he had never addressed. They listened to him, however with respectful attention to the end of his discourse.

We shall not follow the debate, except to note two or three points of Dr. Jewett's replies. His opponent claimed, that since all the lower orders of animals choose their own diet and drink by instinct, it was not reasonable to suppose that man, the lord of all inferior races, was less capable of choosing his than the cattle or reptile. Dr. Jewett replied:

"In the treatment of man, God has certainly made him an exception to the rule stated; for one of the earliest, if not the very first command given to man in Eden, was a restriction on his diet, forbidding him, on pain of death, to eat of the fruit of a certain tree of the garden. Under the Mosaic economy, too, very precise directions were given for the regulation of the diet. They were forbidden to eat the flesh of certain animals. In view of these facts, what becomes of the gentleman's assertion that the right of *man*, as well as of all other animals, to choose his own diet, was so sacred that the Creator had never interfered with it?"

His opponent claimed that the state of Ohio had no right to prohibit the traffic; to which the doctor replied by quoting the unanimous decision of the Supreme Court of the United States, rendered five years previous, sarcastically adding:

"Perhaps the aggregate wisdom of our Supreme Court is equal to that of the gentleman from New York."

His opponent asserted that there was no parallel in the history of legislation to that provision of the

Maine Law that protected a man's liquor in his own
dwelling, and confiscated it when found in his store
as merchandise. Dr. Jewett answered :

" The laws regulating the taking of fish from the Connecticut River and other waters, prohibit fishing on certain
days of the week ; and violation of those laws subjects
boats, seines, and fishing-tackle to confiscation. Cards,
and other gaming apparatus, which a man may use in his
own dwelling, are confiscated when used in a place of
public resort. The counterfeiter loses all his implements,
as well as his money, when the detective finds him out.
And so of a hundred other things. It is a common principle of law that is involved in the confiscation of liquors."

At his last meeting in Cincinnati he arranged to
conduct it upon the principle of questions and answers. Lest there might be backwardness in asking
questions, several temperance men distributed themselves among the crowd for the purpose of interro-
gating the speaker. The arrangement was carried
out to the letter. For nearly an hour questions and
answers followed each other in rapid succession,
and much information was imparted. At length the
great distiller of the city interrupted him by calling
in question a statement made, and the following colloquy followed, greatly interesting and amusing the
audience, and the general public subsequently, when
it was reported by the press :

" *Distiller.* You stated that the manufacture and sale
of intoxicating liquors works great mischief to the state
of Ohio, which no one will deny ; but you also stated that

no corresponding advantages result, which is not true, for many millions of gallons of whiskey are annually exported from the state, adding *greatly* to its *wealth.*

" *Dr. Jewett.* Sir, you are mistaken. Private individuals may add to their wealth by the liquor business, but the state does not.

" *Dist.* That is quite a new notion in political economy, that you can increase the wealth of the individual citizens of a state, without adding to the wealth of the state.

"*Dr. J.* New as it may be to you, sir, it is yet true. When Mr. A. picks the pocket of Mr. B. *he* is the richer by the contents of the pocket-book, but nothing is added thereby to the wealth of the state."

Just here came a loud shout from the listening throng, which for a moment somewhat disconcerted the distiller, but he soon rallied and proceeded thus :

" *Dist.* We were not talking of theft or of other crimes, but of legitimate and honorable business.

" *Dr. J.* Well, sir, by the business of manufacturing and selling intoxicating liquors, men do accumulate wealth, and therefore pay heavier taxes for the support of the state government ; but meanwhile thousands are made so poor by that same traffic, that they pay little or no tax at all, and thus the state is a loser rather than a gainer by the entire liquor business, even in a money point of view — not to speak just here of its immense loss in the health, happiness, and morals of its people.

"But I wish to call your attention, sir, and that of the crowd around us, to another point, which perhaps you have not considered. Pork is one of the great staples of Ohio, and the state exports an immense amount annually, five-sixths of which, I am informed, is corn-fed, produced by the farmers of the state, while one-sixth is still-fed pork, of an inferior quality. This gets so mixed with the farmer's pork, while passing to the great markets of the country, that it cannot be distinguished until it reaches the consumer. That fact being well known, depreciates the value of western pork in the aggregate, often three or four dollars on the barrel below the price of pork produced and packed in the eastern states. Thus the farmers of Ohio are losers to an immense amount, that the distillers may sell, *above its real value*, their miserable still-fed pork. That, sir, is one of the ways in which Ohio is enriched by the liquor business."

Here came another shout from the listening throng, but the veteran distiller still stood his ground, and made another point thus :

"*Dist.* That is but one half the truth ; the other half is, that the smoked meats produced by the distillers bring up the price of the entire aggregate exported, as they are a better article, and are preferred in the markets.

" *Dr. J. Why* are they preferred?

" *Dist.* It is no use denying it, the fact is notorious.

" *Dr. J.* I have not disputed the fact. I only wish to know *why* they are preferred, that is all.

" *Dist.* It is no use to quibble about the matter. Meet the fact, and dispose of it if you can."

He seemed to suspect that the doctor might make some bad use of any explanation he might make of the fact stated, and sought to avoid it, but the doctor still thrust the question upon him.

" *Dr. J.* Why are the smoked meats of the still-fed swine considered more valuable? "

At last the distiller responded :

"*Dist.* Well, sir, if you must know, I believe it is because the meats are more tender.

"*Dr. J.* Aye! That is it! Please notice that fact, citizens of Ohio. The smoked meats of the distiller are 'more tender' than those produced by the farmers. I will now explain to you why they are more tender. Causes which lessen the vitality of an animal during life, hasten its decomposition after death. Some diseases of a low type produce such changes in the solid structure of the human body, that parts here and there lose their vitality, run into a state of decomposition, and slough off, while the patient yet lives. Now, still-slops form an imperfect diet for animals, for although you can, by their use, load an animal with adipose or fat, as you may a man by the use of whiskey, yet the tissues of the whole body have but a low degree of vitality, and are at the very verge of decomposition before the butcher ends the life of the animal No wonder that the flesh of such animals, even when cured for the market, is tender. Let those who fancy such tenderness enjoy it. For one, I prefer hams from the cornfed pork, though the fibres be a little less tender."

The colloquy was here interrupted by a peal of laughter from the crowd, and our friend the distiller lost for the moment his good-nature, and declared, with a moderate explosive, the doctor's statement unfounded, or at best an exaggeration.

"*Dr. J.* Hold on, sir. You declare my statement false. Listen a moment to another, and deny it if you dare in the presence of this crowd, who are doubtless acquainted with the facts. A man accustomed to that business is sent daily through those large enclosures

where swine are fed in connection with the great distil-
leries around this city, to examine the swine in every pen,
and when he finds one with a scratch or wound upon him,
as often happens, he is at once withdrawn from the pen
and sent to the butcher; and why? Because, sir, it is well
known by all concerned, that wounds on still-fed hogs do
not heal."

The distiller was so completely vanquished that
he withdrew from the multitude, amidst laughter,
shouts, and clapping of hands.

When Dr. Jewett completed his campaign in Ohio,
his health was quite broken, and he retired to his
farm in Millbury, seeking rest in comparative seclu-
sion until his removal to the West.

XII.

WESTWARD.

OVERWORK was telling upon the doctor's health. Lecturing night after night, with other cares, made heavy drafts upon his nervous system. But more than all, a great sorrow overwhelmed him and the family. His son William, a youth of seventeen years, a bright, talented, Christian boy, was suddenly prostrated by disease. He was late in going to the lyceum lecture one evening, so he ran the whole distance, about a mile, was thoroughly heated, and wet with perspiration, when he sat in a current of air, taking a severe cold, the result of which was a fever that proved fatal. In a few weeks all that was left of that noble lad was laid in the village churchyard.

Willie's death was a severe blow to the doctor and to the whole family. Together with overwork of the brain, his crushing sorrow quite disqualified him for further labor in the lecture-field for the time. He cast about for relief. Just then his son Charles returned from California, where he had been three years.

Here was the doctor himself unable to do his accustomed work, his wife an invalid, his son Charles, twenty-four years of age, without business, and another son, Richard, nineteen years old, anxious for some useful and profitable pursuit. In these circumstances, Dr. Jewett decided to go West. His plans were facilitated, too, by the fact that a neighbor's son stood ready to purchase his small farm. His decision was soon made. He was a man of marked decision of character, and always did what his judgment declared was for the best. He saw that it was best for his family now to go West; and he went.

He purchased a large tract of land in Batavia, Illinois, about one mile from the centre of the town, on the banks of Fox River. Thither he removed with his family in the spring of 1854.

Batavia was one of the older towns of Illinois, settled by emigrants from New York and Connecticut. The Batavia Institute had just been opened there, and the doctor was invited to the position of lecturer upon physiology and agricultural chemistry. This fact, together with literary advantages for his children, drew him to that particular locality.

In disposing of his farm and household furniture, he reserved the family horse and pet dog. Such was his attachment to the animal creation, that he considered these quadrupeds members of his family in such a sense that he could not part with them. On the passage they were intrusted to the care of Charles, who saw them deposited safely in a freight-car, where he fed and cared for them on the route.

The horse readily acquiesced in the change, as if he understood that it was a wise move for the family, to whose members he was strongly attached. But the dog was restive, and even turbulent, under the arrangement. He had never caught the Western fever, and had manifested no desire to emigrate, either for health or pleasure. He made himself as troublesome as possible on the way, and before he had travelled a thousand miles his reputation of being a "good dog," with Charles, was lost. On arriving at Chicago he became desperate, and carried the matter so far that he had the hydrophobia, when a bullet terminated his life. So the horse and dog parted company, the latter going where the hydrophobia usually sends canines, and the former continuing the journey with as much docility and composure as if no affliction had been experienced.

Mrs. Jewett and her daughters stayed overnight with friends in Chicago, while the doctor and two sons went to a hotel. The cholera was raging alarmingly in the city at the time, and Dr. Jewett and Frank were attacked with it on that night. For a few hours they were dangerously sick, but finally obtained relief. One of the sons remembers with what coolness his father lay on his mattress (the hotel was so crowded that they slept on mattresses laid upon the floor), and poured out medicine for himself and son. He had taken the precaution to provide himself with remedies for the cholera. The proprietor of the hotel and his attachés rendered all the assistance possible, but the doctor depended mainly upon himself. On being relieved, he lost no time in taking his family from the town.

Not much of interest transpired on the journey thereafter, except that the doctor, who was never able to ride far without making the acquaintance of strangers in car or stage, found a Canadian emigrant, whom he hired, and took along with all his family, consisting of himself, wife, and three children. As the doctor had six children, with himself and wife, the number who settled on his farm in Illinois was rather imposing. But there was something about the Canadian, whose name was Page, that appealed to the doctor's humanity. The mere fact that he would need extra help on his farm would not have induced him to engage the whole household. But the laborer's son, who was a young man grown, was intemperate; and this fact induced him to engage the crowd, that, if possible, he might save the son. The doctor was always ready to become "all things to all men, if by any means he might save some."

He caused to be erected on his farm the L of a house, designing, at a future day, to erect the main building. Then he built an addition thereto for the Page family; pretty close quarters, of course, but well enough for that country. The doctor proved himself equal to an experienced carpenter in the erection of his dwelling. He worked early and late with the men, his mechanical skill making him second to none in efficiency at house-building. It was not long before the Massachusetts temperance

advocate was transformed into a Western farmer and
professor of physiology and agricultural chemistry.
Nor was his labor in the latter sphere that of a
novice.

His services proved to be of the greatest value to
the institution, highly appreciated by both the pupils
and board of managers.   Dr. Jewett was always
at home in chemical analysis and physiological
investigation.   Agricultural chemistry drew his
attention in early manhood, and he studied into the
nature of soils, and their adaptation to crops of different kinds as well as to fruits and trees.   His love
of nature and interest in the products of the earth
were the occasion of his researches in agricultural
chemistry.

On his farm the doctor was not less successful.
His great crop was corn.   Wheat and other grains
he did not attempt except in a small way.   But
corn yielded its golden treasures over many acres.
Whether "seven ears of corn came up upon one
stalk rank and good," as Pharaoh dreamed, we do
not know ; but the yield satisfied the teetotal farmer,
so that it must have been considerable.

We ought to have told the reader before how the
hired man Page conducted himself; for the doctor
engaged him without a line of testimonial about his
character or efficiency.   Nor did he want any letters
of recommendation.   Dr. Jewett was so sharp a
student of human nature that in less time than one
would take to write a recommendation, he would
learn what sort of a man the stranger was.   He

knew that the Canadian was an honest man, — for he looked him through with his penetrating eyes clear to the recesses of his heart, — and he proved to be. Faithful, industrious, and efficient, he suited his employer well. But his intemperate son was the cause of much trouble. He was the source of real sorrow to his parents. If the doctor engaged the family with the benevolent purpose to reform the son, he was beaten for once. The young man was rough, rowdyish, and incorrigible. He would have his rum at times, let the consequences be what they might. One day he lay in a drunken sleep on the floor, with his mouth wide open, snoring as one who was born to make a noise, when a litter of pigs came into the door, and one of the number, more inquisitive and familiar than his companions, actually thrust his nose into the sleeper's mouth. The doctor made use of the fact thereafter to shame the young scapegrace, by telling how pigs would kiss him when he was drunk. But even this method of reform proved unsuccessful.

At one time of the year the family embraced several nationalities among its members. In addition to the eight original live Yankees, there was the Canadian on the farm, also an Irishman, a Frenchman, and a Swede, while in the house was a Norwegian servant-girl, and, weekly, a colored washerwoman. Yet everything moved on smoothly under the doctor's judicious administration. Clearly he was at peace with all nations. As chairman of the

" Committee on Foreign Relations," his tact and diplomacy served him a good purpose.

Early in the autumn an incident occurred, illustrating the cool and ingenious manner of the doctor to meet an emergency. He had planted an ample patch of watermelons on a piece of ground near the highway.

" Every one of your melons will be stolen," said a neighbor to him. "I don't try to raise any now; it is no use. The young fellows from the village steal every one of them."

Another neighbor said, " Last year I planted a bed of melons in the centre of my cornfield, where I thought nobody could find them; and don't you think the thieves found the patch, and they were so mad that I tried to conceal it, that they stole the melons before they ripened, and stuck them on the posts around the field, — splendid great melons, — and pulled up all the vines. You can't raise a melon."

The doctor listened attentively, and simply answered, with that sly, curious twinkle at the corner of his eye that many knew so well, "Perhaps so · we'll see."

When the time arrived to protect the melons, the potatoes around the patch, together with weeds, had grown so as to nearly conceal the melon vines. The doctor put up stakes around the patch, with pulleys on the top of them, through which he ran a wire clear around the patch, and thence on the ground, hidden by the grass, to the corn-crib, twenty rods

distant or more, where it was attached to a bell. In
the night the melon thieves would rush for the
patch, hit the wire, when the bell in the corn-crib
would sound the alarm.

The doctor had planned his campaign well, and
now he issued his orders. "Load both guns with
powder; you two, who sleep nearest to the crib,
have one ear open; when the bell rings, spring out,
fire the guns, and after the rascals."

There were five or six men, including his two
sons; and all were anxious for the sport. It was a
sort of mock warfare, in which enough of reality
was mixed to make the affair very exciting. It was
arranged, however, who should be on picket duty.
The doctor was fond of experiments, and this one
was in a new line altogether. It would test his
generalship. If the truth were told frankly, it
would appear that the doctor himself was second to
no one on the farm in real interest in the fun.

We do not know how many nights the parties
watched; not many, however. At eleven or twelve
o'clock one night the bell rang out the alarm.
"Bang! bang!" went the guns in an incredibly
short time, and almost instantly the doctor appeared
on the scene, shouting at the top of his voice,
"Shoot 'em!" The thieves took to their heels and
dashed through the cornfield, where they could be
heard running for some minutes, as if they expected
a bullet would bring that marauding expedition to a
serious close. Did not the warriors laugh when the

victory was won? Did not the general in command
glory in the exploit?

The melons were saved — and such a crop of
them, some of them almost as large as a man could
lift! When fully ripe, the doctor selected two of
the largest, and sent one to each of the neighbors
hitherto alluded to, *with his sincere compliments.*
It was a capital joke, thoroughly appreciated. It
was settled, in Batavia, that Dr. Charles Jewett
could raise watermelons, and, what was more difficult, he could *keep* them, too. His watermelon war
gave him great notoriety.

However, he was *sold* afterwards, if never before.
Two young men called at his house one day, saying
" that a sick woman over the river heard that he had
some nice watermelons, and she would relish one
if the doctor would be so kind as to send it." Of
course he responded. Two hours afterwards, the
young men returned to say "that the melon proved
to be a white-meated one; and the sick woman
would relish a red-meated one best." So the doctor presented them with another. On the next day
he learned that there was no such woman in the
region, and that the two young men and their companions had a treat with the two melons.

Pigeons and quails were very plenty on his farm,
and the doctor devised an ingenious method of cap-
turing them in winter for food. They came in
flocks to the corn-crib when the ground was covered
with snow. The crib was set up three or four feet
from the ground, the space underneath enclosed

except on one side. The doctor boarded up that side, leaving space for a door, so arranged by a cord running from it to the house that it could be instantly closed when a sufficient number had entered the trap. Any day of the winter, almost, when the family wanted game for a meal, this device proved successful.

From the first Sabbath that the Jewett family became residents of Illinois, they were regular attendants at the Congregational church, and were connected with the Sabbath school, except Mrs. Jewett, whose feeble state of health did not permit her to attend the latter service. Here, as elsewhere, the doctor identified himself, heart and soul, with the work of religion, and his influence was highly valued. He was an ardent admirer of the young pastor, Rev. Wm. E. Merriman, and regretted to lose any of his ministrations, even at the prayer-meeting. The latter place found him an earnest and active helper.

The family had been residents of Illinois but a few months before the members, one after another, were attacked with the ague. Every one but the doctor had been attacked at the end of a year. Their home was in a malarial district, and ague was the inevitable consequence. At one time all of them were suffering from its effects at once, except that the "shakes" did not attack all on the same day; and Mrs. Jewett's ague was *dumb*, that is, without shakes. Still it was necessary for them to rise early in the morning and hurry through the work, to be ready to "shake." None of them could do both at the same time. The doctor began to think that ague did not dare to attack a stalwart farmer like himself, but he counted without his host. At the end of a year, or thereabouts, sure enough, the ague had him fast. In its merciless clutches, the doctor shook as violently as any of his children. The first hard, rousing shaking completely disgusted him; and his interest in Illinois farming was pretty well shaken out of him. He resolved to abdicate and remove still further west, where he could defy ague as successfully as he did the melon-thieves. To be beaten and cowed on his own premises by ague, or anything else, was a new experience for him.

Add to this affliction the fact that the Institute had not flourished as its ardent patrons expected, and the reasons for Dr. Jewett's removal from Illinois were ample. He sold his place at once without any sacrifice, resolved to keep moving westward till the ague should despair of ever troubling him. Charles had already explored Iowa and Minnesota, falling in love with the latter territory, where he had pre-empted a claim two miles and a half from the "Fari-bault" Trading-Post, at the junction of the Canon and Straight rivers. All the government claims between the "Post" and the locality Charles selected had been taken at that time, although few of them were occupied. Charles's claim was on a fine rolling prairie, half-way between the two rivers, without a tree, shrub, or stone. The chills and fever were unknown in that vicinity; the climate was healthy and invigorating, and the soil deep and rich. The town consisted of the "trading post," which was made of hewn logs very neatly joined together, a handsome framed house belonging to the son of the trader, Mr. Alexander Faribault, after whom the town was named, and six log and slab houses.

So soon as the doctor sold his farm at Batavia, he prepared to remove to Minnesota. The plan was to leave the female members of the family with one son in Illinois until autumn, when a dwelling would be erected for their reception. The doctor and his other sons would repair at once to the new home, preëmpt claims for himself and Richard, pitch a tent in which to dwell through the summer, and plant and sow for their first crops. Mr. Page declared that he would go with the doctor if it was "to the jumping-off place," and that where he chose to abide, he and his would abide. So Mr. Page and son joined the emigrants. The boy Frank went as errand-boy for the tent and professional dish-washer.

A wagon drawn by a yoke of oxen, the doctor's favorites, was loaded with tent, tools, cooking-utensils, provisions, and whatever a tent life of five or six months demanded; and Mr. Page drove it to the Mississippi River, whence it was boated to Hastings, and thence driven again inland forty-two miles to Faribault. Dr. Jewett's ox-team was the first one to go up what is now called "Jewett Valley," in honor of the teetotal pioneer.

Going up the Mississippi, the doctor found some old friends on the boat from Whitinsville, Mass., bound for St. Paul. When they learned that Dr.

Jewett was emigrating to Minnesota, they abandoned
the idea of going to St. Paul, and decided to unite
their fortunes with the doctor's.   " If the place suits
you, and you think it is a good location, we have
such confidence in your judgment as to believe that
it will suit us," they said.   Subsequently several
families followed the doctor to his new settlement,
constituting quite a colony of old friends.

It was a season when there was a rush for claims,
so that lively times followed their arrival.   The
doctor preëmpted claims for himself and Richard
adjoining that of Charles, and one of them was a
"woodland claim," that all might be supplied with
fuel.   Some one, according to the custom, had
selected a claim near by, and put up a stake with
his name, but had not occupied it.   The law
allowed a person thirty days to secure a claim
after driving down his stakes.   At the expiration of
thirty days, if he had failed to occupy it, his right
thereto ceased.   Charles had watched that claim.
for Mr. Page, and the thirtieth day had arrived without the appearance of the would-be proprietor.   At
twelve o'clock midnight of that day the man's right
would expire.   So Mr. Page took counsel of the
doctor, and both together were on the ground at
midnight to drive down their stakes; and both were
at the land-office at Hastings by the time it was
open to the public in the morning.   The claim was
secured to Mr. Page; and in the course of the next
day another claimant put in his appearance, to learn

that promptness is indispensable in dealing with the government of the United States.

With planting, sowing, fencing, and preparations for house-building, the doctor's hands were full, and a jollier man than he was in this novel field of labor never drove a stake on Minnesota soil. The timber for his house had to be transported from Minneapolis, sixty miles distant, over a road that would discourage any man but a pioneer. There was not time to fence his fields wholly, so that watching night and day through the summer, to keep the cattle out of the corn, was necessary, in lieu of a fence. The doctor had watched rumsellers so much in New England that it was an easy matter for him to "sleep with one eye open" to keep cattle out of the corn. Many a night during that summer his quick ear caught the sound of live-stock in the cornfield, after which he posted without stopping to arrange his toilet. A letter that he wrote to his wife that summer says:

"DEAR WIFE: Tough as an Indian and about as black, dirty and ragged, would be a fair description of your husband at present. The weather to-day is very hot, and, following as it does an abundant fall of rain, vegetation advances with great rapidity. Our neighbors who were here in the winter or early spring so as to get in their crops in season, are now luxuriating on as fine vegetables as one could desire: green peas, beets three and four inches through, and potatoes of good size for any season of the year. We are going to send up the valley to-morrow for a supply of new potatoes. The potato crop promises to be abundant. We got a little bit of a wetting last night, as we had a severe thunder-storm with a high wind, which made our canvas roof surge to and fro smartly. . . .

"Our buckwheat is all in, and all but one acre or two is up finely, and looks well. We have eleven acres of that crop and eight of corn, potatoes, beans, squashes, turnips, &c. The storm threshed down our potatoes, corn, and beets badly; but as the plants are all young, few broke off, and the main part is lifting itself up under the hot sun of the day; and in two or three days, if we have fine weather, no vestige of the storm will be visible on our planted fields. We have not one fence completed around our corn and potatoes, and have to watch it closely daytime and nights. I am on it as soon as there is light enough to see cattle across it in the morning; and this morning it was so dark when I got out on the border of the field that I could not see across it, and lay down on some fencing-poles and waited for daylight. All our folks were soundly sleeping in the tent. No material damage has been done our crops yet. With good luck we will have it enclosed in two days more. The next job is to fence our buckwheat field. We are congratulating ourselves upon the prospect of having a good supply of lime for building purposes, as a kiln that will turn out a thousand bushels is to be burned this week. It was all ready to fire last Saturday. We have found a splendid bank of gravel on Charles's claim, for making concrete; and, as the chance of getting lumber in time and in sufficient quantity looks rather dubious, we shall try the concrete. We shall first put up a small building, with hen-house, smoke and carriage room, and see how strong the mass appears. If we are satisfied with it, we shall go ahead and put up our tenement with that material. We shall be able to get lumber enough for door and window frames, and the doors and sash we shall buy and bring over from the river. Every day the confidence of our whole company in the move we made increases, as does our confidence in the excellence of the soil and climate. Not a case of ague has been *heard* of in the region since we have been here."

The letter continues at some length, and finally inquires how Mrs. Jewett feels about undertaking such pioneer life. The doctor was prepared to abandon life in Minnesota unless "his better half" was perfectly satisfied to live there. The reply of Mrs. Jewett is characteristic, and so well justifies Dr. Jewett's opinion of his wife, as frequently expressed to near friends, that a portion of it at least should be laid before the reader. A woman must be one of a thousand who will uncomplainingly rear a large family of children, and "knock about from pillar to post" as suits her husband's convenience in the work of reform. She says, in her reply :

" I see notices of your lectures in several papers, saying that you are the ' same old sixpence' as when you left Massachusetts, ' as funny as ever,' &c. ; so that I perceive, whatever may be your state of mind out of the desk, in it you seem the same. . . . . By the time you get home everything will look so enchantingly lovely that you will be desperately in love with all your possessions, from the fish in the middle of Fox River to the bullfrog piping his bass in the marsh a mile in the rear ; not to mention the mistress of ceremonies who presides over your affairs in your wearisome absence. Such days appear to stir up the spark of immortality within, reminding us of that new life to which we shall come forth after our wintry sleep in the tomb. Could we be other than glad, did we let the teachings of nature, aided and confirmed as they are by Revelation, prompt us to more hopefulness? At times how insignificant seems earthly wealth! and how utterly unworthy an immortal being this constant struggling, striving, toiling even unto death to obtain it! . . . I wrote you a long, long letter a few days since, though I did not by any means exhaust the subject. I do not know — yes, I *do know* — that I need not, at this date of our acquaintance, explain my sentiments in regard to any plan you may think for the best, because it did not immediately concern my own private or individual ease and comfort. The good of the whole is my good, and will ever be while life is continued. I did not know but you might infer that I should be unwilling again to change our home should it be thought best. I was thinking of yourself. I can only say that the most I fear, or the greatest trial I should have, would be the hurry and perplexity necessarily producing in weakened frames nervous irritability, that is harder to witness and endure than fatiguing labor simply. This (Batavia) is a most delightful spot of earth, but I can leave it; I would not say without regret, for I am not insensible. In my constitution, locality is strong; so is affection; I am strongly attached to friends; and there is *one* friend for whom, with lengthening years and increasing cares, my affection has proportionately increased. His home is mine, though 'it may be in the wilds of an unsettled territory or on a rock in mid-ocean. His name I hope will be on the marble that covers my dust; by it I hope to be called forth by the awakening trump of the archangel, and by it known until I receive (if such should be my blessed portion) that ' white stone with a new name,' ' to him that overcometh.' Let that sentiment be my epitaph."

The same letter contained the following original stanzas :

> " I go, dear husband, gladly go,
> Though wild the region be,
> Where'er thy wandering footsteps roam,
> Still there 's the home for me.
>
> " I go ; my purpose still to cheer
> Thy rugged path the while ;
> Our aim nor wealth nor fame shall be,
> But Heaven's approving smile.
>
> " And when in death our sleeping dust
> *One* marble covers o'er ;
> United in that ' Better Land,'
> No change shall part us more."

On the fourth of July of that season, the settlers, whose number was rapidly increasing, conducted the first celebration that was ever observed in that part of the territory. Dr. Jewett delivered the oration, which was received by his pioneer audience with unalloyed satisfaction. Nobody but Dr. Jewett could have delivered such an address in a wilderness, crammed so full of the wittiest wisdom and the wisest wit. The settlers will never forget that characteristic oration.

In August of that season Dr. Jewett was applied to for two weeks' labor in Minnesota, in behalf of "freedom and temperance" both. He was offered fair pay, too, for his service ; and seventy-five dollars added to his treasury just at that time, would be a substantial help. He accepted, and wrote to his wife from St. Anthony, August 19, 1855 :

"DEAR WIFE: I have just listened to a discourse on the Tenth Commandment; and how it rejoices me to know that while it forbids the desire of possessing the wives of other men, it does not forbid a desire, however ardent, for the companionship of one's own wife. If it did, I see not how I could possibly avoid breaking it hourly. Oh, how I long to see your face once more and to be assured by your own sweet voice of your continued love and your well-being. Not that I doubt the former; but such affection as has from our childhood, or from our youth at least, existed between us, is never tired of assurances, but like the miser would still be hoarding up its uncounted treasures. I saw men to-day walking to and from the house of God, in company with their wives and children, and I felt alone. Well, the time will come again, I trust, when I too will take my loved ones to the house of worship. I have for three evenings addressed the citizens of this place and Minneapolis (on the other side of the river) on the question involved in the coming election, Anti-Nebraska and Temperance. I am to speak again to-night, and to-morrow night at Excelsior, on the edge of Lake Minnetonka, twenty miles distant. My appointments extend to the 29th. I shall allow them to give out no more at present, because I want to be on our claims pushing on our operations there, and getting our domicils ready for you and yours."

This extract introduces the reader to Dr. Jewett's industry in Minnesota, his unfaltering interest in the cause of liberty and temperance, and his plans concerning his pioneer life. We shall omit further details, and pass directly to the removal of his family to their home on the prairie.

XIII.

PIONEER LIFE.

MRS. JEWETT was obliged to pack up and move to Minnesota without her husband. His engagements prevented his return; and then he knew very well that his wife was equal to the task. He arranged, however, to meet her and their two daughters at Hastings, on the Mississippi. Their route was to Chicago, thence to the Mississippi, where they embarked on a steamer up the river to Hastings. The distance from the latter place to Faribault, their destination, was forty-two miles, and the road was in a very muddy condition, caused by heavy rains. The reader may judge of the depth of the mud from the fact that the doctor had procured a wagon with springs, to convey his wife and two daughters to their new home; but a portion of the way the daughters were compelled to walk, for fear of breaking the springs to the vehicle, so severely racked and jolted by the perilous state of the road. The girls actually waded through mud knee-deep.

One night they stopped at " Sod Tavern," a public-house that derived its name from the material of which it was built. Both the walls and roof were made of sods. In the night there was a tremendous thunder-shower, such as the inhabitants were accustomed to in that part of the country. The doctor and his wife were startled by the rain coming down upon them through the sod roof in a stream. Before they could escape from their exposed situation, both of them were quite wet with water that had percolated the sods above, and consequently was as dirty as it was limpid. The landlord directed Mrs. Jewett to get into bed with his two "little boys," who were sleeping where the roof did not leak, while the doctor shirked for himself in another corner of the soddy establishment. They survived this unexpected introduction to pioneer life, however, and in due time reached their destination.

The doctor was building a house, but it was not completed, so that there was no shelter for his family, except the tent, on his claim. There was a small cabin on the claim of Mr. Nutting, near by; and that was vacated for their accommodation. Their nights were spent at the cabin; but the days at the tent, in cooking for the men, who were rejoiced to have genuine cooks who understood the business, after their miserable mock cookery for six months.

The house was soon completed — a building eighteen by twenty feet, with loft and cellar. The former was reached by a ladder in one corner of the room, made by nailing slats upon the studs; the latter through a trap-door cut in the floor. A *trap*-door

it was indeed; for notwithstanding their good inten-
tions to guard it well when open, Frank went
through it once with a handful of wood in his arms,
and Lucy, with a butcher-knife in one hand and a
dish in the other. Both of them found that such a
sudden descent into the cellar was more perilous
than congenial. But their bruises healed rapidly,
and they were soon as good as new.

The lower floor was one large room at first,— parlor, sitting-room, and kitchen in one,— the loft being
devoted to lodgings, where the whole space was
divided into sleeping-apartments by means of curtains. The space was so fully occupied in this way,
that lodgers were obliged to stand on their beds to
undress. The furniture of the house was not imported, — the doctor was a stickler for home manu-
factures. Ever since he made that bureau for his
prospective bride, he felt competent to furnish a
house on a Western prairie without calling to his
aid skilled European or American labor. He constructed several three-legged stools that were really
more useful than chairs, since the occupant was
obliged to exercise skill and tact to maintain an
upright position upon them. There was not a stool
for each member of the household; so a seat, long
enough to accommodate five or six persons, was
put up on one side of the room, hinged to the ceiling, and when not needed it was let down out of
the way. This always served for a seat to one side
of the long dining-table, which the doctor made
also. Several boxes, in which bedding, iron-ware,

and crockery were brought, were appropriately fitted and arranged for tables and sink. Shelves were erected on one side for tin-ware, crockery, &c. All the bedsteads used were of the latest Jewett pattern, destitute of carving to be sure, but capable of furnishing as much genuine sleep as the most approved French styles. In one corner of the room the family grist-mill was set up; it was like an old-fashioned coffee-mill, only somewhat larger. Through this hand-mill all the corn and other grains used in the family were run. It was a slow method to prepare meal for cooking, but "many hands make light work;" and there was no lack of meal. A farmer living several miles distant heard that Dr. Jewett had a grist-mill, and away he went one day with as much grain as he could carry on his wagon, rejoicing that civilization had reached Minnesota with one of its most useful inventions. The doctor thought that the farmer's countenance would furnish an artist with a good subject, when he was introduced to the hand-mill in one corner of the room. To the doctor it was one of the best jokes of the season, though he really sympathized with the disappointed man when he saw him starting homeward with his load of unground corn. He believed, as we have seen, that "the beginning of a good cause is never small." We suspect that, when he looked at that load of corn and then at his mill, that he must have questioned the truth of the maxim.

This house answered for the first winter of pioneer life. In the spring following, it was enlarged by the addition of an L, and the large room of the main house was divided into three, a sitting-room and two bedrooms. While the L was building, Mrs. Jewett came near losing her life. Boards were placed over the timbers that the family might have passage-way into the wood-shed. In some way a board was slipped from its position, when, stepping upon it, Mrs. Jewett fell through upon the ground beneath, the board striking her a fearful blow in the face, seriously injuring her nose. She was taken up insensible, and for some time serious apprehensions as to the result greatly troubled the family.

The house was plastered after the family occupied it; and cold weather setting in, it was scarcely dried through the winter. Yet no member of the family took cold, the dry atmosphere out of doors furnishing a good antidote. All enjoyed uninterrupted health, except some annoyance experienced from the lingering effects of the ague; and Mrs. Jewett's *dumb* ague was made to *speak* by the climate, so that she shook herself as effectually as any of them had done. But a few months' residence there carried off the remains of the dreaded disease.

Having made his house comfortable for winter, and put two stoves into the large room, the doctor turned with tender heart to the cattle. It was not customary to erect barns or sheds for cattle in that country; but his heart was touched by the sight of his poor dumb creatures huddling together for warmth in the face of wintry blasts. So he erected a comfortable shed for them, with straw-thatched roof.

The first winter was spent in preparing fencing for the spring. It was necessary to go three miles for the material, and this necessity exposed them to the blinding snow-storms of that region. It required great courage and caution to find the way home in a storm. As a wise precaution, the doctor cut poles, and, after tying a strip of black cloth upon the tops, set them up, two or three rods apart, along the whole way to the forest. By the aid of these they could find their way home in the most driving storm, unless darkness overtook them. In the latter case, the family set a light in the window, and waited with some anxiety for their coming. The sleds used that winter were made by the doctor. A cart also, used in the summer and autumn, was his handiwork.

The winters of Minnesota were cold indeed. All that winter the frost did not melt on the windows. When a light was put in the window on a stormy night, to guide travellers or any returning member of the family, one of the children would sit by it, and, with a cloth dipped in hot water, remove the frost from the pane that the light might shine through. One day a man, going with them to Hastings, would have been frozen to death on the sled, had not the doctor resorted to a resolute remedy. The man protested against interrupting his sleep, and begged to be let alone when his companions shook him up. Finally, they rolled him from the sled, and, by the most active and persistent dealing, compelled him to walk and live. Nearly every one froze an ear, nose, finger, or hand. The doctor froze his nose seriously, and for three months it was red as a toper's; and more than one pioneer told him that his nose was a "disgrace to a temperance lecturer." Richard froze one of his ears, and afterwards the same ear was frozen again, one cold night when he was in bed and asleep. When out of doors, riding or walking, in the coldest weather, they were wont to watch each other, so as to give timely warning when ears or faces were freezing.

In the house, two stoves were kept running night and day in the one large room. The females wore shawls also, all the time, in order to be comfortably warm. At night they put on hoods when they retired. These were especially necessary in a driving snow-storm; for the fine, dry snow blew in at every crevice, notwithstanding the house was shingled. Directly over the beds cotton cloth was tacked to the roof, between the rafters, and yet snow would sometimes beat in and fall upon the beds. In some parts of the loft, after a very furious storm, there would be several bushels of snow to remove.

Soon after the family occupied the new house, Mr. Faribault, by the advice of General Shields, waited upon the doctor to see if he would take his two sons, eight and ten years of age, into his family, to teach them the English language, and care for them. Mr. Faribault was a Frenchman, and his

18

wife an Indian squaw; he was a man of considerable wealth, and would pay reasonably for the service. The doctor's house was not constructed exactly for a boarding-school, but then he could easily adapt it to the circumstances. Somehow he had a wonderful faculty to make a little room answer for a good many people; and they appeared to get along just as well as a few would. Then doubtless, as the doctor had welcomed Irish, French, Swedes, &c., all at once to his family, he had an irrepressible desire to try an Indian. So the boys were received, and remained there a year or more. The doctor won their affection and confidence, and so did the whole family. They were nervous, fiery little fellows, proud and haughty, requiring tact and management to interest and control them. But in the doctor's hand an Indian was just as plastic as an American, and the young savages improved from day to day, and finally became quite Yankee-like. The doctor treated them as he would other boys, and made kites, carts, and tops, to amuse them. The habit of his early life served him a good turn in the "conduct of Indian affairs."

Indians were at first a source of anxiety and fear to the feminine part of the household; but the doctor lost no sleep on account of their presence. At first they were disposed to frighten the new-comers if possible. But when they yelled to the doctor, he yelled back again with an imitation and power that must have made them suspect he was of Indian descent. At the same time he met them more than

half-way for conciliation, and worked himself into
their good graces successfully. Their visits were
frequent and generally friendly. Their chief demand was for whiskey; and when they could not be
made to believe that the doctor had nothing to do
with the article, they were somewhat demonstrative.
One Sunday two Indians came for whiskey, when
the doctor, with all the family except Mrs. Jewett
and one of the daughters, had gone to meeting.
That Mrs. Jewett was frightened we need scarcely
say. But she treated them to food, and finally succeeded in convincing them that there was no whiskey in the house. At another time an Indian called
for water. The youngest daughter, by mistake,
handed a pitcher of hot water to him, from which
he took a swallow, when his eyes flashed vengeance
for a moment; but he was made to understand that
it was a mistake. At another time the same daughter went to the shed in the evening with a lantern to
get potatoes for breakfast. While filling her pan,
two large Indians, hideously painted and wearing
an extra amount of feathers, appeared before her.
Evidently they intended to frighten her, and they
did of course. One of them dangled his tomahawk
in front of him that it might glisten in the light of
her lantern. She lost no time in returning to the
house, the Indians following. On entering the
room, pale as any snow that ever covered the prairie, she said, "Indians, father," and stepped behind
him. The Indians courteously responded, and,
looking at the girl, they indicated to the doctor that

she was afraid of them, and proceeded to say what the doctor could not understand. At that time a. French girl, who had lived among the Indians, was working for the family, and she conversed with them. They said that they liked the little girl and would buy her; that they "would give *ten* cents for her." That offer did not obtain her. After this the doctor procured a watch dog, which the Indians held in mortal terror. They would come within hailing distance of the house, and call out to have the dog taken care of. It is a singular fact that nearly all dogs, horses, and oxen hated Indians, and would manifest their hatred emphatically. The presence of an Indian would render one of the doctor's oxen almost unmanageable.

At one time the doctor was going to the woods for the day. It was in the winter, and he carried on his sled provender for the oxen and a jug of coffee for the men. Several Indians met him, and rather authoritatively demanded "that jug of whiskey." They were assured that it was coffee and not whiskey, but they would not be convinced till the doctor poured some of it out into the snow.

We have adduced these facts that the reader may readily appreciate the doctor's tactics in subjugating wild Indians. One day he observed that several squaws, who came into the woods to cut dry limbs from the trees for burning, had very small and dull axes. He exhibited his own to them, heavier and very sharp, and showed them how easily it would cut the driest limb. He learned that they had no way of sharpening their axes ; so he made one of the number understand that he would sharpen her axe if she would bring it to the house at a specified time. The squaw was prompt, and the doctor soon put a keen edge upon her axe. A more delighted squaw than she, with her sharp implement, was never seen on a prairie. That she carried a very favorable report to her uncivilized sisters was proved to the doctor by the appearance of a bevy of them on the following day, with axes to be sharpened. He found that somebody besides Yankees and politicians had " axes to grind." As his object was to conquer the red men and their " better halves " with kindness, he did not shrink from the unexpected burden of labor imposed. If sharpening axes would open the way to their hearts, then he believed in that sort of gospel. Another man might have been suspicious that he was sharpening axes for his own beheading, but the doctor did not dream of such a thing. He was after a treaty of peace with the tribes of the forest, the Sioux and Chippewas, who were then waging war with each other, and he fully expected to succeed. His tactics proved to be eminently sagacious. The squaws had found a model pioneer. A man who would sharpen their axes without money and without price, must be a better friend to them than any Indian agent whom the " Great Father " had sent into their domains. The axe treaty became a fixed fact.

The doctor was wont to extract teeth for any suffering neighbor or traveller who stood in need of such service. After winning the confidence of the Indians, he offered his services to them in that line, and they were accepted. One day an aunt of the two Indian boys, who were still in his family, came to see them. She was suffering with the toothache. The doctor examined the tooth, and proposed to pull it. He took her to the door-step, where he performed the operation. She was a ponderous woman, as fat and disgusting a squaw as ever darkened his doors. Putting his arm around her neck, with his hand under her chin that he might hold her firmly, the tooth was out in a trice. But the dusky lady swooned and fainted clear away in the doctor's arms. In the midst of the scene, who should appear but Squire Mott, now a leading citizen of Faribault; and he exclaimed, "Oh, doctor, who ever would have thought of beholding this!"

However, such dental courtesies had their effect, no doubt. Perhaps their importance entitles them to be known as a tooth treaty.

At another time he came across a squaw in the woods who was trying to bind up a severe cut on the leg of her son. He had cut his limb badly with a hatchet. The doctor expressed his sympathy for the boy, and offered to dress the wound himself. She gladly accepted his offer, and seemed grateful for the service rendered. Ascertaining where she lived, he told her that he would come to her *tepee* (house) the next day with suitable bandages, and dress it again, — all of which gratified her very much. On the next day, taking with him a quantity of court-plaster and bandages, he found her "tepee," and dressed the limb more elaborately. Of course, the kind act gave him prestige among the children of the forest.

At still another time he was going several miles, when he overtook a squaw bearing a heavy burden. He stopped, and motioned to her to ride on his sled, and directed her to sit on a box he was carrying. She gladly accepted his invitation. When she laid down her burden, he inquired, by signs, what she had there.

"Pappoose," she replied —(her baby).

"Indian or squaw?" asked the doctor, meaning "boy" or "girl."

"Indian," she said.

And he learned that the child was dead, and she was carrying it twelve miles away for burial.

The doctor carried her as far as he went, for which the sorrowing mother was very thankful.

The family had not been long in Minnesota before they learned that a pioneer's house must be a free hotel. Sometimes as many as four travellers would call for food and lodgings in a single night. With his characteristic kindness, the doctor provided bedding with which beds for several visitors could be extemporized at short notice. Several extra plates at the table were often required. During the second winter of his residence there his house was crowded with permanent residents. The doctor invited Rev Mr. Willey, of Maine, who was in feeble condition, to spend that winter in his family for his health. He

also invited an intemperate young man to do the
same, thinking that he might reclaim him. He also
gave a home to a carpenter, that winter, in his
house, though the young man did a little work in
his line for him. Still another young man, the son
of a personal friend of the doctor's, whom he thought
might be benefited, spent the winter there by invitation. And all this was without pay—a free gift!
Nor did the recipients enjoy the hospitality so much
as the doctor enjoyed his acts of kindness.

Nor was this all. During that winter Mrs. Jewett
proposed to teach her children; and the neighbors
hearing of it, besought her to teach their children also.
There was no school in Faribault yet, of course.
Quite a number of new families who needed instruction, had settled there within the year. She had
three of her own children to teach, and " more could
be taught as well as not." The doctor entered into the
project with all his heart, and the result was a day-
school of fifteen scholars, taught without charge.
The following season there was such a rush of emigration thither that a public school was established,
and Mrs. Jewett taught it in her own house until
sickness prostrated her.

There was no place of Sabbath worship within
many miles when Dr. Jewett went to Minnesota. It
seemed strange and sad to him, amidst the impressive silence and enchanting verdure, to reflect that
there was no public recognition of God, whose care
and goodness were so manifest in the beauty and
grandeur of nature. A friend, who rode over the

green prairies with him, recalls with what touching pathos he recited the words that Cowper put into the mouth of Alexander Selkirk in the island of Juan Fernandez:

> "Religion ! what treasure untold
>   Resides in that heavenly word !
> More precious than silver and gold,
>   Or all that this earth can afford.
> But the sound of the church-going bell
>   These valleys and rocks never heard,
> Never sighed at the sound of a knell,
>   Or smiled when a Sabbath appeared."

As soon as possible he established a Sabbath school and public worship in his own house. Making known the situation to the Eliot Church in Newton, Massachusetts, which he helped to establish, they sent him a Sabbath-school library of two hundred and fifty volumes.

Unwittingly the doctor came "around into the ministry," as, in his boyhood, the neighbor said he would. It was a treat to the families for miles around to have Sabbath worship established; and a few, who lived five or six miles away, came with ox-teams. Benches were extemporized by placing boards on blocks of wood of suitable height. The doctor conducted the services, which consisted of prayers, singing, and the reading of a sermon or an exposition of the Scriptures. The exposition and remarks by the doctor were highly valued by the audience for their practical character. Few theological professors could excel Dr. Jewett in clear, original, and bright expositions of the Bible. He was never dry or dull. An occasional flash of wit *would* appear, lighting up the subject with a halo. The conclusion was that a good minister was found in the mirthful pioneer. Nor could any one tell in which sphere the doctor proved himself the more efficient, — on the farm, in the woods, as a mechanic, physician, temperance lecturer, or preacher. He interested them so much in whatever he did that comparisons were out of the question.

One intelligent woman from Massachusetts, almost as keen as the doctor at repartee, disliked the country very much. Her husband removed thither at the doctor's suggestion, so that she felt at liberty to discuss the matter freely with her old friend. Half in earnest and half jocosely, she would berate the West, and declare that there was no beauty or profit in the land that she should desire it. Again and again the wit and logic of one came into collision with that of the other, and many a time hearty laughs were enjoyed by listeners over the spicy encounters. One Sabbath morning the doctor was not quite ready when the time of service arrived, and he gave the hymn-book to this lady, asking her to select a hymn for him. She did so, and put a mark into the book. On opening it to give out the hymn, he was taken aback to find the hymn,

> " Oh, what a wretched land is this,
> That yields us no supply ! "

If the doctor was ever vanquished by a woman,

he was then. Had it been other than a religious meeting, there would have been an explosive laughter. As it was, the religion of that service was considerably diluted by the merriment occasioned.

Within two years after settling upon the Minnesota claim, so many people had taken up their residence in Faribault, that Dr. Jewett proposed the organization of a church at the centre of the town. So the place of worship was transferred to another dwelling at the centre, and a church was organized with seven members, Dr. Charles Jewett, his wife, daughter, and two sons, constituting five of the number. Now, the population of that town is over six thousand, the membership of the church two hundred and twenty-five, Sabbath school more than two hundred, and a congregation of over half a thousand. And the church is but twenty-three years old.

Dr. Jewett was not satisfied with worshipping in a dwelling and school-house; (after the erection of a school-house the Sabbath services were held in it.) He proposed, within a year from the organization of the church, that a house of worship should be built. Many families had settled at the centre of the town, though few of them had money to contribute to the object. Dr. Jewett was earnest and persistent. He was prepared to make sacrifices himself, and he would write to Eastern friends for contributions. At length the interest awakened justified the effort. A subscription paper was circulated among the people, and at the same time the doctor wrote to

Rev. Jacob Ide, D. D., of West Medway, Mass., and others, soliciting aid. Dr. Ide published the communication of Dr. Jewett in the Congregationalist of May 9, 1856, with remarks of his own. Dr. Ide said:

" The following letter from Dr. Jewett is one of great interest. Though the churches, in the present state of things, cannot respond to the call, which every individual church at the West might be disposed to make, yet such are the circumstances of the community in which Dr. Jewett is located, and such are the feelings of the friends of temperance and religion in the commonwealth toward him for his long and self-denying and effective labors in the temperance cause, that they will, it is believed, deem it a privilege to respond to the affecting appeal which he now makes for a little assistance at their hands. Medway will cheerfully pay the tax which is laid upon her."

The letter of Dr. Jewett filled a column and a half in the Congregationalist, and was regarded as a valuable document for the information it contained about the resources and promise of Minnesota, together with its moral and spiritual necessities. We have only space for the doctor's earnest plea for help based on the reasons advanced.

" REV. AND DEAR SIR: Worn and wearied by hard service in the temperance cause, I thought to secure a little release from responsibilities, and some relief from severe toil, by removing westward, and devoting myself to the quiet labor of cultivating the soil. Well, here I am, where the circumstances that surround me call for as severe and continuous labor as I have ever been called to perform, though I think the character of the service more conducive to bodily health than that to which I have been accustomed. I am, as you see by the post-mark, in the territory of Minnesota, sixty miles south of St. Paul, forty west of the Mississippi, and in latitude forty-four; on the very outskirts of civilization, where the Indian chases the deer and the farmer follows the plough over the same acres, where barbarism and social refinement meet and mingle, and where heathenism and infidelity must be met on their own ground, and conquered by Christian faith and Christian love. . . . Last summer a few of us, feeling our responsibilities and spiritual needs, sustained at the village, two miles and a half distant from my residence, religious worship, through a large portion of the season, where only the summer previous had stood more than a hundred lodges of the Sioux Indians. . . .

"There are here about twenty male members of Congregational churches, and perhaps as many females, who will unite in the formation of a church; and the seventeenth of May is fixed upon as the time for organization. We have as yet no place of worship, and hold our meetings in private houses. We want to build a church as early in the summer as possible, as there is no private house in the village or on the neighboring prairies large enough to seat one half the number who would attend on our worship if we shall be able to secure, as we hope to, a faithful and able religious teacher. But how we are to accomplish what we so ardently desire, puzzles our bump of calculation not a little, and draws pretty heavily on our bank of faith. . . .

"Our old friends in the East must help us a little, until we can get fairly on our feet, and then, with the blessing of God, we hope to stand and become, in turn, helpers of others. . . .

"Minnesota is to be, I believe, the New England of the

West, and exert, when it shall take its place among the
states of the Union, a decided influence, and that, too, on
the right side of those great questions which are now
agitating the country.

"The followers of His Holiness the Pope, ever ready
to seize on the best points, have contracted to have a
church built here early in the summer. Oh! shall that
be the first church-edifice in this lovely region? God and
his faithful people forbid!"

This call was quite liberally responded to in Massachusetts, the ladies of Dr. Ide's church contrib-
uting forty-five dollars. The church in Millbury,
where the doctor lived six years, gave thirty-five
dollars; the neighboring church at Whitinsville presented a bell; and the Eliot church at Newton,
which gave the Sabbath-school library, contributed
more than a hundred dollars, accompanied with their
prayers and blessing. We suspect that, when the
doctor received the latter gift, he must have been
satisfied as never before with his sacrifices in found-
ing with others the aforesaid church in Massachusetts. It was a *paying* operation, if for nothing
else than to take a part in the benevolent work at
Faribault. In less than three years from the time
that Dr. Jewett settled in Faribault, he had the pleasure of seeing a Sabbath school and church organized,
and a house of worship erected. As he expressed it,
"we had a church-edifice completed, a bell hung in
the tower, awakening the prairie echoes, before one
half the people who went there to worship had their
own houses properly covered and provided with
comforts."

This Christian enterprise alone is all the monument that Dr. Jewett need to have. It was born in his large, loving heart, and cradled and nursed by his watchful interest and prayers. The result is far better than he devised; but it is according to God's rich grace towards men who lay foundations in faith and love, without regard to personal aggrandizement. It was true missionary work that he performed, casting seed upon all waters; and he lived to behold the remarkable transformation — "the wilderness and solitary place to blossom as the rose."

HOUSE BUILT BY DR. JEWETT IN MINNESOTA. — GRINDING AXES FOR THE SQUAWS. — See page 277.

XIV.

PIONEER LIFE CONTINUED.

DR. JEWETT came near losing his life in 1856, by drowning in Cannon Lake. His wood-lot was on the other side of the lake — three miles distant — and he went thither to work, with his two sons and two hired men. It was in the summer, when mosquitoes were abundant, and laborers were obliged to wear thick clothes to protect themselves from these pests. At noon, when the doctor and his men and boys were eating their dinner, the two yoke of oxen, chained together, started for home across the lake, and they were not noticed until they had waded quite a distance into the water. One of the sons present (who is now Professor of Chemistry in the Imperial University at Tokio, Japan) shall tell the remainder of the thrilling tale :

"Father immediately unfastened the horse, which stood near by, and led her by a zigzag course down the steep bank to the water's edge. Here he mounted her, and rode into the lake as fast as possible, to get ahead of the cattle before they should reach deep water, where they must swim. He was urging his horse forward so intently that he did not notice when the cattle went beyond their depth; and so he continued until his horse began to swim. At once he saw that the horse was too light to sustain his weight long, and he attempted to turn her about by causing her to swim in a circle; but she soon sank under his weight, and he was obliged to slip from her back and attempt to swim to the shore. The wind was blowing hard against him, causing the waves to beat into his face, greatly retarding his progress. His thick clothes and heavy shoes, also, hindered him so much that he could make very little headway. He wrenched off one shoe, that happened to be untied, but was unable to remove the other. Filling his lungs with air, he dropped down to the bottom of the lake, untied and removed the shoe, and succeeded in regaining the surface of the water without strangling. Parker and I were running up and down the shore, hand-in-hand, trying to keep in sight of father; and when he descended to the bottom to remove his shoe, we thought he was drowned, and began to cry as hard as we could. The men on the shore, also, were running about, vainly looking for some way of getting help to father. After removing his shoes, he got on a little better, though he still made but little headway against the wind and waves. He was becoming exhausted, and every little while would try to touch bottom, but was unsuccessful. At last, having lost all his strength, and, as his limbs straightened out, dropping down into the water under the conviction that he must drown, his toes just touched the bottom, leaving his head out of water. He said that if he had not touched bottom just when he did, he must have drowned, as he could swim no further. After wading to the shore, he directed the men to run to the cabin of a Frenchman on the shore, and get him to go out in his boat to unchain and unyoke the cattle, now swimming

19

about in a circle, that they might swim out. Father sat down upon a large stone exhausted, and there watched the Frenchman until he separated the oxen (a work requiring great skill and carefulness), and all of them swam to the further shore.

"Father was now alone with Parker and myself, and he said, 'Now, boys, let us thank God for my deliverance.' We three knelt around the big white stone on which he had been sitting, and there he thanked God fervently for preserving his life."

Dr. Jewett engaged in farming with all his heart. As we have said already, he was greatly in love with agriculture; and tilling the soil in that country where it was so productive, was doubly enjoyable. He planted and sowed from twenty to thirty acres annually, wheat, corn, potatoes, buckwheat, oats, and turnips, turning his attention to fruits as soon as possible. It was a novel experience to him to cultivate corn and potatoes in rows half a mile long; and he used to introduce a little pleasantry into the labor by stopping to shake hands with his men as they met in the field when ploughing or hoeing from opposite directions. They had travelled so far, and been absent so long in ploughing or hoeing from one end of the field to the other and back, that congratulations were fitting, he thought.

To him there was something impressive and grand in the thought of tilling those thrifty acres, so far away from "city or busy mart;" and often he came from his fields into the house repeating Cowper's lines :

"I am monarch of all I survey ;
My right there is none to dispute ;
From the centre all round to the sea,
I am lord of the fowl and the brute."

He introduced the best varieties of corn, potatoes, and fruits that were known in the East. His numerous friends in Massachusetts were glad to assist him by sending scions and seeds of fruits. The letters of several of his correspondents speak of such gifts forwarded. In addition to the more substantial products of the earth, he introduced currants, raspberries, gooseberries, strawberries, plums, the crab-apple, and Chinese sugar-cane. One of his letters before us, written when he was on a trip to New England, speaks of having gathered over one thousand cuttings of currants, of the best varieties. We are told by a resident of Minnesota, that varieties of corn, potatoes, and fruits, introduced by him into that and other states, are still raised; and that he often meets with parties who say, that they not only removed to Minnesota in consequence of what Dr. Jewett wrote and said about it, but also are raising the kind of produce that he introduced. An amusing incident, illustrative of his promptness and ingenuity to meet an emergency, is told of him in this connection.

He wrote to a friend in Rhode Island to forward to him as many kernels of a certain kind of corn as could be carried in a letter. He was waiting for it when it arrived. He put it to soak in a saucer under the shed, and went into the field. Presently his little daughter came running to say that " the rooster has eaten up your corn." " Sure of it ? " said the doctor ; " was it the rooster ? " " Yes, sir ; he was eating the very last of it when I came to the shed."

Dr. Jewett sought the rooster hurriedly, and in an incredible short time he was caught, decapitated, and his crop made to yield up its stolen contents. The Rhode Island corn was recovered, and the doctor gloried in its golden ears at harvest-time, though his rooster lost his head in the operation.

His love of agricultural pursuits appears prominent in his letters. We think that four-fifths of his letters speak of the fruits of the earth. No matter with what subject a letter begins, he is quite likely to introduce agriculture or horticulture, one or both, before he closes it. A few extracts from his correspondence when absent from home, on this point, will be read with interest :

" This weather makes me quite homesick. I want to get into a garden somewhere. I have an unconquerable love for the soil and its cultivation. . . . Please have R. cover over the boxes that contain the apple-seeds, so that they will not feel the warmth of the sun and start too soon."

" To the gentleman who sent you the gourd-seeds, I wish sent a potato of the ' Shaker Russett ' variety. You know those big ones that we dug before I left. Make a little bag, say one-half of one of those bags I sent the apple-seeds in, cut up a big potato, leaving an eye on each piece ; leave the pieces a little longer than a walnut ; then put them in the bag to the amount of half a pound or a pound, sew them up nicely, and forward by mail to Dr. J. L. Free, Stewartstown, York County, Pa.

"Also, cut off a few slips from the Jabe Reed apple-trees, cutting them the length of a long envelope, or about eight inches long, seal the end of each graft with wax, and send them to Nelson Brooks, Union Village, Courtland County, N. Y."

"The new breaking should be cross-ploughed this autumn, so as to turn up about an inch and a half or two inches of soil deeper than the prairie plough went, so that the frost, the coming winter, may act upon the soil thus turned up, and it will slack up in the spring as mellow as ashes, and help to cover the wheat that should be sowed in the spring as early as possible."

"The east flat of twenty-five acres will make a splendid cornfield next year, and rotation of crops is desirable. Cropped with corn one year, it will produce far better wheat the next year."

"I sent you from Lancaster two more small potatoes, said to be a very superior kind. I think myself they are identical with the Irish Flukes; but they say not. If they come through safely, take good care of them. . . . Look once in a while at the apple-seed box, and see that nothing disturbs it."

"Pretty soon it will be time to expect frost in Minnesota. When the first frost comes it is generally light, and will not injure the vitality of the corn; but soon afterwards I would have the seed-corn picked — six or eight bushels of the finest ears. If the corn in drying shrinks a little, it will not hurt its vitality at all. Are your tomatoes ripe? Did the chickens eat them up? How about the

pumpkins in the garden and in the field? Is the corn below the barn pretty ripe? Tell me everything."

"I went out yesterday to a great bed of spearmint by
the roadside, and gathered a lot of the seed, as it was fully
ripe, which I shall bring home with me. Sowing it by
the roadside, down where my spring crosses, it will secure a supply of that convenient 'yerb' for all time. It
is well to have such things about."

"I mailed you yesterday two bags of apple-seed, which I
wish put into a box of moist sand, after soaking the seeds
six hours. Mix them thoroughly with fine, clean sand, so
that in the spring I can take a riddle and sift the sand out
before planting them in proper seed-beds. I wish to
raise some thousands of stocks. When two years old
we will graft Siberian Crab of the finest kinds on them,
and the Red Astracan, Famosoe, and Duchess of Olden-
burg. These will stand our climate."

"I wish now especially to remind you that the time is
fast passing when it will do to cut off the currant cuttings.
The new shoots that grew last year are what we want.
Those from the great English bushes I would have kept
separate. I shall take up a good many of them and sell
when I get there."

"I got of the friend with whom I stop here about five
pounds of the Early Rose Potato which is so famous.
It is the most splendid potato in existence, very early,
excellent in quality, and yields enormous crops. From
three pounds a man here raised NINE BUSHELS."

"You speak of the seed-corn. No matter how thoroughly ripe corn is, it must be dry to resist the action of

the frost. If ever so ripe, and a little damp, freezing will destroy its vitality. It will not dry sufficiently in the crib. I think it will be found in the spring that only that which was brought in and dried will sprout."

" Do not forget to have F. take up and bring with him the seeds which we put into the ground last autumn. There were two boxes of cherry-stones, and a box of the upland cranberry. Fruit is one of the essentials, whether we keep our farm to live on, or whether we shall sell. The amount of fruit on it will make it attractive to pur-chasers."

" You did right in the sale of the cow, and your plans are arranged as I should have expected of a lady having superior executive abilities."

" Please send in an envelope some seeds of the Hub-bard squash to Rev. H. H. Bensen, Mineral Point, Wis., and Rev. Calvin Warner, Plattville, Wis. Put up some of the pure blood seeds also, and send to Mr. Lee, Depot Master, Neponset, Ill., and say to him a part of them are for Rev. Mr. Barnes. These gentlemen are among my most active friends."

" I mailed to-day a bag of a new variety of peas, which, when green, are bouncers; and they do not require tall brush, growing only two and a half feet high."

" I was glad to hear that the seeds reached you safely, though you did not speak specifically of having received seeds in bags at three different times. First I sent a bag that I hired a boy to get for me. Then I sent two bags with pieces of white cloth sewed on them. The last con-tained four full quarts of seeds, and cost me only one dollar besides the postage. The last two bags I sent from Elmira. That makes five, containing in all nine quarts of seeds. Did they all reach you? The potatoes came safely, you say. Keep them separate from all others."

"I have gathered, in my travels, two packages of seeds, which I send, one of spearmint and the other of penny-royal. I got them in my walks for exercise. We will scatter them next spring where they will have a good chance, and they will take care of themselves as the dandelions did. I have never seen either in Minnesota."

"I send you a paper of sweet corn to-day, and some freshly imported ruta-baga seed. I would sow some of the ruta-baga where the York cabbage-plants were raised last year. Has the ground beyond the barnyard been ploughed? Has C. received the plough I sent him; and how does it work?"

Dr. Jewett left Minnesota in 1858, but he retained and rented his farm, and lived again in that state in 1867 and 1868. The foregoing extracts cover that whole period. They show that the doctor was an enthusiast in agriculture and horticulture, and that his knowledge of both extended to the very minutiæ of the business. We can readily believe the statement before mentioned, that Dr. Jewett introduced the best varieties of grain, vegetables, and fruits raised in Minnesota. If that and the neighboring states lacked apple-seed, it was not the fault of the doctor.

Nor was his interest in the tilling of the soil confined to Minnesota. As already intimated, his entire correspondence abounds in testimony of his interest in this direction. Wherever he lived, he had a garden to cultivate, if nothing more; and neighbors declared that he would gather the largest quantity of productions from the smallest lot of land of any man in town.

From other correspondence, not relating to the Minnesota home, we make a few extracts.

"We had on our breakfast-table this morning ⌊St. John's⌋ some of the finest potatoes I ever tasted. On inquiry, I found they were called 'Black Kidneys.' All assure me that they were never equalled by anything in this province. I sallied out after breakfast, and found some in a provision store. I bought a peck; also a half peck each of two other kinds, the 'Copper,' and 'Our Own.' On the top are a half-dozen 'Calicoes,' and four of the 'Lawrence.'"

"If I can fish up a pint or a quart more seeds in my travels, I shall be very glad, and will send them through by mail. The grape-vines may be covered with earth any time. The grape cuttings need not be taken up this fall, but covered with the soil just where they are.

"Save the seeds of that great sunflower. The best way is to cut off its head when ripe, and hang it up to the roof, so that the mice cannot reach it."

"I came across a new variety of the squash here, the seeds of which I shall secure and bring home — the 'Canadian Marrow.' That is the shape,* and the color that of a rich cream. They say that when growing, and quite young and green, it makes the very best summer squash possible, while, when ripe, it is the richest squash for boiling or baking."

* Referring to his drawing of the squash.

" Tell Mr. H—— that he may have that entire lot for two years if he will fill it thoroughly with leaves; and when he wishes to take up the trees for transplanting, will leave a few, at proper distances, for standards. It would make a first-rate lot for nursery purposes, but needs to have the soil lightened up with vegetable decay."

" I am partly of the opinion that the earth filled well with a deep coating of leaves will be greatly improved for fruit-growing, as it will keep the ground light and open. Our soil consisting largely of silex or sand, and alumina, or the elements of clay, needs vegetable humus to render it jus right. I purposed to have a rack made, with rounds about four feet high, and a top round or rail on purpose to draw leaves. I would have the front end put to-gether permanently, and round across the bottom from side to side, so that it could be lifted off the wagon whole; but for convenience of unloading I would have the back end to take out."

His correspondence shows that friends in Maine, Massachusetts, Connecticut, and other parts of the country, frequently sent to him in Minnesota, scions, cuttings and seeds. Apple, plum, pear, cherry, currant, corn, potatoes, are among their generous contributions. One correspondent informs him of over a thousand scions forwarded in a box.

During the last twenty years, Dr. Jewett occasion-ally lectured upon agriculture. Had the Batavia Institute flourished, he would have cultivated a few acres of land belonging to the Institute for the pur-pose of giving practical lessons upon agriculture to the students. In his lectures upon agriculture, he gave a chemical analysis of different soils, and their adaptation to different crops and plants; also the chemical composition of plants, and their uses for the growth of animals; the food that should be given for growth alone, and that for fattening cattle.

He spent the winter of 1854 in New England, lecturing upon the agricultural resources of the West. He had maps of Minnesota, Illinois, and Iowa carefully prepared under his own eye, from which he showed the formation of the sides of many of the rivers into bluffs and table-lands. He took with him to the East, long narrow boxes containing large slices of the soil, obtained by digging down the whole depth of the loam, and cutting out pieces to fit the boxes, in which their shape was preserved. Some of these were over three feet long, rather ponderous to transport for lecturing purposes, but very practical in their use, as every man could see for himself the richness of the soil. Dr. Jewett's lectures were very popular, and his parallelograms of soil caused many a New England citizen to emigrate thither. A journal in Manchester, N. H., where he lectured before the Lyceum of the city, spoke as follows of his effort:

"Dr. Jewett is well known as one of the most entertaining and useful public lecturers in this country. The last fifteen or twenty years of his life have been devoted mainly to the temperance reformation in the New England states. He is now a farmer in Batavia, Illinois, and is also connected with some institution of learning in that section, as a lecturer upon physiology, chemistry, and agriculture, and has recently closed courses of lectures upon these subjects. His lecture before the Lyceum was upon the prairie country of the West, its natural formation into river bottoms, second bottoms, bluff and rolling prairies, and how it happened to have this formation; its geology, geography, climate, and natural resources in soil and minerals. Also the manners, customs, and conditions of the people, agricultural implements, and method of tilling the soil, and the variety and abundance of the harvests. The subject was illustrated by three large maps and one beautiful diagram; and these, in connection with the doctor's practical views and humorous anecdotes, and pleasing free and off-hand manner, rendered the evening's entertainment one of the most interesting and instructive with which our Lyceum has ever been favored. The audience listened an hour and fifty minutes, manifesting unusual interest and delight to the last."

At the close of one of his lectures upon the West, a gentleman in the audience arose, and inquired: "Would not such soil be excellent for the cultivation of tobacco?" That question was a little too much for the doctor. Straightening himself up, with lightning in his eye, he answered: "I presume it would; but I would see every acre of my quarter-section sunk so deep that a lake should occupy its place, before one acre of that splendid soil should, with my consent, be used to supply with a filthy, poisonous weed the depraved appetites of men, and to abet the nuisance of tobacco-smoke, cigar-stumps, and stale quids." That was emphatic.

We have no data from which to estimate the extent of Dr. Jewett's farming in Minnesota, except a single memorandum dated September, 1868, on which is the amount of wheat raised upon his own farm and that of his son :

"On my farm   .   .   505 bushels
On Charles's   .   .   764   "

Total, 1,269   "
Also 999 bushels of oats."

The doctor's experience in horticulture caused him to invent a way of making and printing convenient tags for fruit-trees, in 1866. It was done by the same kind of a machine that is used for stamping buttons. Strips of zinc, of the requisite length and width, for the name of the fruit were provided ; then the "die" was used the same as type, except that the "die" raised the letters on the one side and depressed the metal in on the other.

Dr. Jewett's pen was employed considerably, during his pioneer life, in producing articles for the press, respecting the resources of Minnesota and the whole West. No writer ever did more in the same time to induce emigration thither. He was so well known throughout our own country and the British Provinces, and public confidence in him was so implicit, that his representations were at once accepted. His writings, too, bore internal evidence of thorough acquaintance with the West, in its social, agricultural, political, scientific, moral, and religious capabilities. The following extract from an unpublished article found among his papers, will be read with interest :

"The prairies of Minnesota, which constitute more than half of its surface, are much more rolling than those of Illinois, and consequently better watered. The soil differs in one important particular from the soil of all the prairie states below, in containing a much larger portion of silex, or sand, which renders it more friable, increases its absorbent power, and brings forward vegetation more rapidly. The soil varies in depth from one to three feet, and is rich in all the elements of fertility. . . .

"The peculiar composition of our soil renders it quite unnecessary to stir in the spring ground ploughed the previous autumn. We can throw on the wheat, oats, or barley at once, and cover with the harrow; or if we aim at a crop of corn, we apply the marker, and proceed to plant at once; and by so doing we get a better crop than we do where the ground is ploughed in the spring. All the edible roots and vegetables grown in temperate climates, we can produce in Minnesota by simply scattering the seed on well decomposed soil, and covering with the harrow or rake. As there are few weeds the first two or three years, no labor with the hoe is required. When, however, weeds begin to show themselves among growing crops, great care must be taken to make their destruction complete, otherwise such crops of them will be produced as no eye in New England ever saw.

"The subsoil of our prairies is very peculiar. It is a gravelly loam; and a considerable part of the pebbles which constitute the gravelly portion are of limestone in a state of partial decomposition. The spade will cut through them as it would a lump of very soft chalk; and when thrown up and exposed to the influence of the elements, they crumble to a fine powder.

"I scarcely need to inform your readers that in a rich, new soil containing a good share of silex in its composition, and in a latitude as high as 44° north, we produce abundant crops of potatoes of excellent quality.

"We have the winter of Central Vermont and New Hampshire, and yet we have the summer of Philadelphia, proven, if it were doubted, by the fact that we ripen the southern corn which cannot be ripened in Massachusetts.

"Our progress in establishing the arts of civilization may be judged from two or three simple facts. Two years ago last May I visited Faribault, which then contained one framed and half a dozen log houses; now it has a population of more than *eighteen hundred*, with all the institutions of a New England village. Two years ago last winter, I, with the aid of other members of my family, were accustomed to grind, in a hand-mill, during the evening, the corn for next day's use. Now we have three fine flouring mills, with all the modern improvements, within three miles of my door, and they have been running all winter on wheat of our own production."

Dr. Jewett appeared to attach a kind of sacredness to the objects and products of nature. His manner of handling and speaking of them, accompanied by his intense enthusiasm over them, and his natural reverence for God who gave them, contributed to this end. His letters as well as his conversation denote this. A friend sends one of his epistles, from which we extract the following :

"I watch the miracle of growth in my garden daily with a pleasure which is quite apart from the thought of the increased money value of its products. What a miracle is growth! How the carbon, oxygen, hydrogen, and nitrogen are welded or wedded together in such various and beautiful forms no chemist this side of heaven can tell us. Shall we learn the unknown truths of this world *there?* Will the acquisition of knowledge, coveted and unattainable here, constitute a part of the employments and enjoyments of the better country? "

If any man in the world ever tilled the soil under the full, deep conviction that he was at work on " God's plantation," that man was Dr. Jewett. Probably his admiration of nature contributed largely to this disposition of his to treat the soil and its products sacredly, as many of his personal friends have noticed. We have seen him make a dinner of apples, all the while discoursing upon the delicious qualities of the fruit, the " miracle " of its production, and the goodness of the Great Giver. We have many times seen him come in with an apple or a pear in his hand that he had purchased on the street — a rare variety that he had not raised — and tell of its excellences; then carefully wrap it in paper and lay it in his carpet-bag, to exhibit to other friends, as if there attached to its growth or quality some remarkable natural phenomenon that God's children ought to see and respect.

On his deathbed, this characteristic of the man was no less conspicuous. When the expressed juice of the orange was given to him, he beautifully christened it " golden drink! " " blessed juice! "

The second year of his residence in Faribault there was a demand for a hotel, and his son Richard, though not a professional carpenter, and only twenty years old, was employed to frame it. Dr. Jewett rather objected to putting so much responsibility upon an inexperienced youth, but was silenced by the reply, " He is equal to it, for he possesses the ingenuity of his father."

While he lived in Minnesota he was unexpectedly called to perform a surgical operation, and the circumstances furnish further proof of his wonderful tact and efficiency in any and every position. A neighbor accidentally discharged the contents of a heavily-loaded musket into his own leg. The limb was so mutilated that amputation or death was inevitable. There was no surgeon within two or three hundred miles, and the unfortunate man was too poor to employ one if there had been. Dr. Jewett, too, had sold his surgical instruments ten or fifteen years before. What could be done? Dr. Jewett resolved to amputate the limb, for he could do it without money and without price.

He took his razor out of its handle and put it into a handle made for the purpose; then he sharpened a fine carpenter's saw as well as he could; and with these pioneer instruments he amputated the limb. With pure spring water to bathe it, and a generous, suitable diet, the patient prospered finely, and not many weeks elapsed before he was well again, minus one leg.

The doctor maintained his interest in the anti-slavery and temperance causes, and frequently spoke upon the latter subject in his own and other towns. His old friends in New England, among whom were Hon. Neal Dow, Rev. John Pierpont, and Lucius M. Sargent, kept him well posted upon temperance movements in the East, while his new friends in the West did not allow his talents to rust for want of opportunities to speak.

He lectured too, as we have seen in a previous chapter, upon Shakespeare and Burns, to the no small delight of the people of Faribault, who verily believed that the cities of the East could not furnish a better public reader than they could boast in their townsman, Dr. Jewett. We find a letter from a medical gentleman in Maine, who lived in Faribault at the time of which we speak, and he says to the doctor :

"Reading a paper called *The National Temperance Advocate* (1870), I saw the name of Dr. Charles Jewett connected with it. Is this the Dr. Jewett I have heard lecture on temperance in the city of Boston so many times? Is it the Dr. Jewett who lived in Minnesota in 1856, and who recited the Scotch poetry in the village of Faribault? If so, you are indeed a veteran, and the right man in the right place."

The last year of the doctor's pioneer life he represented Faribault in the legislature of the state. No particular issue was before the people except the general reformatory questions ; and the doctor was a marked man to represent these, so that public attention was directed to him as the best exponent of progressive ideas. The political campaign was a close one, and Dr. Jewett was elected by only about twenty majority. The result of the election was not known on the morning it was necessary for the representative-elect to start for St. Paul, the capital. To go into the village to take the stage, and learn that his opponent was elected instead of himself, would be too much of a joke for even a noted joker. So, putting his trunk into his wagon, the doctor drove near to the village, and sent a messenger forward to learn the facts. The messenger learned that the doctor was elected, and returned to conduct him into the village.

It was while Dr. Jewett was in Minnesota that the friends of temperance in England made a special effort to secure his labors in that country. Hon. Neal Dow, who spent several months in great Britain, was delegated to induce the doctor, if possible, to visit Great Britain, and we find a letter from that gentleman, strongly urging him to accede to their request. But Dr. Jewett never visited the mother-country. It could not have been because of poverty, since good pay for his services awaited him there. We think the chief reason was, that it was too far from home — that HOME of which we shall hear more particularly in future pages. If he was at all ambitious to spread his fame in that distant land, that ambition was brought into complete subjection to his love of home and family. His friends at home deeply regret that their friends abroad had no opportunity to see his pleasant face and hear his voice.

An extract from a letter by D. W. Humphrey, Esq., of Faribault, will close what we have to say of Dr. Jewett's pioneer life:

" We often recount to our children and to each other little reminiscences of our early days here and our visits

to Jewett Valley, and our frequent intercourse with Dr.
Jewett and family. We have many things to remind us
of those early days. Among others, we have still some
of the plum-trees which we got from Dr. Jewett over
twenty years ago, he having selected the seed from wild
plums in the woods ; and our currant-bushes are all from
the Jewett farm, and from slips the doctor brought from
Wisconsin or Illinois. The many pleasant visits between
here and the farm are so many pleasant memories. Mrs.
Humphrey used to say, when we were about to go to Dr.
Jewett's, ' Now let us get all our work done, for we can't
get away before night when we once get there.'

" There was a fascination in his conversation that always kept us in spite of any resolves to come away
early. And when he came here his hurry was usually
forgotten. If once he commenced to quote poetry, Shakespeare, and Burns, and Burleigh, and sometimes his own,
would flow in a constant stream and in such a manner as
to keep our rapt attention. He was by all odds the best
reader and reciter I ever heard, and I have heard plenty
of professed readers and elocutionists. One did not think
of Dr. Jewett, but saw and felt and believed all he recited.

" I recollect once, some thirty years ago, he came into
an office in Westfield when I happened to be alone. I
had known him some years then. As he turned to go
out, something brought up Shakespeare, and he recited
from memory Hotspur's apology to the king for his denying his prisoners to him, when, all smarting with his
wounds, the popinjay with pouncet-box comes to him and
discourses about spermaceti for bruises, and how, only for
these vile guns, he himself would have been a soldier,
&c. It was really wonderful. I was his only hearer ;
but I doubt, had the audience been thousands, if he could

have rendered it better. I never heard that recitation equalled.

"One winter's day, perhaps twenty years or so ago, he drove up to our door here (we were on the bare, unfenced prairie then) and said: 'I was going home by way of the lake, where I have a grist; and as it would make me late home should I be delayed there, I thought I would just call and give my horse a few oats; and, sister (he always called Mrs. Humphrey sister), if you will let me have just a bowl of bread and milk, I'll soon be off.'

"After eating his lunch, he said: 'Now I will lie down on this lounge just twenty minutes for a little nap. Remember to wake me in twenty minutes.' With that happy faculty for sleeping when he made up his mind to, he was asleep seemingly as soon as he lay down. It seemed a pity to disturb him, and we let him sleep about an hour and a half. As he awoke and sat up, he made some apt quotation of poetry, and one thing led to another, and for over an hour he talked and gave extracts from various authors, in his very best vein, and made that afternoon one of our pleasant memories. His hurry was forgotten, and not till the sun was just dropping into the prairie did he leave, and then concluded he would let the grist go till to-morrow, and make the best of his way home."

The friends of temperance in Massachusetts greatly needed Dr. Jewett's labors, and they did not allow him to rest longer. In 1858, the Massachusetts Temperance Alliance applied for his services, and repeated the application with emphatic appeals, before the doctor consented. At last, however, he gave an affirmative answer, arranged with his son to run his farm, and returned to his old battle-ground.

XV.

DR. JEWETT IN THE REBELLION.

ON his return to Massachusetts, Dr. Jewett settled in Malden, after a few months' residence among his old neighbors in Millbury. He entered at once upon his temperance work, receiving as hearty a welcome as was ever tendered to a great and good man. Public attention was so thoroughly engrossed by the outrages perpetrated, in different parts of the country, by pro-slavery enthusiasts, that the cause of temperance was pushed aside. The threatening attitude of the South towards the national government, also, was awakening solicitude throughout the North, making temperance labor more difficult and discouraging.

The old plan of membership, by the payment of one dollar or more annually, was adopted by the Alliance, and several agents were put into the field. A monthly organ of the society was published under the direction of Dr. Jewett, and the " new departure " was inaugurated as successfully as the most sanguine could expect in such times. As formerly, the doctor responded to the demands for labor wherever required, from Cape Cod to Berkshire.

The war-cloud gathered, however. It appeared no larger than a man's hand at first, but it rose and spread rapidly, darkening the political horizon, and causing unparalleled anxiety and alarm. The people of the North lost their interest in social reforms, and even in business, and widespread depression followed the manifest consternation. Civil war was dreaded as the direst calamity, and yet it was inevitable. The little cloud had enveloped the whole heavens, and the thunder of hostility was muttering from afar.

In these circumstances, the temperance movement was embarrassed, and the hearts of its stanchest advocates failed them. It was quite impossible for the best friend of the cause to maintain a deep interest in it, when his loyal heart was bearing about such a burden for the imperilled country as it never carried before. The work was crippled; agents were listened to with indifferent attention, and the society was compelled to abandon its noble plans, and wait for more propitious times. Dr. Jewett resigned his position.

The doctor had returned to Massachusetts with quite a debt upon him for the purchase and stocking of his Minnesota claim and those of his two sons. It proved far more expensive to stock those Western farms, and to erect dwellings upon them, than he had anticipated; and for the money he borrowed a high rate of interest was demanded, so that a heavy burden was upon him. Add to this, long and protracted sickness in his family, and the reader will not wonder that it was rather a gloomy period for the doctor when the outbreak of the rebellion forced him from his position. However, he was not long in deciding What next? With the clearness of a prophet, he saw that a long conflict was before the country, and that it would greatly embarrass, if not entirely hinder, the work of reform in which he was engaged. Casting about for a solution of the difficult problem, he concluded to return to the West, where the temperance work could not be more hindered than in the East, while he would be nearer to his farm, if compelled to withdraw wholly from temperance labor, and return to agriculture.

He removed to Wisconsin, May 1, 1861 (his oldest son, who was a clerk in Boston, remaining), to labor for the Wisconsin Temperance Society. He selected Menasha for his residence, because, in addition to tolerable school facilities, two of his sons could work in a pail-factory in that thriving village. More sagacious and wise than many others, he prepared for the worst.

As his temperance labor was fragmentary during the war, it will occupy but a small place in this chapter. The chief interest of himself and family was in the overthrow of the rebellion, to which they contributed more largely, as will be seen, than most families of the country.

Dr. Jewett was always a vigorous foe to slavery. His heart was with the early anti-slavery workers, though his labors were limited to the cause of temperance. All the anti-slavery champions of that early day were temperance men and women, though those engaged in temperance were not all anti-slavery advocates. From the time he began public life, he made himself known as a foe to slavery. Aided by his wife, he circulated petitions to Congress for the abolition of slavery in the District of Columbia, and for other objects. On his professional routes he distributed tracts upon the sin and curse of slavery, and by conversation converted many persons to his anti-slavery, as he did to his temperance, views. From the time that the matter became a subject for ballots he voted against slavery. He believed that no Christian man should cast a ballot that "he would not gladly open to the eye of the Master before carrying it to the polls;" and a ballot that meant "traffic in human beings" he would not dare to show to Him.

The passage of the Fugitive Slave Law wrought upon him powerfully, as it did upon other true Christian men. He stamped it under his feet, and blushed for his country's shame. The rendition of slaves under that law outraged his humane feelings. Five hundred such men as he in Boston, on fire with opposition to the wicked business, would have prevented the rendition of Burns, in spite of government bayonets, or left the sacrifice of devoted lives upon the altar of liberty. He became at once a volunteer station-agent on the "underground railroad," and his house at Millbury was known to fleeing fugitives as a safe rendezvous. He fitted up a place under a stairway in his dwelling, where footsore travellers, with "skins not colored like his own," might be secreted. Here they were fed, comforted, and instructed about the journey towards the north star. He kept an anti-slavery horse, too (the faithful beast that he took with him afterwards to Illinois and Minnesota), and with her he carried these dusky children of the South over to Worcester, to take an early train for their Canadian Canaan. He enjoyed that blessed service full as much as he did addressing the Hampden County rumsellers after he got them into jail.

His children remember one female fugitive slave, who came to their home very much exhausted by her hurried journey. Her feet were bare, blistered, and bleeding, and her nervous system completely prostrated by fear and over-exertion. A noise in an adjoining room or in the street would cause her to start as if she thought the slave-hunter was at hand. In her sleep at night she uttered startling screams, dreaming that her pursuers had seized her and were taking her back to bondage.

Southern "barbarism" in Congress, the outrages of "border ruffians" in Kansas, the multiplied wrongs of slavery in the South, the truckling schemes of some Northern politicians, and kindred evils, added to the horrors of the Fugitive Slave Law, called forth Dr. Jewett's bitterest invective against the traffic in human beings. Friends recall, too, with what evident pain and disgust his heart turned away from these things as he recited, in his inimitable way, from Cowper's graphic pen:

"Oh, for a lodge in some vast wilderness,
Some boundless contiguity of shade,
Where rumor of oppression and deceit,
Of unsuccessful or successful war,
Might never reach me more! My ear is pained,
My soul is sick, with every day's report
Of wrong and outrage with which earth is filled.
There is no flesh in man's obdurate heart;
It does not feel for man; the natural bond
Of brotherhood is severed as the flax
That falls asunder at the touch of fire.
He finds his fellow guilty of a skin
Not colored like his own; and, having power
To enforce the wrong, for such a worthy cause
Dooms and devotes him as his lawful prey.
Lands intersected by a narrow frith
Abhor each other. Mountains interposed
Make enemies of nations, who had else
Like kindred drops been mingled into one.
Thus man devotes his brother, and destroys;
And worse than all, and most to be deplored,
As human nature's broadest, foulest blot,
Chains him, and tasks him, and exacts his sweat
With stripes, that Mercy, with a bleeding heart,
Weeps when she sees inflicted on a beast."

No patriot in the land was more thoroughly aroused by the first gun fired upon Fort Sumter than Dr. Jewett. He was prepared for any sacrifice, as the sequel will prove, to save his country and abolish slavery. "God is above all," he wrote, "and out of this He will bring about His purposes of mercy, I doubt not, to an oppressed race."

Soon after the doctor removed to Wisconsin, he received a letter from his old friend John B. Gough, containing a draft for *five hundred dollars*. "We had scarcely had time," said the doctor, "to wipe a few stray tears, before the reception of another letter was announced, containing a draft for *five hundred dollars* more, from L. M. Sargent, author of 'Temperance Tales.'" This unexpected and timely aid was a great relief to Dr. Jewett. It was proof, also, of the esteem and confidence of tried friends.

From the outbreak of the war, his son John desired to enlist. He was far from being robust, having a physical tendency to pulmonary complaints; and his father thought it was presumptuous for one so frail to undertake the duties of soldier-life. But in Wisconsin his health improved; and after the lapse of a few months, he put in a new and more earnest plea. On the Sabbath evening that he united with the church, he was sitting on the piazza with his mother enjoying the view of Fox River and Winnebago Lake. The evening was very beautiful, and the scene impressive.

"Mother," said John, "have you any objection to my going into the army?"

The question was unexpected, and for a moment his mother's feelings were indescribable. At length she answered:

"John, you are a child of God. Your Heavenly Father loves you better than your father and mother, and if you think it your duty to go, I have nothing to say, only to commit you to his care."

She added words about his health, hardships and exposures of army life; to which he replied by saying: "I have tested my endurance lately by exposures. I have purposely been wet all day when fishing. I have been out in all sorts of weather, and I am better now than ever. I can go better than Charles or Richard; for Charles has a family, and Richard has a good situation in Boston. I have no excuse for staying at home; and I feel mean and dissatisfied with myself to remain at home when so ·many go who have more reason to stay at home. I think it is my duty to go."

Dr. Jewett was laboring in Iowa at the time, and only three or four days remained in which John must decide, if he would join the Tenth Wisconsin Regiment, with several of his companions. He telegraphed to his father for permission to go. His father, after telling him of the special risk on account of the condition of his lungs, closed his reply with these trustful words: "But decide for yourself."

He enlisted, and joined the Tenth Wisconsin Regiment, November 25, 1861.* A few months after, Richard enlisted in Boston, and joined the Sixth Massachusetts Regiment, from which he was transferred for meritorious conduct to the position of first

---

* John was passionately fond of a gun, and was an expert marksman. In Minnesota he used a rifle with which to shoot gophers (a little ground-squirrel), taking off their heads nearly every time. The gopher would run to his hole, stop at the entrance, and stand up on his hind legs to look at his pursuer, and just in that nick of time John would cut off his head with a bullet. One morning, when the family were at breakfast, one of the younger children came running in, saying, "A big hawk is sailing by!" John caught his rifle and ran out, and before his father rose from the table the dead hawk lay at his feet.

lieutenant in the lamented Colonel Shaw's colored regiment — the Fifty-fourth Massachusetts. It was gratifying to both Richard and his father, that he should become an officer in the first colored regiment raised for the war.

Dr. Jewett's eldest son, Charles, in Minnesota, was one of the first to offer himself when the First Minnesota Regiment was raised. So many young men, without families or farms, offered themselves, however, that the authorities advised the fathers of families, especially those who were running farms, to wait until their services were absolutely required. So Charles did not become a member of that regiment; but subsequently he did become a member of Colonel Sibley's regiment, and went to fight the Sioux Indians. At the close of that campaign he returned to his farm, all the while uneasy that he was not a soldier of the loyal army. He resolved to hold himself in readiness to take the place of one of his brothers, if either should fall in battle. And he did, as we shall see.

After having lived about a year in Menasha, the doctor was invited to labor for the State Temperance Society of Illinois, with headquarters at Chicago. He had accepted and removed thither when Richard enlisted at Boston. He became so thoroughly absorbed in the issues of the war, and the duty of patriotic citizens to support the government, that he almost decided to offer his own services as surgeon. He wrote to his wife, who was then in Chicago:

" Neal Dow, I see by the papers, is authorized by the War Department to raise a regiment in Maine for the war. Had I best offer myself for a place in the medical department? Write immediately. This will reach you to-morrow morning, and may be you can get your reply into the one o'clock mail."

He would not decide without the consent of his wife; but he was in great haste to obtain that, so that his application might be on its way. But Dr. Hollister and other physicians interfered, saying it would be presumptuous for a man of his years, and with his heart troubles, to go into the service. Still, his heart was there all the while.

Next to going into the army to care for the sick and wounded soldiers, subsequently he showed his interest in them by writing and publishing "The Wounded Soldier's Friend," the object of which was to show this class how to assist themselves in the absence of a surgeon, or when first wounded, and alleviate their own sufferings. The little tract of sixteen pages contained advice relating to all the usual casualties of war, illustrated by cuts, so as to make the counsel more intelligible. It was one of the most valuable pocket companions that was given to soldiers during the struggle. The style in which it was written was suited to engage their attention and confidence. He naively introduced his little treatise thus :

" Your principal business on the field is, of course, to make wounds, to multiply them among the enemies of your country. Keep cool, therefore, in action, and send

your leaden despatches with as much care as though the
issue of the battle depended upon you alone. If wounded
in battle, make it a matter of patriotic principle, never to
withdraw a fellow-soldier from the lines for one moment
to aid you, if by any possibility you can help yourself; for
in taking even one man from the ranks, you weaken our
force just so much, and increase your own risk of falling
into the hands of the enemy, weak and wounded, a prisoner of war."

His letters to his wife and family are full of the
war — more war than temperance in them. No matter what subject he was writing about, the rebellion
was sure to be mentioned before he had proceeded
far. A few extracts from his letters will show his
animus from the time Fort Sumter was assaulted.

"We fear that the garrison of Sumter will be forced
to surrender, and then there will be a howl of delight all
through the region of traitors. God reigns, however, and
it will be for the best in the end. Our last news was that
the flag of Sumter was half-mast, as a sign of distress to
the fleet outside ; and it was thought that the fort was on
fire within. We shall wait the issue with impatience."

"I presume that John has gone. He is in the hands of
God, though God does not often work miracles to save us
from the result of our decisions, if they be unwise. John
is a good fellow, but restless and full of the spirit of ad-
venture. He will make a good soldier. He will die
sober, if he dies. I fear for his health, for reasons stated
in my letter. . . . The Lord be with you and the family.
I am glad that John united with the church before he
went, and I hope he, as well as the others who have

taken upon themselves the vows of the Christian, will walk worthy of their profession."

"It helps digestion to see things working so well just now in connection with the war movements. They will have some hard fighting in Kentucky soon. Will our John be where the bullets are whistling? Pray, dear wife, — God will hear you always with favor, I think, — pray. I will pray, too. Tell the children to remember John in prayer now especially."

"The roar of cannon and the peal of bells are now heard throughout the West over the fall of Fort Donaldson. How many homes have been desolated by that sanguinary struggle! But there was no help for it. It was the key to the very centre of secession. The Tennessee and Cumberland rivers open to the head of navigation and traversed daily by our gunboats, almost impregnable to any shot they could send from any temporary battery on shore, and the condition of Secessia will be very uncomfortable. Our boys missed the chance of a fight at Bowling Green, as Secessia took to its heels. . . . If I knew there was a real need of surgical aid at Cairo, I would jump into the cars and go down as soon as through my present appointments."

"Oh, how I wish this dreadful war was over and our dear sons safe at home! How uncertain is all the future!"

"It is a great grief to me that I must bid you prepare for the worst so far as our son John may be concerned. You must look over the list of the killed and wounded, when it comes, with a mother's hopes, but also with a mother's fears. The last battle, at Murfreesboro', was terrible beyond compare. God grant that our dear boy may not be among the buried ones. Time will reveal. Mean-

21

while, be strong of heart and prepare for the worst. Pray ! "

" There are in Buel's division at Nashville seventy thousand troops. Mitchell is general of that division which John is in. Look out for Buel's division, or Mitchell's portion of it. The troops are as yet tolerably healthy. May they continue to be! We shall have stirring news from that quarter soon. God grant that it may not be to us heart-rending."

" Secesh has to move rapidly down the Mississippi with our Foote at his rear."

From a letter to John we extract the following:

" I see by the papers that a forward movement is soon expected of the force with which you are connected, and I will steal a moment from pressing duties to let you know that you are the object still of strong parental love and of daily prayer; and that we are in constant anxiety lest some of those casualties incident to war may fall to your lot, though we hope not.

" Take good care of your health as far as possible. You will stand a great deal better chance to have health than those who have no control over their appetite. In hot weather we need less food than in cold. Lean meats and bread, with fruits, milk, and eggs, when you can get them, will always be good. Keep as much as you can out of the damp evening air. Keep the skin clean, drink the best water you can get, and trust in God. Should God in his mercy allow you to return to us safe and sound, we will rejoice together and thank Him for it, and try to show our thankfulness by the obedience of our lives. Try to exert a good and saving influence on those around you who may not have been so highly favored with Christian parents, brothers and sisters, as you have been. . . . God protect and guide you, my son, and return you to your friends laden with rich experience of his mercy."

"I hope the war will soon come to an end. Things are looking like it now, though I think we shall have one terrible battle with Lee's army when Sherman moves up so as to co-operate with Grant. Grant will try to avoid it by closing communications to Richmond, and seeking thus to bring Lee to surrender without a fight. If Lee evacuates Richmond, moves further south, Grant will follow him and Sherman will be on his skirts. Sheridan will come down from the Valley and join the chase, while Thomas will come in from the West. Whether our dear boys will have to share the perils of other battles before the war ends, we cannot know."

These extracts show that Dr. Jewett kept posted thoroughly upon the movements of the army, exhibiting considerable knowledge of military tactics. There is before us one letter, however, penned at Chicago, at the time Massachusetts soldiers were fired upon in the streets of Baltimore, which shows that the doctor comprehended the situation like a general who was commissioned for the war. A liberal extract will show its animus :

"The city is in a blaze of excitement in consequence of the news from the collision in Baltimore. Illinois will soon have her full quota in the field. The earnest work will be on the line of the Border States. Both armies are working towards that line. The Gulf States would rather have the battle on the Border States than on territory where the black population doubles the white. The shock will be terrible, and thousands will bite the dust;

but I can see that the hand of God is in the whole matter. It was fortunate that the rebels struck the first blow, and that the old flag was struck by rebels. It has stirred the patriotic pride of thousands, as it would not have been stirred had Sumter been successfully defended. Then it is well because it brings the struggle at once in reference to the capital, the defence of which is more difficult and yet more important than any other single point. It needs now only an attempt of the rebels to seize the capital, — one conflict there, to thoroughly arouse the whole North and call forth all its energies. If it be successfully defended, the result will be glorious, and will strike a hard blow on treason all over the country. If *they* are successful for the time in getting possession of it, they will be driven from the ground if it cost fifty thousand lives, and will be followed by a war in which the watchword will be, Liberty to the captive through the entire South, and death to Slavery on this continent. Thousands who are now enlisting under the excitement of the hour have no sympathy for the slave; and yet, in the wonderful providence of God, they are going to fight for him and his liberation from bondage. Thousands, who have been all their lives execrating the negro whenever he was named in their hearing, are now going to risk their lives in a conflict where the principle contended for is at the bottom of slavery or freedom. Three fourths who are going South by present enlistment from the West, who did not, before the struggle opened, belong to some military company, are of that stamp. How wonderful are God's ways!"

The doctor wrote the foregoing letter when he was on a flying visit to the West, to make preparations for the removal of his family thither. While he was in Chicago, he was invited to address a Triennial Convention of Ministers, upon the "state of the country." Other speakers were to participate, among them the celebrated Dr. Post, of St. Louis. Dr. Jewett's address was the favorite one of the evening to the large assembly. In pathos, logic, eloquence, and power, the doctor never surpassed that effort, perhaps. He was called to address soldiers there, also, as one remarkably adapted to such work. Often thereafter, during the war, he was called upon here and there, to address soldiers marshalling for the war.

But to return to Dr. Jewett's engagement in Illinois. The friends of temperance purposed to employ him three years, expecting to raise the money for his support in five-dollar subscriptions. But the war continued longer, and made heavier drafts of men and money than was anticipated, at the same time absorbing public interest to such a degree as to greatly embarrass the temperance cause. And yet Dr. Jewett continued his work two years in Illinois. No other lecturer could have commanded the attention of the public at all during that period of unprecedented excitement. His great ability and universal popularity secured a hearing for him when other men would have been ignored.

In Chicago his children enjoyed excellent school advantages. Three of them were connected with the High School, where they took three of the five prizes offered. A cit'zen remarked that " if there had been five Jewett children in the school, all the prizes would have been taken by them."

At times, during Dr. Jewett's philanthropic life-work, it seemed as if Providence directly guided him to certain apparently lost men, to save them. There was such a case in Chicago. A teamster, by the name of Davis, was a notorious drunkard. Nobody expected or thought that he could be reformed. Dr. Jewett's attention was directed to him, and he studied his case. He became acquainted and talked with him. He was sure that man could be saved. He resolved in his own heart that he should be. He befriended him, took him to his house, instructed him, offered him a home, and finally won his confidence. The teamster occupied a poor tenement in the suburbs of the city, and in his yard were currants. He told the doctor that he might have the currants if he would send his boys to pick them. Afterwards, when the boys went to his house on an errand, they found Davis hanging to a rope. The sequel proved that he had been on a spree, was so ugly that his wife left the house with her children, in great fear; and finally, becoming sober, he had attempted suicide by hanging himself. The rope proved to be too long, so that he was not dead, though he was insensible. The boys gave the alarm, Davis was cut down and restored to life. Dr. Jewett lost no time in going to him, took him to his house, induced him to sign the pledge, and held to him until he became a Christian. The doctor had the satisfaction of seeing his family reunited, all happy beyond expression, and all bowing around the altar of prayer.

In one thriving town a committee waited upon him for further labor, and of one of them he wrote to Mrs. Jewett thus :

" One of the men most deeply interested in my coming here was clerk for John F. Pond, of Providence, R. I., with whom I had so many encounters years ago. How strangely things come round. Twenty-five years have passed, and the man who was then the severest of my bitter opponents, is now paying his money to reward me for teaching the same doctrines that I then taught."

During the last year of the doctor's stay in Chicago, his youngest daughter had a severe and dangerous illness. His eldest daughter was in the East, and his son Frank was fitting for college in Philadelphia. It seemed absolutely necessary that he should devote his attention wholly to his suffering daughter, who, he feared, was having her last sickness. He countermanded all his engagements, and became at once the sole nurse and physician in that sick-room. Week after week he devoted himself to her with unremitting and loving care, and finally had the inexpressible joy of seeing her convalescent. Then, still sitting by her bedside, watching with tender solicitude, with pen in hand, he prepared that pamphlet, " *The Temperance Cause, Past, Present, and Future ; or, Why we are Where we are ;* " in which he presented, in a clear and able manner, his plea for a financial basis for the temperance reform.   The document has had a wide circulation throughout the Northern states.

When Richard was transferred to Colonel Shaw's colored regiment, he made a flying visit to Chicago, where he met his affianced at his father's, and was married.   His wife remained with the family until the close of the war.   The family of Charles also came from Minnesota, where he had enlisted, and continued with Dr. Jewett's family until their reunion in Minnesota, at the close of hostilities.   The doctor believed that his soldier-sons would feel more at ease if their families constituted a part of his own household.   And no man could have enjoyed the arrangement more thoroughly than Dr. Jewett did.

The press of Illinois paid noble tribute to Dr. Jewett's temperance labors in that state.   The clergy of the commonwealth placed him at the head of the list of temperance advocates.   At the close of his first year's service, the Christian Association of Chicago sent out a circular to the clergy and leading temperance men, and we doubt if ever there was so unqualified admiration of a temperance advocate expressed on paper.   We have many of the responses, and the following is a fair sample of them all:

"I have consulted with several of the friends of temperance, and all agree with me in the opinion that Dr. Jewett is the best temperance lecturer who has ever visited our place.   The good he accomplished by his visit cannot be estimated by dollars and cents, and I should esteem it an irreparable loss to the cause in our state were his labors to cease, and most sincerely hope that arrangements will be made to continue him in the field."

To return to the doctor in the rebellion. What sort of material did he furnish for the defence of his country in his sons? We should be most happy to quote entire letters of theirs from the manuscripts before us, to show the intelligence, patriotism, affection, manly bearing, and religious principle that pervades them. But a single brief extract from the letters of each is all the space that can be given to them.

John wrote:

"I read a chapter in my Bible every day. Here in camp one has to watch and pray, for there are temptations on every side. Nothing but prayer and watchfulness can keep the Christian. Several of the boys in our tent, some of them Good Templars too, drank wine on the first night of our march. I am persuaded that a man may join all the temperance societies in the world, and if he has no principle, he will drink. . . . I knew that my first battle was at hand, and I cannot express my feelings at that moment. I silently prayed that the Lord would shield and protect me, and I never before experienced so fully the joy of reliance on Divine Power. I became utterly unconscious in respect to what might befall me, and yet I was aware of all the dangers we should encounter. I was prepared to fight, and my musket felt lighter."

Richard wrote:

" There is little but self-interest and self-comfort among a majority of soldiers. They only see the present hour, and never ask what would be their condition if the re-

bellion is not crushed out completely. I hope and pray
that the Lord will not much longer leave this work of
emancipation to politicians, but will take into his own
hands the righting of the wrongs of the oppressed ones.
It may be that our government will go down in the strife;
but I have the confident belief that such will not be the
case. It is a glorious privilege to have the Christian's
hope and promise that ' all things shall work together
for good to them that love God!' I find that as faith in
men and human governments is shaken, it but drives me
to the Throne that is eternal.

" When I think of the sons you have in the army, I feel
that you must have especial calls upon your attention;
but I do not suppose that you expect one of them to be
cowardly, or to prefer his own good to that of the country. . . . I know that you will pray for me, that I may
be kept from the temptations of camp-life, and be enabled
to do my duty as a soldier in both armies — that of the
country and that of the Lord."

Charles wrote:

"I am very thankful to God for all his mercies to us
as a family. I am much obliged to mother for her letters
and good wishes, and am comforted and strengthened in
knowing that many prayers daily ascend for my protection
and safety. I trust that the Lord will permit us to meet
an unbroken family, after I have fulfilled all his will in
the service of my country."

It was such material as this that made our loyal
army, with all its faults, the grandest army of the
world. But for this leaven of personal piety, the
temptations and vices of the camp and field must
have jeopardized our cause and dishonored our flag

far more than they did. It was a source of pride
and satisfaction to Dr. Jewett, as long as he lived,
that his name was so honorably identified with the
late struggle for national existence through three so
noble sons.

John was killed in the battle of Chickamauga, on
the 19th of September, 1863. A Menasha companion was near him when he was wounded. A bullet
penetrated his lungs when he was lying on his face
firing at the foe. Putting his hand up to his mouth,
and finding blood flowing therefrom, he remarked,
" I am mortally wounded. Send my things to mother." (By arrangement with his mother, before leaving home, each read the same chapter in the Bible
daily.) Then he crawled away into a wooded place,
turned himself upon his back, clasped his hands
across his breast, and passed to his eternal reward.

Said a member of the company :

" Well, John Jewett was the best fellow in the whole
company. I don't believe there was a day, during the
whole time he was in the army, that he did not read his
Bible and pray. We could never persuade him to join us
in any of our scrapes, nor to drink a drop, nor even so
much as to smoke or chew."

At the time of his death he was a non-commis-
sioned officer in his regiment, but had been commissioned a second lieutenant in the Fifty-fourth Massachusetts (colored), in which his brother Richard
was an officer. The commission was on its way to
him when he fell, but did not reach him until the

All-wise Master had transferred him to "the general assembly and church of the First-born in heaven."

Among Dr. Jewett's papers has been found a poem that he wrote upon John's death. It is entitled "The Christian Soldier's Death." On the back of the slip is written, in his own handwriting, the following paragraph, forwarded to him by one of John's comrades: "He looked as if some one had laid him out, — his eyes closed, and his hands clasped upon his breast. There was no expression of pain upon the countenance. He looked like one who lay asleep." The first and last verses of the poem are as follows:

> " The fatal ball had pierced his breast;
>   His life was ebbing fast;
>   One more grim foe to meet! and then
>   Life's conflict will be past.
>
> .   .   .   .   .
>
> " No sign of pain those features show;
>   Hands folded on his breast;
>   By FAITH he slew his last dread foe,
>   And won a peaceful rest."

Richard was wounded twice. First, in the assault upon Fort Wagner a ball struck his sword when it was raised in the excitement of battle, the force of the ball bending the sword so that it was useless thereafter, at the same time driving it against his head with such violence as to inflict quite a severe wound. But for the intervention of the sword the ball must have passed through his head, and killed him instantly. Second, he was seriously wounded in the battle of Olustee, Florida. He was captain of Company E, and was leading on his men in one of the most sanguinary conflicts of the war, when a ball struck the lower jaw on the left side, passed along under his ear, and was extracted from the neck. Although this was a serious wound, Captain Jewett was back again to his post within a few weeks. In these and other battles other rebel bullets flew very near him. At one time he sent to his young wife his blouse with a bullet-hole over the left shoulder, his cap with two holes through it, one of the missiles grazing his scalp; also a fragment of one of General Beauregard's shells, that exploded near him, to be made into a card-basket for his centre-table.

A correspondent of the New York Tribune, who was at the battle of Olustee, wrote :

" The Fifty-fourth Massachusetts, which, with the First North Carolina, may be truly said to *have saved the forces from utter rout*, lost about eighty men wounded and twelve killed. The only officers hurt were Captain Jewett, Company E, wounded in neck; First Lieutenant Henry W. Littlefield, Company H, wounded in right hand ; and First Lieutenant E. G. Tomlinson, Company C, wounded in foot."

Richard entered the service an entire stranger; was selected by Colonel Shaw for his fitness to take a command in his regiment; was promoted to a captaincy; for many months was on staff duty, most of the time acting assistant adjutant-general; then ordnance officer for the division.

As soon as Charles learned of John's death, he
made preparations to leave for the war. Knowing that he stood in readiness to take his brother's
place, the War Department offered him the commission that was sent to John. He accepted it and went
immediately to General Casey's Military School in
Philadelphia to qualify himself for the position. He
passed examination and reached his regiment just in
season to take his wounded brother Richard to the
North. His record in the army was worthy of his
parentage. He was never wounded; but he came
out of the army at the close of the war, physically
disabled to cultivate his farm in Minnesota, or even
to live in that climate, and at great sacrifice was
compelled to seek a warmer locality in the South.

There was a time when Dr. Jewett had great
anxiety for a class of very useful public men in Illinois. He was satisfied that armed disloyal men,
secretly moving about among the people, would not
scruple to assassinate them. The efficient war governor of Illinois, Richard Yates, was one of them.
From a letter of Governor Yates to Dr. Jewett, we
learn that the latter, in his anxiety, had written to
him on the subject. The governor's reply shows
that Dr. Jewett comprehended the situation exactly :

"Your letter concerning danger to be apprehended from
disloyal men who are armed, &c., &c., is received. I have
been fully advised for many months of the truth of which
you speak, and have made every effort in my power to
prepare the government for emergencies, but so far have
not succeeded.

" We have no sufficient militia law, and no arms. The arms which I received for state defence have been transferred to the one hundred days' regiments. When they return, the state will be in condition of defence, with both men and arms.

" The department at Washington has under consideration plans which I have submitted for state defence, and I hope will act upon them soon. For the present, we are indeed in a bad condition, and have been for a long time, without any fault of mine."

Dr. Jewett was in Norwich, Connecticut, working for the Connecticut Temperance Union, when the rebel army surrendered, making preparations for the removal of his family thither. On the memorable April 10, 1865, he wrote to Mrs. Jewett:

" Oh, that you could have heard the steam whistles of this city about an hour since. There are many steam-engines in the city, locomotives on the railroad, steamboats, and manufacturing establishments operated with steam-power, and all their throats were wide open at just twelve o'clock, and were open for about half an hour. Such music! It was followed by the ringing of bells; and now the cannon are pealing from the heights around the city. Lee's great army has surrendered. The end is now near at hand; but, alas! no clanging bells or booming cannon can awake from his sleep our dear, dear John. Blessed, dear boy! Is he conscious of the triumph which his toils and his blood helped to purchase? These questionings have arisen, I am sure, in your own mind. We cannot know now, but shall know hereafter."

Dr. Jewett resided two years in Chicago; then removed to Evanston, a few miles from the city, that his invalid daughter might enjoy the country air, and his expenses be lightened. The family were there when peace was declared; but he removed them to Norwich immediately, where he welcomed his surviving soldier-sons home from the war.

XVI.

GUERRILLA WARFARE.

DR. JEWETT'S temperance work, after the civil war, was fragmentary, chiefly in consequence of the heart-disease, which slowly but surely advanced. He could not endure continuous labors as formerly. Frequent and long periods of rest became a necessity. Then, too, the unsettled state of the country, together with the heavy drafts made upon all classes by the war, made it still difficult to raise money to support the temperance work. For this reason his labors were in places widely separated, from the British Provinces to Minnesota. He called it " Guerrilla Warfare."

At the close of the war he was laboring for the Connecticut Temperance Union, with headquarters at Norwich. There his family were reunited, and his eldest daughter soon married to Professor A. T. Smith, son of President Smith, of Naperville College, Illinois. The doctor was happy again in his family, but not in his work. It was difficult to raise funds for the cause he loved. He worked against wind and tide. The public appeared to be apathetic, and the doctor lacked that hearty, gener-

22

ous support that he felt must be accorded to him in order to be successful. He resigned, and resolved to return to Minnesota. His eldest son had already returned to his home there; Richard, also, had gone thither to settle, instead of returning to Boston; Frank had entered Yale College; Parker was living in Providence, Rhode Island; and the married daughter had taken up her residence in Iowa. His wife and youngest daughter only were with him. At the same time he received an urgent invitation to labor for a season in Kansas. That would be near his farm and friends.

During this period of his residence in Norwich, his inventive genius struck out anew. A friend says that "he was ever studying to lighten labor, and make it more pleasant and attractive." The instance before us is, perhaps, an illustration of that propensity. He had previously manufactured a "Fruit Drier," consisting of a frame four feet long, perhaps, and half as wide, the bottom being of basket-work, that the air might circulate through the fruit. The basket-work was braided by hand, and he conceived the idea of a machine to weave it, thereby greatly facilitating the manufacture. He succeeded in constructing such a machine that did the weaving admirably; and he then applied for a patent on the "Drier." He failed to secure the patent, because "the inventor of a similar 'Fruit Drier' in the state of New York had made application in advance of him." His invention, however, was well received, quite widely circulated, and highly prized.

Some months after he failed to secure the patent he was in New York state, and saw the "Fruit Drier" that was patented in advance of his, and he wrote to his wife, "It is no more like mine than a hawk is like a handsaw."

As we have frequently referred to the products of his inventive and mechanical ingenuity, we may add here, that the occasions for its exercise were numerous. On one of his lecturing tours in the northern part of Massachusetts, he wrote to his wife, from a town where he delivered several lectures, that he had employed his daytime in constructing a useful apparatus for her in doing housework, and should bring it to her on his return. It proved to be an "Apple Sifter," constructed like a crank-churn, and was very convenient and useful in sifting stewed apples.

Since his death we have looked about his homestead, to find his "apple-drying house." We remembered of his return from a rest of three weeks at home, one autumn, to the Massachusetts Temperance Alliance, in whose employ he was. He rehearsed his labors in constructing an "Apple-drying House," in which the fruit of his orchard could be dried by heat; and he had tested its value by drying twenty bushels of apples or more. We found it, — a little building that would hold from twelve to twenty of his "Fruit Driers," one above another, together with a small-sized cooking-stove, so arranged that it could be fed on the outside. Here the labor of drying apples, away from flies and dust, was materially simplified and promoted, producing an extra quality of dried fruit, clean, white, and delicious.

A handcart stood near by, and Mrs. Jewett remarked, pointing to it, " The doctor made that."

" Made that? " we replied.

" Yes; he brought the wheels from Amesbury, Massachusetts, and made it himself."

A rod distant was a wheelbarrow. Pointing to it, Mrs. Jewett said, " He made that, also. He purchased the wheel, but made the barrow."

" Anything else that he made? " we inquired.

" Yes; you must go into the wood-cellar, and see his ' shaving machine.' "

Whether it was an apparatus to relieve men of their beards, without the intervention of a barber, we did not know ; but we followed on, down through the bulkhead into the cellar.   There we found a very simple machine for making shavings to kindle fires.   In one minute the house-girl, or other member of the family, could make shavings enough for kindling a rousing fire.

" He said that he could use it, also, for making hoe-handles and axe-handles," remarked Mrs. Jewett, " which he has always made."

We were thinking about the " jack-at-all-trades," but could not apply the remainder of the adage to him, in the presence of such skilful handiwork, when Mrs. Jewett added, " There is another thing he did : he was accustomed to make the baskets we used in the family.   He has often been into the woods, where he split the material, and made a basket before returning."

Passing along into the garden, on a green plat we observed some sort of frame-work erected, as if for gymnastic performers, and we inquired its use.

" He erected that for the Chinese boys who board with us, for exercise and sport."

Could anything be more practical? Who ever tried harder to lighten labor and make it a joy?

Dr. Jewett returned to Faribault in 1867, where he left his wife and daughter, while he proceeded to Kansas to fulfil his engagement there for the State Temperance Society. He stopped long enough with his old friends at Faribault, however, to deliver a lecture upon the " Battle of Gettysburg." He had recently visited the scene of that bloody conflict, and was able to instruct and interest his audience upon the locality and details of the battle, as well as its place in the overthrow of the rebellion. The people enjoyed his lecture exceedingly.

It was his first visit to that thrifty state, but his fame had gone before him, and the whole temperance public were on tiptoe to hear the distinguished speaker. The invitation extended to him at that particular time grew out of a systematic and resolute effort to secure effective legislation against the liquor traffic. Commencing his labors at Manhattan, he visited the principal towns and cities, in some places delivering more than one lecture. Although the people were expecting a " treat," their highest anticipations were more than realized, and they flocked to hear him as they had rallied to listen to no other lecturer. Crowds greeted him everywhere. Religious societies opened their places of worship gladly to him; preachers welcomed him to their pulpits, and town authorities offered their public halls without charge for his meetings.

In the midst of his labors an accident cut short his work. While in the yard of Dr. Amory Hunting, at Manhattan, who was the apostle of temperance in Kansas, he trod upon a rusty nail, the result of which proved quite serious. Physicians feared the lock-jaw; and the opinion of one of them was that in the East, lock-jaw could not possibly have been prevented. It was thought best, at last, that the doctor should go to friends in Chicago, to which place his wife could be speedily summoned in case he grew worse.

His indomitable will and great courage sustained him in fulfilling quite a number of appointments. while suffering acutely. Rev. R. D. Parker says:

" He came to my house in Wyandotte, arriving the second day of April; and notwithstanding his sufferings he lectured on that and the following evening in my church, and went, on April 4th, to Independence, Missouri, lecturing there on two evenings, and then, on Sunday, April 9th, he spoke again to crowded houses, morning and evening, in my Wyandotte church."

Rev. Dr. Cordley gives a graphic account of his last lecture in the city of Lawrence, illustrating his wonderful power to control even physical pain, or holding it in abeyance, while he sent conviction to

the hearts of a delighted audience. Dr. Cordley
says :

"He lectured several times in Lawrence. The last time
he gave a course of six lectures, on six successive evenings.
His audiences increased from night to night, both in number and interest. At the last lecture the hall was literally packed. During the whole six days he was quite
unwell and was suffering extremely from an injury to his
foot. The last day he was hardly able to leave his room,
and his foot was so painful that he could not stand upon
it. His friends tried to persuade him to postpone his lecture; but he said that if he could get to the hall he could
talk a little while sitting, and then close. He was carried
to the hall, helped upon the stage, and seated in an easy-
chair. Leaning forward on his cane, he began to talk in
a very feeble but clear manner. As he proceeded, his
voice grew stronger, and his form grew straighter. The
crowd seemed to inspire him; and after a few minutes
he arose from his seat, supporting himself on one foot and
on his cane, and finally threw the cane aside, and stood
out on the platform erect. His infirmities all seemed to
leave him, and he poured forth a stream of eloquent logic
which held the audience spellbound for an hour and a
half."

While the doctor was in Kansas, an amusing
scene occurred at Topeka, the capital of the state.
The legislature was in session, and the friends of
temperance were making an effort to amend the
license law, so that no man could take out a license
unless his application was indorsed by a majority
of the adults, male and female, of his town or ward
of the city in which he lived. The liquor interest

sent despatches to Leavenworth, to summon the fraternity to Topeka on the day when the great discussion would occur, thinking that such a crowd might prevent the passage of the Act. On that day, too, the friends of temperance held a convention in Topeka, and it was largely attended, for Dr. Jewett was to be there. The railroad on which most of the rumsellers and their patrons would come, was situated on the west side of Kansas River, and Topeka was on the east side, and the bridge that spanned the river had been carried away, so that people were ferried over in boats. On the morning of that eventful day a whole car-load of liquor-sellers and their patrons from Leavenworth arrived at the depot on the east side. But their enthusiasm and amiable temper were suddenly taken out of them, when they found that during the night previous the ice in the Republican Fork River, a tributary of the Kansas, had broken up, and it was rushing down the latter with an impetuosity that threatened destruction to any boat that attempted to cross. Not a boatman dared to risk his life to carry a passenger over. The rumsellers were compelled to wait on the west side of the river, while the temperance men held a most enthusiastic convention on the east side; and the legislature passed the temperance Act by a handsome majority. The rumsellers waited for the ice to run past until they were tired, and then returned to Leavenworth, while the temperance men remained in Topeka overnight, and in the evening celebrated the glorious victory in Representative Hall. Dr.

Jewett never felt better in his life, and his eloquent
and witty speech made all his hearers feel the same.
It was doubtful, however, whether he enjoyed the
legislative victory as much as he did the discomfiture
of the rumsellers, whom the Great Proprietor of the
Kansas and its tributaries so sorely vexed on the
west bank.

In order to introduce another fact furnished by
Rev. Mr. Parker, we mention a remarkable illustration of Dr. Jewett's imitative powers and command of the passions, in a series of photographs —
facial expressions showing the progress of intemperance from the first social glass to the last in the
road to ruin, used particularly in his lecture on the
"Three Stages of *Drunkenness*." He was lecturing
in a town of New Hampshire, and was entertained
by a clergyman who was formerly a photographer.
His taste for the art was so great that he had a pho-
tographic room fitted up in his own dwelling, where
he experimented for improvement and pleasure. He
listened to the doctor with rapt attention, and was
much impressed by his dramatic ability and mimicry.
Further illustrations in this line at his own house
after the lecture caused him to request the doctor
to sit on the following day, that he might take photos of those facial expressions.

Rev. Mr. Parker speaks of this power, though
illustrating another line of thought instead of drunkenness, as follows:

"When Dr. Jewett canvassed the state of Michigan in
behalf of the Prohibitory Law, I was a student in the

university at Ann Arbor, and saw, at a state fair, a set of
photos (daguerreotypes perhaps), showing his emotions
at different stages of the work. They were very striking.
I wish I were good with the pencil, I could almost repro-
duce those pictures from a memory of nearly thirty years :
the bright, hopeful, natural look with which he undertook
the work ; the grand, high look when he was fairly at
work ; the courageous, determined, warrior-look as he
pressed the enemy to the wall; the face all wreathed in
smiles of satisfaction as he heard the election was carried
for the law ; then the questioning, indignant surprise when
appeal was made to the Supreme Court ; and finally the
rage, the very thunder-cloud of wrath, when the law was
declared unconstitutional."

Next we find Dr. Jewett laboring in Ohio, under
the auspices of the "Good Templars." Although, like
most of the temperance advocates, he preferred open
organizations, and had no taste for the regalia, pass-
words, and ceremonies of the secret orders, yet he
cheerfully conceded to them a sphere of usefulness,
and co-operated with them heartily in prosecuting
the good work. He even joined them, and was a
true, loyal member. He said publicly :

" Had I believed there was anything morally wrong in
the formation and support of these organizations, I certainly should not have joined and worked with them.
My opinion of their moral character I have further indicated by commending them oftentimes to congregations
of the people at the conclusion of my public discourses,
and urging them to connect themselves therewith. I have
done so, not because I believed them the best calculated
to serve our purposes, but because they were eminently

useful, and the best existing at the time in those localities ; and I did not feel myself at liberty to throw cold water on the efforts of earnest brethren by questioning, before a mixed audience, the wisdom of their choice as to the forms through which they would labor."

Ill health interrupted the doctor's labors in Ohio, and in the early part of 1868 he went down into East Tennessee with his wife and daughter to spend the summer with his son, whose infirmities, occasioned by hard service in the war, forced him to sell his farm in Faribault, and seek a warmer climate. He was located on the Cumberland Plateau, a beautiful region, especially inviting to invalids. The result of that visit was, that the doctor purchased a small farm at Pomono, near his son, and subsequently sold his Minnesota farm. One inducement to this step was the fact that the health of his son-in-law was completely broken down, and the doctor thought that a residence there might restore him, in which he was sadly disappointed. His disease continued to progress, and finally, after three or four years of suffering, he passed away, leaving a void in the family which only springs from the sense of personal worth.

At Pomono the doctor was twenty-five miles from a place of public worship, in a region that had been cursed by slavery so long as to leave its blot upon everything. "Poor whites" and poorer blacks, without schools, preaching, or decent homes, elicited his sincere pity. He established worship in his own house ; also a Sabbath-school, with his son-in-law for superintendent; but it was difficult to gather there the population specially needing such privileges. Several northern families had settled in that vicinity, six or eight perhaps, in a radius of five or six miles; and they were glad of these privileges. A few only of the natives, who lived in squalor and wretchedness, could be reached. Some idea of the wretched condition of the "poor whites" may be formed from the wonder with which they viewed the articles of household furniture and apparel. One said to another, describing the wonderful things seen in Dr. Jewett's house, "Don't you think, they have knives and forks to eat with, and they have a broom and dust-pan, as they call them."

From a letter that Dr. Jewett wrote to the "Temperance Advocate" of New York, we extract the following:

"To be serenaded at the break of day by the whippoorwill, and attend a full concert of the feathered warblers at sunrise, in the month of March, is to a northern man quite a pleasant novelty. I have enjoyed it here for some days in my new mountain home. Not less have I enjoyed my strolls in these grand old woods, where, in almost every walk of a mile, I startle the deer and see them bound away through the forest in their own peculiar and magnificent style. Those misguided souls who urge that alcoholic stimulants are needful to give *power to muscle*, ought to see a herd of deer move off on the double-quick when startled by the approach of their worst enemy, man. Thirty feet is but an ordinary leap for these teetotalers; and our field fences of the mountains, ten rails high, are apparently no more in their way than a three-foot fence would be to a trained athlete. There is muscle for you, dear, boozy beer-drinkers!"

Dr. Jewett was very much benefited by his stay in Tennessee, so that in September of that year he felt strong for labor again. He accepted an invitation to spend a few months in the province of Ontario, West Canada. While performing his work there, he received an invitation from the National Temperance Society at New York to become an editor of its organ, the "Temperance Advocate," and to lecture also in that state. In 1869 he accepted the last-named position and entered upon its duties, his family remaining in Tennessee. This separation from his family was not congenial to Dr. Jewett, and in 1870 they joined him, keeping house across the river in Williamsburg.

The doctor occupied this position three years, proving himself, as before, in the editorial chair, a workman that "needeth not to be ashamed, rightly dividing the word of truth." His services were highly appreciated by the numerous patrons of the Society, his facile and able pen, like his voice, instructing and pleasing them always.

While engaged in editorial labors, Dr. Jewett prepared and published a volume entitled, "Forty Years' Fight with the Drink Demon," in which he recorded the leading events of the temperance cause during his connection with it. The volume furnished still further proof of his sincerity, industry, and rare ability.

Dr. Jewett became thoroughly convinced that the

time had come for him to establish a permanent home, where he might spend the remainder of his days. He was satisfied that his public labors must soon close altogether, or, at least, that he would be able to devote but a portion of his time to the lecture-field. In these circumstances, a permanent home was indispensable.

He withdrew from the National Temperance Society, removed to Norwich, Connecticut, and purchased a piece of land, on which he proceeded to erect a house. He possessed nearly enough property then to pay for a comfortable home; but it was in the hands of friends in New York, who had invested it with property of their own. Just when he was expecting to command the principal, augmented by a large income, *he lost every cent of it.*

We recall the day when the news of his loss reached him. He was sitting in the room of the Massachusetts Temperance Alliance. The letter was put into his hand, and he opened and read it. We noticed that he sat silently gazing at the floor, but thought of nothing unusual, until he said, rising from his seat, " God's will be done." An explanation followed. We find a letter, which he wrote to Mrs. Jewett at the time, from which we extract the following :

" The letter came upon me like a clap of thunder. I see nothing now before me but the prospect of losing all I have. If I do, it will necessitate the sale of *our home.* Rather than struggle on under that load, and perhaps kill myself with hard labor to redeem the property, I had rather at once submit it to the inevitable, put it in shape to sell, and let it go, pay my notes, and be out of debt. We are told not to lay up our treasures upon earth, where, &c. Perhaps we have erred in promising ourselves too much happiness in the possession of so good a home. If so, God forgive us, and make us content with one less desirable. . . . Thank God, we have wealth in our good sons and daughters, reputations untarnished, a past record we are not ashamed of, and in any case there are left us, and will be in the event I am now compelled to anticipate, sources of happiness to which many are strangers. . . . I think we are to be tried by one more disappointment in relation to our earthly home and possessions. God grant that we may not be disappointed in relation to our home ' not made with hands, eternal in the heavens.' Let us take care that there be no mortgage on that! God's will be done!

"Yours — ' cast down but not destroyed.'"

Providence however favored an arrangement of his affairs, so that he retained his house, though none of his money was ever recovered.

Dr. Jewett's allusion to their "wealth in sons and daughters" leads us to say of the son, in whose collegiate education he was so deeply interested, that he was graduated at Yale College with honors in 1870, served as teacher in the Norwich Free Academy two years, earning money to pay his expenses one year at the university of Gottenburg, Germany; and in 1876, by recommendation to the Japanese government by the president of Yale College, he was appointed Professor of Chemistry in the Imperial University at Tokio, Japan.

We cannot refrain from adding part of a letter which the doctor wrote to Mrs. Jewett just before his son left for Japan :

" I fear I shall not reach home to see Frank off; but it would not help the matter. He well knows that he carries with him to that distant land, not only the respect and confidence of his father as a man, but a father's love, which never knew a chill since I first saw him in his mother's arms. I shall follow him to Japan with *prayer*, and another article the name of which begins with the same letter, *pride*. As to his course there I have no fears, and of his complete success I have no doubt. He carries with him all the elements of success — a good brain, a good constitution, a thorough education in his department, an educated and enlightened conscience, a firm resolve to do his duty, and a fixed trust in God. To the Divine guidance and protection I prayerfully and hopefully resign him. God bless the child — the man — the teacher — the Christian gentleman ! "

Dr. Jewett's misfortune compelled him to devote more time to the lecture-field than was consistent with his health, and much more than he designed to give to it. Some of the time, after he began to build his house, he was in the service of the Massachusetts Temperance Alliance. He gave courses of lectures, during this period, in the prominent towns and cities. He gave a course of six in Cambridge. At the close of his course he was to rest an evening at his friend's, George D. Chamberlain, Esq., and quite a number of people were invited to meet him there on that evening.

When the company had gathered, and the social intercourse just begun, Mr. Chamberlain stepped forward, and thus addressed the doctor:

"For many years you have been a servant of the people, and the friends here desire to intrust a little matter to your care. Long years ago, in the state of Rhode Island, was a young physician whose professional prospects were unusually bright. He beheld the ruin occasioned by the sale and use of intoxicating drinks, and his heart and hand were enlisted to remove the curse. Many, in different parts of New England, discovered in him sterling qualities for a great work; and they besought him to enter the field against this great enemy of the race; and their request, he thought, was the voice of the Master. Leading medical men advised him to remain in his profession; but after careful deliberation, he responded favorably to the call, turned away from his brilliant professional prospects, and consecrated his powers to the removal of intemperance. Many, many years have elapsed, and some of late have lost sight of that young man. They have looked in vain for his name among the Pierponts, Sargents, and others of the great and honored dead. And now, sir, we desire to intrust this to your care," (handing him a roll of bills,) "and if you can find the young man, now grown old with cares and years, deliver it to him, and tell him for us that he has our fervent prayers and our most cordial support."

The doctor was taken by surprise. Rallying his self-possession, and bidding emotion down, he wiped away his tears, and said:

"Friends: While I did leave my chosen profession to engage in the temperance work, I have always felt that I

23

did it at the call of duty. The way has sometimes been rough, but I have found, all through my long journey, just such warm-hearted friends as I find here to-night."

Here he appeared to have some trouble with both throat and eyes (and most of the company were in tears), so that his attempt to return thanks and express his gratitude proved well-nigh a failure; and the whole company speedily adjourned to the dining-hall, where a bountiful collation soon choked down all superfluous emotions.

There were eighty dollars in that roll of bills; nor was it pay for his lectures; pay for them came from another source. It was a free gift, a spontaneous tribute to his ability and worth.

We recall another time, while the doctor was in the service of the Alliance, that one of the wealthiest men of the state presented him with a hundred-dollar bill, on the morning after he lectured in the rich man's town, saying, "That is for you, not for the Alliance. I wish to present it to you as an expression of my confidence and esteem. Use it as you please."

He did use it as he pleased. In his generosity he divided it equally between the treasury of the Alliance and his own pocket.

It was during his final labors for the Alliance that Dr. Jewett wrote his last poem, entitled, "The Harvest of Rum." It was printed in a neat pamphlet of sixteen pages, illustrated with five excellent cuts, and was widely circulated. Its motto was that inspired passage, "Whatsoever a man soweth, that shall he also reap." The poem opened thus:

" Ho ! to the reapers the harvest has come,
  And the crop that was sown by the sellers of rum
  Must be gathered in — no word like fail ;
  Some to the almshouse, and some to the jail.
  Aye ! gather the crop that rumsellers have sown,
  Till the wheels of the pauper-cart shall groan
        With the fearful weight
        Of the wretched freight ;
        Creak, creak, creak, creak,
        Every day of every week.
  Come, stir up your team ; ply whip and goad,
  For rumsellers' crops make a heavy load."

Dr. Jewett delivered a course of temperance lectures in Halifax, Nova Scotia, after his return to Norwich. The press of the city pronounced them as "thoroughly philosophical and scientific, appealing both to reason and conscience with great power." Being there over the Sabbath, he was invited to preach part of the day at the Presbyterian church. He accepted the invitation, and took for his text, Mark vii. 24–30, containing the history of the Syrophenician woman. Subject, Faith : its trial, importance, and rewards. The audience listened with as profound attention to his sermon as they had to his lectures, and were as profuse in their praise of the former as they had been of the latter.

The doctor's labor, during the last three years of his life, was performed with much weariness and pain. The only rule under which he could labor at all was, short lecturing tours and long intervals of rest.   He lectured in the states of New York, New Jersey, Pennsylvania, and Maryland, with an occasional lecture in New England, impressing his thoughts upon his hearers as successfully as ever, and enlarging the army of his admiring friends.

XVII.

DR. JEWETT AMONG THE CHILDREN.

DR. JEWETT loved children passionately. Children loved him. The attraction was mutual. What a magnet is among metals, that was Dr. Jewett among children. He *drew*, and they were inclined *to be drawn*. Introduced into a family of them, he was at once *en rapport* with them. He carried about with him a photograph of three little girls, sisters, belonging to a family in which he often tarried. They were in his pocket when he came home to die. Letters already quoted speak of this element of power in his character. Others mention it more fully. One clergyman says :

"After he had been at my house once, my children would hop up and down when they learned that he was coming again. The doctor was one with them, and such a fund of stories as he had to draw from seemed to astonish them ; all of the stories acted out, and enforcing good lessons. With pencil in hand, he would make them just the happiest creatures by drawing the picture of anything they asked him to sketch."

Another writes :

"It was only lately that he made his home at my house.

We found him one of the most agreeable guests we have ever known. *The children were delighted with him,* and he seemed to enjoy talking with them greatly. He had a pleasant word for all, and every visit made us more ready to receive him again."

From another letter we make the following extract:

" Even my children mourn his death. They loved him ardently; and no greater treat awaited them than his coming to our house. It was the assurance of an extra good time. That thousands of adults like myself will miss him sadly is very true; but think of the children who will miss him, too!"

From Kansas another writes, in whose house the doctor suffered from a wounded foot:

" One of the cherished memories of my daughter, now sixteen years old, is of standing behind the doctor as he sat upon the floor, his foot swathed in wet bandages, combing and brushing his hair. She was four years old, and just tall enough to reach, and the child's prattle and attention seemed to divert his mind from his sufferings."

The author of the last quotation furnishes an illustration of the doctor's tact in putting all the members of families into which he was introduced at ease, and upon the most familiar terms. Addressing the mother of the household, he assured her that he always enacted and executed a *prohibitory law* against all extra cooking, and extra steps, for him, adding, "I always make my own apple-pie with bread and apple-sauce, and I don't want any woman to do it for me."

One of the most amusing scenes, in this connection, occurred in Williamsburg, N. Y. A little girl of only three years, Daisy by name, was very fond of the doctor. She was always happy in his presence, and he was as happy as she. He allowed her to lather his face when he shaved, which pleased her greatly, so that she would laugh and prattle at the top of her voice with every stroke of the brush, and putting her tiny hand upon his face where the razor had been, sure to find a "wuff" place requiring additional lather. For a half hour the doctor would prolong the operation for the sake of ministering to the unalloyed pleasure of the "wee thing," as well as for the amusement of lookers-on. Sometimes he added other sources of enjoyment to the little creature, such as "sliding down hill" on her mother's dress-board.

He addressed the young in public with remarkable tact and power, so as to leave impressions that were never obliterated. One clergyman says:

"I owe my earliest impressions of interest in the temperance cause to Dr. Jewett's lectures in ———, Mass. When I was a boy, he gave a course in the town hall, which was crowded to hear him. I recollect very well a piece of poetry of his own that he repeated, exposing the meanness of rumselling."

And he goes on and repeats the verse quoted in a former chapter, beginning, "I'd sooner black my visage o'er," together with its effect upon a young rumseller who read it, causing him to abandon the business. And this after the lapse of about forty years! This writer adds:

"I heard the doctor afterwards in Cleveland, Ohio, and he had lost none of his power to instruct and interest. His thorough knowledge of all phases of the subject, his clear, logical statement of principles, with his quaint humor, made him the most interesting and effective lecturer I ever knew. No man has ever done more to form a correct public sentiment on the subject of temperance."

Another clergyman writes:

"My earliest recollections of Dr. Jewett had much to do in shaping my future on the temperance question. When I was a lad he came to Scituate, Mass., invited by the late Rev. Samuel J. May. Both took tea at my father's house; and well do I remember how fascinated I was with his conversation, and his witty rhymings as he recited them. Although I had signed the pledge, I distinctly recollect that interview greatly strengthened my faith in the principle of total abstinence. Also I remember when it was noised abroad that Dr. Jewett would lecture in the evening, a great crowd assembled to hear him. I have him in mind now as he personated the drunkard, and so admirably was it done that the entire audience was convulsed. I remember it as if it were but yesterday. He was a great mimic."

Meeting an old acquaintance on the cars, we said, "You must have been familiar with Dr. Jewett; any incidents in his life that you recall?"

"Why, sir," he replied, "the first temperance lecture that I ever heard was by Dr. Jewett. I was a mere boy, and can tell you the whole plan and argument of that discourse to-day. At that time the plea was that liquors

were indispensable to health and strength, and the doctor
exposed the folly of it. He imitated an old man of eighty,
who pleaded that his long life was due to the moderate
use of intoxicating drinks. Then he imitated his aged
wife, tying a bandanna handkerchief about his neck, and
reproducing her little, trembling, feminine voice, as she
maintained that liquor ' did her old man a heap of good.'
' It is a delusion,' remarked the doctor; ' but suppose it
were true, and that these two aged people have not been
injured by the drink, and even have been benefited, shall
we set this single case over against the thousands of drunkards that fill dishonored graves, and the tens of thousands
of criminals that fill our jails, and paupers that crowd
our almshouses?' Boy though I was, I saw the point,
and I think that every other boy and girl in the audience
did; and we remembered it because he enforced the truth
by his perfect mimicry."

Within a few years Dr. Gould of Hartford, Conn.,
paid a noble tribute to Dr. Jewett by introducing
him to his congregation as " My father, and teacher
of my boyhood, in the Temperance cause."

When Dr. Jewett became an agent of the Massachusetts Temperance Union in 1840, the " Cold
Water Army " was enlisting the children far and
near. The secretary of that society, Nathan Crosby,
was deeply interested in that department of work,
and his efficient labors had awakened much interest. Joined by Dr. Jewett just at that time, he was
greatly encouraged. Rev. M. P. Parish was an
agent of the society also, and these three men had
charge of the movement, and made it a power in
the state. They printed pledges, not only on paper

but on pocket-handkerchiefs, badges, and banners. They manufactured mottoes, badges, and banners by thousands, and organized Cold Water armies throughout the state. Reports of "children's meetings" in those days, numbering one thousand and two thousand in country towns, and three thousand and upwards in cities, were not unusual.

Dr. Jewett was at home and enthusiastic before such swarms of children. Many thought he excelled in addressing boys and girls, although they could not see how he could improve in addressing adults. At any rate his success was complete, and the children in every part of the state flocked to hear him; and he was invited often to address children in other states. Nor were his "talks" mere twaddle, but instruction of the highest type, enforced by anecdote, illustration, and wit. He drew upon his dramatic and imitative powers largely, sometimes making his juvenile audience almost wild with excitement. He could be a staggering, loathsome drunkard before them, or a hapless, half-starved drunkard's child, begging for bread. They could see in him the sober, kind, loving father, trying to make his children and their mother happy in a pleasant home; and they could see, too, the drunken father, savage and ugly, a terror to his children, and making home a dreaded place. No other lecturer could instruct them so thoroughly in all these things.

We recall his attacks upon cider, christening it "WORM-JUICE." Appealing to the boys especially, he caused them not only to laugh and shout, but to turn away in disgust from that "decoction of rotten apple and extract of worm." He would portray the cider-mill before his eager listeners with its pile of half-decayed fruit, "left to partially rot that there might be more juice and tne worms fatter," so vividly that we could see the fat, lusty worms smashed up with the rotten apples, and scarcely help believing that the resultant flowing into the tub was composed of very poor apple-juice (because the fruit was rotten) and the liquid part of worms, in about equal parts. From that time, in our youth, we have avoided cider-mills.

Poetry was a prominent instrumentality which the doctor employed to reach the hearts of children — his own composition and that of others. He also drew largely upon the standard poets, as Shakespeare, Burns, Cowper, &c., to interest them. With his tact, power to represent character, forcible and eloquent recitation, he was able to make quotationo from the best poets, and fascinate his juvenile audiences. Here is one from Cowper, that a gentleman remembers to have heard the doctor recite inimitably, nearly forty years ago, to expose and condemn the plea, "Rum must be sold, and I may as well sell it as others."

> " A youngster at school, more sedate than the rest,
> Had once his integrity put to the test:
> His companions had plotted an orchard to rob,
> And asked him to go and assist in the job.

"He was shocked, sir, like you, and answered, 'Oh, no!
What! rob our good neighbor? I pray you, don't go.
Besides, the man's poor, — his orchard's his bread;
Then, think of his children, — for they must be fed.'

"'You speak very fine, and you look very grave:
But apples we want, and apples we'll have;
If you will go with us, you shall have a share;
If not, you shall have neither apple nor pear.'

"They spoke, and Tom pondered: 'I see they will go;
Poor man! what a pity to injure him so!
Poor man! I would save him his fruit if I could,
But by staying behind will do him no good.

"'If the matter depended alone upon me,
His apples might hang till they drop from the tree;
But, since they will take them, I think I'll go too;
He will lose none by me, though I get a few.'

"His scruples thus silenced, Tom felt more at ease,
And went with his comrades the apples to seize.
He blamed and protested, but joined in the plan, —
He shared in the plunder, but pitied the man!"

An illustration of Dr. Jewett's ability to charm a
child by reading or recitation is found in the following fact. A few months before his death, after he
was brought home sick, and when he appeared to
be improving, a mother called upon him with her
little daughter. The child and aged patient were
soon on the best of terms, conversing, laughing,
and having a pleasant time. At last the doctor asked
her if he should not recite "The Death of Little Joe,"
from Dickens? She indicated her desire to hear it
in a gleeful way. So the doctor leaned forward in
his arm-chair and began it. The child's interest

deepened as he proceeded, tears gathered in her eyes, and her lip quivered as he drew near the end; and when he closed, she burst into tears and wept as if her little heart would break. A higher compliment could hardly be paid to a reader.

The "Union" published a monthly paper for the "Cold Water Army," and when Dr. Jewett assumed the charge of its publications, he introduced a novel feature into this juvenile periodical. It was a rhyme department, with the picture of his "Patent Rhyme Grinder" for turning out poetry, made like a gristmill, turned by a crank, the boy, Irish Jimmy, turning it, a hopper full of "facts" feeding it, while the doctor sat taking away the columns of "machine poetry" as it was delivered. We furnish an example of his work entitled "Strangulation, or The Distiller's Disaster." A noted Boston distiller fell into a fermenting vat, and but for the timely aid of workmen would have died by strangulation. Dr. Jewett appropriated the rather serious accident (he was wont to use passing events in this way), and the following appeared in his paper as the result of his effort:

"*Dr.* Hold, Jimmy! I have no time to hear more of Mistress McGowan's lecture on Strangulation; but, as you seem to be quite interested in the matter, suppose you put the facts in your Patent Rhyme-grinder, and turn us out something for the Journal.

"*Jim.* Faix! I'll do it.

(*He brings out the machine and commences operations.*)

" I'll sing you a song that is rare and queer,
  Of a nager that fell in a vat of beer,
Which was rendered so fine as he slowly decayed,
  That the liquor was praised,
  Its price was much raised,
The business increased, and a fortune was made.

"*Dr.* Jim, you make strange work. You were going to grind out a song from facts that occurred in this Western world, and your very first verse is about an old affair that happened twenty years ago on the other side of the Atlantic.

"*Jim.* Niver mind, doctor, jewel. I'll come to it directly. (*He turns again.*)

" One Haman, the Scriptures relate,
  Got mad at the Jew, Mordecai,
And built for him, outside the gate,
  A gallows some fifty feet high.
' Ha, ha ! ' said his wife, ' they will yet learn to fear us, —
  These stiff-necked, obstinate Jews ;
Now go to the party with Ahasuerus,
  Be cheerful and banish the blues ;
  Come, hurry, my honey,
  Drink wine and be funny.'

He went; and, bad luck to him! made such a bother,
He got himself hanged jist, instead of the other!
And he couldn't complain of the way it was done,
For they let down the drap on a plan of his own.

"*Dr.* Worse and worse, Jimmy! You are farther
from your proper subject than before. You have wandered in point of distance as far as Persia; and as to time,
you have made a jump backward of more than two thousand years. What next?

"*Jim.* Troth, ye're mighty pertickular! If you don't
be aisy stoppin' me, I won't grind at all, at all; and ye
may turn ye'self.

"*Dr.* Well, let go the crank, and I'll give you a specimen of my work off-hand. (*The doctor now turns, while
Jimmy looks on in amazement.*)

> " The fire glowed bright beneath the still,
>   And fiercely boiled the foaming flood,
> Destined the drunkard's veins to fill,
>   To scorch his brain and fire his blood.
> The workmen cheerily plied their tasks,
>   When in the great distiller came
> T' inspect the work; and now he asks
>   ' How boils the flood? How burns the flame?'
> Vexed that the hell-broth cooks so slow,
>   He mounts a vat with careless tread,
> To stir the mixtures vile below,
>   But slips, and plunges over head!
> Panting and gasping hard for breath,
> He would have yielded there to death;
> But helping hands were now applied,
> Which dragged him up the slippery side;
> And forth from that fermenting vat,
> Resembling much a drowned wharf-rat,

> Bedaubed with yeasty slime and foam,
>   Fragrant and dripping as he passed,
> This great distiller sought his home, —
>   By sad experience taught at last
> This truth, contained in Holy Writ:
> *Who for his neighbor digs a pit*
> *Will some time tumble into it !* "

This production is worthy of more attention than the doctor's fun over it seems to warrant. The poem possesses much of real poetical excellence, while the ingenuity and humor involved in its conception and plan are remarkable.

So much enthusiasm was created among the children by this "machine poetry," that at one place where the doctor lectured, the boys and girls crowded around him, and one of them asked, "Did Jimmy come with you?"

At one time the doctor was in Berkshire County. A boy carried him from a railroad station one day to a village over the hills four miles distant. As usual, the doctor found company in the lad, and soon both were on the most familiar terms, the former seeking to interest and benefit the boy, while the latter listened eagerly to the wise counsels of his stranger-friend.

"See there, my lad," exclaimed the doctor, pointing to an old hemlock that had fallen partly over, and was resting upon a young, stout, black birch.

"See what?" answered the boy, inquiringly.

"That aged hemlock supported by that neighborly birch. There is a lesson in that for you, my lad."

"I see the hemlock," replied the boy, "but I don't see the lesson."

"Well," replied the doctor, laughing, "I am in-clined to think that the old hemlock can be seen more clearly by a boy like you than the lesson it teaches; but I guess I can help you to see the les-son as distinctly as you can the tree. What do you say to that, my little man?"

"I should like to see the lesson," responded the boy.

"Well, then," continued the doctor, "you see the old hemlock was getting infirm, like an aged man who totters with years; and that smart young birch said to it: 'My good neighbor, you are not so strong as you used to be, and you cannot stand very well without help. Now, the next time a storm comes, do you just lean over upon me, and I will hold you up. I cannot tell how long I shall be spared to do it; but any way, you lean on me.'

"So when the next gale blew over the hill, the weak, old hemlock leaned upon its kind-hearted young friend, and there it has rested ever since. Now, my boy, there is a beautiful lesson in that; don't you see?"

"I think I do," replied the boy, with a smile that almost run into a laugh.

"I think you do, too," continued the doctor. "That is *brotherly love and respect for the aged.* How much better it is to be kind and generous to others than it is to be unkind and heartless! And how blessed it is to see young people respectful and

24

attentive to the aged! Remember that, my lad. One of these days your parents, if spared, will be old and infirm, and perhaps poor and needy, when you are a strong, noble young man. Say to them, as that young birch said to the hemlock, 'Father, mother, lean on me now; you are too aged and weak to take care of yourselves, and I shall love to have you lean on me.' Now, my little fellow, don't you think that is a good lesson?"

"Yes, sir," answered the lad with an emphasis that denoted character.

The doctor continued his counsel and pointed out some of the temptations that lure the young into vicious ways, not omitting to speak of intoxicating liquors ; and, before his destination was reached, the young driver understood that he was carrying the temperance lecturer — Dr. Charles Jewett.

By the time they reached L—— the boy had received more real valuable instruction to qualify him for practical life than he ever possessed before. Besides, he had made the acquaintance of the most interesting passenger whom he ever carried anywhere — a man he could never forget as long as he lived.

Arriving at his stopping-place, the doctor shook hands with the boy, supplementing his good lessons with other pertinent counsels, and hoping that he might meet him somewhere "when he became a man ; " and then dismissed the matter from his mind for other and sterner duties.

Not so with the boy: he never dismissed that interview from his mind. He returned to his home enthusiastic over the experience of that day. The interview with Dr. Jewett was rehearsed to his parents and to others. His playmates came in for a share of his pleasure, as he rehearsed over and over the remarks of his droll passenger. The old hemlock was not forgotten. He passed by it many times thereafter, and it was always *leaning*, and the "smart young birch" was ever saying, "*Lean*, I love to help you now."

More than twenty years afterwards, when that boy had become a citizen of Chicago, Ill., he read an advertisement in the paper, that Dr. Charles Jewett would lecture on temperance in the city the following evening. The Berkshire boy was there of course. Nothing short of a broken limb or small-pox could have kept him away. An eager listener he was, too. He had more reason to listen than any other person in the hall.

At the close of the lecture he approached the doctor with the familiarity of an old friend, extending his hand, and saying, " Do you remember when we met first, doctor? "

" No, I do not," replied Dr. Jewett, not recognizing the gentleman as any one he ever knew.

" Do you remember delivering an address, many years ago, in the town of L——, in Berkshire County, Massachusetts? "

"Oh, yes!"

"Well, how did you get from the railroad depot to that village?"

"A boy took me over."

"Yes, that is it. I was that boy. It was in the winter, and I took you in a sleigh." And the gentleman went on to relate the circumstances as we have recorded them above, all of which had passed from the recollection of the doctor.

"Let me tell you, Dr. Jewett," added the merchant, "I never forgot your words or that lesson. They have done me good through all the years since, and have reminded me very often of the love that is due to a brother-man, and the respect that belongs to the aged. If the right sort of a boy would make the right sort of a man, from that moment I resolved to be that boy."

Dr. Jewett prepared and published a little work of thirty-two pages, entitled, "The Youth's Temperance Lecturer," designed "to convey to the mind of the youthful reader as much truth in relation to the causes and consequences of intemperance as is possible in so few pages." It was illustrated with seventeen telling cuts, the product of his own brain, and treated of such subjects as "How Distilled Spirits are made," "How Wine is made," "How Ale and Beer are made," "How Cider is made," "The Wholesale Liquor Dealer," "The Tavern Bar," "The Grog-Shop," with the consequences, as "The Drunkard's Home," "The Drunkard's Boy," &c. This little work received a hearty welcome from the temperance public, and passed through *thirty* edi-

tions. It became really one of the temperance educating forces of its day, put, as it was, into the hands
of children who are the men and women of to-day.
It contained several poetical effusions adapted to the
class for whom the book was written. We furnish
one sample. It closes his description of the process
of distilling liquors :

> " They put molasses many an hour
> Into vats and let it sour;
> When it is as sour as swill,
> Then they pour it in a still.
> Under it they put the fire,
> Till it burns up high and higher.
> Now the poison, hot and strong,
> Trickles through the pipe along,
> Till it drops into the cask.
> Little readers, do you ask,
> Why they turn molasses sweet,
> Which is given us to eat,
> Into rum? I'll tell you why:
> 'Tis that foolish men may buy
> And drink the poison stuff and die."

The doctor frequently wrote poems to order for
the gratification of personal friends and the public.
The following was written within a few years, by
request, for " Little Robert's Speech," at the " Band
of Hope Meeting," in Chicago ; the subject,
GRANDPA.

> " Few boys have grandpas so good as mine ;
> He is eighty years old, to be sure,
> And never has meddled with brandy or wine,
> But drank of the water pure.

He does not smoke, or chew, or snuff
  Tobacco, but hates the poison stuff;
So he's hale and hearty, and hobbles about,
And though rather lame, it is not with gout;
Very few, of his age, are half so stout;
To be sure he ain't spry as he used to be,
When he was a boy like you and me.

" He used to go out with us boys to the grove,
  To gather the nuts as they fell;
But now he's too lame, so he sits by the stove,
  And the queerest stories he'll tell,
Of how, when a boy, he could climb with ease
To the very tops of the tallest trees,
And shake down the walnuts as oft as he'd please:
But now dear old grandpa ain't smart at all,
And scarcely can climb o'er the garden wall.

" He laughs at the pranks we children play,
  And seems so happy and glad;
And he tells us all about the way
  They played 'em when he was a lad;
How they built snow forts, and stormed them, too;
How they scuffled and scrambled, and snowballs flew;
And all the wild frolics the boys went through.
Why, boys, we laughed till our sides were sore,
While he told us all that, and a great deal more.

" He once had a horse — so I heard him say —
  That was famous for speed and power;
For, hitched to a gig, light wagon, or sleigh,
  He could trot his ten miles to the hour;
But now ' Old Gray,' with his shambling pace,
He thinks is the very best horse in the place,
Though you'd lose if you bet on his legs for a race;

But grandpa would choose, for a drive, Old Gray
To the very best horse you have seen to-day.

" One day, as he sat in his old arm-chair,
  From the yard he had just come in ;
And dear old grandma was combing his hair,
  When she chucked him under the chin,
And, said she, ' Good man, your locks were brown,
And very much thicker on temples and crown,
When first you came to this blessed old town ;
You were then just twenty, and rather wild.'
And grandpa looked up in her face and smiled.

" He gave us a temperance talk last week,
  About thousands destroyed by drink ;
And as he talked I saw on his cheek
  A tear ; and I could not but think
That perhaps some loved one, young and fair,
A brother, or son, had been caught in the snare ;
But to ask him about it I did not dare :
But I'll tell you what, boys, I've heard enough
To make me afraid of the poison stuff.

" No wine *these* lips shall ever pass,
  Nor ale, to muddle our brains ;
Poor swearing Sam may swallow his glass,
  And be an old bloat for his pains ;
Our drink shall be of the crystal spring,
For poor-house board is not the thing,
Or the gallows-rope a desirable swing :
The poor-house, and prison, and gallows-rope
Will rarely be used by our ' Band of Hope.' ' "

The audience that listened to Robert understood
very well who " Grandpa " was.

We close this chapter with the following poem, entitled "The Ambitious Toad." The doctor was climbing to the summit of a high hill one morning, when he espied a toad going up also, with which he held this poetical colloquy. It has afforded pleasure not only to children, but also to many of their parents :

"Ho! fellow-traveller, which way now?
　Art toiling up the steep,
Over whose rough and craggy brow
　The morning sun doth peep?
Art proud, and dost the vale despise?
Or dost thou hop for exercise?

"The poet Milton doth relate
　That one, of angel birth,
With pride and devilish hopes elate,
　Once visited our Earth,
And took thy shape, to work his plan
Of ruin to poor thoughtless man.

"And hast thou, since that fatal day,
　Partaken his ambition?
And art thou toiling up this way
　To better thy condition?
Poor toad! I fear that, after all
Thy pains, like him, thou'lt get a fall.

"Yon bird doth weary on the wing
　Before it reach the top;
And dost thou hope, poor, silly thing,
　That, with thy labored hop,
Thou'lt safely reach the hill's green crown
And gaze about upon the town?

" Danger awaits thee, shouldst thou gain
 So high an elevation :
Thy blood those rugged rocks may stain ;
 For, toward that lofty station
The hawk pursues her airy road, —
And hawks, you know, will eat a toad.

" Go, get thee down, nor look behind,
 But ' fling away ambition ; '
And for the future be resigned
 To thine obscure condition ;
For, sure, *contentment* is the road
To happiness, for *man* or *toad.*"

XVIII.

DR. JEWETT IN THE LECTURE-FIELD.

DR. T. L. CUYLER'S opinion of Dr. Jewett, "Our Nestor and Achilles of Reform;" and that contained in a letter just received, which says, "As a lecturer, Dr. Jewett stood at the head of the list;" express about the average verdict of press, pulpit, and individuals concerning the doctor in the lecture-field.

We have spoken of several qualities that eminently fitted him for this sphere of action; all of which derived advantage from his habit of reading. We have seen already that he read the new medical works, kept posted upon the progress of art and science, and was familiar with English and American literature. Such books as the lives of Edmund Burke, Byron, and Byron's associate, Shelley, Hampden, Washington, Lee, Jefferson, with the speeches of Burke, Hastings, Webster, and other orators, Macaulay's Essays, Junius's Letters, and kindred works, he studied carefully, almost as carefully as he did Shakespeare and Burns; History and Travels, and miscellaneous volumes, he read rapidly. He could read very rapidly when he pleased, and possessed remarkable tact for gleaning from books whatever was valuable to him, and discarding all else. His mind was not only active but discriminating, and he would get as much information for future use out of a valuable daily paper as many readers do out of a library.

He was wont to converse about subjects connected with his reading, and often related the substance of a conversation that he had with Daniel Webster about Burke and reading character. The doctor opened the subject by speaking to Webster of his reply to Hayne, commenting upon the language as strongly Saxon. Mr. Webster replied: "If you want to think in brass and speak in iron, study Burke. He has made men his study. If you want to study men as individuals, read Shakespeare; but to know how to govern men in masses — to study them — read Burke. Why," he continued, " Burke wrote a better history of the French revolution before it took place than was written afterwards."

The idea was directly in the line of the doctor's practice, impressing him all the more on that account.

That such a habit of reading contributed largely to the doctor's ability in the lecture-field, both as speaker and writer, is quite obvious. It served to invest his speech and composition with dignity, even where wit made them lively. His eminently philosophical and practical style of speaking and writing derived some of its attractiveness from this source. Even a story, by his manner of telling it, acquired the character of instruction and argument.

He wielded an able pen, and was thoroughly convinced that voice and pen together were indispensable in his work. Whatever he wrote was sure to be read, as whenever he spoke he was sure to be listened to with close attention. Some of his best articles for the press were dashed off at a single sitting, when his soul was all on fire with his theme; and some of the most telling speeches he ever made were extemporaneous — uttered when he was so full of thought and emotion that he must speak or do violence to his nature. Hon. Neal Dow says, that Dr. Jewett delivered the best address that he ever heard, on either side of the Atlantic, at a temperance convention in Cleveland, Ohio, and that it was wholly extemporaneous. The reason is found, not only in the fact that he was ready, quick-witted, and prompt by nature, but also that his mind was thoroughly furnished with material, well digested and classified, for just such an occasion.

There is but one testimony on this subject. We must content ourselves, however, with only a few testimonials of the many at hand.

The celebrated pulpit orator of Brooklyn writes:

"SARATOGA SPRINGS, July 19, 1879.

"MY DEAR BROTHER: I heartily wish that it were in my power to make some valuable contribution to your biography of our glorious, and now glorified friend, Dr. Jewett. It was more than an admiration for a brave and sagacious reformer that I have long felt for him; I thoroughly *loved* him. In one of the best pieces of manhood which our Heavenly Father made in those days, He placed a noble, tender, unselfish heart. Divine grace mellowed and sweetened a character which might otherwise have been rather rugged; and there was a poetic element which beautified it as I saw the laurel blossoms lighting up the rocks and forests of the Shawanyunk Mountains a few days since.

"I first met Dr. Jewett in Trenton, N. J., about the year 1852. He attended one of our state conventions in company with our friend, Neal Dow. I never shall forget the flash of that eye, or the keen thrusts of the scimitar which he wielded in that speech; it pierced to the joints and the marrow. When our Lafayette Avenue Church Temperance Society was organized, he came on and spoke several times to large and enthusiastic audiences. We have had all the most eminent advocates of our reform in that pulpit, with one or two exceptions; but the best *educating* work was done by Jewett's clear brain and masterly expositions. He was never dry or tedious. At the end of his keen sentences there often came that merry sound which was something between a laugh and a ' chirrup,' and it always put his audience into a lively humor. At my house he was the delight of the family. How he used to pour forth his favorite passages from Robert Burns, whose best poetry he knew by heart! His stores of anecdotes were large and racy; they were his own, and the man who stole them was easily detected in the larceny. As a contributor of original thought to the temperance movement the doctor stood first. On the medical aspects of the question, and that of a permanent pecuniary basis, he spent his chief strength. Other men made the temperance reform a matter of occasional thought and effort. But he studied it, prayed over it, lived for it; it was the very core and fibre of his whole existence. I doubt if he ever spent an hour without having this great master-purpose of his life in his mind. Grand old 'Great-Heart'! What blows he struck! What sparks of bright kindling thought flashed from every stroke! How nobly he gave himself to the holy cause, ever crying out 'this *one thing* I do!' How completely he finished up his work, and what a crown hung over his dying head! Whomever else I may see in heaven, I shall be sure to look for my valiant and beloved 'companion in arms,' Charles Jewett. Would that I could put upon paper all that lives in my heart about him. Yours teetotally,

"THEODORE L. CUYLER."

Just before John B. Gough left for Europe, in 1878, he inaugurated a movement to raise a testimonial fund for Dr. Jewett, and addressed to him a letter, from which the following extract is made:

"We [himself and wife] have often spoken of you, and wish we could see you before we leave. What a grand work you have been permitted to accomplish for temperance! Long before I knew or cared anything for the great principle, you were at work, and had been since 1826. Many of us have reaped in fields you have sown, and I wish you to understand that there is one who fully appreciates the great work you have done. I am glad to know that you are able to-day to deal such vigorous blows against the old enemy, and I trust that for years your bow may abide in strength. . . . May God bless you and yours, and bring to you in rich profusion the blessing and the peace and prosperity that you have been instrumental in procuring for others."

Hon. Neal Dow once wrote of him:

" I do not know where or when we first met, but my frequent intercourse with him is among the green spots in my memory. I honor him for his unselfishness, his indomitable perseverance, his great courage — moral as well as physical — and a heart tenderly alive to the woes of his fellow-men, and for the great ability with which he has played his part in the long and painful struggle to exterminate the traffic in strong drink. He is thoroughly sound on every question relating to the causes and cure of that hideous national sin and crime, Intemperance. We have not in all the country another temperance speaker who addresses himself as he does to the understanding, heart, and conscience of his hearers."

Twenty years ago Lucius M. Sargent, author of the " Temperance Tales," wrote in the Boston Evening Transcript, as follows :

" We trust that, without disparagement of any other man's labors and successes, we have done rightly in placing the name of Dr. Jewett and Mr. Gough at the head of the present article, and recognizing the inestimable services which they have rendered in their friendly warfare against man, to save him from himself. Between these able advocates the difference is very striking ; and each, in his own way, appears to us, compared with all others, to be *facile princeps* (easily the chief). Dr. Jewett is a man of education, a physician, and a scholar. We have been familiar with his effective labors in this holy cause for thirty years. . . . Though his addresses are descriptive and full of pathos, humor, sarcasm, and powerful exhortation, he is a lecturer in the scientific sense of that word."

Miss Julia Colman, the distinguished writer and authoress, says:

" Dr. Jewett was the providential instrument of great good to me. I had seen enough of the evils of drink to make me abhor and grieve over them, but I could find, in all the usual modes of temperance work, nothing that seemed to me adequate to the emergency, nothing that probed the difficulty and promised success. If alcohol was a good creature of God, good in its place, and yet in that place continually ensnaring men to their destruction, what could be done? . . . . At this crisis I came across the report of an address by Dr. Jewett, describing the origin of alcohol, detailing its effects, and giving an impression of its utter worthlessness. It just met my wants. God had not made alcohol, and it was not necessary to the well-being of man. From that time, whatever I could find from Dr. Jewett's pen was perused with profit. . . . When he afterwards delivered a course of lectures in the Clinton Avenue Congregational Church, Brooklyn, (to an audience of women engaged in the crusade,) I drank in every word. He was so lucid and simple that the dullest could comprehend, and it seemed to me that his ideas ought to set people to work everywhere. . . . Some years subsequent to the above series of lectures, he addressed a crowded audience in Brooklyn, giving practical instructions and answering inquiries about the medical aspects of the question, when some one asked, What tonic could be given to a convalescent instead of wine? He showed that the great need of the patient was for air, gentle exercise, and simple and wholesome diet, with all gentle ministrations and hygienic surroundings; and especially that the food should be given by whomever the patient loved best; for ' Love is better than wine.' The idea, and its presentation in a Scripture quotation to such a body of intelligent Christian women, was extremely happy, and made a deep impression. I never heard him without profit, nor read his writings without advantage." *

The following are some of the subjects upon which he lectured:

"Alcohol a Cerebral Poison."

"Alcohol a Narcotic."

"Alcohol and the Eliminating Organs."

"Three Stages of Drunkenness—Excitement, Bewilderment, and Narcotism."

"Alcohol condemned alike by Scripture and Science."

"The Law and Tendencies of Artificial Appetites."

"The Warfare of the Liquor Trade on all Useful Trades and Occupations."

"Characteristics of Intemperance; seen in its Effects on Communities, States, and Nations."

"Intemperance as a Vice of Individual Man."

"Prospective Results of the Traffic in Intoxicating Liquors."

"Instrumentalities for Removing the Curse of Intemperance."

"Intemperance the Giant Curse of the World and the Master Vice of Man, and *why* it is so."

"Harmony of the Divine Word with the Teachings of Science, relative to the Effect of Wine on Human Life and Welfare."

"An Argument against the Use of Alcoholic Liquors,

---

* From a large number of valuable letters from friends, and tributes by the journals of the country, we designed to select and publish several pages, but material has accumulated to such an extent that we are compelled to omit them.

25

drawn from their Origin and their Chemical Relations."

" What Views of Intoxicating Liquors and their Relation to Human Welfare did the Spirit of God communicate to the Minds of the Prophets?"

" Alcohol a Non-nutritious Element."

" Why Intemperance is the most Destructive Vice."

" Alcoholic Enslavement: its Philosophy."

" Alcohol as a Stimulant."

" The Law of Increase in the Use of Narcotics."

" Total Abstinence, and its Benefits."

" Alcohol in Medical Practice."

"Means of carrying forward the Temperance Cause to
a Complete Victory."

" Popular Errors relating to Intemperance."

" Incidental Supports of the Liquor Traffic."

" The Literature of the Temperance Cause."

" Obstacles to the Progress of the Temperance Reform."

The following briefs of addresses, as reported by
the press, will show, next to quoting the addresses
entire, his originality, directness, and sound logic :

" Why our Work is Difficult."

1. Apathy to the appalling evils of intemperance, owing
to the fact that the mind grows callous to the view of un-
relieved suffering.

2. That excessive drinking changes the structure of the
drunkard's brain, so as to make his reform difficult.

3. The world is in a state of revolt and unrest : the
devil keeps it satisfied by narcotics.

LECTURE PRELIMINARY TO A COURSE OF EIGHT LECTURES.

1. The need of using every means of temperance education, especially the press.

2. Observation not enough ; the world must study.

3. God works through us, else prayer would be the best excuse for laziness.

4. Tillage in nature means continual warfare against weeds, thorns, and thistles ; so in this moral reform, grog-shops do not need protection or cultivation.

5. Public opinion must be revolutionized : and such is the case in most of the New England states. Comparatively few people now offer liquors to every visitor.

6. Why drink to the President any more than eat a breakfast to the President ? Because conscience needs the peg of patriotism to hang the drinking custom on. The custom needs bolstering, and so people get others to drink with them.

7. Liquor saves tissue ; yes, but how ? Thus : all action, whether "of brain or muscle, destroys tissue, and when a fellow gets muddled with alcohol, there is not much destruction of tissue."

HARMONY OF THE BIBLE AND SCIENCE.

1. As to the origin of the mischievous agent, and the point at which danger commences.

2. As to the specific relation of the dangerous agent to the human constitution, Science declares, and the Bible clearly indicates, that alcohol is a *Brain Poison.*

3. As to the relation of the habit of drinking intoxicating liquors to other vices.

4. As to the *measure of personal peril* to which the drunkard exposes himself.

5. As to the influence of wine-drinking customs among

the people to produce drunkenness, and seriously to imperil all public interests.

6. As to the point at which we are to commence our resistance to the influence of the dangerous agent.

7. As to their estimate of abstinence as a principle or practice.

OBSTACLES TO THE TEMPERANCE REFORM.

1. Its fundamental truths are not understood.
2. It has no financial basis on which it rests.
3. The strength of the liquor traffic is overrated, for it is founded on lies.
4. A want of self-sacrifice among temperance men.
5. Parents cannot believe that there is any danger to *their* children, and so do not teach them.

PECULIARITIES OF INTEMPERANCE.

1. In its origin.
2. In its universality.
3. In its destruction of all good.
4. In destroying the power to produce.
5. No mitigating circumstances to afford consolation.
6. Its constant operation.

PROPS OF THE LIQUOR TRAFFIC.

1. Secrecy.
2. Falsehood.
3. The Entire Devotion of the Liquor-Dealer's Political Power to support the Traffic.
4. The Influence of Fear in our Camp.

INTEMPERANCE A VICE OF INDIVIDUAL MAN.

1. It adapts itself, as no other vice, to both sexes, all ages, classes, and conditions of men.

2. It seizes upon all occasions, sacred, social, and patriotic, joyful and afflictive, and turns them to its own account.

3. It crushes all the powers, faculties, affections, interests, and hopes of individual man, unlike most other vices.

4. It is the pioneer of other vices.

A Temperance Sermon.

" '*By their fruits ye shall know them.*' — Matt. vii. 20.

" Looking at the liquor traffic, what are some of its fruits?

" 1. What fruit has it borne to the individual?

" 2. What fruit has it borne to the manufacturing and agricultural interests?

" 3. What fruit has it borne to the family?

" 4. What fruit has it borne to the state?

" 5. What fruit has it borne to the church?

" And there is no help. The evil cannot be *regulated*. The business itself is an irregularity, and you cannot *regulate* an *irregularity*. You must *extirpate* it — *annihilate* it. 'Every tree that bringeth not forth good fruit is *hewn down*, and cast into the fire.' "

We have no recent lecture of Dr. Jewett written or published, for he did not commit one to writing during the last thirty years of his life. The subjects, skeletons, and characteristic extracts from reports, lectures, and newspaper articles, however, will give the reader a good idea of Dr. Jewett in the lecture-field.

Brief extracts from the doctor's speeches and writings will confirm the statements quoted from individuals and the press.

Pleasure in Reform Work.

"It is one of the felicities of a life devoted to some grand reform movement, that it brings one in contact with the best spirits of the time and country, and secures, even to a plain man, ennobling friendships. Had I been worldly-wise, stuck to my profession, looked out for the 'main chance,' and turned all my energies in that direction, I might, perhaps, have acquired wealth; but I would not exchange the memories of the last forty years, devoted to the temperance reform, for a good many shares of bank or railroad stocks. Now, I can call around me, by the aid of memory and a little imagination, a host of the good and true, with whom my work has made me acquainted. I see them even with closed eyes. They come trooping at my call from all parts of the compass. I am charmed with their shadowy presence, until, possessed by the illusion, I am almost ready to rise and exclaim, 'Mr. President, and Gentlemen of the Convention!'"

Intemperance destroys the Producing Power.

"If I with a hammer should break the lamp before me, you would say it was a wrong act. I have destroyed an object of interest as well as of use. There is the history of the world in that lamp. Noah did not light the ark with lamps constructed like this. The means employed by the patriarchs to give light when the sun had gone to bed, were, I suppose, quite rude in comparison with this. Each generation added something to the facilities for producing light, and so on, age after age, until we have such as this before me. Hence the lamp before us affords other matter for reflection besides the light it furnishes. It were surely a wicked act to destroy, wantonly, an object of so much interest and, at the same time, so useful. But, sir, when you have crippled the intellect which planned that piece of mechanism, and palsied the hand that fashioned it, you have done a most foul and accursed deed, which neither men nor angels can repair. And that is what alcohol does."

No Alcohol in Nature.

" People vainly suppose that alcohol strengthens and supports. Nutritious articles are the product of nature alone. We can take sugar, for instance, and resolve it into its three elements, oxygen, hydrogen, and carbon ; but all the chemists in the world cannot take these three and make sugar. The sugar-cane, the sorghum, the beet, and our maple trees can do it, but man cannot. The vegetable and animal world growing (composing), produces substances nutritious for man. Alcohol is not produced by composing matter in any instance in creation, but by decomposing matter entirely. Sugar putrefying makes alcohol. Alcohol is a stage in the process of decay and death. It putrefies humanity, physically (as many a bloated form testifies), socially, and morally."

Ladies, Beware !

" The signs of a drinker remind me of a vessel that has sprung a leak and hoisted a flag of distress at sea. The water increases, the pumps are choked, and all despair ; yet the flag still waves. Just so when the system springs a leak at the mouth, the word is, ' All hands to the pumps !' and the flag of distress is hung out upon the nose. The eyelids also look as though they were bound with red ribbon. Ladies, when you see a young man bearing these signs, beware ! "

Alcoholic Medication covers Disease.

" It was remarked by Miller, the great surgeon of Edinburgh, ' Alcohol cures nothing, but it covers up a great deal.' It is illustrated by the trick of the jockey, who has a foundered horse to sell. The purchaser is coming on the morrow, and to-night he takes a knife and adroitly severs the nerves of sensation just below the fetlock. The horse in the morning travels without any show of lameness. But is he cured? No: the founder is covered up. The sundered nerves do not telegraph the disease to the brain. The telegraphic wire is cut. The founder is there the same as ever. So the patient who submits to alcoholic medication has his disease covered up. His nerves of sensation are blunted and refuse to carry any intelligence to the brain. The man or woman is deceived; and I am sorry to say that often the physician, either consciously or immorally, is a party to the deception."

INTEMPERANCE IS CONSTANT.

"War blows his bloody trump, and dire alarms
  Convulse the earth, while nations rush to arms;
Earth's lap is with her bleeding children pressed,
  Each with his bayonet in his brother's breast."

" And were the terrible scourge to continue its ravages without intermission for centuries, the earth would be unpeopled. But war ceases. The industrial pursuits of life, the public morals, education, the arts and sciences, and in short all the interests of humanity, have time to recover, in part at least, before the evil is repeated. Pestilence is not always sowing the air with the seeds of death. Frost, drought, famine, fire, and storms execute their messages of wrath, and then for a season bid us farewell. Not so, however, with intemperance. Its work of death goes steadily on, winter and summer, by night and by day, in seasons of plenty and when famine stalks abroad. If, like war or pestilence, it would occasionally afford the suffering earth a little respite, men would have an opportunity to contrast their condition during such periods with their condition during its visitations; and their eyes would be opened. But no such respite is afforded."

UNIVERSALITY OF INTEMPERANCE.

" Storms may baffle the skill or defy the power of our seamen, and make sad havoc with our commerce; but while the noble ship is going to pieces on the rocks of our hard New England coast, and men and merchandise are by every surge consigned to destruction, the good people, ten miles in the interior, are, it may be, sleeping in safety in their beds, or pursuing, without interruption, their ordinary avocations. The storm does not assail their immediate interests, nor threaten their lives. *But this curse of intemperance scatters its wrecks as well over the interior as on the coast.*"

REMOVAL OF INTEMPERANCE POSSIBLE.

" If a man can make a copper kettle for Satan, and set it boiling, I can dash cold water on the fire, and with a sledge-hammer break the kettle in pieces. ' But such a course would be contrary to law.' Then legalize it by your will and votes, and make me sheriff of the county, and, God helping me, it shall be done. Muscles and sledge-hammers were never better employed than they would be in demolishing those accursed structures which, swallowing up, as they do, immense quantities of fuel and the fruits of the earth, while thousands lack for fire and bread, sent out in turn a ceaseless torrent of disease and death upon a suffering world. If men can erect a grogshop in one of our beautiful villages, fill it with the materials of mischief, call about them the reckless and the vile, and set to work to ruin our youth and curse all the interests of society, — why may not the strong hands of the sober and moral portion of that community empty the vile concern of its inmates and contents, and bar its doors against their return? ' Why, it would be contrary to law!' Then amend your laws, and let their sanction be given to such a righteous work."

PROHIBIT THE TRAFFIC.

" You know that in a bowling-alley there are two parties — one who make it their business to bowl down the pins, while the other picks them up and arranges them again on the alley. While the boy is picking up the pins, you will often hear the other party uttering the language of encouragement and commendation — ' That is right, my little fellow! Pick them up, my brave boy!' &c.; and occasionally they will toss him a penny or two to encourage him. What does all this mean? Do they admire the arrangement of the pins, and will they allow them to stand thus? By no means. They have bowled them down repeatedly, and intend to bowl them down again. Thus it is with rumsellers. While we are content to pursue the course recommended by some, and confine our efforts to the lifting up of those whom their accursed traffic has bowled down, even the rumsellers will pay us a compliment — ' There, now; that is true temperance!' at the same time meaning to bowl them down again. Sir, I am willing to join my fellow-citizens in further efforts to rescue the fallen; but I ask them in turn to join me in saying to these unprincipled men, ' Roll again at your peril!'"

ALCOHOL A DECEIVER.

" You understand, doubtless, that alcohol is always the product of decay. Obtain it from whatever source you may, the death of the vegetable from which you obtain it must precede its formation or extraction. Vitality cannot co-exist with it. No vegetable contains it while its life continues; but when all vitality is extinct, then fermentation takes place, and alcohol is the first product of the process of decay. Now, in all its influence on society and man, alcohol seems to retain this character of incompatibility with the principle of vitality. Death must precede its march, and tread closely on its heels. Yet, while it is doing the work of death, *it promises and counterfeits life.*"

RUMSELLERS.

" It is very amusing to see the rumsellers laboring so industriously to place themselves in the attitude of persecuted individuals, and almost enough to draw tears from granite to listen to their pathetic appeals for public sympathy. The language of a distinguished comic poet of England would not be out of place in their mouths, —

'Pity the lifted whites of both my eyes,'

" Sir, the traffickers in intoxicating drinks are the last men who ought to complain of persecution. They live, not by a legitimate business which returns to society an equivalent for the goods or money they extract from it and employ for the sustenance of their useless lives, but, on the contrary, as they grow rich, others around them, to a still greater extent, must grow poor; for the article with which they supply their customers not only does them no good, but positive evil, unfitting them for the discharge of their duties to God, their families, and society at large. As a poisonous mushroom grows most luxuriantly when it sprouts from a heap of decaying vegetables, so a rumseller fattens and thrives in exact proportion to the decay and rottenness of society around him."

The Eliminating Organs expel Alcohol.

" When you inhale the strong odor of liquor from a man who has been drinking, it is because his eliminating organs are at work.   His lungs are throwing off its vapor. . . . Drinking men know how to treat a companion who is drunk.   They don't know the philosophy of it, but they know the fact that it is necessary to get him in an upright position and then give him exercise.   By doing this the blood will gravitate from instead of to the brain, and the exercise will increase the activity of the lungs so that the vapor of the liquor will more rapidly pass off.   The poor fellow may object — may talk about his ' cons-tu'sh'nal right, yer know,' and may choose to lie down in his drunken stupor like an ' ind-pend't cit'zen of this free country, yer know ; ' but his companions ' train ' him, and by and by he gets sober, because the eliminative organs have been set actively at work and have performed their office."

Secrecy of the Liquor Traffic.

" Our opponents have sought to hang an impenetrable veil around those establishments where factitious wines and adulterated liquors are prepared, with which the mass of liquors are both imposed upon and poisoned Enough, however, has been learned of those liquors, and the destructive and disgusting materials employed in their manufacture, to associate them forever in the minds of those who have investigated the subject, with the delicate compound prepared by Macbeth's witches, some of the precious ingredients of which were, as enumerated by the second witch, —

'Fillet of a fenny snake,
  In the caldron boil and bake ;
  Eye of newt, and toe of frog,
  Wool of bat, and tongue of dog,
  Adder's fork, and blindworm's sting,
  Lizzard's leg, and owlet's wing, —
  For a charm of powerful trouble,
  Like a hell-broth boil and bubble.' "

LOGIC OF FACTS.

"Array these facts on paper, and put a copy into every family, until they shall be made to reflect, to feel — ay, and to speak — until they shall be prompted to exclaim with the poet, —

'Shall tongues be mute when deeds are wrought
  Which well might shame extremest hell ?
Shall freeman lock the indignant thought ?
  Shall mercy's bosom cease to swell ?
Shall honor bleed ? Shall truth succumb ?
Shall pen, and press, and soul be dumb ? '

"Let the enemy talk of *constitutions* and *inalienable rights* and *free trade*, to the end of the chapter ; but let us talk of FACTS — of soul-stirring FACTS of daily occurrence, and from those facts reason out the duties and obligations of those we address, by plain and logical argument. Study the subject in all its relations, and make yourselves familiar with every argument by which the right and the truth may be sustained, and then grapple boldly with the enemies of truth. Join issue with them, wherever they may be met, — in the public meeting, in the columns of the public journals, in the social circle, in the stage-coach, in the rail-car and steamboat, — and pray God for strength and victory."

Laughable Side of Vice.

"Every vile system and every debasing vice has about
it certain points or phases which render it fair game for
ridicule, and expose it to the laugh of good men. The
poet, Pollock, in his 'Course of Time,' makes hypocrisy
appear not only a sin against God, but so supremely ridiculous that the spirits of even good men cannot resist the
inclination to laugh at it, even before the bar of final judgment.

> 'The righteous smiled, and even Despair itself
>   Some signs of laughter gave.'

"No wicked system that curses this earth presents so
many ridiculous aspects as that with which we are con-
tending. Think of a human being outside of an asylum
for idiots, sucking a mint julep through a straw! Think
for a moment of distinguished gentlemen around a public
table bobbing and bowing to each other across it, and
drinking to the health of 'her Majesty,' or 'our President,'
or 'Count von Bismarck!' Why not eat breakfast to
'her Majesty' or 'our President'?"

The doctor's reports to the Union from the lecture-
field, when he was agent, were regarded as models.
He called wit, sarcasm, logic, as well as his familiarity with Burns, Shakespeare, and other poets, to
his aid, making his reports very spicy and readable;
thus:

"A division of the house was called for, and a separation promptly between alcohol and water, without the aid
of retort or copper kettle. Then came the tug of war!
No evasion, no concealment of sentiments or wishes for
any one who voted. What was a man to do who re-

gai led his character, from whose soul the love of rum or the love of pence had not extinguished all sense of justice, all regard for the prosperity of the town or the welfare of its inhabitants? Most fortunately there was a door on the side of the house occupied by the miscalled liberals. Let them devoutly thank their stars for once! To the door numbers of them rushed; and,

> 'As bees buzz out wi' angry fyke,
>   When plundering herds assail their byke,'

so eagerly rushed they out, glad to escape for once, having their own noses counted with some others, about the complexion of a ripe strawberry. The count gave fifty for rum, one hundred and seven for water, — more than two to one. Our new friends and faithful allies, the Washingtonians, stood side by side with the old regulars, and together they triumphed. Let no one henceforth deny that there is a distillery in ——, one that separates rum from water, —

> 'Quicker by far than some desire,
>   Without the aid of worm or fire.'

" As your last journal contained no report from me, and as the field of my labors for the past month has been in a part of the state distant from the metropolis, I know not but you may have come to the conclusion ere this that I had quit the field, and given it up entirely to our late but efficient allies. If so, you are quite mistaken; for I am yet ' on hand and to be had.' It is not best for all the old regulars to quit the field because we have been reinforced, but rather with renewed energy —

> 'Attack the foe; break through the thick array
>   Of his thronged legions, and charge home upon him.
>   Perhaps some arm, more lucky than the rest,
>   May reach his heart, and free the world from bondage.'

"Whatever other errors or vices may properly be charged to us in the account for August, we are sure that idleness will not be of the number. We have worked hard. We have more than once thought of those touching lines in Hood's 'Song of the Shirt,' —

'Work ! work ! work ! while the cock is crowing aloof ;
Work ! work ! work ! till the stars shine through the roof.'

" In this village the wife of an intemperate man closed a life of suffering in death. 'After life's fitful fever she sleeps well.' It is, however, sad to think she was deserted by her husband in that hour when most she needed support and sympathy. He took his hat and moved towards the door. She followed him with an eye that looked unutterable things, and, with what strength the great destroyer had left her, she exclaimed, '*Dear husband, do not leave me now !*' But he went, and she was left to struggle *alone*. She breathed her last in about twenty minutes after he left the house. From our souls we execrate the influence that could tear a man away, at such a moment, from his wife. When we look upon the scenes of wretchedness and guilt, the want and woe, the disease, despair and death, which visit the earth through the influence of the traffic in rum, and when we realize that all this is known and understood by those who are, for paltry gain, vending the poison by wholesale and retail through a suffering community, we are sometimes led to exclaim, with Campbell, —

' Where sleeps thy shaft, O vengeance ? — where the rod
That smote the foes of Zion, and of God ? ' "

XIX.

"TABLE TALK."

IT was in conversation that Dr. Jewett's remarkable versatility appeared to best advantage. His tact, wit, humor, wisdom, and mental force came into full play here, and he instructed, electrified, amused, and "set the table in a roar." And what was equally remarkable with his conversation, it made little difference whether his listeners were educated or not, a group of professional gentlemen or the "tin-pail brigade." He could adapt himself to circumstances with such remarkable facility and suddenness, that no emergency caught him napping. His sallies, from "grave to gay," and from gay to grave, were so unexpected and natural, that old and young, educated and ignorant, were held spellbound.

In 1842 Dr. Jewett was on the cars, when fifteen or twenty railroad laborers, called the "tin-pail brigade," entered at a certain station. Some of the number found seats, others stood. The doctor greeted them with one of his broadest smiles and a jocose remark, and was soon on the freest terms with them in conversation about railroading, dignity of work, and

26

Robert Burns.   He began to recite from the Scotch
poet, accompanying the recitation with the most appropriate action, to the inexpressible pleasure of his
illiterate audience.   They left their seats and gathered around him, with tin pails in hand, hanging
upon his lips entranced to the end of their trip, part-
ing with him there as with an old friend of twenty
years' standing, each countenance beaming with
pleasure.

Nor did he compromise dignity, or lower the
standard of intellectual taste, in ministering to the
enjoyment of his uncultured listeners.   Every one
in the car was deeply interested; and there were
refined and educated people among them.   James
Russell Lowell, the distinguished poet of Cambridge,
was there, although Dr. Jewett was not aware of his
presence.   He was a delighted listener, too; and,
subsequently, he celebrated the event in a poem of
twenty-two stanzas, entitled, "*An Incident in a
Railroad Car*."   It opened thus:

> "He spoke of Burns; men rude and rough
>   Pressed round to hear the praise of one
> Whose heart was made of manly, simple stuff,
>   As homespun as their own.
>
> "And when he read they forward leaned,
>   Drinking, with thirsty hearts and ears,
> His brook-like songs whom glory never weaned
>   From humble smiles and tears.
>
> "Slowly there grew a tender awe,
>   Sun-like, o'er faces brown and hard,
> As if in him who read they felt and saw
>   Some presence of the bard.

> "It was a sight for sin and wrong
> And slavish tyranny to see,
> A sight to make our faith more pure and strong
> In high humanity.

> "I thought, those men will carry hence
> Promptings their former life above,
> And something of a finer reverence
> For beauty, truth, and love."

We have not space for the whole poem; but it continues, expanding the thought that, under the rough exterior of the "poor and untutored," there is a heart that will respond to the "higher" and "nobler" sentiments of life when touched by one who is master of the art. This fine poetic tribute of Lowell illustrates and confirms much that has been said of Dr. Jewett, in this department, on previous pages.

Many of his admirers can appreciate that scene. They readily recall the whole-heartedness and abandon with which his wit, wisdom, and mimicry could make such an occasion memorable. Such a mixing up of instruction and sport, talent and drollery, anecdote and argument, pathos and fun, yet without offending good taste or degrading intellect, they cannot associate with any other person of their acquaintance.

A clergyman writes:

"The half can never be told. The charm of the man was in his presence. Brave old soldier! A more delightful guest never crossed our threshold. We were always glad to see him. His conversation in the home was charming. His fund of anecdotes, witty sayings, and shrewd observations was endless. His good sense and practical wisdom always impressed us. He ought to have written a book on the management of children."

A temperance-worker says:

"Dr. Jewett was often at my house. He always stopped with me when he came to town. It was a treat to have him in my family. He was the best conversationalist I ever knew. My family would turn night into day any time to hear him converse. Such pithy sayings, such wise remarks, such genuine wit as he would pour forth for hours, I never heard from any other man. And then he would make it all so spicy with pertinent quotations from British and American poets, with whose productions he seemed perfectly familiar."

A few years ago Dr. Jewett lectured in a town in New Jersey, where an influential doctor of divinity was settled. He was told that the distinguished preacher was not much of a temperance man, and he was inclined to accept the information as correct. He was assigned to the minister's house for entertainment. After the evening lecture, when he had stretched himself out upon the minister's lounge, somewhat exhausted, the host said:

"Dr. Jewett, what do you think of the gospel as a reformatory agent?"

"Great, wonderful!" replied Dr. Jewett, perfectly satisfied what was coming.

"I mean its power to save the drunkard, and do up this temperance work," added the preacher.

"I understand you; nothing like it, perfectly marvelous, only let it reach the heart," answered Dr. Jewett.

"I did not know that your opinions accorded so nearly with my own; those are my sentiments," continued the minister. "If men would become Christians they would not become drunkards."

"And if drunkards would become Christians, they would be drunkards no longer," responded Dr. Jewett.

"Well, doctor, what need then of this outside temperance work? Why not give ourselves to preaching the gospel wholly, and let that accomplish the work?" remarked the minister, with an air of confidence in his position.

"The case is just here," replied the doctor, rising from the lounge. "I was educated for a physician. I am called to a patient who is in a state of asphyxia from over-eating, and is nigh unto death. I know that the gospel is just suited to his spiritual necessities; but I shall not spend a moment in exhortation or preaching; *I shall give him twenty grains of ipecac at once.* You must get the rum out of a man before you can put the gospel in."

That sally of wit converted the conservative doctor of divinity into a radical advocate of temperance.

We remember once at our supper-table, the doctor was criticising the manners and customs of the times, when he summed up his discourse in this sentence :

"People nowadays make unimportant things important, and important things unimportant."

He had furnished illustrations of his remark in advance, as, "Many parents bestow more attention upon the dress than they do upon the moral culture of their children." "Some men are more anxious to have their houses furnished well than their heads." "It seems as if many good people even think more of money than they do of morals." "Youths appear to want to grow up into a good business more than into good character."

"Do you suppose that he was *called* to the work of preaching the gospel?" inquired the doctor concerning a minister whom the small company were criticising, and one whom the doctor himself knew to be without talent or eloquence.

"He thinks so, no doubt," answered one of the number.

"But do *you* think so?" urged the doctor.

"Perhaps I do not understand what a *call* to the ministry is," was the reply.

"Well," added Dr. Jewett, "between us and the ceiling, I should say of that man, as the good old lady said to her nephew, who was a preacher nobody wanted to hear, 'James, why did you enter the ministry?'"—and he imitated the old lady's voice. "'Because I felt that God *called* me to it,' answered James, with a serious air. Wiping her spectacles with her handkerchief, and seeming somewhat troubled, she responded, 'James, are you sure it was not some other *noise* you heard?'"

Dr. Jewett had a way, in conversation, of repeating poetry from prominent authors in response to some remark, often without adding a word of his own. The following are examples.

Calling upon a family to spend the night, where he had often been, his salutation on entering the house was, in Cowper's lines:

"Now stir the fire, and close the shutters fast,
Let fall the curtains, wheel the sofa round,
And, while the bubbling and loud-hissing urn
Throws up a steamy column, and the cups
That cheer but not inebriate, wait on each,
So let us welcome peaceful evening in."

On listening to a sad tale of filial ingratitude, he remarked in Shakespeare's words:

"How sharper than a serpent's tooth it is
To have a thankless child."

His attention being called to the starry heavens on a beautiful evening, he replied, from Shakespeare:

"Look, how the floors of heaven
Are thick inlaid with patines of bright gold;
There's not the smallest orb, which thou behold'st,
But in this motion like an angel sings,
Still quiring to the young-eyed cherubim;
Such harmony is in immortal souls:
But whilst this muddy vesture of decay
Doth grossly close us in, we cannot hear it."

An allusion to immortality, brought out the following lines from Campbell:

" This spirit shall return to him
    Who gave its heavenly spark ;
Yet, think not, sun, it shall be dim
    When thou thyself art dark !
No ! it shall live again, and shine
In bliss unknown to beams of thine,
    By Him recalled to breath ;
Who captive led captivity,
Who robbed the grave of victory,
    And took the sting from death ! "

In conversation with several temperance advocates about the late Lucius M. Sargent, the doctor
expressed the opinion that in " graceful rhetoric, combined with keen satire and powerful logic, no American has excelled him, especially in controversial
writing," adding, " an English poet has expressed
my opinion :

" The arrow, polished, in his hand was seen,
    And as it grew more polished grew more keen ;
He seemed to sport and trifle with the dart,
    But while he sported, drove it to the heart."

And this, in our opinion, has equal force when
applied to Dr. Jewett himself.

Riding with an intelligent lady, the conversation
turned upon the varied conditions of life, when the
doctor expressed his belief, that God's grace was
sufficient to make a person happy in spite of circumstances ; that " a good man is satisfied from himself,"
whatever his condition in life may be, quoting
Burns's lines :

" It's not in titles nor in rank ;
    It's not in wealth like Lon'nun bank,

> To purchase peace and rest;
> It's not in making muckle mair,
> It's not in books, it's not in lear,
> To make us truly blest;
> If happiness ha'e not her seat
> And centre in the breast;
>   Nae treasures nor pleasures
>   Could make us happy lang;
>   The heart aye 's the part aye
>   That makes us right or wrang."

Sitting by his wife in the evening when she was engaged with her needle to meet the pressing demands of the family, and the children were gathered for their evening pastime or tasks, he repeated Burns' lines:

> " Wi' joy unfeigned brothers and sisters meet,
>   An' each for other's welfare kindly spiers;
> The social hours, swift-winged, unnoticed fleet;
>   Each tells the uncos that he sees or hears;
> The parents, partial, eye their hopeful years;
>   Anticipation forward points the view,
> The mother, wi' her needle an' her shears,
>   Gars auld claes look amaist as weel 's the new;
> The father mixes a' wi' admonition due."

Friends remarked in his presence about the love that a youth of his acquaintance bore for his affianced, when he at once responded again from the Scottish bard:

> " O happy love! where love like this is found!
>   O heart-felt raptures! bliss beyond compare!
> I have pacéd much this weary, mortal round,
>   And sage experience bids me this declare:—
> If Heaven a draught of heavenly pleasure spare,
>   One cordial in this melancholy vale,

> 'Tis when a youthful, modest, loving pair
> In others' arms breathe out the tender tale,
> Beneath the milk-white thorn that scents the evening gale."

Passing along the street with a friend, their attention was called to a company of youths jumping a fence to test their agility. The scene turned the doctor's conversation to the buoyancy and hope of youth, and the real beauty and winsomeness of such a scene as that before him, closing with this stanza from Burns:

> " I am a bending, aged tree,
> That long has stood the wind and rain ;
> But now has come a cruel blast,
> An' my last hold of earth is gane ;
> Nae leaf of mine shall greet the spring,
> Nae simmer sun exalt my bloom ;
> But I maun lie before the storm,
> An' ithers plant them in my room."

This is but an illustration of the general character of Dr. Jewett's conversation. Many times we have heard him slip in quotations, in both prose and verse, that invested the interview with an indescribable charm. In conversation with friends upon public questions, quotations from the speeches of Burke, Hastings, Webster, Corwin, and others, were common. He was just as likely to call quotations to his aid when riding in the cars or at work in his garden, as he was in the social circle or at the fireside. A friend recollects with what tender spirit he addressed a little bird in his garden, reciting Burns's entire poem, beginning thus:

> " Ilk hopping bird — wee helpless thing,
> That in the merry month of spring
> Delighted me to hear thee sing."

We must limit this chapter to a few of the doc-tor's apothegms, which added to the attractive, in-structive character of his conversation.

" Alcohol may stimulate to increased action, just as a whip may impel the horse to extra efforts; but neither the alcohol nor whip impart any strength. It is poor reasoning, that, because the stomach can bear a stroke or two of the whip to get it out of the quagmire, it can live on lashes."

" The trouble is, that, while people are opposed to in-temperance and kindred vices, they are not opposed to their *causes*. They want to continue the causes in opera-tion, but avoid the consequences. God won't let them."

" Benedict Arnold was a rumseller and drunkard Three of the most important defeats sustained by our country in the Revolution were caused by men who died drunkards. Had a sober crew been on board the Chesa-peake, the brave Lawrence never would have had to cry, ' Don't give up the ship!' Drunkards can't save the lib-erties of this country."

" You remember that inimitable scene in Faust, where Mephistopheles takes a gimblet and draws wine out of the dry table. The wine turned to fire in the stomachs of all who drank it, and they became wild and mad, and seized each other's noses, cutting them off with their knives, thinking the noses were bunches of grapes. There is more truth than poetry in that description. ' Wine is a mocker,' and it burns in the brain, and maddens men till they cannot tell a nose from a bunch of grapes."

" A man may do a right thing in a wrong way; but he cannot do a wrong thing in a right way. For there is no right way of doing wrong. If there were, it is a question whether he would not be as badly off in doing right in a wrong way, as he would be in doing wrong in a right way."

"I am sick of the half-hearted and ignorant efforts of hundreds who have a place in our societies of various kinds. To hear men declaiming against tippling, and pausing now and then to eject from a dirty mouth the juice of tobacco, a poisonous and filthy weed, chewed for no purpose but abnormal sensations and excitement, — it makes me sick. When I see so many of our rank and file smoking and chewing, burning a half dozen ten-cent cigars per day, and yet declaring themselves too poor to pay for a temperance paper which might instruct them in a better way, I am half inclined to exclaim with the despairing Eneas :

'What hope, O Panthus ! Whither shall we run ?
Where make a stand, or what can yet be done ?'"

XX.

DR. JEWETT A MODEL REFORMER.

DR. JEWETT possessed the elements of a model reformer. Chiefly they were born with him — tact, wit, humor, decision, courage, talents, sympathy, love, and principle; nurtured from childhood, and matured by industry, patience, and close observation into stalwart qualities. In this respect he did more for himself than all the world beside did for him. Gibbon says that "every person has two educations, — one which he receives from others, and one, more important, which he gives to himself." The educa tion which Dr. Jewett gave to himself was vastly greator than that which he received from others. Nature provided him with excellent material, and he made the most of it possible.

The celebrated English merchant, Samuel Budgett, was wont to say that a "man's success in life depends upon tact, push, and principle." Whatever these three qualities may do for a business or professional man, they alone will not make a genuine reformer. They constitute an important part of the outfit, but, without other qualities, can make but the commonest worker in this line. That Dr. Jewett possessed these to an eminent degree, and others no less marked and valuable, the previous record furnishes abundant proof.

His tact was remarkable. He knew how to use his powers to advantage. His methods of working indicated to every observer that he knew what he was about. He adapted himself to circumstances with singular ease. He controlled emergencies readily. Not only was "necessity the mother of invention" with him, but also the father of thought, application, and force. If one method of doing was impossible, he found another that was just as good. If too poor to get what he wanted, he took what he could get, and made it answer his purpose well. If he lacked the wherewith to purchase surgical instruments, he made them. If he needed cart or wheelbarrow, and his income was more limited than usual, he could easily manufacture them. He could doctor the body and the soul as well. He could be master of physic and the rostrum, or a practical mechanic and farmer. His resources, in this regard, appear to have been equal to any occasion.

When such tact is combined with talents, success is easy. In this way often a man of very ordinary abilities, with tact, achieves more in practical life than one who has ten times his talents without tact. Emerson expresses it thus :

> "Tact clinches the bargain,
>   Sails out of the bay,
> Gets the vote in the senate,
>   Spite of Webster or Clay."

As a reformer Dr. Jewett's tact was a cardinal quality. It served him well in dealing with all classes of men, as he necessarily did. When appetite and avarice assailed him, his tact always managed them. Discordant elements, grave difficulties, violent opposition, and even treachery itself, were largely modified by its agile exercise.

The doctor possessed sound COMMON SENSE, which enabled him to use his powers to the best advantage. In popular parlance men mean about the same thing when they say of a man he has "sound judgment," "tact," or "good practical knowledge." Yet there is this difference : Common sense involves mental and moral resorces behind it, of which the latter may not be an exhaustive exponent. Dr. Jewett possessed a fund of ability, by whatever name called, existing in conjunction with tact, and perhaps, in an important sense, part of it. We call it common sense.

This gave power to Dr. Jewett as a reformer. The usual appellations applied to this class, as "fanatical," "pig-headed," "impracticable," "foolish," did not set well on him. Whoever labeled him thus knew that he had put on the wrong label.

As already hinted, Dr. Jewett's sound sense served him a good turn in all circumstances. It was not serviceable in one place and useless in another. Some men have good sense in some things, and the opposite in others. That college professor who replied to the grocer's inquiry, — "How much coffee do you want?" "Well, I declare, my wife did not say, but I should think a bushel would do," — had not common sense in common affairs, however much practical wisdom he might have possessed in his special department. But Dr. Jewett's common sense controlled his acquisitions and natural powers, — his zeal, temper, language, learning, wit, humor, and logic, — and was available everywhere. Macaulay said of the Duke of Monmouth : "He had brilliant wit and ready invention without common sense." Dr. Jewett possessed the same with common sense ; and so they served him a noble purpose while they were comparatively useless, if not injurious, to the Duke.

His WIT was second to no quality in making him a model reformer. Often, in battling against the appetite and avarice of men, as Dr. Jewett was compelled to do in his work, keen, sparkling wit enabled him to manage his audience, keeping them in good humor and eager to listen. Neither rum-sellers nor their emissaries were in the habit of trying to cough, hiss, or stamp him down. However unpalatable the truth he spoke, they listened; for the doctor's rule was, the more unpalatable the dish the more wit to season it for swallowing. Stern logic and just severity might compound the pill, but wit must sugar-coat it. In all reforms, *witty* advocates, other things being equal, have experienced little trouble with disturbers of public meetings or the mobocratic spirit.

Dr. Jewett once replied to a remark about his wit -- "Wit is like fire, a good servant, but a hard master." He set a careful watch that his wit should serve only as a servant.

"Wit never grows old," it is said. The born sparkle always sticks to it. This, too, is an advantage to a reformer. His physical force will abate with age. The old-time dexterity and strength must flag. But genuine wit retains its youth. It is "more ruddy than rubies. Its countenance is as sapphire," whether twenty years old or three-score and ten. Was not this true of Dr. Jewett? Whoever saw him on the rostrum, in the last decade of his life, without thinking and perhaps saying, "young as ever — appears just as he did forty years ago"? It was his wit, flashing in his eye, enlivening thought, vivifying sentiment, rejuvenating action, and reinforcing age with youthful spirits. It was the same in the social circle. A friend in whose family Dr. Jewett often found rest and congenial society, furnishes an illustration of this fact. The doctor came just at night suffering quite severely with his heart. It was but three or four years ago. The family left him on the lounge when they went to the weekly evening prayer meeting. On their return he was there still, suffering less, though weary and distressed. He inquired about the meeting. He wished to know what was said. While one was rehearsing what A said, he quoted a text of Scripture that the speaker might have employed to enforce his words. And the same was true of B's and C's remarks — a passage of Scripture was ready for each one. By and by, uncon-

27

sciously, he glanced off to the poets, quoting from them on this and that topic, both grave and gay — Cowper, Burns, Young, Shakespeare, and others, interspersing anecdotes and wit in rapid succession, forgetting debility and pain and even that he had a heart; finally sitting bolt upright to enter into the occasion with body, mind, and soul, as if renewing his youth, keeping the whole company, young and old, interested and every now and then "in a roar" until the clock struck twelve — midnight, all surprised at the lateness of the hour.

The spontaneity of his wit increased its power. Often he evoked laughter without meaning it. His wit was so natural and genuine that it appeared to be essential to his speech. We recollect hearing him one Sabbath evening when his whole heart was in harmony with the sacredness of the day; and he put one of his points so quaintly and triumphantly that the audience laughed. After the meeting, with some anxiety, he inquired why the audience laughed, saying it was far from his intention to make them laugh. We assured him that it was all right — that if there was no occasion for an actual laugh, a broad smile was very appropriate in the circumstances.

Dr. Jewett's COURAGE was another element of his power as a reformer. He appears to have been oblivious to fear. He was put into many perilous places, but was never scared. He expected opposition and abuse. He knew that difficulties and dangers would arise. He understood well that the temperance cause must push its way in the teeth of wicked men and devils. Yet his courage was equal to the demand. He was as near *fearless* as any man could well be. Though friends feared for him, he did not fear for himself. Nor was it reck- lessness. Such a man as he is not reckless. It was the courage of a soul in earnest to discharge personal duty at the call of God. He thought not of popularity, greatness, or renown, but simply how to do the most and best for humanity; and his courage was a state of heart incidental to that heroic, Christian purpose.

LOVE OF THE CAUSE was still another element of his success as a reformer. He loved it better than anything else in human work — better than the medical profession, better than agriculture and hor- ticulture, better than literature and science, better than wealth or distinction. All of these he relin- quished for the privilege of advancing a cause that he loved. And when he had nearly worn himself out by hard service, he wrote:

" Had I sacrificed my ' hobby,' as some called it, and devoted myself to my profession, and acquired wealth, that wealth could have added nothing to my personal happiness, or that of my family, and would now be a miserable possession as compared with the memories of a life devoted to the reformation, education, and elevation of my fellow-men."

The words quoted prove that not only LOVE OF THE CAUSE, but also LOVE OF HIS KIND, was a prominent factor of his ·life as a reformer. Every

chapter of this book, and almost every page, furnishes proof of the statement.   He lived for others,
not for himself.

As the editor of a prominent journal in the town
where Dr. Jewett lived and died, said:

> " In his life he has touched, with an uplifting power,
> millions, and never one with a down-pulling power.   He
> has always made the world better, and never made it
> worse.   He has builded society, never demolished it.
> His life has been given, without pay, to his countrymen ;
> working for human weal, and not for honor or pay."

Dr. Jewett took the BIBLE FOR THE BASIS OF THE
TEMPERANCE REFORM.   It was not enough with
him to be a *Christian* reformer ; the Christian reformer must plant himself upon Christianity in his
methods and hopes.   He saw no victory, near or
remote, outside of the Bible.   That must provide
not only the tactics of war, but its munitions as
well.   Hence, he was as familiar with the Bible as
the commander is with the arsenal.   He understood
exactly what ordnance it could furnish.   He felt
strong, confident, and bold when reinforced by the
Scriptures.   Then he was master of the situation,
commanding both reason and conscience.

Here was the secret of Dr. Jewett's steady, persevering and consistent course.   While some reformers drifted into doubt and unbelief, renouncing former respect for God's Word and His Church, the
doctor maintained his hold upon both as vital to
success.   No minister or Christian layman ever

expected other than the most emphatic words from him, for the Bible was guide and counsellor on the temperance question. Hence he was welcome to pulpits, Christian conventions, and ecclesiastical bodies. Public confidence, personal respect, and admiration were secured by his fidelity to the Word of God.

His SPIRIT as a reformer was highly commendable. He was sharp but kind in controversy, even when he "flayed his antagonist alive." A sally of genuine wit was very likely to accompany the application of the knife, so as to modify the pain. He never became angry in the hottest contest, though he excelled most public speakers in the use of sarcasm and invective. The lance of the most chivalrous knight never went straight to its mark more surely than the doctor's polished invective. We have seen him when his attack upon the liquor traffic was a tempest of denunciation, lightning flashing from his eye, thunder rattling in his voice, and his logic a flaming bolt splintering all before it. His earnestness was the strength and rush of a tornado. Yet there was not a particle of malice or madness in his heart. He closed the assault by causing the audience to explode with laughter.

He often employed words that read harshly, though at the time they seemed to listeners well chosen and select. In the little volume of addresses that he published thirty years ago he said:

" If the language employed to express my opinion of the liquor traffic, and of the vileness and inhumanity of those engaged in it, should be considered by some unwarrantably harsh, I shall not be surprised; and I will say, with perfect frankness, that its employment was not a slip of the tongue or pen. At the risk of my character for amiability, I will confess that my feelings on this subject are much stronger than any language I have employed."

He was not *partisan* or *sectarian*. He mingled with all political parties and sects harmoniously, yet without compromising his principles. He was as religious at the polls as he was at the altar. He believed in carrying religion into politics. He always voted, and voted where he believed his ballot would tell the most for liberty and temperance. Hence he scratched ballots or bolted, according to conviction. He was formerly a Whig, and then a Republican; but he was prompt to criticise either party when untrue to the principles they professed. So in the church, he was a decided Congregationalist without being *denominational;* but his denominational views were to him no reason why he should not labor harmoniously with all Christian denominations in the cause of humanity. His views are expressed clearly in the following paragraph from his pen :

" The same is true of sectarian prejudices, which serve to hinder men from working together in any movement for the good of community. Religion never hinders its possessor from aiding even bad men in a good work. The disciples of our Lord, when directed to distribute the loaves among the starving multitude, did not display the littleness of their souls by inquiring who of the hungry throng were Pharisees and who Sadducees. They fed them indiscriminately. Men of different sects, who have in exercise the spirit of the gospel, will kindly work together to feed the hungry and to clothe the naked, to reform the vicious, or remove from society sources of common danger; but let the parties whom you desire should work together for the promotion of a cause bear but the name of Christ, without his Spirit, and they will be as unsocial, jealous, intractable, and obstinate as the devil could desire."

The consciousness of being right, morally and logically, seemed to lift him above criticism. He cared more to be right and just than he did to parry assault. He pressed forward towards the mark for the prize, regardless of the spears and arrows that critics in the rear hurled at his back. Hence there was little comfort to critics in assailing him. He was more likely to crack a joke at their expense than to slap them in their faces. He often took the wind out of their sails by accepting their criticisms. Again, a pat illustration or shaft of wit turned the edge of their attacks in a twinkling. Altogether he was as nearly invulnerable as a public speaker could well be, in the presence of critics. It was difficult to pierce his armor; and if it were pierced, he would turn the assault to real practical advantage.

It is evident that Dr. Jewett did not ride a " hobby." This charge is usually brought against reformers, whether true or false. It never could be charged with any show of fairness against Dr. Jewett. Neither was he " impracticable," as this class are said to be. Such wisdom and conscientious effort as characterized his life raised him above such accusations. If, as Madame De Staël said, "a historian is almost a statesman," then a philanthropist like Dr. Jewett is almost a philosopher; and philosophers are neither hobbyists nor enthusiasts.

XXI.

DR. JEWETT IN THE FAMILY.

"A RARE man in society — a model in the family," — says one. "To know Dr. Jewett thoroughly, it was necessary to see him at home," says another. "Tender, affectionate, merry, intelligent, instructive, and a decided Christian, his home was an Eden without the serpent," writes a third. That his home (the place where his family was), whether in Rhode Island, Connecticut, Massachusetts, New Hampshire, Illinois, Minnesota, Tennessee, or New York, was the dearest spot on earth to him, no acquaintance ever questioned.

The birth of his first child was to him one of the most interesting and important events of his life, equalled only by the subsequent births in his family. He comprehended its meaning as few fathers ever do. The ordinary ideas that are expressed by the term "*baby*," at such a time, did not appear to possess his mind so much as those higher and grander thoughts about its future in this life and the next, as well as the weight of responsibility his new charge imposed. To see him so lovingly dandle the

"wingless angels," as he called them, on his knee,
toss them in the air, talk to them out of a *mother-*
heart really, and caress them like a woman, was
enough to convince any beholder that he found
society with the little helpless ones. And further
on, as they grew older, to witness his boyish demonstrations with them, joining in their sports, rollicking with them on the floor, playing horse, ball, and
top to amuse them, gave proof that he still adapted
himself to their society. But that was a small matter in comparison with the higher thoughts that invested childhood from the Godward side. Just here,
to illustrate further, we quote a paragraph from a
letter of his to Mrs. Jewett, in 1874, after she had
received an unfortunate Swedish girl into their family with a child (that was to bear through life the
shame of a mother's sin) to care for, in the exercise
of a true benevolent spirit:

"I am anxious to hear how you get on with home affairs, and how the sick baby is doing, if indeed the little
wingless angel (every babe is that) is still with you.
Whether it live or die, I shall always be glad that we
gave it quarters with us, not in a manger, but in our own
comfortable home. '*Inasmuch as ye did it unto one of
the least of these, ye did it unto me.*' It is not the
amount of suffering we alleviate or prevent, which gives
character to the act in the sight of God, but *the spirit*
which prompts it, and that can be as distinctly manifested
in the case of a little helpless mortal as in the case of a
man or woman of years and borne down with infirmities.
But there is no need that I lecture *you* in relation to matters of human duty."

There is something peculiarly touching in the loving spirit of a man almost seventy years old, whose heart thus folds the stranger-waif to itself, doing it for the Master. It is especially so in a father who has had thirteen babes of his own to handle and caress.

A complete history of the names of Dr. Jewett's children would be interesting in itself. We can only say, however, that it was perfectly natural for the first daughter to be named Lucy : Dr. Jewett would have consented to no other name than that of its mother. It was natural that the name of the first son should be Charles ; Mrs. Jewett would have consented to no other name than that of the child's father. When the next son was born, Dr. Jewett had been reading the life of Richard Henry Lee, and he was so much gratified with the character, that he appropriated the name. In like manner, when the third son was born, the doctor had been reading the life of that English statesman, John Hampden, and he showed his high appreciation of that Englishman's character by naming his boy for him. All the other names of his children have a history, and the reason for them is found in some demand of kinship, hereditary claim, or personal friendship.

At the earliest possible age, the doctor familiarized the minds of his children with *work*, as a discipline. He dreaded idleness, because of its demoralizing effects. It might be some simple thing that he required them to do, like drawing water, bringing in wood, washing dishes, taking care of the baby — something that was helpful to the family.

He believed in a time to play; and no father ever spent more hours to make the playing of his children both pleasurable and useful than he. He could make kites, carts, tops, and balls for them as well as he made them for himself and others in boyhood. But, as early as practicable, he aimed to unite amusement and utility. He sought the useful in the pleasurable. His boys were not more than six or eight years old when they were introduced to mechanical labor. A turning-lathe was fitted up, with bench and tools to correspond; and they were taught to manufacture articles; perhaps sleds, carts, and bow-and-arrows, for sport, and crickets, milking-stools and boxes for use. There was a great amount of fun in this for them as well as excellent discipline. It was play and work combined.

Order was the first law of his family. This was secured by implicit obedience. His children *obeyed* from their very babyhood. In no family was there ever more cheerful obedience; and yet no visitor ever witnessed any particular effort in that direction. It appeared to be secured without effort. Like planets, the children moved in their respective orbits, as if by some organic law of the household. Dr. Jewett used to claim that it was because they revolved about their mother, crediting the order, obedience, and beautiful harmony of his home to her. Be that as it may, he co-operated. His family government was of the republican form. He gov-

erned by consent of the governed. He was president, and his children constituted the co-ordinate
branches, presided over by their mother, by virtue
of her office as vice-president. Every measure
adopted became the stronger because each branch
of the little republic had indorsed it. The president
never found his hands tied because the co-ordinate
branches refused to vote supplies. On the other
hand, the co-ordinate branches never found themselves badgered and oppressed by a dictatorial executive. A veto was never demanded. The bare
statement of his wishes, in a fatherly message, was
sufficient to secure co-operation and harmony. The
result was a model family government, as every man
and woman conversant with the facts will testify.

His letters to Mrs. Jewett, in his frequent and
long absences, contain many paragraphs like the
following :

" The family I am with are cursed with a dissolute son.
Already I see one reason for it in a shilly-shally, milk-and-
water course in governing their children, that fails to
secure obedience. God be thanked that he gave us the
wisdom and firmness to train our sons to habits of obedience, and to exact of them a decent regard for the pro-
prieties of life. We have our reward in a family of sons
who know how to conduct themselves with propriety in
any company and under any circumstances, and who will
not crimson their parents' cheeks with shame by their
rudeness."

No visitor in Dr. Jewett's family ever witnessed
any disorder or trouble among the children, no

interruption of parents when talking, no lack of harmony among themselves; nor did he ever hear unkind, boisterous, or defiant language. Each seemed to live for the other, and all the happier because of each other's enjoyment. Within three or four years we heard the doctor refer to his family, and say, that "he feared he was not sufficiently thankful to God for the blessing enjoyed in his children;" adding, of the six sons reared to manhood, "not one of them, to my knowledge, ever drank a swallow of intoxicating liquors, smoked a cigar, chewed a quid of tobacco, or uttered a profane oath, and not one of them ever gave me an hour's anxiety in his life." Blessed father! Happy children!

A unique and fascinating feature was imparted to Dr. Jewett's home by the decidedly literary and moral character with which he invested it. Not only his strong affection, wit, humor, ingenuity, versatility, and tact, were called into requisition, but his talents and piety as well. His knowledge of English and American literature, his familiarity with science and art, his acquaintance with books, his criticisms of authors, his discussion of the current topics of the day, his elocutionary powers, his remarkable use of Scripture and favorite hymns, all contributed to the enjoyment and culture of his family. This was one of the attractions which induced acquaintances to ask a place for their sons in his household. After he returned to his home with his final sickness, he received a letter from a refined lady of his acquaintance, asking a place for her son of sixteen years, in the coming spring, in his family. Her son was going to college, and she frankly expressed the opinion that the culture he would receive in the doctor's family, through the spring and summer, would be of more practical advantage to him than continued drill in the schoolroom.

For several years past Dr. Jewett boarded students in his family, Americans, Chinese, and Japanese, and his moulding influence upon them was remarkable. They learned to regard him with the affection and confidence of sons. Two interesting Chinese students were members of his family at the time of his death, and they mourned for him as sons mourn for a father. A Japanese student, who was a member of his family a few years since, became a strict teetotaler, though no direct influence was employed to make him such. The doctor's magnetic power unconsciously caused him to walk in his steps. At the dinner-table of a distinguished public man, he declined to sip the wine that was passed, and in his simple-hearted honesty, said, "Dr. Jewett thinks that wine is not only unnecessary, but perilous, and so I must decline to take it." A fine tribute to the doctor's influence. He now resides in London, and in a letter of lamentation over the doctor's illness to his daughter, after hearing of it, we find this beautiful sentiment: "Pray do not think I am forgetting you ; but, on the contrary, you and your family are often remembered and mentioned to my heart by my good friend whose name is MEMORY."

The doctor's habit of quoting prose and poetry in

conversation, and reciting at length from Shakespeare, Burns, and others, as an exercise in elocu-
tion, was nowhere more conspicuous than at home.
At the table, in the sitting-room and garden, whether
having company or not, this was a frequent exercise.
Whole evenings at the fireside were spent in this
way.   Neighbors and friends often came in to enjoy
the entertainment.   And when the young people or
the older people of the town proposed a public entertainment to raise money, or for social good, Dr.
Jewett must read Shakespeare, recite Burns, or contribute something in his way, to the interest of the
occasion.   A citizen informs us that one of his last
public acts of this kind in the town was the recitation of Tennyson's "Grandmother."   Arrayed as an
ancient dame, his false teeth removed from his
mouth, his voice suggestive of feminine antiquity,
the imitation was so nearly perfect, that the audience
could scarcely believe they were listening to a familiar neighbor, and a man too.

The doctor was wont to draw out the opinions of
his children relative to the books they read, as well
as a synopsis of the same.   Also, to call their attention to the excellences of certain writers, citing
illustrations from their prose or poetry.   At table,
and in the family circle, he would frequently propose that each one should recite poetry upon a given
subject, as "Spring," the "Tempest," "Youth," from
any author familiar to them.   Sometimes he would
give out a subject, and request that quotations from
authors relating to it be collected for future use.

Often his memory would furnish quotations from a dozen standard authors upon a single subject. Then again, he would recite and explain a whole poem, showing its fine points, contrasting it with the productions of other authors on the same subject, thus occupying considerable time by the effort.

As Dr. Jewett was necessarily absent much of his time lecturing in different parts of the country, letters to his family were frequent and numerous. They were characteristic of the man. He said in letters just what he would have said by voice. They were penned for no one but his family, never dreaming that a line of them would be seen in print; and so much the more they show the heart of the husband and father. It was a treat to him to love and to be loved. To him there was nothing unmanly or soft in the frankest and freest expression of it, but rather it was ennobling and charming. The soul that did not overflow with it sometimes was not much of a soul in his estimation. Hence, his letters home revel in love. Through them he saluted, embraced, and kissed his dear ones. The following extracts from letters to his wife will illustrate :

" Oh, how I wish I could drop in upon you. I want to see how you look and manage as boss of the whole concern. Write often and long. Reading letters from home is more than half my comfort. Tell me everything going on from attic to cellar. Kiss Lizzie for me " (she only of all the children was at home) ; " and, Lizzie, please kiss your mother on my account."

" I long to get news from the nest, and to be assured

28

of the continued health of the old bird and the young ones."

" I thank you for your kind wishes and earnest prayers. I have had the benefit of both for thirty-six years. God be thanked for my family! I have no bank or railroad stock, but my home stock I can boast of with a glad heart."

" I am counting the days and the hours until I shall be under your care. I can think of nothing so likely to put new strength and courage into the old worn frame as the light of your countenance and the ministrations of love by you and my dear daughter, who, I know, will do all she can for her lover *par excellence.*"

" I am most provokingly disappointed. I came down to take the one o'clock train to N——, that I might chat a couple of hours with my wife and children, and take the three o'clock train to M——. *The one o'clock train has been discontinued*, and I must now whistle by you at the rate of twenty miles an hour, gazing wistfully, as I pass, at the little cottage which holds my treasure. I am to be with the ladies at W. this evening at a temperance levee, where, as the fair ones flaunt by me, I shall inwardly exclaim with Robert Burns:

'Ye are not Mary Morrison.'

Allow me to congratulate you on your safe arrival at the new home and on your mother's improvement on the score of health. No other improvement is possible. My own health is by no means perfect. I have trouble in the region of the heart in addition to the old chronic complaint of depravity."

" It is but six o'clock in the morning, and I hope that you and dear Lizzie are still under the blankets, enjoying that sleep which is 'kind nature's sweet restorer,' or as Will Shakespeare has it, which 'knits up the ravelled sleeve of care.' " . . .

"One of the troubles I have to contend with in this sort of labor is, to be unable to communicate directly with my family. Well, there is a much worse trouble than that — *to have no family to communicate with.*"

"I am meeting with great kindness, and see folks enough, in all conscience. But a man who has a wife and children is alone in a crowd when they are far away."

"As to considerations that may decide my choice of location, I cannot detail them with pen or pencil. They must be whispered into your private ear at short range."

Going from place to place so rapidly, Dr. Jewett was often troubled about receiving his letters.

"I am so hungry for news from home! 'Any letter for Dr. Jewett?' — my heart all the while beating at one hundred and ten or thereabouts with joyful expectation. The postmaster looks over the list, and, with a coolness that is absolutely shocking, replies, 'None, sir, none.'

'From glorious height of expectation,
Down to the bottom of creation.'

Down I go with a plunge. A cold shower-bath just after getting out of a warm bed, would give you some idea of the effect."

To one of his daughters he wrote, during the late civil war:

"DEAR LIZZIE: I received your excellent epistle to-day. I am quite obliged to you for detail of matters about home I love the *detail*. With detail, I can almost see home, and see how things look, while general statements are quite unsatisfactory. I would kiss you in *detail* for your excellent letter, but for the great distance and the expense involved in bringing our lips together. With yours and your mother's letters, I know almost all about you, though you did not say a word about Lucy. Am I to understand that she has married, and so has ceased to be a member of the family? Let me know at once. . . .

"The news from the elections is glorious. Oh, if we whip out the Copperheads, and then the rebels, and then the rumsellers, and then, finally, or during the struggle, all the little devils that strive to nestle in our own hearts, what an everlasting triumph we shall have! Remember me to all our neighbors and friends, and kiss your good mother on both cheeks for me.

"God bless and guide you aright. You know the con-ditions — 'Ask, and it shall be given you ; seek, and ye shall find ; knock, and it shall be opened.' No promise of gifts unasked for.

"Love to Lucy, and a big lump for yourself, from

"Your affectionate

FATHER."

Dr. Jewett employed satire with great effect at times. In a letter to his other daughter, who was absent in Chicago, in 1870, he employed it upon the forthcoming Musical Jubilee in New York city, where he was editing the Temperance Advocate. It appeared ridiculous to him to employ anvils, cannon, and the explosion of rocks in Hell Gate, and call it a "Musical Festival ; " and so he "took off" the affair thus :

"Lizzie is absent at a rehearsal of oratorios for the great Babel of noise, *alias* the coming Musical Festival. Beside the trumpets, big drums, anvils, and heavy artillery, there are to be forty cats, with a spring patent clothes-pin on the tail of each, attached side by side to a twenty-foot pole, and placed just over the orchestra. On the edge of the front gallery, at a distance of one yard from each other, will be placed one hundred and fifteen screech-owls, and twenty fat Dutch-women, weighing one hundred and eighty pounds each, are to spank an equal number of babies, under the special leadership of a great musical genius just imported from Kam-Scat-ca for this great occasion. Twenty-seven experienced gentlemen are to file saws of the largest saw-mill pattern, as an accompaniment to a quartette of four lumber-wagon wheels revolving on dry axles. The last performance of the great occasion will be distinguished by the screaming of all the aforesaid instruments, aiding the trained voices of all the prima-donnas to the number of three thousand, with the simultaneous screaming of the whistles from the East River tug-boats, and will conclude by the explosion of forty tons of powder in the big rock at Hell Gate. The excavation in the rock is nearly completed, but the explosive material will not be placed in situation until the day before the explosion. The hulk of a dismantled man-of-war, loaded with Chinese fire-crackers, will be anchored over the rock, and will be fired by the same electric discharge which will explode the contents of the great rock. Don't you wish you could be in New York on that orful occasion?"

Dr. Jewett held "the fashions" in contempt. He never spent much time at the toilet himself, as all his friends know very well. In one letter he wrote:

"You spoke of material for a dress. What kind would you like? If you wish it to be sent so that you can make it up immediately, I will buy and forward it at once.

Don't, for pity's sake, decency's sake, and my sake, allow
the cry, ' It's the fashion,' lead you to tolerate the *drag-
gling skirt abomination.* I beg pardon for admitting the
possibility of such an outrage on propriety by your consent; but I know how tailors and dressmakers clamor for
' the fashions.' "

To one of his sons, about to engage as a clerk,
he wrote :

" If you have commenced service with Mr. C., spare
no pains to render yourself so useful that he cannot do
without you, and there is no danger that you will be out
of business. It will be a fine school, in which you can
perfect yourself in the practical affairs of the counting-
room, so as to qualify yourself for some more responsible
position. Spare no pains, as you love your father, to
render the situation of your excellent mother as pleasant as possible. The tendency in your nature that you
will have the most difficulty in controlling and keeping in a proper state of subordination to reason and conscience, will grow out of your strong social nature. You
came very honestly by it, for it was your father's besetting
sin ; and had I not labored to control it, it would have
been much in the way of my advancement and success in
business. When I was in the Medical College at Pittsfield, Mass., though often invited, I did not spend half a
dozen evenings in social parties during the two winters
I spent there. It was a great self-denial ; but I knew that
if I gave way to my social feelings, it would block my
way to success by interfering with my studies, diverting
my thoughts therefrom, &c. A knowledge of our weak
points, or strong tendencies, will enable us, with proper
decision, to keep all right. I advise you to read John
Foster's essay on ' Decision of Character.' It is admira-

ble. Every young man and young woman, sufficiently developed mentally to understand him, should read Foster. Do not spend your time in reading novels. If you indulge at all in reading works of fiction, read the works of Sir Walter Scott, Goldsmith, The Scottish Chiefs, and the works of Dickens. Works of fiction should, however, form but a small part of a young man's reading. History, philosophy, biography, travels, and scientific works, — these should form the staple of a young man's reading. Study the poets some, — Shakespeare, Milton, Gray, Burns, &c., — and the Word of God daily."

To his son preparing for college, he closed a loving letter thus :

" Let me know your wishes always without any reserve ; and be assured I shall always do my best to serve one whose entire character and course have thus far met the approbation of your parents, who are pretty exacting, and in whose present promise of a respectable and useful future we have so much grounds for confidence."

> " They [parents] in their children lived a second life ;
> With them again took root ; sprang with their hopes ;
> Entered into their schemes ; partook their fears ;
> Laughed in their mirth ; and in their gain grew rich."
>
> POLLOK.

" God bless and prosper you, is the earnest prayer of
" Your earthly father,

C. JEWETT."

It will be seen that Dr. Jewett made the Bible a guide in the family as he did in the temperance reform. All interests clustered about it. All counsels and authority were derived from it, or were in

harmony with it.   It was not only read, but studied.
It had its place not only in family devotion, but it
was treated as by far the most important book of
reference in the house.   Much of it was treasured
in the doctor's memory, and quotations therefrom
were as likely to add variety to intercourse at the
table, or the interchange of thoughts on different
subjects at other times, as quotations from the poets.
Indeed the doctor was wont to recite portions of it,
as he recited Shakespeare, to show its dramatic
power.   He maintained that it was unequalled in
this respect.

Dr. Jewett signed his letters in a great variety of
ways.   Not only his character, but his feelings and
mental moods, were indicated to the family by these
signatures.   Wisdom, wit, humor, tact, love, impatience, confidence, piety, mind, heart, soul — all
appear in them.

"Yours since 1828, only more so." (Time of betrothal.)
"Yours, as on the 5th of May, 1830." (Time of mar-
riage.)
"Yours, in love and much weakness."
"Yours, altogether, entirely."
"Yours always."
"Yours, feeble, but hopeful."
"Yours, jubilant."
"Much love equitably distributed."
"Yours, tried and troubled."

To his wife, when expecting her to meet him at
a given place, he closed a note thus :

" Don't try to get everything ' fixed ' before you start.

"'Just as *you are*, without one plea.'"

" C. J."

Writing to a friend to whom he felt under great obligations, he signed himself:

" Yours, fraternally, externally, internally, and eternally.

" C. JEWETT."

We have given but a glance at Dr. Jewett's correspondence. The variety of subjects upon which he treated in his letters is wonderful, perhaps a dozen topics in a single letter. Theology, science, art, mechanics, farming, apparel, cows, vegetables, grain, books, schools, fruit, liberty, slavery, the country, temperance, government, and too many more to be named, are all treated of, often, in singular juxtaposition.

XXII.

DR. JEWETT IN THE CHURCH.

D R. JEWETT loved the church. To him it was
indeed a *sacred* institution — God's " human
agency for the conversion of the world." He denied
that the church had any weapons of *defence*. He
claimed that her weapons were those of *aggression;*
that it was her duty to assault sin, and not stand on
the defensive against it. Hence he maintained that
the church should be foremost in every necessary
reform ; that she was not only delinquent, but disloyal whenever and wherever she failed to take this
position.

He possessed qualities that made him efficient
in the church. He was a *live* member. His native *reverence* was large. In certain localities,
where Nature appeared in her grandeur, he felt like
uncovering his head, as he did in a house of worship. When practising medicine in Greenwich and
Warwick, R. I., he occasionally passed a high rock,
situated in a romantic spot, where he felt constrained
to alight, uncover his head, and pray, before passing
on. This was his almost invariable custom as he
went that way, enjoying it most at night, when a

deeper and more impressive silence pervaded the scene. Here is the proof of a born element of character that early made him a hopeful subject of divine grace, and thereafter was prominent in his Christian experience and work. He once thrilled an audience in the city of Providence, by saying, in his impressive way, "I thank God for bringing me into this beautiful world of His, even if there were no hereafter. I have enjoyed so much that my heart swells with gratitude to Him daily."

Dr. Jewett was a *spiritual* Christian. A common opinion is, that a radical man cannot be a *spiritual* man. But Dr. Jewett was both. He ever maintained the most radical views as to the removal of slavery, intemperance, and other evils. He held that the Bible taught total abstinence and prohibition of the sale of intoxicating beverages; that Christ preached and practised total abstinence, and did not make alcoholic wine at the marriage of Cana, or use it when he instituted the supper; and that his followers are in duty bound to discard the use of all intoxicating beverages, under all circumstances. The following quotation shows his position exactly:

"When the mind of the Christian man is enlightened on the subject, he can no more put alcoholic liquor in his stomach, and keep a conscience void of offence, than he could swallow daily a moderate dose of any other poison. All the discussion as to whether it be a sin *per se* to drink a glass of alcoholic wine, is a waste of breath. The answer to two simple questions will settle the matter: Is alcohol a poison, at war with vitality? If so, does the

Christian man know the fact? If he is acquainted with
that fact, he compromises his Christian character if he
meddles with it, unless prescribed by some medical ad-
viser."

Nothing grieved him more than to see professing
Christians lending the power of example to wine-
drinking; and ministers, Christian editors, and laymen, supporting, directly or indirectly, the drinking
customs, and interpreting the Scriptures to favor the
same. It seemed to him one of the gravest offences
for a man to use the Bible to support even the smallest evil. "If anything is wrong, rum-selling and
rum-drinking are wrong," he claimed; "and the
Bible is opposed to all that is wrong." Hence, he
grieved when the Bible was used, indirectly even,
to sustain wine-drinking. Once he was delivering
a course of lectures in a town where he unwittingly
wounded two or three church-members by his criticisms. It was suggested to him that he smooth the
matter over at his next lecture. How well he reduced the suggestion to practice may be learned
from his words. "I do solemnly aver," he said to
his audience, "that I did not know there was a
drunkard in this church."

About being radical, we have heard him say,
"Christ was the most radical person who ever lived.
He condemned sin in every form. He never com-
promised with it — he fought it. He always 'laid
the axe at the root' of every evil. He used no
temporizing policy. We are not as radical as Christ
was, though we ought to be."

He believed fully in the power of the cross, and the duty of personal consecration to Christ. Public worship, the prayer-meeting, and all means of grace, were helps to this end. The one leading thought and desire of his heart was, that his children should early come to Christ; and his joy seemed to be complete when the last one of his large family became a Christian, and united with the church.

Though giving his life to the cause of temperance, his heart was deeply interested in every benevolent enterprise and work of the church. Missions, foreign and domestic, found in him an earnest friend and champion. He always kept posted, too, upon the grand work of evangelizing the world; and no class of pious workers shared his reverence and sympathies more than missionaries. If the whole membership of the churches of our country should contribute as largely as the doctor did, in proportion to property, to carry forward the work of missions, there would be no lack of money.

Revivals of religion appealed to his spiritual emotions. He believed in them, and was never happier than when he was permitted to participate in promoting them.

He was a man of *prayer*. Not simply as a duty, but as a privilege, he valued prayer. Indeed, more than that; he regarded it as an absolute *necessity* to the Christian. "Prayer is the Christian's vital breath," — he believed it with all his heart. And he carried everything to God in prayer.

He was a *conscientious* professor of religion.

Hugh Miller said of the honest mason with whom he served his apprenticeship, "He put his conscience into every stone that he laid." That is the sort of conscientiousness that characterized Dr. Jewett's piety.

His *submission* under trial was always noticeable. A clergyman writes :

"He was at my house after he had lost all his property — property upon which he was depending for support in his old age. His contentment and cheerfulness under the loss surprised me. I have often thought of it since. It certainly taught me a lesson of trust in Providence which I never have forgotten."

Concerning that trial he wrote to Mrs. Jewett (in addition to a letter quoted in a former chapter) :

"Evidently, Providence does not mean that I shall be rich, but have just enough to live on daily. God says, Trust in me ; go on with your work, and verily thou shalt be fed ! That is good."

Other pages show his hearty submission under severe afflictions. He believed that Divine grace was just as ample for heavy sorrows as for light ones.

With all this experience he nevertheless had a very humble view of his own Christian attainments. One of the poetic quotations that he was wont to use related to his coming to Christ, and is expressive of the spirit in question. It was from Cowper :

"I was a stricken deer that left the herd
Long since ; with many an arrow deep infix'd

My panting side was charged, when I withdrew,
To seek a tranquil death in distant shades ;
There was I found by One who had himself
Been hurt by the archers. In his side he bore,
And in his hands and feet, the cruel scars.
With gentle force soliciting the darts,
He drew them forth, and heal'd, and bade me live."

A note from his pastor, Rev. C. T. Weitzel, says :

" Paul's description of the true Christian — 'Not slothful in business, fervent in spirit, serving the Lord,' might be applied with singular appropriateness to Dr. Jewett. Conspicuous among his rare qualities was a Paul-like singleness of aim. He was, in a noble sense, a 'man of one idea,' in the same sense in which Paul was that, when, in preaching to the Corinthians, he determined not to know anything save Jesus Christ, and him crucified.

"Dr. Jewett's success was also due in no small degree to his knowledge of human nature, his uncommon skill in approaching men of all kinds, his mastery of the subject to which his life was devoted, and his abounding good-humor and courtesy under all circumstances. This last did his cause incalculable service in rendering acceptable Dr. Jewett's bold, uncompromising utterance of truth as he saw it.

"Above all, he was a whole-souled Christian ; and, as he approached his end, he might well have said with the apostle, 'I have fought a good fight, I have finished my course, I have kept the faith.' "

XXIII.

SICKNESS AND DEATH.

ON the fifteenth of November, 1878, Dr. Jewett left home for a brief lecturing tour in Pennsylvania. He was in a better physical condition, apparently, than he had enjoyed for two or three years, since he had not spoken in public for several months, and had exercised freely in the open air. He delivered but few lectures, however, before the "old enemy" (as he called the heart-disease) assaulted him seriously. Medical aid, however, relieved him so much that he was able to return to his home in Norwich Town, Conn., which he reached December 8th.

His family physician administered amyle at once, to expand the muscles and arteries, that the movement of the heart might be easier. The effect of this medicine was magical. Under its influence, Dr. Jewett improved so rapidly that hopes of his restoration were entertained.

In January, however, the disease assumed so serious an aspect, that he could not lie down, or sleep in a chair, only as anodynes were administered. His two sons in Minnesota were summoned by telegram; and the eldest remained with him until his death.

The son put up a rest, consisting of a bar across the bed of such a height that his father, bolstered up in bed, could throw his arms over it, and, with a pillow, be far more comfortable than was possible in a chair, and obtain more sleep. Dr. Jewett was removed to the bed, where he occupied the sitting posture until he died, on the third day of April.

He was better and worse alternately, often suffering more than language can describe. In these paroxysms of pain his stalwart frame seemed to writhe and rally itself as if waging a successful contest with death. One day, in his anguish, he exclaimed to his wife, "Oh, what must have been the agony of Christ? This is agony. His was much more. But I must learn to bear it."

His sufferings were so intense, that for days his teeth would strike together so as to be heard across the room. Dr. Peck remarked, " He literally gnashes his teeth with agony."

On the eighth day of March he felt that the struggle would soon be over, and expressed a desire to see all the members of the family, and to say his last words. His wife expressed the hope that he might be spared yet longer to the family; to which he replied: "Perhaps I may; but if I say what I wish to say *now*, I shall be all ready." Then, in the most tender and happy manner, without a tear moistening his eye, he addressed his wife, referring to their long and happy union, the goodness of God to their large family, and the prospect of a speedy reunion in heaven.

In like manner, also, he addressed his two daughters and son separately, speaking of things peculiar to the experience of each one, and pouring forth his gratitude that all of them were devoted followers of Christ.

He gave directions about his funeral, and expressed the wish to be buried in the family lot in Lisbon, eight miles distant. He spoke of the funeral services, and requested that his friend, the author, with whom he had labored so much, should be invited to address the assembly. Then, leaving his "love" for several dear absent ones, he kissed each member of the family, and, exhausted by the effort, reposed his head upon the rest, as much as to say, "All ready."

Thus closed an unusual scene, the occurrence of which, in its grave, peaceful, happy details, were impossible outside the Christian faith. Not a tear was shed by a person present; not a word was spoken, except in a calm, cheerful voice. As if their loss were his unspeakable "gain," loving hearts rose higher than personal sorrow, and smiled their joy at his glorious victory over death and the grave. It was the triumph of Christian faith on both sides, when tears seemed out of harmony with that exultant joy that could say, "For me to live is Christ, and to die is gain."

Subsequently his mind wandered, and at times he was very delirious, requiring both tact and strength to control him, although he was still compelled to occupy a sitting posture in bed, and was of course exhausted and weak.

The last time that he conducted family devotions (and it was at his own request), his wife passed him the Bible, when, adjusting his spectacles, he opened to the eleventh chapter of Matthew, and read, in quite a strong voice, the last three verses, namely : " Come unto me, all ye that labor, and are heavy laden, and I will give you rest. Take my yoke upon you, and learn of me ; for I am meek and lowly of heart ; and ye shall find rest unto your souls. For my yoke is easy, and my burden is light."

He closed the book, and passed it to Mrs. Jewett, at the same time removing his spectacles. Waiting, thoughtfully, a moment, he said, " Let me see that again." Mrs. Jewett passed him the Bible again. Readjusting his spectacles, he opened it, and re-read the passages, remarking as he returned the book, " Blessed words ! blessed words ! " Bowing his head upon the bar in front of him, he led in prayer audibly, and with the beautiful simplicity of a child. He prayed that God would bless the remedies used for his restoration, if best ; make him submissive and patient in suffering, and prepare the loved ones for His will.

Dr. Jewett had expressed the wish that " he might pass away without a hard struggle ; " and he died, about nine o'clock on the morning of April 3d, 1879.

The news of his death was telegraphed over the country, and the public journals paid noble tributes to his memory. From Maine to Minnesota the tidings were received by a host of friends with saddened hearts; and at hundreds of family altars the afflicted household was remembered with tears and fervent prayers. Letters of sympathy and condolence came to the stricken ones from near and far. In Great Britain, also, the news of his death was received with demonstrations of sorrow; and the English press spoke in the highest terms of his life and character.

Even before his death, when the news of his sickness was telegraphed over the country, letters of friendship and profound sympathy to him were received from individuals, temperance conventions, and societies, churches, and other bodies. An unusual scene transpired in the Pilgrim Church of Cambridgeport, Mass., on the Sabbath evening before the doctor's death. The house was crowded to its utmost capacity, and some reference being made to Dr. Jewett's labors, as well as to the fact, that if living, he was nigh unto death, the service was turned sympathetically into one of commemoration of his great life-work. It was thought to be one of the most interesting and profitable meetings ever held in he church; and it closed by a vote to instruct the clerk to send the following telegram to Dr. Jewett early on Monday morning:

" Dr. Charles Jewett.

  " Dear and Respected Friend: Our hearts are with you, and our prayers ascend for you."

The motion to send the telegram was adopted by the entire assembly rising, presenting a scene of profound interest, consecrated by many tears.

We regret that a large number of letters, resolutions by temperance organizations and other bodies, and tributes of public journals, that we selected for insertion here, must be omitted, as already our space is fully occupied, excepting only the following poem from Dr. Jewett's old friend, George S. Burleigh, the poet:

CHARLES JEWETT.

BORN SEPTEMBER 5, 1807. DIED APRIL 3, 1879.

A noble life, well rounded to its goal!
  A gallant race well run!
I see the crowning of a worthy soul;
  I hear the sweet "Well done,
Faithful and true, unbettered by the best
For loyal service. Enter into rest!"

If they may sorrow who have lost a friend,
  Then all things pure and glad
Shall be his mourners. Champions who defend
  The innocent, wronged or sad,
Truth's lover and Virtue's guardian, by whose side
His keen steel flashed, will weep that he has died.

But, if the fulfilled stature of a man,
  That, like a star, defies
The blight of years, — a heart whose clear blood ran
  For truth that never dies, —
May lift a proud love o'er the shafts of loss,
Then this man's life shall crown our sorrow's cross!

A loving life, that made home beautiful
   With more than wealth could buy ;
A life of service to the golden rule
   That wheels the orbs on high, —
By all that sweetened his own hearth's delight,
Sent forth to rescue withered homes from blight.

World's honors, incense of the flattering crowd ;
   The market's glittering prize ;
Civic or martial wreaths, the garlands proud
   That tempt Ambition's eyes ;
Though clear within his ample grasp, apart
From his high task drew not his steadfast heart.

Above the lute of pleasure, and the clang
   Of clarions blown for fame,
The long, shrill shriek of murdered mothers rang ;
   The wail of orphans came ;
With sob and curse, and idiot laugh and whine
Of manhood blasted in the drench of wine !

Behind the sceptre and the shield of law,
   Counting their bloody gain,
The gloating villains of this woe hè saw,
   Caressed by Fashion's train !
Then rose the Hero, sank all soft desire,
His eye was lightning, and his blood was fire !

Then his long war of " forty years " began,
   On Virtue's deadliest foes ;
Flashed his wit's falchion in the battle's van,
   Fast fell his broadsword blows,
And his keen scalpel's pitiless surgery
Let slip the wind of many a bloated lie !

On, in the darkness, faithful as in light;
   If earth below grew black,
God overhead was everlasting Might
   To him, who turned not back !

On, never resting, till that great heart's tide
Broke its own barriers, and he sank and died !

Here drop the curtain, looking up through tears
  For light of larger faith,
To see the harvest of his all-ripe years
  Sown by the Angel Death :
For a true life goes broadening from the grave,
Through untold time, to bless, inspire, and save.

The funeral services took place in the Congregational Church, at Norwich Town, Conn., on Saturday, April 6, at 11 o'clock A. M., Rev. Messrs. Weitzel, Davies, and Thayer officiating; the latter delivering the address. Mr. Thayer closed his remarks as follows :

"To me, the sadness of this hour is relieved by the grandeur of the life that has closed. I know what I am saying when I use that word, grandeur. The career of a man consecrating himself to the defence of a principle for half a century, regardless of reward or fame, intent only upon the triumph of his cause as a boon to suffering humanity, is both exceptional and grand. In comparison with the ambitious contests for distinction in field or senate, and even in the schools of science and halls of learning, it is godlike. Divested of those selfish aims which mar the world, and animated with the Christian spirit that was in the Master, such a life challenges the admiration of men. Thus, our dear friend and stalwart reformer of his day has closed his earthly mission, and passed on like a conqueror that he was ; and never, never could a ransomed spirit at the gates of immortality more appropriately adopt the apostle's language of triumph : 'I have fought a good fight' — who will deny it ? — 'I have finished my course' — rounded it like an orb. 'I have kept the faith' — true to the end. 'Henceforth,' through eternity, 'there is laid up for me' — all ready, waiting for his coming — 'a crown of righteousness' — not of flowers that fade, nor of diamonds that perish, but of everlasting purity — 'which the Lord, the righteous Judge' — not mortal friends like himself, but the Lord of glory, to whom he prayed in his extreme suffering one day, " O Thou, who knowest what agony is, help me to bear it," — 'He shall give me at that day' — without one doubt. Glorious end of his earthly life! Thrice glorious beginning of his immortal life!"

The following hymn, written for the occasion, with the benediction, closed the solemn ceremonies:

"Rest, Christian worker! sweetly rest
　　From age and cares, and toils and fears;
In life-long labors, wrought and blest,
　　Thy seventy are a hundred years!

"Men die; but truth, like God, lives on,
　　Victorious through the mortal strife.
Thy cause, O worker! is at dawn,
　　Instinct with an immortal life!

"Well done. The Father calls thee. Go;
　　'Tis ours to worship and adore,
Glad that we had thee long below,
　　We weep to see thy face no more.

"Great God! before thy throne we bow.
　　Thou lent us this dear life, to be
A benison to earth, and now,
　　With thanks, we give it back to Thee."

XXIV.

EULOGY BY HON. NATHAN CROSBY, LL.D.

HOW shall I eulogize Dr. Charles Jewett? With whom shall I compare him? or where shall I look for a field of life-labor like that of the cause of Temperance? Shall I group him with Edwards and Marsh, with Delavan and Neal, with Hunt, Taylor, and Mathew, with Pierpont and Sargent? Shall I say, and defend the claim, that no cause of benevolence this side of the New Testament gospel is its equal in its love and good will to man, and is, of itself, the great underlying power — a forerunner of the gospel? Shall I say that no young man or old man, at his early day and all his days, saw and felt the dangers of the use of intoxicating drinks, and the only way of escape from their untold evils, as did Dr. Jewett? I think I can safely say that no man ever devoted, as he did, fifty and more years, in a " Fight with the Drink Demon ; " nor has any man been so ably and thoroughly qualified and equipped for the fight as he. .   .   .   .   .   .

He was an educated physician, and gave earnest study and investigation, professionally, in all the hygienic and physiologic influences of alcoholic liquors upon man. He believed intoxicating liquors, used as a beverage, were hurtful and dangerous, insidiously and irresistibly forming an uncontrollable appetite for them; that they demented him, enfeebled him, demoralized him, unmanned him, changed his manhood to brutehood, and from a blessing to a curse.   .   .   .   .

He brought to the controversy intelligence, great conversational powers and eloquence, logic, poetry, anecdote, wit, satire, great love of right, of humanity, benevolence, Christian charity and faith, unfailing zeal, indomitable courage and perseverance.

By day and by night, in the street, the field, the shop, and the school, the old and the young, the rich and the poor, the seller and the drinker, the tempter and the tempted, he admonished and entreated.   He pressed moral suasion upon them, and he appealed to the law.   .   .   .   .

Dr. Jewett formed early an enlarged judgment of the character and value of the temperance cause. He was a temperance man and worker before he studied medicine, but after he had been admitted to the practice, and had lectured somewhat upon temperance, he became impressed, by the exhibition of anti-temperance strength, that something more than taking pledges of abstinence was wanting to make sure progress in the cause.   The people were to be stirred up to the examination of the original question, Whether alcoholic drinks were injurious to men in health?   Want of professional success did not turn him to the cause, but a conviction that the physiological aspects of the case should be presented by a physician whose theories and opinions could be verified by fact and science. . .

Dr. Jewett's profession opened to him the opportunity and duty of healing diseases by his skill and remedies, but his philanthropy and education induced him to change his profession of healing diseases to preventing them, believing and knowing how largely sickness and death were chargeable to intemperance.

He regarded the advocacy of the cause as next in responsibilities and value to the mission of the Saviour. . . . The noble Christian men of the land had inaugurated the cause, and prosecuted it with great success, down to the Harrison Gray Otis petition to the legislature, when the hosts of distillers, rumsellers, and drinkers rallied in unexpected numbers to defeat wholesome legislation upon the subject. Dr. Jewett, at this juncture, came to the front, by engaging in the service of the Massachusetts Temperance Union in 1840. He was singularly successful. He did not pretend to be graceful, but he did wonderfully impress his hearers with the conviction that he was master of his subject. He possessed peculiar qualifications for a public speaker. He had such command of every topic and feature of the subject, that he could at any moment vary his discussion as he saw the interest of his hearers rise or fall; as he found them doubting or believing; wide awake, or otherwise. He seemed intuitively to read the mental operations of his hearers, so as to amuse or solemnize; his eyes would delight and pierce, but his frown was withering; and his mimicry, when called for, was inimitable. Other men often excelled him on special occasions; but the year in and out, no man in the enterprise was found of equal power and success. . . . The pressure of public interest in the Washingtonian, or Reformed (Baltimore) Drunkards enterprise, and the disintegration of the Union ranks, which followed, led Dr. Jewett to drop his Massachusetts commission only, not at all his mantle or his zeal. He saw, as none other man did, the value of the cause to the world, and that it must be successful in America to secure its blessings to the nations. .   .   .   .   .

He left only the ephemeral labor of organizing societies, addressing cold-water armies, picnics, and evening talks, and prepared his able, inimitable lectures upon the physiological questions involved in fixing the value and use of alcohol by man, for man, and in man. This became his great field of labor. His facts were well put, his reasonings clear and pungent, his anecdotes illustrative, but incisive. His hearers were certain soon to forget any want of oratorical grace, in the fire-flashing eye and varied expression of his face; he gained easily, and held strongly, intently, their interest, to the end of his discussion. .   .   .   .

Dr. Jewett is eminently the apostle of temperance. Edwards, Marsh, Dow, and others, devoted only a few years to his many. He devoted his life, staff in hand, with a pack upon his back and sandals on his feet, leaving his domestic pleasures behind him, to preach salvation from Alcohol in all its forms, that there might be peace, prosperity, and good will among men. He impressed his fearful warning upon every town in Massachusetts, and upon many of the states of our Union, against the strength of the liquor traffic, against the insidiousness of liquor-drinking, against the ravages and degradation of intemperance, and cried aloud, and often, and everywhere, that safety could be found only in total abstinence from their use, and from all trade in them; that the sharpest vigilance against their approach must be established, and irrepressible efforts used to prevent their use in all time to come. He was a model advocate of reform. In all the houses of the people, where he found the prophet's chamber and guest-table, his conversation was pure and instructive; he had no doubtful dogmas or ultraisms to disseminate; no tares to sow; or gossip, or unkind innuendos to scatter along his path. He was social, chatty, and amusing, turning wit and anecdote to good account; always leaving behind him happy influences and grateful acknowledgments, while receiving plaudits and benedictions from all. His years of labor rolled on to more than his "threescore years and ten." When his frame shook upon the weakening foundations, when his last teaching and warning were given, and his last steps had taken him homeward for new strength and comfort, as had been his wont for fifty years, he found and accepted the reward and blessing: "WELL DONE, thou good and faithful servant, enter into the joy of thy Lord."

INDEX.

illustrations are as characteristic of the humor and originality of childhood, as is the story itself.

Aunt Tabitha's Trial. By L. O. COOPER. 12mo. With full page illustrations. Elegantly bound in cloth, gold and ink. $1.25

Fresh and pure as a mountain stream, and as charming for the beauty and freshness of its style, as for its sweet and helpful lessons. All in all it ranks among the most fascinating stories of the year and can be read by no person, old or young, without charm and suggestion, and stimulus to better living.

Abiding Peace. By Rev. A. B. EARLE, D. D. 16mo. Cloth, extra. Gold side and back stamp. 50 cts.

"This beautifully published volume is written in a clear and calm style, and is a persuasive statement of the believer's birthright."—*Zion's Herald, Boston.*

All Things. By FRANCES RIDLEY HAVERGAL. Cloth. 25 cts.

One of the most suggestive and helpful of the many works of this very popular author.

After the Battle. Per dozen, 20 cts. Per hundred, $1.25.

A story of the war, making clear and simple the way of pardon and peace.

Are These Things So? By REV. EMORY J. HAYNES, pastor Tremont Temple, Boston. 16mo. Cloth, $1.00.

Any Book mailed postpaid on receipt of price.

ANDREWS, REV. EMERSON.

Pearls of Worlds. $1.00.

Living Life. $1.00.

Revival Sermons. $1.00.

Travels in Bible Lands. 60 cts.

Youth's Picture Sermons. 50 cts.

Revival Songs. 40 cts.

Beulah Land. By Mrs. M. CARTER. Handsome 16mo. Portrait and illustrations. $1.00.

This autobiographical volume is the thrilling story of a life of faith that shows the spirit and devotion of the old-time men and women of faith to be as mighty to mould character as ever. It is a book for hours of religious devotion, and will give the reader inspiration and instruction.

Beyond. By HERVEY NEWTON. . Elegant square 16mo. Laid paper. Cloth. 60 cts.

A presentation of the known facts of the conditions, occupations and characteristics of the world beyond.

We can best describe its character by an

EXTRACT FROM THE PREFACE.

The pictures and descriptions given by Revelation of the country " Beyond," are full enough to show it superior to the most favored bits of Eden of which this world knows. A real land, with homes, music, personal recognition, freedom from sorrow and from sin, the society of the Lord himself. They show the life there to have many of the conditions and pleasures that give this

Any Book mailed postpaid on receipt of price.

world its chief charm, with none of the infirmities, and with many added enjoyable conditions.

An author widely known in the Old World and the New, says: •

" Those who doubt the recognition of friends in heaven should read 'BEYOND'! Those who do not doubt, but want confirmation of their belief should read 'BEYOND'!! Those who mourn dear ones gone before, and long for a realizing sense of the joys and occupations of the departed should read 'BEYOND'!!! This book is a poem, not in rhyme and metre, but in lofty sentiment, glowing imagery, and beauty of expression. It is a gem in clearness, purity and brilliancy. It is a book of fervent devotion, of holy love, and of the comfort of the Holy Ghost."

" Its pages do for the reader what the pen pictures of travelers in the East do for people at home."—*Central Baptist, St. Louis.*

" The book is excellent, and will help the Christian citizen on his way to his new country,"—*The Evangelist, New York.*

" Devoutly and impressively written and will afford rich subjects for meditations." *Zion's Herald, Boston.*

Better Life (The) and How to Find It. By REV. E. P. HAMMOND. 16mo. Cloth. 50 cts.

For young men and women who have not realized the peace and joy there is in believing in Jesus.

"Young ministers who are seeking to learn what manner of presentation of Gospel truth is most likely to be blessed of God, will do well to study this book."—*The Revival.*

Between Times. By I. E. Diekenga, "The American Dickens." Cloth, gold and black. 16mo. 75 cts.

In this breezy volume of story, sketch, and poem, Mr. Diekenga has satire for folly and meaness, humor for the ludicrous, and tender charity for adversity and helplessness.

Any Book mailed postpaid on receipt of price.

"We have not seen among recent publications a fresher, sprightlier, or more original book. There is not a dull page in the book. The author has come to be known as the "American Dickens," and is master of verse as well as prose." — *Western Recorder, Louisville, Ky.*

Bible Teachings from Nature. By Rev. J. Byington Smith, d. d. 12mo. Cloth. $1.50.

The author has happily conceived the idea of making the world with its charm and grandeur, the interpreter of Revelation, with its comfort for human souls and light for human feet. Lovers of the forms and graces in which the earth bedecks itself, and Bible students will alike find delight in these charming pages.

"The author writes like one who loves the Bible, and who finds in it mines of wealth for the intellect as well as the heart."—*Saratoga Daily Journal.*

"In a charming manner Dr. Smith brings the beauty and wonder of earth and sky to light up the Word."—*Journal and Messenger.*

Bible Studies and Life of Rev. George F. Pentecost. Edited by P. C. Headley, under Mr. Pentecost's supervision. Extra large. 12mo. Cloth. With Portrait. $1.50.

Mr. Pentecost's Bible readings, are valuable to all lovers of God's Word.

Bringing in Sheaves. By Rev. A. B. Earle, d. d. With Portrait. 12mo. Cloth. $1.25.

This work, crowded with sketches, incidents, helps and lessons, from the author's long experience, is invaluable to all who would be successful workers for Christ. It also contains four of his

---

Any Book mailed postpaid on receipt of price.

sermons, a single one of which is believed to have been the means of bringing twenty thousand souls to Christ.

"Nothing has for a long time been published, better adapted to arouse holy zeal in the cause to Christ."—*Methodist, New York.*

"One of the most remarkable books ever given to the public." —*Western Recorder, Louisville.*

Calls to Christ. By REV. W. R. NICOLL, M. A. 16mo. Cloth. 40 cts.

Designed for Christian workers in leading to the awakening and conversion of the unconverted.

"Full of simple, solemn, searching truths." — *Presbyterian Monthly.*

Can I Find Jesus? By S. G. KNIGHT. Per dozen, 10 cts. Per hundred, 60 cts.

Charles Jewett, Life and Recollections. By WM. M. THAYER, author of "From Log Cabin to White House," etc. With Steel Portrait. 12mo. $1.00

Dr. Jewett's brilliant talents, his wit and humor, and his consecration to the work, gave him the foremost place among temperance workers at home and abroad. In reducing the price from $1.50 to $1.00, we seek for it the widest circulation in this time of special temperance activity.

"Immensely entertaining,"—*Rev. T. L. Cuyler, D. D., in N. Y. Evangelist.*

"Every page is aglow, making the book throughout as interesting as a novel."—*Christian Mirror, Portland.*

Any Book mailed postpaid on receipt of price.

Capital for Working Boys. A Book for boys in any condition, rich or poor. By Mrs. JULIA E. M'CONAUGHY. " Log Cabin to White House " Series. Illustrated. Handsome 12mo. Silk cloth ; profusely ornamented in Gold and Ink. $1.00

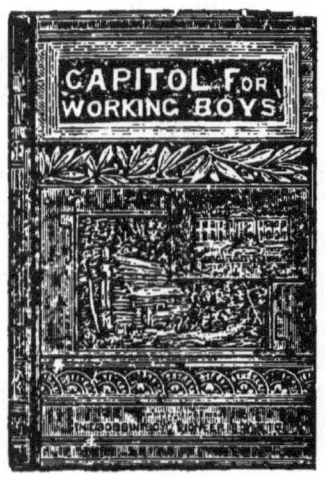

This is a genuine boy's book, suited alike to poor and rich. Every parent, anxious to see his son rise to manliness, honor, and usefulness, every young man who desires to make the most of himself, and all who desire to read a book of practical helpfulness, will do well to obtain this volume on the conduct of life.

" It is one of the books that will be read and re-read, and shape character and action for life."—*Advocate and Guardian, N. Y.*

"It enforces those principles that are the key-note of success. It is almost impossible for an employer to confer a greater benefit, upon any clerk than to present him with this book."—*American Grocer, N. Y.*

Charles Sumner. By WM. L. CORNELL, LL.D., and Bishop Gilbert Haven, D. D. With the leading Eulogies. Illustrated. 12mo. Cloth. $1.50.

These eulogies, by the leading men of the nation, are masterpieces of thought and expression ; invaluable to every professional man, student, and public speaker.

Any Book mailed postpaid on receipt of price.

Character (Building A). For young men. By A. P. PEA-
BODY, D. D., LL.D., Professor of Theology, Harvard
College. Elegant square 18mo. Cloth. 30 cts.

" No words can well overstate the excellence of this volume."—
Morning Star, Boston.

"Many whole libraries have no more of real value in them than
these pages."—*Congregationalist, Boston.*

"Marked with the grace and culture of this widely known
scholar."—*Yale Courant.*

Cottage to Castle. The boyhood, youth, manhood, old
age and death of Gutenburg, and the fascinating
story of his skill, faith, perseverance and triumph in
the discovery and use of the art of printing. By
MRS. E. C. PEARSON, author of "Ruth's Sacrifice,"
"Our Parish," etc., etc. Elegant 12mo, fully illustrated. $1.25. Gilt edges, $1.75. Library Edition, $2.00

"The history is one full of romance and well told."—*Harper's
Magazine.*

" The story of Gutenburg's trials, is most graphically told."—
Boston Traveller.

" Clear, comprehensive and impressive."—*Literary World.*

Don't Spend Your Money for Rum. Words and
music by Mrs. M. Carter. Quarto. 25 cts.

A touching story in verse, set to music and accompaniment,
suited to temperance gatherings and the fireside.

Any Book mailed postpaid on receipt of price.

Dollars and Duty. By EMORY J. HAYNES, Pastor of Tremont Temple, Boston. Large 12mo., of over 456 pages. Cloth. Richly embellished in gold and ink designs. $1.50.

" A quaint and interesting story, given with fidelity to all sides of human nature, and specially well told."—*The Critic, New York.*

" Characterized by the brilliancy and vigor and beauty which distinguish the public utterances of the author."—*The Interior, Chicago.*

" Written with a grace and charm that cannot fail to attract attention."—*Journal of Education, Boston.*

" Dramatically and eloquently written."—*Zion's Herald, Boston.*

" We wish every young man in the country could read this admirable book."—*Central Baptist, St. Louis.*

" A charming book upon vital and significant phases of our social and religious life."—*The Standard, Chicago.*

" The new work by the pastor of Tremont Temple reminds one forcibly of a book which was very popular a quarter of a century ago, entitled " Life in a Country Parsonage," and which wrung tears from many an eye which is old now. Its title, 'Dollars and Duty,' declares its character immediately. A young man, the son of a clergyman, has presented to him the choice between a princely fortune and the ministry of God. He chooses the latter, but it seems to be a case in which the Scriptural prophecy, 'Seek ye first the kingdom of God, and all these things shall be added unto you,' is fulfilled, as the wealth comes to him with his wife. The story is charmingly written, reminding one, in its religious tone, and sharp, terse sentences, of the writings of the late William M. Baker."—*Daily Globe, Boston.*

Dot. By ANNIE LUCAS, author of " Nobody's Dar-

Any Book mailed postpaid on receipt of price.

ling," "City and Castle," etc. With twelve full-page illustrations. Handsomely bound. Cloth. $1.25.

An inimitable story of life in the great city. For its truthfulness to life, originality and tenderness, mingled with light and shade, the book will be read with absorbing interest.

EARLE, A. B., D. D.

The Morning Hour. Octavo. Cloth. $2.00.
Bringing in Sheaves. 12mo. Cloth. $1.25.
Abiding Peace. 16mo. Cloth. 50 cts.
Rest of Faith. 18mo. Cloth. 40 cts.
Sought-out-Songs. 25 cts.
The Human Will. 18mo. Cloth. 25 cts.
Work of an Evangelist. 18mo. Cloth. 25 cts.
Title Examined. 18mo. Cloth. 25 cts.
Two Sermons. 18mo. Cloth. 25 cts.
Revival Hymns. 18mo. Cloth. 25 cts.
For Eternity. Per hundred, $1.50.
Growing, Because Abiding. Per hundred, $1.50.
Why Not Now? 32mo. Per hundred, $1.25
Evidences of Conversion. Per hundred, 60 cts.

Eva's Physician. By the author of "Lessons of Trust." Per dozen, 35 cts; per hundred, $2.00.

Any Book mailed postpaid on receipt of price.

From Log Cabin to White House. By WM. M.
THAYER, author "Tact, Push, and Principle," etc.
Elegant 12mo, of nearly 500 pages. With portrait
of Mr. and Mrs. Garfield, his mother, and other illustrations. Gold and black designs. $1.50.

This work is the one popular life of President Garfield, for
young and old, in steady demand.

"It is because all this is made very clear in this life of President Garfield, that we predict for this literary venture an immense success."—*London Literary World.*

" I know of nothing in the whole range of Sunday-school literature so fitted to be helpful to our American youth as 'From
Log Cabin to White House.' "—*Warren Randolph, D.D., Sec. of
the International S. S. Committee.*

From Pioneer Home to White House. The life of
Abraham Lincoln. By WM. M. THAYER, author of
" Log Cabin to White House," etc. Elegant 12mo.
Illustrated. Uniform with the other volumes of this
notable series. $1.50.

The charm and inspiration of President Lincoln's character,
portrayed by this popular writer, make this a volume of special
value to young and old.

From Tannery to the White House. The Life and
Memoirs of Gen U. S. Grant—his boyhood, manhood, personal history, public life, sickness, and

Any Book mailed postpaid on receipt of price.

death. By WM. M. THAYER. Companion volume to his famous family life of Garfield, "From Log Cabin to White House," of which over 250,000 copies have already been sold. Elegant 12mo, of nearly 500 pages. Illustrated with portraits, scenes, and places. Fine cloth, profusely ornamented. $1.50.

This work supplements for family use, for old and young, the voluminous work by General Grant, which, with its records of his public life, goes into the libraries, while this is read at the fireside.

"This work, written in a very absorbing style, is an unfolding of the entire life of the great General, from birth to death." *The Morning Star, Boston.*

"'From Tannery to the White House' is destined for family circle reading, and will doubtless be as popular as the author's 'Log Cabin to White House.'" *St. Paul (Minn.) Pioneer Press.*

"Of Mr. Thayer's 'Life of Garfield' a quarter of a million copies have already been sold. This volume will probably exceed in popularity its predecessors. Mr. Thayer's books sell without puffing, requiring only a public announcement." *Zion's Herald, Boston.*

For Eternity. By REV. A. B. EARLE, D. D. 32mo. Per dozen, 25 cts; per hundred $1.50.

A new and searching appeal to prepare and work for eternity.

Any Book mailed postpaid on receipt of price.

vealed by Jehovah for the guidance of believers in the minutest affairs of the daily life, and the clear apprehension of His will.

" This volume is the very marrow of the gospel. It will enrich every reader and is a delightful companion."—*Church Union.*

Grandmama's Letters from Japan. By MRS. MARY PRUYN. Illustrated. 16mo. Cloth. $1.00.

Mrs. Pruyn, one of the leading ladies of Albany, in social position and benevolent enterprise, was widely known for her work in Japan. These letters should be in every home and Sunday-school library.

" Mrs. Pruyn was a close and intelligent observer."—*Evening Journal, Albany.*

Growing Because Abiding. By REV. A. B. Earle, D.D. New and revised edition. 32mo. Per dozen 25 cts. Per hundred $1.50.

HAYNES, REV. EMORY J.
Dollars and Duty. $1.50.
Are These Things So? $1.00
Temple Pulpit. $1.00.

HAMMOND, REV. E. P.
Harvest Work of the Holy Spirit. 12mo. Cloth. $1.
Sketches of Palestine. 16mo. Cloth. 75 cts.
Jesus, the Lamb of God. 16mo. Cloth. 60 cts.

Any Book mailed postpaid on receipt of price.

Little Ones in the Fold. 16mo. Cloth. 50 cts.
Better Life and How to Find It. 16mo. Cloth. 50 cts.

Hand Book of Revivals. By REV. H. C. FISH, D. D.,
author of "History of Pulpit Eloquence," etc. 12mo.
Cloth, gilt and black. $1.50.

A manual for successful revival work,—indications, hindrances,
objections, means and methods; preaching, prayer, and singing;
evangelists, inquirers, converts, Sunday-schools, etc., etc.

"The best book on revivals, for its specific uses as a hand-
book, we have seen. Wise in counsel, practical in aims."—*Christian Intelligencer, New York.*

"More complete and judicious than any work hitherto produced on this great subject."—*Christian at Work, New York.*

Harvest Work of the Holy Spirit. By REV. P. C.
HEADLEY, author of "Women of the Bible," etc, etc.
12mo. Cloth. $1.00.

Suggestive of revival methods, as illustrated in Rev. E. P.
Hammond's labors in England, Scotland, and America.

"The record is one of great interest."—*The Observer, New York.*

Havergal (Miss Havergal's) Story. Compiled from
her Letters, Diaries, and other writings, by L. B. E.,
author of "Lessons of Trust," etc., etc. Elegant
12mo. Cloth. Red edges. 60 cts.

Miss Havergal's popularity and influence, have for their key,
her symmetrical Christian life and character. This runs through

Any Book mailed postpaid on receipt of price.

HEADLEY, REV. P. C.

Harvest Work of the Holy Spirit. $1.00.

Bible Readings and Life of Geo. F. Pentecost.
Edited under Mr. Pentecost's supervision. $1.50.

History of the Temperance Crusade. By MRS.
ANNIE WITTENMYER. Octavo. Over 800 pages.
Illustrated. Cloth. $2.50. Full gilt, $3.00. Library
edition, half morocco. $3.50.

A thrilling record of woman's consecration, self-sacrifice, and courage. Mrs. Wittenmyer, as a leader of the temperance army of women, has given the public such a book as can hardly be surpassed.

"In some respects it rivals 'Uncle Tom's Cabin.'"—*The Christian Woman, Phila.*

"A record of one of the most wonderful movements in the world's history."—*Cleveland Earnest Christian.*

Home and Country (Poems of). By PROF. JAS. A.
MARTLING, the California poet. Large 12mo. Illustrated. Nearly 600 pages. $2.00.

Prof. Martling writes with rare grace and beauty, and his poems include almost every topic of heart and life, home, nature, love and duty, country and city.

"I think the Professor's verses very striking and beautiful and the lines (referring to his poem on Death) exquisitely finished."—*Wendell Phillips.*

Hon. Wm. E. Gladstone says of his translation of the first book of the Iliad, "It seems to me to do him great credit."

Any Book mailed postpaid on receipt of price.

Lessons of Trust. By L. B. E., author of "The Jewel Found," "How I Found Jesus," etc. Elegant 16mo. Cloth, red edges, 75 cts. Full calf, $2.00.

Comparatively few are the authors who have so large a circle of readers. "Lessons of Trust" is marked by the same clear apprehension of Spiritual things, as this author's other works, and takes its place with the devotional books that are kept at hand to give comfort and direction in the hours of trouble, or question, or temptation.

"A sweet and comforting book."—*The Advance, Chicago.*

"Admirably adapted to help those who are inclined to look on the dark side. Well written and beautiful in form, a most appropriate gift-book." — *The Journal and Messenger, Cincinnati.*

"'Lessons of trust' is a very handsomely-published religious gem. From significant initial letters, we suppose the volume is from the pen of the accomplished and devout wife of the publisher. It is a delightful and profitable manual for hours of meditation."—*Zion's Herald, Boston.*

Life, Letters, and Wayside Gleanings. By Mrs. B. H. Crane. Octavo. Cloth. With Portrait, $2.00.

Mrs. Crane, as the gifted wife of a former prominent New England pastor, gives not only the history of a family and a life, but she has interwoven recollections of the olden time, incidents and lessons of great interest and value, in her own matchless style, which is the very soul of poetry itself.

"A charming book for the home and fireside."—*Watchman, Boston.*

Any Book mailed postpaid on receipt of price.

Log Cabin to White House Series. These volumes,
designed especially for young men and women, boys

and girls, but alike
fascinating to all
ages and classes,
have reached an ag-
gregate sale of over
300,000 copies.
This series is uni-
formly and sumptu-
ously bound in fine
cloth; richly embel-
lished in gold and
black. The six vol-
umes put up in a neat box, $8.25.

I. From Log Cabin to White House. By WM. M.
THAYER. The life of James A. Garfield, with
portrait and illustrations.

" Will fascinate old and young."—*Manchester,* (*N. H.*) *News.*

A better biography for boys was never printed."—*London
Christian.*

II. From Tannery to White House. By WM. M.
THAYER. The life of Ulysses S. Grant, with portrait and illustrations.

" A work of solid merit, and likely to achieve as wide popularity as the companion volume."—*London Jewish World.*

Any Book mailed postpaid on receipt of price.

www.ingramcontent.com/pod-product-compliance
Lightning Source LLC
Chambersburg PA
CBHW052338110726
47901CB00005B/1281